PRAISE FOR **BILL HILLMANN** AND *THE OLD NEIGHBORHOOD*

"A raucous but soulful account of growing up on the mean streets of Chicago, and the choices kids are forced to make on a daily basis. This cool, incendiary rites of passage novel is the real deal."

—**IRVINE WELSH**, AUTHOR OF *TRAINSPOTTING*

"Hillmann's prose is sharp, his dialogue is righteous and the F-word hits the reader square in the face like belt-fed .50 caliber ammunition. *The Old Neighborhood* is a wonderful first novel."

—**THOM JONES**, AUTHOR OF *THE PUGILIST AT REST*

"Tough and real and filled with a remarkably interesting cast of characters, this is a novel in the great Chicago tradition. Nelson Algren would have loved it, as I do."

—**RICK KOGAN**, *CHICAGO TRIBUNE* SENIOR WRITER & COLUMNIST, **WGN RADIO** HOST, AUTHOR, AND CHICAGO LEGEND

"Bill Hillmann's *The Old Neighborhood* is like a right hook to the chin with brass knuckles, crackling with both bravery and urgency. Brilliantly evoking Nelson Algren's *Neon Wilderness* and Richard Price's *The Wanderers*, the novel is unflinchingly honest in its depictions of class and race, a deft portrait of our sometimes-less-than-fair city."

—**JOE MENO**, AUTHOR OF *HAIRSTYLES OF THE DAMNED*

"Bill Hillmann writes with a furious humanity and wide open heart."

—**TONY FITZPATRICK**, RENOWNED ARTIST AND AUTHOR

"Hillmann describes in detail the horrifying, hilarious and moving events of a childhood dominated by a heroin-addled career criminal of a brother. The story is like something from a Scorsese film."
—*THE SPECTATOR UK*

"A dark, urban tale."
—RESONANCE FM LONDON

"Bill Hillmann's *The Old Neighborhood* is as good as it gets. The generosity, style and passion of his story gripped me from the beginning and convinced me as few other books have that here was a writer to be reckoned with. Chicago has a new literary star in its firmament."
—JOHN HEMINGWAY, AUTHOR OF *STRANGE TRIBE* AND GRANDSON OF ERNEST HEMINGWAY

"Bill Hillmann, a veteran of the streets, the boxing ring and the staging of knock down drag out literary happenings finally gets his say in novel form. We love its raw authenticity. Bill Hill is the Rill Dill..."
—KENT AND KEITH ZIMMERMAN, AUTHORS OF *HELL'S ANGELS, ROTTEN, AND OPERATION FAMILY SECRETS*

"Bill Hillmann has written a top notch novel."
—MARC KELLY SMITH, ORIGINATOR OF **POETRY SLAM** AND THE HOST OF THE **UPTOWN POETRY SLAM**

"Hillmann paints such vivid scenes of the north side, I feel as if I am right there. I've always believed that this part of Chicago and these neighborhoods deserve more literary attention than they have ever gotten. Hillmann's novel delivers, showing the side of Chicago that those who grew up and worked here would recognize. His language is powerful and his characters lively. The central murder scene is so well conceived it was like I was working it as a cop. Hillmann is a writer worth keeping an eye on, writing about a city that is just aching for the right storytellers."

—MARTIN PREIB, AUTHOR OF THE INTERNATIONALLY ACCLAIMED MEMOIR *THE WAGON* AND VETERAN CHICAGO COP IN ROGERS PARK

"Bill Hillmann takes you deep inside what it's really like growing up on the streets in a tough Chi-town neighborhood. Excellent read."

—FRANK CALABRESE JR., FORMER CHICAGO MOBSTER AND AUTHOR OF *OPERATION FAMILY SECRETS*

"*The Old Neighborhood* is a rib-wrenching look at man's desperate desire to survive and rise above even the most harrowing of circumstances. His dialogue is crisp and true. He captures the street and its ethic in a way anyone who has come out of such an environment can relate to. But the story itself is one that any reader, anywhere, will come to care about because it is as basic as life itself—live every moment to its fullest because that moment could easily be your last."

—JOE DISTLER, LEGENDARY BULL RUNNER IN *PAMPLONA* AND *NYT* PUBLISHED ESSAYIST

"It's an exciting read, hard to put down. It brings back memories of the neighborhoods on the North Side, the speech patterns, it takes me back there. It's a great book."

—DAVID DIAZ, FORMER CHICAGO GOLDEN GLOVE CHAMPION, '96 US OLYMPIAN AND WBC LIGHTWEIGHT WORLD CHAMPION

A NOVEL BILL
HILLMANN

 CURBSIDE SPLENDOR CHICAGO

THE OLD NEIGHBORHOOD

CURBSIDE SPLENDOR PUBLISHING

This is a work of fiction. All incidents, situations, institutions, governments, and people are fictional and any similarity to characters or persons living or dead is strictly coincidental.

Published by Curbside Splendor Publishing, Inc., Chicago, Illinois in 2014.

First Edition
Copyright © 2014 by Bill Hillmann
Library of Congress Control Number: 2014933482

ISBN 978-1-940430-00-3
Edited by Leonard Vance
Cover and author photos by Jacob Knabb
Designed by Alban Fischer

Manufactured in the United States of America.

www.curbsidesplendor.com

THE OLD NEIGHBORHOOD

A SENGSTACKE NEWSPAPER

CHICA...

Daily

The Big Week...

VOL. LXV — NO. 41

JANUARY 17...

FEAR GRIPS

Police Escort Black Students

By TED LACEY
(Daily Defender Staff Writer)

Racial antagonism flared up on a smaller scale all last week, precipitating T h u r s day's massive disturbance at Nicholas Senn High School, 5900 N. Glenwood, according to Principal Thomas Coffey.

"This was building up for most of the week," he said. "Tuesday we had a Spanish-speaking boy arrested, Wednesday we arrested a black girl who was said to have assaulted a teacher and there have been two or three fights among the girls along racial lines."

He and his human relations coordinator and his security officers have been trying to determine why the atmosphere at Senn has been so explosive, but no conclusion has been reached yet, Coffey said.

"When you live in a changing situation, it's hard to say why these things do happen. You can just as well ask why people are people and don't like

some other people," he said.

"We are a large school—we have close to 3,300 kids here—and they are pretty cosmopolitan. At the last racial count, we had about 394 blacks, 30 of whom live within our district and the rest of whom are permissive tranfers from other areas. There are 354 Orientals and American Indians, 88 Puerto Ricans, 337 Spanish-speaking students other than Puerto Rican and the rest are Caucasians. Many of the Caucasians are Appalachians."

The disturbances Thursday prompted C o f f e y to tighten security measures at the school, he said. "We have a lot of police protection here," he said, but additional juvenile officers are being brought in to ride out the storm.

Thursda... with most students masse to station b... cars.

The stu... ors that white str... the TJO... get" blac... students the scho... they wait cort.

The mal... ed files file of g... down Ridg...

Two bla... Daily De... turbance day by m... acting d... services tin Luth... White stu... rogatory walked ou... said.

SENN HIGH

...fternoon ended
...he school's black
...g escorted . on
...Bryn Mawr "El"
...f a dozen squad

...had heard rum-
...bers of militant
...gangs, including
..., were "out to
...dents. The black
...ed anxiously to
...ditorium where
...r the police es-

...ck students form-
...both sides of a
...as they walked
...to Bryn Mawr.
...tudents told the
...r that the dis-
...sparked Thurs-
...t white students
...ectfully during
...rating Dr. Mar-
...King's birthday.

...made loud de-
...ments and some
...e black student

Another black students said
that white gang members fired
two shots into the balcony of
the auditorium, triggering the
disturbance.

Coffey said, however, that
there was no shooting and no
fighting. "There was more fear
and more wild rumors t h a n
what actually happened Thursday," he said. "Yesterday
(Wednesday) there was fighting, but not today."

"Many rumors began spreading during lunch. We saw gangs
forming and were able to dis-
perse them. There was no
shooting and no knifing, but
there was an awful lot of high
tension and excitement and an
awful lot of rumors."

Coffey said some of the TJO
gang members walked out of
one of two memorial services,
but that there were no major
disturbances during those as-
semblies.

"The TJO's are some of the
toughest gang members in the
city. The older members have
police records. They come from
the immediate area surrounding Senn High School."

A black student told the Daily
Defender "many of the black
students I've been around have
said we are outnumbered, but
at the same time they are
not about to be beaten. They
are aware of what is going
on. TJO is known as a hate-type
organization, and from what
I've seen, I believe it."

The service that the white
gang members behaved rude-
ly during "was a memorial
service for a man who preach-
ed non-violence," the b l a c k
student said. "Is people like the
TJO's and other involved in
the disruption cannot respect
a man like Dr. King, then I
don't think they could honor
anyone who believes in human
rights and freedom."

PROLOGUE

THE MUSCLED-UP, NAVY-BLUE '65 IMPALA sat elevated on ramp jacks above the white slab of the two-car garage. Pungent oil spilt in a steady bead to the tin pan below. You watched it empty as you crouched beside the car with your head craned downward. Your long arms stretched down—hands planted flat on the concrete. The veins bulged and crisscrossed the bulbous knots of your forearms like strings of lightning.

The garage door burst open, and a teen with a buzzed scalp panted in the doorway. He wore a brown jean jacket and construction boots. The gray winter sky illuminated his smooth cheek.

"It's going down! It's going down over at Senn right now! Dey're runnin' dem niggers out de neighborhood!" he yelled.

Moments later, you briskly walked east down Bryn Mawr Ave. toward the Red Line "L" stop. Large clots of salt-blackened snow lined the edges of the sidewalk; the freezing weather preserved them, shin-high and sloped, like tiny mountain ranges. The teen knew not to talk to you. He knew he'd get no response. He was afraid to even look at your hawkish scowl and the broken and re-broken nose. They sent him to deliver the message and show you where. That was all.

This silent, negative charge radiated from you. You ground your teeth and stomped on in Chicago's burning January freeze—a freeze that can paint a man's face and hands red in seconds. A rumble of shouts and honking car horns built to the north. When you got to Wayne Ave., you peered down the narrow corridor of the one-way street, which intersected with Ridge Ave. at a forty-five degree angle. An immense, calamitous procession ambled slowly down Ridge. You quickened your pace to a jog and cut down Wayne. As you approached Ridge, you saw a long line of leather coat-clad city police officers with their powder-blue chests peeking out near their collars. The cops'd taken one of the southwest-bound lanes and surrounded a parade of over a hundred black teenagers. Traffic skirted slowly around them. An awestruck young mother eked past in a brown four-door Buick. Her young boys' faces were glued to the window in back.

At first, you could only see the black boys' faces, which were stoic and resolved. Their feet slipped on the thin films of ice. They were twisted at the waist with their arms locked elbow-in-elbow to create an intertwined shield of bodies. A black kid with a fuzzy gray skull cap and a black quarter-length pea coat bugged his eyes out at the faction of white hoodlums across the street who stalked them from across the way. They were just a few feet up the sidewalk from you. The black boy muttered, "Mothafuckas," quietly.

Then, you saw the girls inside the arm chain. One thick-boned, dark-skinned girl pressed her school books tightly to her chest. Her full lips pursed. Her eyes darted from her snow boots across Ridge to the gang of white thugs that bellowed cat calls at her. All the white hoods were clad in tight jeans and tan construction boots. Their hair was either buzz-short or slicked back tightly to their scalps. One of them was a head taller than the rest. His hair was swirled back in a ducktail, and his dark-brown jean coat read "T.J.O." in black, block-shaped letters high across the back. He had a jagged, angular face and wild eyes. His large Adam's apple yo-yoed along his narrow throat as he cackled. You knew him as little Kellas. You'd kicked his ass a hundred times while he was growing up, and you got him hired on as a laborer at a high-rise job a few months back when he dropped out of school. He showed up until the first payday, cashed the check, and vanished. He was like another little brother to you.

Kellas craned his head back like a rooster. His scratchy voice careened over the others: "Come on, baby! Don't be shy! Bring that big, nasty fanny on over an' sit it down right here." He yanked at the crotch of his black jeans, and the gang erupted into laughter. A smirk slithered across the lips of a young, pudgy copper in an ankle-length trench coat. The cop looked down. His polished black boots stomped atop the salt-faded, yellow dotted line while his maple billy club swung in circles from the strap around his wrist.

You followed behind this group of rambling roughnecks, keeping your distance. Your wide hands flexed and gesticulated with the burning sensation there in your palms that always appeared when you itched to give somebody a smack—the kind of slap that leaves the recipient snoring on the sidewalk. The teen ran up to Kellas and yanked at his coat sleeve, then pointed back at you. Kellas turned and grinned maniacally. He raised his palm towards the marching students. His eyebrows hiked upward. You grimaced and your face flushed red.

"Who's dat?" someone asked.

"Dat's the leader of Bryn Mawr," Kellas replied.

You walked on—your jutting chin tucked into your throat. The procession reached the three-street intersection at Bryn Mawr, Broadway, and Ridge. The white gang halted at the sharp peninsula where Ridge and Bryn Mawr touch. There were fifty or more now. They spilt out into the streets. A short, stout guy with acne bubbled across his cheeks stumbled out into the street and puffed his chest out.

"WHAT'D MARTIN LUTHER KING EVER DO FOR ME?" he yelled, his vicious tone piercing the bedlam.

You walked up beside Kellas, but he didn't turn. He kept his gaze on the mob of black and blue that encompassed the high-schoolers.

"You told me there was gonna be a fight," you said, baring your teeth. "They look like they just want to go home."

"And we're seeing 'em off," Kellas replied, smiling. Then, he cupped his hands around his mouth, leaned back, and rocked up on his tip-toes to yell, "GOOD RIDDENS, NIGGERS!" The wind whirled and frayed his greasy, dark-brown hair, and it wimpled up in thin strands like tentacles.

The procession stopped traffic in all directions. The honks of car horns rose in a steady, long, mournful chorus that encircled the procession in the melodic agony of the city. The police and students crossed Broadway—a slow, sad parade. They sifted up toward the Bryn Mawr "L" stop.

You watched them for a while. Thin trails of steam rose from their mouths and nostrils and accumulated and congealed into one misty haze above the procession. The hoods roared at your sides. Their laughter felt like pinpricks in your earlobes.

"Fuck this," you spat. You turned away down Bryn Mawr and walked home.

PART ONE

CHILDHOOD

CHAPTER 1

THE LAST EXIT ON LAKESHORE

IT BEGAN AT THE CARNIVAL.

Those magic nights—the whole of St. Greg's Parish strolling over from the bungalows and two flats and apartments mix-matched throughout the neighborhood. There were the games, the shouts of the carnies, the swirling thunder of the Tilt-A-Whirl, lights flashing, pulsing; the colors of yellow, red, green, and blue exploding like fireworks against the walls of the church; the old nunnery; the high school; and the grammar school that encircled it all like a towering red-brick fortress. The structures trapped the cacophonous noises so they echoed with booms that bounced from wall to wall. And there was the crying joy of the children and the wild in their eyes and the running and no knowledge of anything else.

The carnival sat on top of the school parking lot. The exits were the alley to the east behind the priest's house, the tunnel that cut through the school and led out onto Bryn Mawr, and the narrow opening between the church and the nunnery.

I was nine years old and hanging out amongst the big metal

rides near the beer tent with some kids from the block. Lil Pat was drinking with the other hoods in the beer garden behind the rectory—something he'd been doing for years even though almost none of them were of age. Father McHale loomed near them in his black priest suit. Beads of sweat rolled down his huge bald head. He kept an uneasy eye on the youngsters guzzling back beers from clear plastic cups.

Lil Pat was the tallest of 'em. His shoulders were set close, and only his profile revealed his large, low-hung pot-belly. They were somewhere between greasers, cholos, and jocks. Some wore shirts with sports logos, or sweatpants and Dago T's, and some wore oil-stained Dickies. Some had buzzed heads, and others had slicked back hair with the sides almost shaved. Their voices rose and fell in that squeaky Chicago slang. They were a dying breed. The great white flight was siphoning their numbers. The neighborhood was changing.

"Aye, Joey," Lil Pat yelled. "C'mere," he said, waving his hairy knuckled hand. He'd walked up to an older woman and a redheaded kid my age. I jogged over.

"Hey, did you ever meet Ryan?" Lil Pat asked.

I shook my head no.

"Well, he's Mickey's nephew," he said, nodding towards where Mickey stood. Mickey's stout build poured out of his Dago T. His face flexed as he spoke to the hood next to him.

I looked at the kid in front of me—Ryan. He was like a mini-Mickey. His hair was in a short buzz cut, and he had the same pit bull face, but softer, rounder, and covered with a spattering of dark-brown freckles. He wore old, grayed Adidas with thick blue laces that made me wonder if he was very poor.

"Well, shake hands or somethin'. Jesus," Lil Pat said, furrowing his brow and shaking his head. "What's wrong wit you?" He slid his palm the wrong way through my slicked back hair, so I had to fix it.

"What's up?" Ryan and I said at the same time. Both of us looked down.

I noticed a thick gold bracelet on his wrist.

"Nice gold," I said.

"Thanks," Ryan replied, looking at the tips of my scuffed up Air Jordans. "Nice rope. I got one like dat at home."

"Well, you two go on an' play," Lil Pat urged, dragging his fingers through his trimmed goatee and mustache. "An' stay outta trouble you little shit." We both smiled.

Ryan and I made quick friends, and soon we were laughing and playing with the other kids—white, black and Mexican kids—dipping and dodging through the maze of grown-ups.

■

THE GUNSHOT WAS ABRUPT. It sent a torrent of reactions through the mass of people. Some of the hoods dove under the folding tables. Father McCale smirked and jammed both of his index fingers in his ears like it was a firecracker. No one seemed to know which direction it had come from. I saw it though—the fire from the barrel. I watched Lil Pat run and jump the beer garden fence in the direction of the tall, skinny Assyrian kid who held the pistol to his leg. A line of gray smoke leaked from the barrel and slithered up his wrist. The confusion continued as the Assyrian sprinted down the alley with Lil Pat and Mickey giving chase close behind. Ryan and I darted after them as they ran down the alley and turned right. A wild, menacing laughter erupted from Lil Pat and Mickey. I glanced at Ryan sprinting beside me. He looked as scared as I felt. We ran as fast as we could, but they pulled away from us as we turned at the T in the alley. Their shoes clapped the pavement as my Jordans slipped on the dusty, pebble-ridden concrete.

They sprinted across Ashland Ave. and through the Jewel parking lot. Ryan and I crossed Ashland. A rusty pickup truck honked its horn as we cut in front of it. My heart banged in my ears. Across the half-empty parking lot, the Assyrian disappeared through the front door of the pharmacy, with Lil Pat and Mickey close behind. The laughter rose to high hilarity. As we approached the pharmacy, I heard the screams from inside, but no gun shot. We stood there at the open door as the neon-green light from the sign in the window poured out and stained the sidewalk at our feet. We peered in at the long rows of shelving units that ran back to the counter; there wasn't a soul in sight, just the screams and a deep, leaden crunching. Then, the sound dampened. The laughter plummeted to a bubbling, demonic gurgle. There was a blur of motion. Ryan grabbed my arm and pulled me toward another doorway. We crammed in and pressed our backs to the glass door. Lil Pat emerged from the drug store with Mickey right behind him. Their laughter fizzled into a popping giggle. Their hands were as red as butchers' to the forearms, and there was a bulge in Lil Pat's blood-speckled waistband. As they jogged out, Lil Pat's shirt rose up above his belt, and I saw the wet wooden pistol grip. They glanced up and down Clark Street, wild-eyed, and then hung a left and disappeared into the darkness of the side street.

The screaming continued inside. It was a woman's voice, and it was the only voice that could be heard. There was a quick panting between each scream. I listened as I hid there with Ryan beside me. Our chests heaved. The patter of Lil Pat and Mickey's steps dissipated. We entered the drug store wordless. The woman screamed like she was falling into an endless, black abyss, it rang in my ears. Trembling, we walked towards it. I saw the dark-red puddle on the floor slowly expanding like a shadow across the green and grey tiles. I walked closer to the puddle's edge where I saw the young man motionless—eyes still open. A deep crack above his eye ran up his forehead and into his hair. Thick blood oozed slowly from the wound, wetting his frizzy black hair. His bottom jaw hung open and was cocked to the side of his narrow, dark face like it had been dislodged from its hinge. The woman screamed deeper into the abyss, crumpled on the ground with the phone trembling in her hand. Her torso shook terribly. The puddle enveloped her legs and soaked the underside of her brown nylons. I looked at them in silent mourning—for the young man and something that I hadn't words for. We slipped out of the store as others poured in through the doorway.

We walked towards home in the quiet—our heads hung. The weight of it all around us. The air was thick, and the carnival roared on in the distance. The sound of the children's joyous screams rose and fell, but I had no urge to return. We walked down Clark to Hollywood Ave., where the yellow sign of the corner store glowed stale and flickered. We stood there under it a while.

"You think dey're gonna get caught up?" I asked.

"Naw, there ain't nobody gonna rat dem out."

"Shit… He was dead wadn't he."

Ryan didn't answer. We walked down and crossed Ashland with the sirens floating in the air. Ryan went his way to the north, and I went home. I went up to my room and sat on the bed a while in the dark as the orange-yellow of the streetlight seeped in through the window. I thought about God. I thought about heaven and if Lil Pat could ever go there now. I wondered if I could go there now that I knew what I knew and was never gonna tell. I held my crucifix and prayed to Jesus that he wasn't dead. After the others had gone to sleep, I went downstairs to the TV room and watched the reports of the murder.

And that was the birth of Pistol Pat.

■

WHEN I WAS A LITTLE KID, all I ever wanted to be was the baddest kid on the block. At least that's what I thought I longed for;

deep down, all I wanted was for my family to stay together, but I didn't find that out 'til later.

My Ma got pregnant with Lil Pat when she was thirteen and the old man was fourteen, and they had to go down to Tennessee to get married 'cause at their age it was illegal in the State of Illinois.

The far North Side was a strange place back then. Uptown and Edgewater were full of hillbillies from West Virginia who came looking for work, found it, and stayed. Their hillbilly family vendettas came with them. Rifle volleys resounded over Sheridan Ave. from one low-rent high-rise to the next. Folk music flourished. John Prine, Steve Goodman, Fred Holstein—all of them spewed out of the North Side of Chicago.

At first, my family lived on the second floor of my grandmother's two-flat. It was right there on Olive Ave. in-between Ashland and Hermitage Ave. in the St. Greg's Parish. The old man had evolved from street thug, to car thief, to cat burglar, to repo man. In other words, he'd gone pro. And Ma was babysitting. They had three raccoons and a fox as pets. Then, they had Blake. He was a sick baby—had a heart defect—but don't worry, he grew up to be probably the biggest and strongest of the brothers. Richard was born a couple years later, and everybody said, "Look at the size of the feet on that kid! He's gonna be a giant!" but he never broke six feet.

Ma started to worry that my Dad was only gonna give her boys, and she really wanted a little girl. So she thought of adoption, but DCFS was already breathing down her neck because she was running an illegal babysitting outfit out of the apartment, though the only thing illegal was that she had too many kids. What DCFS didn't understand was that Ma was really good at taking care of ten to twelve kids at a time, in addition to her own.

She'd read an article in the Trib about adoption and found out that you could adopt kids from third world countries really easy. She and my old man looked into it and started saving. Next thing you know, they're on a flight to Puerto Rico to change planes and head to the Dominican Republic to adopt a little girl.

My Dad had earned himself quite a reputation as a tough guy in quite a tough neighborhood at quite a tough time in Chicago. Well, he ends up in the pisser at the airport in Puerto Rico, and he says when he walked in there was a uniformed cop standing at the door. So there he is pissing at a urinal when three "Spanish guys" (they weren't from Spain, though) walk in and step up behind him in this empty bathroom. Pin-prickles dance up his back and neck. The three of them stood in complete silence behind him, though all the other urinals were open. Dad figured they weren't gonna wait for him to finish, so he didn't wait either. With his thang hanging out in mid-stream, he spun around on them. He said he'd never kicked anyone in the face harder in his whole life, which means something because he had a long, storied history of kicking people very hard in the face. At the end, he grabbed the last of them by the head and broke the porcelain urinal with the guy's cheekbone. When Dad walked out, the cop at the door had evaporated. Interpol grabbed him, and my Ma didn't know where the hell he was 'cause he didn't inform her that he was going to the john.

Anyway, somehow they made it to the Dominican Republic. An adoption agent took them miles inland along winding dirt roads to a tiny village full of huts. They literally lived in a shack made of scrap metal and salvaged wood with chickens and lizards running around on the dirt floor. The girl's family was comprised of thirteen children from two fathers—the first had passed. My parents went for the infant, but the birth mother urged them to also take the second-youngest in the belief that her children would get a chance at a better life in America. The negotiation took place as giant, black hornets swooped in to kill the tarantulas. The second-youngest was a little girl about to turn three, and somehow Ma convinced Dad, so they came home with not one but two little, dark-brown, frizzy-haired angels. They named the youngest Rose and the older one Jan, but they'd forever be known as Jan'n'Rose and have their names be confused by all of our family, even though Rose was much lighter skinned and taller than Jan, who was dark and small-framed with a fiery temper. I came into the picture about a year later. A "late-in-life baby" my Ma always said, but she was just twenty-seven. It was a different time.

■

LIL PAT BECOMING A MURDERER didn't spark off out of the blue. We could feel it coming—in the family and in the neighborhood.

The TJOs sprouted up in Edgewater in the '60s. The original name was the "Thorndale Jarvis Organization." They were a fairly organized stone greaser gang that hung out right under the Thorndale stop on the Red Line directly across from the huge dark brick armory where I took gymnastics as a little boy. Their real estate ran between there and the Jarvis stop on the Red Line. Under the leadership of Joe Ganci and Bob Kellas, the gang flourished, and membership skyrocketed to over 200 members in the early '70s. At one point, there was a whole juvenile courtroom full of TJOs on a variety of charges. The judge's name was Reynolds, and he was known for his hot temper and quick wit. After he'd sentenced the twelfth TJO to appear that day, he looked up and said, "What is this TJO crap anyway? These guys are nothing but a bunch of Thorndale Avenue Jag Offs."

The name stirred uproarious approval through the entire courtroom, and the gang forever changed the official name to the Thorndale Avenue Jag Offs.

The older TJOs had slightly biker-ish leanings and at times called themselves "Thieves Junkies and Outlaws." Eventually, they garnered the attention of Sonny Barger and his crew, and the Hell's Angels would sporadically stop by and pay the neighborhood a visit while on their countrywide tours of wreaking havoc. It was around then that the TJOs began dealing heroin. Some say it was the Angels that biked it in, concealing it in their fuel tanks, but others say it was the Mob, who Ganci and Kellas started doing low-level hits for. Those hits eventually got the both of them pinched on a murder rap, but during the months-long trial, they both miraculously escaped from Cook County Jail in a week that saw seven inmates escape, including one who was in the county hospital for a stab wound and just walked out of the front door in broad daylight. Needless to say, it was a bad week for those friendly confines that the regulars lovingly called "California" due to its location on California Ave. Both men were caught within weeks. Ganci took the plunge and got natural life, and Kellas got ten on conspiracy to commit murder.

Mickey's big brother and Ryan's dad, Rick Reid, took charge and brought the TJOs into the '80s until he got in a traffic dispute on Clark, ripped a guy out of his car window, and beat him to death in front of his wife and child. In the process, he nearly exposed the long-running extortion ring the TJOs had going with the businesses on Broadway and Clark, between Thorndale Ave. and Foster Ave. Word was that Rick went into a bar across the street while the ambulance hauled the guy away, and the police began to question people on the sidewalk right in front of him. The entire neighborhood claimed they didn't see anything. Mind you, the assault occurred in the middle of a busy Saturday afternoon on Clark. All the press brought on a big two-year investigation in an attempt to link heroin, extortion, murder-for-hire, and all-around Chi-town All-Star thuggery. The smart-ass TJOs decided to sue the City of Chicago and the Chicago Police on charges of harassment, and it actually got before a judge before being thrown out for its utter ridiculousness.

In the mid-'80s, Kellas was released from prison and regained the reins from an up-and-comer nicknamed Wacker. Word was that Wacker headed the murder-for-hire division of the gang. The TJOs enjoyed a short reign in the North Side heroin distribution ranks through newly acquired friends Kellas made during his stay in Joliet Correctional Institution. Then, a nobody buyer approaches him wanting to purchase two kilos of heroin for $40,000 dollars. Now, the TJOs were top dogs at this point for a long stretch of real estate—from Uptown to Howard Street—so it wasn't out of their reach and reputation, but sensing that there were no Mob ties or muscle involved, Kellas and Wacker get greedy. They set up a deal in the Carson's Ribs parking lot at 2:30 p.m. on a Friday—the same time school lets out at Senn High School, which is across Clark and down a block.

They decided to bring a newly acquired MAC 10 UZI with an extended clip in place of the two keys of H and figured they'd negotiate from there. Afterwards, they'd head over to pick up their girlfriends at Senn and see how the young bucks were holding down the courtyard, 40 stacks the richer.

They show up rolling in a souped-up, dark-green Mustang convertible with racing slicks. The guy is there just like they talked about. They all exit on the side of the Carson's. They ask to see the green, and he asks to see the brown. They show the MAC 10, and the guy starts stuttering. Then, Wacker sprays the side of the guy's Cutlass with a short burst from the MAC 10. A briefcase is handed over. They jump in the Mustang, and off Kellas and Wacker roll, already counting the money. Suddenly, a U-Haul truck flies out of nowhere and T-bones their Mustang. Thirteen DEA agents pour out with their guns drawn and firing. Wacker crawls out of the mangled muscle car and empties out what's left in the extended clip. One of the DEA agents shoots him in the head. The bullet strikes his skull at an angle above his left eye, scorches through the flesh between his scalp and skull, ricochets off his hard Irish bone, and exits the back of his head. He passes out but survives, scarred for life. A giant wave of kids vacating the school walk past, astonished at the sight. The co-leader of the TJOs lies there presumably dead with a bullet hole in his head. A mob forms. The Chicago Police also arrive. There are more arrests, but finally it simmers down. Both of them go away for assault on federal agents and conspiracy to distribute heroin, which, when it's all settled, leaves Kellas with a thirty-year sentence. Since it's Wacker's first felony offense, he gets ten years. Now, we're getting into the mid-'80s and the rise of Mickey Reid, Fat Buck, and my big bro, Pistol Pat.

CHAPTER 2

DA

I USED TO WALK MY NEIGHBORHOOD a lot as a little kid. We called it Edgewater back then, but nowadays most people call it Andersonville. At first, I walked with my grandfather. His nickname was Da, which was my mom's first word. Some babies say, "Dada," but Ma just said, "Da," and it stuck. We never called him anything else. All us kids walked with him over the years, running his weekend errands, getting ice cream and then early lunch at McDonald's until we aged-out. It was our own little familial tradition, precious in its simplicity. Da was a sharp, good-looking old man who dressed well in collared shirts and slicked back his thick, black hair in immaculate columns. He worked the streetlight truck for the city and was the precinct captain in the neighborhood. He was a milkman before operating the streetlight truck, and to this day, I can't come in contact with either without thinking of him. After Da got sick and couldn't walk anymore, I started to walk the neighborhood collecting envelopes for Lil Pat.

It was an easy job: walk down Clark, step into a shop, and say "Collection" to the person at the register. They'd hand over an envelope, and I'd walk to the next one. I'd finish it in about an hour. Lil Pat would cruise the neighborhood around then and check in on me once in a while. He'd slowly ease past with a grin, and I'd give a nod if everything was fine and all the envelopes had been handed over. If not, I'd shake my head and he'd stop to chat. He'd keep track and go back and talk with the shop manager himself. I'd finish right by Hollywood. He'd pull up, I'd jump in and hand over the envelopes, and he'd give me twenty bucks. It was like a second allowance, and it kept me stocked up on comic books, baseball cards, and candy. I loved it. A few months after I'd started collecting, I began to figure out what was happening.

My walk shadowed the walk we did with Da. We'd walk south down Ashland to Foster and turn left past the funeral home where Da's wake would be held and I'd crack jokes in a side room with my cousin J, then cry uncontrollably as the priest said the final words.

Then, we'd turn north down Clark. Da's Cocker Spaniel, Sheba, led the way, cutting through the busy mass of old ladies with the little bells jingling on her collar. It was busy as ever on Clark. I passed the crazy Middle Eastern shops with neon-green statues of Buddha glowing in the windows, as well as other strange knick knacks and herbs and candles. I stepped into the ice cream shop where I used to order a Green River Float every time with Da, and my sisters would tease me and try to trick me into ordering something else. The old man in the white smock behind the counter looked down at me, sad, and handed me the envelope. He must have missed Da, too. Da wasn't the same since he got cancer—he was sad and cried a lot. Even then, I kept hope that he could beat the cancer and that he'd be back making his walk like nothing ever happened in no time flat.

I walked to Almo's Shoes, where Almo himself would blow up a balloon for any kid who entered the store, whether his parents were buying or browsing. I didn't get balloons anymore, just the envelopes and the same sad face.

"How is your grandfather?" Almo asked as he placed his hand on my shoulder.

"He's OK," I said. "He's doing real good." I thought that if I said it enough it could turn true. It wasn't true though; he got sicker every day.

I knew the people on the walk worried about Da because he was a good man. They couldn't have really known half of it though—I didn't even know then. When Lil Pat was young, Dad used to beat him a lot. Dad was just an angry, confused teenager. When it was bad, and Dad wouldn't stop beating him, and they thought he might put my brother in the hospital again, Da would throw himself on top of Lil Pat and take the beating for him. He was a nonviolent man. When people were hurt, it made him sad. All of that just oozed out of everything he did with us kids, and it made it easy to love him a whole lot.

I closed my eyes as I walked, and I could hear Sheba's bells ringing faintly. Then, I could feel Da walking beside me in his patient gait. I remembered how we used to hold hands sometimes, and I reached out beside me. I walked square into something heavy and opened my eyes to see an old lady with a curly wig frowning at me. She swore in Swedish and brushed past.

"Sorry," I said, and kept going. I liked to collect the envelopes from the shops that Da never stopped in because I knew they wouldn't ask about him and it was easier. Sometimes, I even had to run around the corner into the alley and cry by a dumpster until I got mad. When I got mad on the walks, I'd start to steal stuff, and I wouldn't feel bad about it, and then I wouldn't be sad anymore.

I finished my walk and stood at the corner of Hollywood and Clark next to the Edgewater Dollar Store, waiting. Two old ladies hobbled by in faded housedresses and smiled at me in the sunlight. I stood proud and dutiful, clutching my bundle of envelopes bound with a green rubber band. The low morning sun cut Clark in half; the east was cast in cool shade, and the west smoldered in a deep, golden haze. The density of the morning bustle was the same on either side, though one was a mysterious calm, and the other vibrant and naked.

A tan Lincoln Continental swayed up Clark, knifing through the light. It eked to a halt across the street, and Lil Pat waved me over from the driver's seat. His wrist sparkled. He chuckled as I crossed. His eyes were hazy-pink and tired.

"How ya doin', kiddo?" he asked.

"Alright," I answered.

"Did dem sand niggers pay up?" A voice crackled from the shadowed cab.

There were four in the car. Mickey Reid sat shotgun. He was the scariest human being I'd ever laid eyes on. He had a large head, a muscular brow, and his scowl was sunken so deep into his face that it never left.

Lil Pat sighed, turned, and snapped, "Give me a minute with the kid, OK? What de fuck?"

I stepped up to Lil Pat's door, and he reached out his big, meaty arm and hugged me to his chest. My belly pressed against the sun-baked sheet metal. His body was warm against my head like he had a fever. Funny how sometimes it's the ones capable of the most horrific deeds who are also capable of the most compassion and the deepest love. Maybe it's that they've seen the dark face of man and what we are capable of that makes them give love this way—to shelter and protect us.

"I love ya, Joey," Lil Pat whispered, then kissed the side of my crew cut.

I giggled and tried to squirm away, but I knew Lil Pat wouldn't let go 'til I said it back.

"I love ya," I squealed, and he finally released.

"Look what I got for you," he said, pulling a silver chain out of a cup holder in the center console. It had a flat, gold crucifix attached to it with immaculate little etchings traced along it. He reached out and slid it over my big round head. It just barely cleared my ears. I reached up and took the cross in my fingers and rubbed the etchings. Lil Pat reached in through the neck of his shirt and pulled out a matching one.

"Now we both got the same one, kid. How about dat?"

"Thanks, Pat!" Just the thought that I could have something he had made my heart swell with pride.

Fat Buck and another guy snored in the back seat. The car stank of warm beer, piss, and cigarette ash.

"Where's the envelopes?" Mickey interrupted, staring straight ahead as a big green vein bubbled up on his forehead.

I knew something was wrong when they gave me the envelope at my last stop—the corner store.

The thin, old man stood stoically at the register. A bright red dot on his forehead glistened like a bloody thumb print—the ink had smeared and dribbled down his black eyebrow before it dried on his wrinkled, deep-brown skin. He sneered at me then tossed the envelope on the counter. I grinned, stretched the rubber band, and slid the envelope in beside the other twenty or so.

"Go now! Get out!" The old man shouted as he came around the counter with the broom. I snagged a sucker off a display tray and ran out the door.

I reached the envelopes into the cab, and Mickey snatched them and thumbed through. He plucked the one out and tore it open.

"Thirteen bucks? Motherfuckers!" he yelled.

Mickey's whole head flared red. These large mounds near his jaw, temple, and above his ear pulsed. It seemed that at any moment each mound would separate, like tectonic plates, and his broiling wrath would finally erupt from him, roar forth and dis-integrate everything it touched.

"Who de fuck gave you de envelope?" Mickey roared. "Was it that cunt or the old man?" Mickey snatched a big air vent in the dashboard and pulled it right off. He reached his hand into the opening and came out with a nickel-plated 9mm semi-automatic. He slid the barrel back until it clicked and shot forward with a sharp, metallic crack. "WHO THE FUCK WAS IT?!"

Lil Pat twisted in his seat, snagged Mickey by his collar, and slammed his head against the far window. Mickey's eyes bulged, but he made no move—the gun laid limp in his stubby hands.

"I told you not to talk to the kid like dat," Lil Pat said.

The two snarled at each other, eyes locked in some darkened collusion. "And put dat fuckin' piece away." Lil Pat released him. "Neighborhood's hot enough as it is wit' out you try'n to be John Wayne every five minutes." Mickey returned the pistol into the stash and fastened the vent.

Lil Pat turned back to me. "Joey, it's OK... Go home. I'll see you at the house later." The warmth in his voice returned.

I turned toward home, then looked back over my shoulder.

"Go on, it's alright," Lil Pat urged as the Lincoln pulled away.

I started for home, then darted into a parking garage across from the corner store. I ducked behind a green Nova and peered out into the intersection. A few seconds later, the Lincoln appeared north-bound on Clark, stopping in front of the corner store. The back door opened, and Fat Buck got out wiping sleep from his eyes with his thick wrists. He looked up and down Clark and nodded back. The other three got out. The young one in back got in the driver seat while Lil Pat and Mickey walked toward the store.

"Hey... Look who it is, my favorite old shitbag!" Mickey spread his arms out, palms open, like he was going to give someone big a hug. He disappeared into the doorway, and Lil Pat stepped in behind him. Then, Lil Pat hoisted his knee up to his chest and booted over a large stack of pop cases just inside the door. They avalanched in a thunderous clang. There were more crashes and a large bang. Mickey raged in demonic tongues—only sparsely decipherable phrases leapt from the doorway. "THEMONEY MOTHERFUCKER! SANDNIGGER, FUCKWITHME, FUCK-WITH ME!" It scared the hell out of me.

Lil Pat emerged from the doorway stuffing bills in his front pocket. He looked back and shouted for Mickey. A cheap champagne bottle smashed through the large front window. It arced slowly in profile with a wake of glass shards sprinkling after it like confetti. Then, it popped on the sidewalk and sent white fizz splurging out over the curb. The window crinkled and fell in chunks.

"I got us some champagne, brotha!" Mickey yelled as he walked out clutching a big dark-green bottle. Lil Pat laughed crazily, but he must have felt my eyes on him, because he looked back at me. His wide grin evaporated, and his mouth hung open in an O. The cross sat dead center in his solar plexus, and the etching threw flecks of the morning light in sharp glints. The old man moaned in defeated agony inside.

They piled into the Lincoln and were gone.

■

I HAD AN IDYLLIC CHILDHOOD. It wasn't all dark. We had the best block parties in the whole city of Chicago. Da being a precinct captain, we were all kindsa hooked up! The fire engines and the cops on horseback would show up and hang out. The jumping bean would spend the whole afternoon on our block. Hundreds of kids from all over the neighborhood would show up to the 1600 block of Hollywood, and we'd have water fights that lasted the entire day—from dawn to dusk. Ma ran the whole thing, so we had dibs on everything, like the ice cream eating contests and the hundreds of water balloons we had in our little above ground pool.

Parts of the neighborhood were as clean as my brother Blake's Gordon Tech letterman's jacket. There was a tradition of ball hawks in the neighborhood, and Blake brought a group of us down there on the Clark St. bus. We tried to catch the home runs during batting practice and spent a bunch of time chasing the home run balls that bounced up and down Waveland Ave. We played baseball in the lot behind St. Greg's gymnasium with racket balls and metal bats and cranked home runs all the way onto the roof of the gym.

Sometimes, my family would escape the city all altogether. We'd head up to Grand Beach during the summer to the old family vacation home that became the family home after Grandpa Walsh dissolved into alcohol. He passed before I was born, but long before that, my old man became the father figure to his six younger brothers. When they were little, all of 'em slept in bunk beds in one room. Grandma dumped a box of clothes in the center of it every morning, and they fought it out. The loser might be out socks or underwear, or worse. No wonder they all ended up so damn tough. They couldn't make rent a lot of the time, and eventually the landlords got fed up, so the family'd have to up and disappear to the old summer house in Grand Beach. It was a place to escape—you could disappear into its winding roads and walk down its steep shored beach and look out across the lake to the city with all that blue in between you and it and know you were safe.

The drive to Grand Beach was always tough on me. I had a serous fear of heights, and the Skyway Bridge was the most terrifying thing to me as a kid. I'd cry and beg my Dad to turn around, then lay down on the floor of the van underneath the bench seats as my sisters and brothers teased me. When we got to the top, I'd stop crying, get up, and look out at the enormity of the lake and the city behind us. We'd be in Grand Beach within the hour, and we'd fish off the shores of Lake Michigan. We caught lake trout and king salmon, and it was always a blast.

Back in the neighborhood, our block was the kind of block where everybody knew everybody. Gossip ran up and down front porches all day and night, and you couldn't walk very far without someone waving to you and asking about your family. The neighborhood was just a nice place to live in, and I loved being a child of Chicago and growing up in the greatest city in the world.

■

AFTER THE MURDER, everything changed. In the weeks that followed, I hung out with Ryan more and more. It was a secret, and like most shared secrets, it brought us closer. I started to have this reoccurring nightmare of Lil Pat and Mickey chasing me—their wild, hackling laughter blaring in my mind. Lil Pat brandished a large, cartoonish revolver with his massive, bubble-fingered hand squeezed tight around the grip. I would run through this neighborhood I'd never seen before in the night with its towering streetlamps looming above and emitting a thin glint of foggy, green light. I could never break away from them no matter how hard I tried.

At the end of the dream, the strange neighborhood would suddenly fall away to darkness. Then, the dead Assyrian would appear—just his face floating in a pool of red. When I saw the Assyrian's face at night, I couldn't sleep, and I'd wake with a horrible terror, panting. A cool silence hovered all around and above me. I'd keep my eyes shut because I knew he was there floating in my room. I'd keep my eyes shut because I was afraid to look at him. I'd keep them shut until the coolness dissipated. Then, I'd slide off the bed to my knees and pray. I'd pray for his soul. I'd pray Lil Pat's soul. I never prayed for Mickey because I knew he had no soul to pray for. It happened every now and then. Over the years, it slowly slid and fell away and was overtaken by something even worse.

CHAPTER 3

THE LAKE

THERE WAS A HEAT WAVE that summer. It was a dry, coarse heat that scorched the lawns yellow and deepened the skin tones of the children. Grandma had told Jan'n'Rose to stay out of the sun so their Afro-Caribbean skin didn't turn black, so they stayed in the house most of the day and walked the neighborhood at night. They'd go over to the apartment building two doors down to hang out with their friend Maria and flirt with the Mexican boys who lived there. They were always on the lookout for Lil Pat, Blake, and Rich, but they didn't mind me tagging along. Maria was tall and thin with long, black, curly hair and thick, purple lips. Sometimes, for a joke, Maria would take me by the hand and lead me into her bedroom. We'd lay together on her bed with the lights off, and she'd moan, calling out my name—loud—so my sisters and the others could hear her in the next room, and I'd kiss her full lips in the dark. She'd gasp quietly with the giggling from the next room flooding in through the thin walls. The scent of her grape lip gloss made my mouth water as it soothed my always-chapped lips. One time, she even let me give her a hickey on the side of her soft, warm neck with the low light of the alley lamps filtering in through her window.

■

I STILL MADE MY WALK to collect the protection money along Clark for the TJOs every Sunday. Ryan started coming with, and we'd spend the afternoon joking about the things we'd stolen along the way. It was a team action: one of us going up to the manager to collect the envelope and buy something like candy for a quarter, while the other grabbed chips or lighters or anything of value to a kid. Sometimes, Lil Pat and Mickey would pick us up and drive us down to Montrose Beach where we would wade out into the blue and marvel at the clear between our feet like a lie. We'd skip rocks and climb on the huge concrete cubes lining some parts along the shore as the older guys drank beer, smoked joints, counted the money, and laughed at the profile of the city they thought they owned.

Ryan lived at the Dead-End-Docks on Paulina Ave. between Thorndale and Rosehill Ave. Paulina dead-ends at Rosehill into this six-foot, concrete, castle-style wall; the same style wall as the ones that encircle Rosehill Cemetery a few blocks west. His alley butted up against the Clark Street. Ace Hardware's loading docks, which made the alley three-times the width of any in the neighborhood. That drew little knuckleheads from all over. They swarmed around back there incessantly. It was like the United Nations of juvenile delinquents: blacks, Irish, Mexicans, mutt whites, Assyrians, Filipinos, and Puerto Ricans. They shot hoops on a plastic milk crate with the bottom stomped out. Someone just nailed it to a wooden electricity pole, and they played with a mini basketball. The alley ended in a big vacant parking lot. A legion of bold, yellow-headed dandelions sprouted up through the cracks in the old asphalt. Past the lot, across Rosehill Ave., there was a row of small houses with full-leaved trees nestled around them. The immense, tan structure of the hospital leered above them—the only present and capable authority.

I was over there one afternoon that August. It was hot out like the inside of an oven set to bake. Ryan and I leaned against the fence separating the alley from the lot. The top horizontal bar was warped in a low-hung bow from the kids jumping it while running from the cops and each other. Ryan had his shirt off, and his thick shoulders and neck were seared red with chalk-white sunblock slathered over them. The heavy freckles were like brown sugar sprinkled up his arms and across his brow and cheeks. He wore gray sweatpants and black and white Chuck Taylors.

This little runt of a black kid named BB spliced a mini basketball between his legs. He had a missing top-front tooth and crazy graphics etched into his scalp. He was in the middle of a lecture on how 'mothafuckin' good' he was at basketball to a disinterested audience. BB made up for his small stature and age deficiency by having the loudest mouth for miles around, and he'd have gotten his ass whooped every thirty seconds if it weren't for his brother being a high ranking Black Stone Ranger.

A gangway gate creaked open halfway down the alley, which led to a large, red brick apartment building. A wooden stairwell snaked down the rear of the structure, and two older black kids sauntered out. Everyone's eyes shot towards them. The first out wore a black Starter cap with a large gold "P" above the brim. The other one had on white jogging pants with the left leg rolled up to his knee and a black pick comb jutted upright from the back of his cone-shaped afro. They all flocked over, and Ryan and I trailed in their wake.

"Krazy Crew!" the one with the hat bellowed, elongating the words. He threw up a quick wrist-flicking hand gesture. The mob of kids instantly echoed it. They formed a "C" with the thumb and index fingers and a "K" with the middle, ring, and pinky on the same hand.

"Monteff," the one with the pick said. "Mama's looking for you, go on inside."

"Awe, T-Money, come on," Monteff cried, throwing his head back in agony.

"Aight, it's your ass, nigga... Speaking of ass whoopins, ya'll been holdin' down the set?" His tall, thin body loomed over us. His Adam's apple bulged.

"Hell yeah. Aw hell yeah," us kids roared urgently.

"We need to hand out any violations?" the one with the hat asked. He mashed his wide fist into his palm high over our heads. "Any mouth shots?"

This sent a shiver of frightened murmurs through the crowd. Even BB got spooked. His eyes bugged, and his bottom lip drooped open.

"Ah, we just fuckin' witcha," the older boys said, bursting into laughter. A sigh of relief hissed from us kids.

"But ya'll need ta get toughened up," T-Money said. "So we gonna have us some boxing matches today."

"How about dangly, old Leroy," BB shouted. "He ain't never fought nobody."

"Yeah?" T-Money asked, furrowing his brow. "Come'ere, Leroy." Leroy sifted to the front. "And who else?" T-Money scanned our faces.

"What about Joe," BB said. "Dat white boy prolly neva fought nobody."

"Who's Joe?" T-Money asked.

All the kids turned and shot their index fingers directly at me. A pang singed through my throat. I'd been in plenty of fights. I was the toughest kid in my grade at St. Greg's, but all these kids were from Pierce—the rough public school down the street.

"You wanna fight?" T-Money asked, baring his yellow-white chops.

I nodded and pulled my t-shirt off. The kids oowwwed.

"Hell yeah," T-Money said. "I like your style boy, you look like you finna whoop ole Leroy."

The boys formed a shoulder-to-shoulder circle about the size of a boxing ring. I slipped my crucifix off and handed it to Ryan. He slid it over his head without a word.

"Twon, get Leroy's corner," T-Money directed, motioning to the other big kid.

Leroy was a little taller than me and skinnier. He wore a white t-shirt with grease stains streaked across the belly and some tight cut-off blue jeans. Leroy twirled his finger through his light-brown afro that sprang out puffy and thick like the tips of cauliflower.

T-Money crouched down to my eye level and gripped his jogging pants as he chomped a wad of Juicy Fruit. "You got him, champ. You just gotta go'n whoop his ass... Hit him like dis." T-Money bobbed on the toes of his black Reeboks. Then, he threw quick-darting punches into the air like he was swatting flies with closed fists. Years later, when I started to box, fighting at park districts around town and then the Golden Gloves, I'd learn that boxing was way more than hitting and getting hit. But I'd always look back at this as my first real bout.

My stomach was uneasy and bloated. The plan was to get him in a headlock, hip-toss him to the ground, and then pound his face with my free hand—a move that had won me most fights. But I was usually angry when I fought. Now, I just felt sick and dizzy as the circle of boys hooted.

"Naw... I betchu Joe's gonna whoop his ass," Ryan sneered at a mahogany-toned black kid who'd just walked up.

BB solemnly stepped into the center of the circle of boys, announcing, "And in this corner," BB raised his small palm towards Leroy, "with a record of zera and zera... dangly, old Leroy..." Laughter rippled through the ring.

"And in this corner," BB said, raising his arm towards me, "also with a record of zera and zera... Whitey Joe..."

Everyone's eyes beat down on me as they giggled and clapped. Mad, eager smiles spread across their faces, and BB waved us both to the center of the ring. Twon loomed behind Leroy, and he glowered down at me. A thin line of peach fuzz undulated above his mouth. T-Money kneaded my traps and shoulders. They walked us up close to each other, and our foreheads almost touched. Leroy and I tried to make mean faces, but they slid from grimaces to grins.

"Rules..." BB said, looking down and scratching his chin. "Fuck... it ain't no rules..." The crowd squealed. "Aight, no bleedin' too much, and no cryin'."

The boys roared.

"Now go back to your corners, and come on out swingin'," BB declared, placing his hands on his hips. "And don't be swingin' like no girls or nothin'."

As I walked back to my corner, Ryan rushed up.

"You got him, Joe... You got him." Ryan's green eyes gleamed. His spiky buzz-cut blazed in the sunlight like a copper crown.

I smirked. My heart pulsed. The yells deafened me. I couldn't think. I just scanned their faces. An obese, light-skinned black kid with a saggy, off-yellow shirt; a little white kid with a blond box cut; a wiry Assyrian kid with a shaggy, loose-curled afro. All of 'em bounced on their toes with the same excited, toothy grins. The ground felt soft and unstable under my sneakers. Their sudden shouts spouted up and swallowed the next.

"Let's get ready to rumble!" BB bellowed, and then stepped back. Leroy and I stood across from each other. We didn't know what to do.

"Go on an' fight," BB ordered, and clapped his hands together.

We walked out in the middle. Both of us awestruck, we smiled and glanced around. Suddenly, Leroy's fist lurched out and cracked my forehead. A loud "Ohh!" rang from the circle. My head rocked back. I'd never been punched like that. I saw the fist, then the blue sky. Then, I was looking back at Leroy again. A howl surged through my ears. It wasn't funny anymore. An orb of broiling energy materialized in the center of my chest. I squeezed my fist, and the energy gushed straight through my arm and bottlenecked at my wrist. Then, it exploded as my fist burst into Leroy's eye socket. His head whipped back, and his smile evaporated.

We commenced to drive our clutched fists into each other's heads. There was no form, no technique. The blows were all guided by complete and blind malice. I heard nothing, thought nothing. There was no time, just the moment. We teetered into the circular wall of boys, and they just shoved us back toward the center.

After a few calamitous minutes, I drew arm-weary. Tears splashed down Leroy's face. His lip sparkled with blood. I couldn't catch my breath. My arms flapped at my sides like two dead lake trout, and I crumpled to the cement. A joyous howl ballooned up around me. The sudden embarrassment wrenched in my heart and hurled me to my feet. I rushed Leroy and dug my fist into his belly, deep, so he cried out. Then, he crumbled to the ground and wept in heavy, tired sobs. T-Money rushed into the middle of the ring waving his hands over his head.

"That's round one. End-a the round," he said, then he grabbed my elbow and led me back to the corner. Twon picked up Leroy.

"That's good, Joe!" T-Money urged. "You got him! You gon' whoop dat marg!"

Ryan stepped up on my side. His bright eyes glowed. There was a hopeful smile on his thin lips. "You all right, Joe?" he asked. "You all right?"

I got a lump in my throat and nodded.

"Damn, Leroy, I thought you was a sucka... You ain't a sucka at all..." BB squeaked. "But you betta not let that white boy whoop you."

When T-Money called out for round two, a few hot tears streamed down my face. I didn't want to stop, and I didn't know why I was crying. The tears infuriated me. I wanted to fight, and I wanted to win. Leroy's bottom lip was split down the center, and bright-red blood glistened across his quivering mouth. A thin stream slid down from the cut and mixed with the tears streaking along his cheek. The bloody tears suffused at his chin, then dribbled down to his shirt in murky, red splotches.

They called for round two, and we went right back at it. We fought toe-to-toe like that for a very long time. It became a battle of wills. I cracked first. The sizzling heat, the surging roars, the bursts of white in my vision—it was all too much. I got dizzy, stumbled, and then locked eyes with the wiry Assyrian kid. He looked worried. It could have been his brother. The dead Assyrian's face swirled up and flashed in my mind—his blood-dampened hair, the frozen scream. I tried to say I was sorry, to tell him that I pray for his brother sometimes. I'm so sorry. Leroy smacked me with a hard punch to the forehead, and I crumpled to the pavement and curled up in a fetal ball.

Suddenly, BB leered down at me.

"One... Two... Three... Four..."

Ryan dashed over and squatted down on his hams beside me.

"Come on, Joe, get up... Please get up."

Ryan's strained face floated over me before the cloudless, stark-blue sky that hovered above. The sun was silhouetted perfectly by his round head. My crucifix dangled down from his neck and swayed over my eyes. *What if he don't wanta be my friend no more.* This cool calm spread over me. I wiped my tears, took a deep breath, and stood up. Then, I walked straight to Leroy and cracked him. He reeled backward, and I unloaded a barrage of shots that bounced his head around like a paddle ball. Finally,

Leroy spun and belly flopped on the cement. His cheek clapped the concrete and kicked up a spray of white dust that caked the whole side of his face. The dust clung to his tears and sweat like flour sprinkled on wet dough.

BB counted over Leroy. My fists felt like hot goo. I heard the low rumble of a Diesel engine, then tires crinkling atop the pebbled alleyway. The obese black kid stepped up behind me and pounded his heavy paw on my back. The others joined him, and their many hands jolted me as I stepped back, heaving. A car door unlatched, swung open, and slammed shut. I craned to see over the ring. There was a light-brown truck just down the alley. Suddenly, Leroy sprang up and drove his shoulder into my hip. We both tumbled to the pavement, sprawling, and I knew I'd roll him. He straddled me and tried to punch down, so I yanked his shirtsleeve downward, reached up, and clutched his mucky, tear-drenched jaw. Then, I twisted and toppled him. As we rolled, a large hand clamped down on my arm and yanked me clear up into the air. My big brother Rich's glossy, steel-blue eyes flashed in mine. His teeth flared at the center of his bristly beard. The wild, brown curls of Rich's shoulder-length mullet swayed fiercely as he ambled through the wall of kids. He knocked BB flat on his backside. I dangled from his grip with the tips of my sneakers scraping the pavement. He snatched his backward, red Marlboro baseball cap off his head. T-Money scampered alongside us with his brow furrowed.

"What? You his brotha or something?" T-Money pleaded. "It was a fair fight. He was doin' fine. He was finna win!"

Rich stomped on. As we got to Dad's old Diesel, he shoved T-Money in the chest. Then, he yanked the passenger side door open and threw me in by my arm. I landed on his girlfriend Nancy's lap.

"Richard, stop it now!" She hissed. Her long, straight brown hair spilt out of her headband.

Rich slammed the door shut on us, then spun around on T-Money, who looked young and frail up next to him. Rich's chest heaved beneath his sleeveless, black Iron Maiden shirt.

"You wanta beat up on my brother, nigger?" Rich spat, then smashed two quick fists into T-Money's face. T-Money tumbled backward and clutched his mug.

BB threw a stone that pegged off the side Rich's head. Rich stomped around the front end of the Diesel, jumped in, and we peeled off.

"FUCKIN' NIGGERS!" Rich screamed maniacally from his window.

A wash of garbage and rocks clinked and banged against the windshield and side panel. Monteff whipped a half-empty RC can that clanked on the windshield and splattered a string of fizzy, brown suds across the glass. The Bronco careened out of the alley.

"WHY THE FUCK YOU HANGING OUT OVER HERE!" Rich screamed, spittle spurting from his teeth.

"They're my friends!" I replied, writhing in Nancy's arms. My head pulsed as lumps inflated along my forehead.

They quarreled as we pulled in front of the house. I hopped out and ran upstairs to my room and collapsed on my bed. My chest heaved as I sobbed. The dark-blue drapes were drawn closed, and they filtered the harsh light. A cool, turquoise haze filled the room. Stone-sized knots swelled on my forehead beneath my scalp—pulsing mounds that itched and burned like giant chicken pox. My hands and wrists felt large and hollow, and a thin film of blood dried on my knuckles.

Light footsteps entered my room. I bawled uncontrollably, lying flat on my back. Jan's pudgy hand appeared, palm up, and her deep-brown fingers spread. A sopping-wet dish rag peeked out from between the gaps in her fingers. Droplets of cool water dripped off her knuckles and spattered on my cheek and brow. She brought her hand close, and the ice cubes jostled in the folded rag. Then, she flopped it onto my forehead. I gasped. The shock-ing chill instantly soothed and deflated the burning knots.

My whole body eased as Jan sat on the mattress beside my arm. Her soft, brown face. Her thick, frizzy hair pulled back and tied with a rubber band. The silky, black curls splayed out over her shoulders as she gazed peace-fully out the window at the head of my bed. The slow breeze parted the drapes, send-ing vertical slivers of light across her chocolaty skin. A thought slithered though my mind: *is she a nigger, too?* Strings of agony coursed down my throat and planted in my heart. She stayed be-side me, silently strumming her fingers gently through my hair. My love for her, my sister, like a giant, deep lake with bright yellow sunlight streaking its peaking surface. I went to say it— to say it all—but it got caught in my throat as the exhaustion billowed up and encompassed me in a heavy, warm fog, and I sank into sleep.

■

I LOVED THEM the way boys love older sisters, and they adored and tortured me equally. When I'd started grammar school, I hat-ed it. I'd fight and refuse to go each morning while Ma was out picking up the babysitting kids. At first, they'd scream at me to get ready, I'd scream back, and we'd get nowhere. Later, they'd bargain and offer to carry me piggyback. More often than not, they'd carry me to school. Grandma saw us a few times as we crossed through her gangway, and she told everyone I was their prince. In a way, I was, I guess, but I was also a despised pest. Once, as I rode piggyback in the falling snow, my boot slipped off. I didn't say anything until we got to St. Greg's in the hopes it'd disqualify me from school that day. They screamed at me the whole way back trying to find that boot. Jan was inconsolably enraged, and Rose was near tears because we'd been late several times that month—all my fault. I don't know how they put up with me. On summer nights, they'd get their revenge.

Jan'n'Rose hung out with their Filipino friend Marge and her effeminate little brother, TeeTee. Jan had this way of turning everything into a military action, so instead of strolling the neighborhood, they'd march. Or, Jan'd march and they'd follow. Whenever Jan saw me, she'd unleash this seething scream and sprint after me. I'd take off running, and the rest of them followed, laughing. It sucked sometimes, but I loved them like that—like every moment of my life they were my sisters. Not my *adopted* sisters, or my *black* sisters, or my *Afro-Caribbean* sisters. Just my sisters—that simple. Our neighborhood was so accepting of us and them that it was like nobody noticed. That fight was the first time it'd been thrust in my face. They were different than me. Even though every fiber of my being knew they were part of me, and I part of them.

CHAPTER 4

QUARK

MY BROTHER RICH was a racist, but he was one of the few individuals in the world who actually almost had the right to be one. He was the victim of a terrible hate crime.

It happened earlier in the same summer as the fight. Rich, Nancy, and another friend of theirs named Garret were walking through some alley in Rogers Park looking for a basement party they'd gotten bad directions to. It was about midnight, and they passed a liter of Old Style amongst themselves. The neighborhood streets were quiet. Suddenly, two black men burst out of a gangway behind them. The first brandished a heavy, muck-covered lead pipe. He surged toward Rich, hefted the pipe over his head, and swung it down hard, nicking the side of Rich's skull and planting deep into his collar bone. Rich's knees buckled. The other one rushed at Nancy and grabbed hold of her shirt. She screamed, instantly reached up, and gouged at his eyes with her nails. Rich staggered and leapt at the one who'd grabbed her and thudded his fist into the guy's head.

"Go!" Rich shouted. Garret yanked Nancy free, and they ran.

The pipe finally found its mark over the back of Rich's head, and he flashed out like the streetlights had been shut off, but Nancy said he never hit the ground. The heavy-set ex-cons snatched him up, blabbering something about guard brutality in Statesville and how they were 'doing this for dem brothas in Statesville.'

The two men dragged Rich into an abandoned basement and ripped his clothes off with their incredibly strong hands while they muttered, laughed, and grunted.

Nancy and Garret ran down the alley screaming for help. Then, they cut onto Clark and ran right out into traffic, waving their arms. The cars swerved and screeched around them. Nancy screamed, "Rape!" then, "Fire!" and a light clicked on.

Rich's mouth filled with blood. Some slid down his throat, and it gargled there as he begged for mercy.

Finally, a police squad swerved up to Nancy and Garret. They jumped in and surged into the alley, where they frantically searched for the gangway. They found it thanks to a red hand smear on a wooden garage siding. When they got down in the basement, the men had Rich's pants down to his knees. The shirtless one was hovering above him, stroking his own semi-hard cock hanging out of his undone pants. The cops pulled out their firearms.

The ex-cons said it was consensual—that Nancy just got jealous. The cops were reluctant to arrest them, and Rich didn't pursue it, so they let them go. The cut on the top of Rich's head wasn't bad enough for stitches, and the bruises eventually healed. Nothing else ever did.

■

MUSIC DOESN'T MEAN MUCH when you're a little kid; it's just sounds and the emotions they produce. None of your identity is aligned with what you listen to. You're a clean pallet.

I was on my way upstairs to my room when I heard laughter

booming out of Rich's open bedroom door. My head still ached from the fight. I reached up and felt the soft lumps along my forehead, now all purple and blue. I could hear Rich over Pantera's fast, rippling metal.

"My baby brother, he was fighting with twenty little niggers at once," Rich roared, his voice all high, squeaky, and excited. "I came up and saved him and beat the shit out of a few of 'em myself. But, man, I'm telling ya, twenty of 'em!"

"OK, Rich. Fuckin' superhero over here. Where is that little rascal, anyways?" I recognized the gravelly voice. It was Sy.

I reached the top of the stairs. It was early evening, and a bright yellow light radiated out of his doorway. I peered in to see four guys lounged on his little bed. All of them had long dirty hair and ripped-up jeans. Rich stood with his back to me and his arms flailing around as he recounted the fight. There was an American flag tacked to the slanted ceiling that hung with the pitch of the roof. A large Iron Maiden poster hung on the wall near the window that showed the skeletal Eddie the Head in a straitjacket with three chains attached to his iron neck collar. It secured him inside a padded room, and his fierce eyes screamed out at you. It read *"Peace of Mind"* at the bottom.

Sy's hair was a greasy, dirty blond tangle that hung down past his shoulders. His beard was mangy and had a tint of red in it. He wore this threadbare, black Metallica t-shirt, bleached white jeans with rips at the knees, and some white high-top Reeboks. I peeked my head in through the door.

"Get over here, you," Sy said, waving me in. "The champ himself!"

He reached out, grabbed me, and threw me in a head lock. I smelled pot and liquor, but I didn't know what the smells were then, and I recognized 'em as Sy's scent. He let me go and stood there. I could feel them all staring at my forehead and eye.

"Now what happened, Joey?" Sy asked.

I took a deep breath. "Got in a fight," I said quietly.

"Well, I can see that," Sy replied, grinning. "Did ya win?"

"Didn't get to finish," I said, and glanced over at Rich, who watched me with his arms folded over his chest.

"Well... Did you get any good punches in?" Sy asked.

I paused, looked down, and scratched my chin. I riffled through my memory—the haze of punches and shouts—then I remembered Leroy on the pavement, and I looked back up.

"Yeah!" I exclaimed. They broke up.

"So he's coming out tonight, huh?" Sy looked over at Rich.

"Yep, Ma even said it was alright," Rich confirmed as he reached over and messed up my hair. "I told her what happened and said it might cheer him up to hear some metal."

My mind raced with wild excitement of where we were headed. I was sure it was some dark pit of dragons and snakes, smoke and roaring noise.

We piled into Rich's rusty Bronco, and the back was stacked to the roof with large black amps, guitar cases, and a drum kit.

"Sy, what's the name of your band?" I asked as we squished in the back seat.

"The Dead Rat Society," Sy growled. "Got a problem with that, kid?" He glowered at me. Metallica erupted as the sputtering engine started, and the Bronco sped down Hollywood.

The show was at a place out on Peterson Ave. called Fautches. I remembered Jan'n'Rose said they had all-ages house music on Friday nights, and they'd even convinced Ma to take 'em a few times. Fautches was a wide one-story converted office space with tall windows that spread across the entire width with tan, vertical track blinds that were always drawn shut. There was a glass door in the middle for the entrance, and the building had a narrow, empty lot beside it that was covered with white stones and garbage. A few bushes lined the club's cinderblock side wall. As we approached Fautches, Rich swerved right, and suddenly the

Bronco barreled over the curb and sidewalk. Everything in the truck sprung up airborn, then it all fell downward on the creaky shocks as the truck bounced. The instruments and amps wobbled. The truck tires rumpled over the stones and stopped near the back of the building next to a steel door.

"You're one crazy motherfucker, Rich!" Sy shouted as we piled out.

Rich got out and swung the rear hatch up. Miraculously, the mountain of equipment didn't avalanche out.

"Here, you carry this," Sy said as he gripped a guitar case, spun around, and bent down on one knee. Then, he lifted it up to me like some sacred relic. "Now you take care of this, champ."

"What is it?" I asked, grabbing the smooth wood handle.

"Excalibur," Sy declared, his eyes closed solemnly. "Now get in there."

I followed Rich, who hoisted a large kick drum.

We walked down a dark hallway. The roaring yawn of a lead electric guitar spilt into the room. We stacked the instruments and amps on the back of the small carpeted stage. The long, narrow room was about half full with slouchy metal-heads—almost all of whom wore black band shirts, bleached jeans, and combat boots—and most had long mops of dirty hair. There was one black dude sitting atop a tall amp near the side of stage. His long, skinny legs dangled almost to the floor. He had a mohawk made outta finger-length spikes of frizzy hair that spouted down the center of his shaved, glistening scalp.

I stood steadfast beside Excalibur's case and gawked at the room. Rich stomped up with a fistful of quarters. "Here," he said, and poured them into my cupped palms. "Go ahead." He nodded to the large arcade in the side room. "The show won't start for a while."

The game room was long and narrow like the concert room. It was filled with manic, pulsing lights. Video game machines lined each wall, and a column of games ran down the middle. It was full of racecar and gun games and crazy, themed pinball machines. I had a blast. Sy came up later and challenged me to a game of pinball. I picked Pin-Bot; it had this intergalactic robot with electricity blazing from its fingertips. Sy was all into it. He leaned in over the machine, and his wild hair splayed on the clear glass plane. Below was the bust of a lit up solar system. The green, red, and blue bulbs pulsed frantically, and the sensors rang as the ball bopped them.

Rich poked his head into the game room. "Hey... Sy, you gonna smoke?"

"Naw. I'm busy whippin' this kid in pinball," he replied without looking up.

"Alright," Rich said, putting his hand through my hair and disappearing back down the dark hallway.

"Smoking," I scowled. "That's what gave my Da cancer."

"Hey," Sy paused and looked down at me. "Well, den I never want to hear about you smokin'. Got it punk?" He slapped me softly on the back of the head.

"I won't, never."

Two blondes strolled up to us and started hanging on Sy. One wore this tight, white tank-top. It was sliced up with scissors on the sides and struggled to restrain her giant pair of plump boobs. She had on a black spandex leotard with a blue stripe running down one leg and these huge hoop earrings. The other was chunky with a loose, nylon plaid shirt on that hung down to her knees. Sy flashed his glowing smirk. I took my turn. Sy teased the ladies as they drunkenly hung on his shirtsleeve. The chesty one twisted her index finger in an oily strand of his hair.

I focused on the pinball machine. I banged hard on the smooth, little buttons. The flippers popped the small, chrome ball and bounced it through the flickering neon lights. The ball incited the spring-loaded boppers to percolate red. When my last ball slipped past the flippers, I was up a few points on Sy. He batted the blonde's hands away and stepped around to the front of the machine.

"Now, ladies, watch how a real man plays the game," he said, glancing at them. "You gotta understand, I ain't been beaten in two years runnin'. I'm the reigning champ of Fautches," he said to the girls as he smoothed his hair back behind his shoulders.

He pulled the spring, let it go, and leaned over the machine. The little ball bounced and rattled. Sy squinted in a crazed focus as he banged the flipper buttons. With his first ball, he racked up some points, making the game even closer. He glanced at me as I bit my fingernails nervously.

The next ball slipped past him.

"Ahhhhh," he exclaimed, and banged his fists against the thick glass. The girls chortled.

"It all comes down to this," he said, glaring at me. "I ain't losin' to this punk kid, no damn way!"

The girls watched Sy pull back the spring on his last ball. His face scrunched excruciatingly tight, and he leaned in on the tilted glass plane. He released, and the shiny ball soared up the narrow channel. It dinged and popped and bumped the score even closer. I bounced up and down on my toes and clenched my fists at my lips.

The ball arced down the slow tilt of the plane, slashing through the colorful planets. Sy tapped the ball with the tip of a white flipper, and it arced up slowly like a pop-fly. Then, it came down, and he just barely nicked it. He let out another long groan, and the girls leaned in and smirked at his agonized face. He whiffed with the flipper, and the ball panged into the black vault.

"Damn it!!! This machine's broke! I want a rematch!" Sy yelled, squeezing his hands around the machine and jolting it savagely.

"He beat you?" the girls sighed and clapped. "Who is this young, sexy little man?" The big-boobed one bent down to my height. Her flimsy shirt drooped, so her milky breasts poured out of her tight bra. "There's a new champion in town isn't there?"

I smiled up at her large, green eyes. She smelled like a whole lotta strong perfume.

"He's so cute," the other one chimed in, gliding her pudgy fingers through my hair.

"Aye, he's all mine," the one with the big jugs declared, smacking the other girl's hand away. Then, she smooched her puffy, wet lips against my cheek. A thick film of lipstick clung to my skin.

"Get away from my little brother, ya skank!" Rich said as he and the rest ambled in through the back hall. "It's showtime, baby brotha." Rich's eyes were bloodshot, and his breath smelled like a musty skunk. He hoisted me onto his shoulders.

Sy and the rest climbed on stage. Rich jogged with me out into the crowd, and by then, the room had completely filled. Sy slung Excalibur around his shoulder; it was a cherry red Stratocaster with white trim. He flicked one of the chrome strings with his pick and it roared. Sy stepped to the microphone.

"You scumfucks ready for this?" he screamed. He leaned out over the crowd and spit out a small, white glob that arced out into the mass of long-haired domes. The crowd spit back, and a barrage of half-crushed beer cans clanked onto the stage.

"We're the Dead Rat Society," he muttered. The music exploded from the speakers. There was more order in this roaring, racing sound. I had a clear view of everything as I sat perched on Rich's shoulders. The front of the crowd immediately twisted into a torrent of thrashing arms and legs. The black punk jumped off the amp and into the pit. The spiral widened into the room. Sy rambled through cutting, indecipherable lyrics, and every few words, the whole crowd would shout a garbled phrase in unison with him.

Rich stayed back where it was calmer. The crowd began to sway. A big circle twisted in the mass of shadowed bodies. Then, another circle opened in the center of them like the eye of a tornado. This circle kicked their legs out savagely, following each other like a Comanche war dance. Their grins morphed into howling scowls.

After a few songs, the front door opened and several guys with pale white shaved heads stepped in. They all wore white t-shirts with red suspenders and had fierce, cold grimaces on their muscular faces. They glared at everyone who didn't look away, until they did.

I'd seen skinheads around before, and I had a vague idea of what they were all about. They slid their way into the chaos, passing us with sly smirks spread across their faces and eyes lit up like they were about to pull a prank. They pushed to the edge of the slam-dance circle, and then they suddenly erupted with forearms, head-butts, and punches. I caught a flash of one of their maniacal faces as he slapped his fist into some tall kid. The kid's long mop of hair exploded in a big swoosh like he'd stuck his finger in an outlet. By the time that song ended, most of the crowd had quieted. It was only the skinheads smashing each other. The kid bled profusely from his nose, and I strained my neck to see a couple girls help him to the bathroom in back. The black guy with the mohawk had stopped moshing. He leaned his back along the wall, nervously, with his arms folded over his chest. His eyes darted around the room.

"This's our last one," Sy said as sweat dripped off his brow and glistened in his light beard. "I want to thank you for being so fuckin' polite."

The crowd screamed. The drums rattled. One of the skinheads threw an empty whiskey pint that just missed Sy's head and broke against the fake wood-paneled wall behind the stage. A couple fat-faced bouncers at the front door pushed into the crowd. Their bulging, neon-green shirts sliced through the darkly clad bodies as the room erupted into high-swung fists and beer sud-bursts. A girl screamed, but the roar swallowed it. The crowd surged backward. Rich staggered into the arcade with me clung to his head and took me down from his shoulders.

"Stay back. It's OK," Rich said, putting himself between me and the chaos. "Fuckin' skinheads."

Two of the bouncers broke through the crowd. They held one skinhead by both arms, and the fatter bouncer clasped him by the nape of his neck. They dragged him out the front door as he fought to break their grasp, and the rest of the skins giggled as they trailed behind.

"It wasn't him. It was that fuckin' nigger," one yelled.

I glanced though the back door of the arcade and saw a black figure stumble down the dark back hallway.

The crowd unleashed an exalted cheer as the Dead Rat Society finished their set. The guys started to break down their equipment, and I followed Rich up to the stage. Sy hopped down and crouched to my height.

"What'd ya think, kiddo?" he asked as sweat dripped off his burly face.

"It was awesome!"

Sy was the coolest. He just had a knack for making the best out of anything. He smiled and combed his sweat-dampened hand through my hair.

I lugged Excalibur and followed Rich out the back door past the bathroom. There was blood smeared all over the white-tiled walls and a dark pool in the sink. As we passed, the guys saw it and burst into laughter. Outside, I noticed two long, skinny legs sticking out of the bushes that lined the cinderblock wall. The black combat boots attached to them crumpled inward on each other. I walked over, stooped down, and peered into the narrow crevasse.

"What," Rich shouted toward the bushes. "Can't hold your liquor?" He set the amp he carried down on the stones and opened the truck's back hatch.

It took a second for my eyes to adjust—it was the black dude with the spiked mohawk. He sat and clutched his stomach. A smear of dark red blood covered the white Dago T. His eyes stared blankly into the bushes.

"You alright?" I asked. I reached out and touched his ankle.

Sy walked up next to me, still chuckling at what Rich had said.

"He's hurt," I said, glancing up at Sy.

Sy bent down and looked.

"Oh shit! Call a fuckin' ambulance!" Sy yelled as the other guys scrambled back inside.

"Shit, man! You OK?" Sy crouched down. The guy looked at Sy and started to say something, then his head just slumped to the side, and he passed out. His thin torso began to slide down the wall. Sy pushed the bushes back and reached in, grabbing him and holding him up.

"What?" Rich asked as he sauntered over.

"He's fucking hurt, Rich!" Sy shouted. "Call an ambulance!"

"Oh shit," Rich laughed. "Them skins got him."

"Wake up, man," Sy said and slapped him lightly on the cheek. The guy seized. A line of yellow ooze slid out of his lips, touched the stones, and then slurped back before just dangling from the corner of his mouth. He started to shake violently, and his legs jerked and kicked up the stones.

"Man, leave that nigger where he lays," Rich said, laughing.

"What the fuck, Rich?" Sy yelled. "Are they calling or what?"

"Come on, Joey," Rich said as he put his arm around my shoulder and led me to the truck. The fat bouncers rushed out of the club.

We left after the ambulance got there. I was in back, scrunched next to Sy.

"Think he's gonna die?" Rich said as he turned slowly onto Peterson. The red and blue ambulance and police strobes spun and spilt onto the crowded street.

"Shit, I don't know," Sy answered. "He looked bad, didn't he?"

"He came to the wrong fucking place," Rich said.

"That guy wasn't doing nothing to nobody, man," Sy said as he slammed his fist into the pleather headrest in front of him. "He was just slamming like the rest of 'em."

"Had the wrong skin tone is all," Rich drawled as one of the others chortled.

"Richard, would you quit that shit already?" Sy sighed. "What the hell they ever do to you?"

"Ahh, they hate me just as much as I hate them," Rich laughed. I thought about Jan'n'Rose and wondered if they really did hate each other. It sure seemed like it sometimes. My mind drifted as we drove home along Peterson, and I thought of the black punker and hoped he'd be OK. *Why do people hurt each other so bad?* I felt the bumps along my forehead. *Why can't we get along?* I closed my eyes and tried to think of nothing as the wind howled in my window. The Assyrian floated in a black haze. His eyes were closed, and his arms were folded over his chest in some ancient burial pose. *Why'd you have'ta die?* His mouth opened, and he whispered, "I ain't dead," then he smiled and vanished.

We pulled up in front of the house, and Rich double-parked. He got out and walked me toward the house.

"Now you know you can't tell Ma or Dad or anybody what happened tonight, right?" Rich said, rubbing my shoulders. "Or else you won't be able to go with again, OK?"

"OK," I said, and started up the front stairs.

"Alright. I'll see ya later buddy," Rich said.

"OK. Thanks, Rich," I went through the front door and didn't tell a soul.

Rich was like that. He could be really good to me sometimes, and he could be a miserable son of a bitch, too. It all depended on his mood that day I guess. But to be honest, when I look back on it, I could see that he really loved me. He even really loved

Jan'n'Rose, too. He was just all mixed up and living in a fucked-up world out there—almost getting raped like that. I mean, that could radicalize anyone. All those crazy radicals out there, all of 'em had either something horrible happen to 'em, or some kind of mental illness, and Rich had both. That made it rough for him, and it was only gonna get worse.

He needed a guy like Simon around. Sy had sense. He could make sense of the world for these guys. He made them feel like what they were going through mattered and had meaning. That respecting each other and being there for each other was what mattered. The whole North Side knew Sy, whether it was because of his bands or just that he was always around the metal scene back then. People just latched onto him. He knew everyone, and everyone loved him. Sy had a sense of right and wrong, too—something Rich had lost somewhere along the way. Without Sy around, I think Rich woulda been doing way worse shit out there in the neighborhood. In fact, I'm sure of it.

SEEDS

MY BROTHER BLAKE was a terribly sick child. He had a hole in his heart the size of a walnut, and they weren't sure if he'd make it his first five years. He literally could have been rushed into surgery at any moment, so Dad even stepped down from his foreman position in order to take on a Union Steward job, (basically, the Union's eyes and ears on the site). He couldn't afford to get laid off and lose his insurance, even for a week, and stewards worked all year round. By the time Blake was about twelve, the hole sealed up on its own. He started playing Pop Warner football with the High Ridge Chargers and ended up being pretty good.

Lil Pat was a brutal big brother to Blake. Don't ask me why. Sometimes, when two eggs hatch, a terrible war unfolds within the nest. That seemed to be the force of nature at work between 'em. Rich told me that when they were little, Lil Pat would do horrible things to Blake. Things like literally holding him down and taking a shit on him, or pushing him out of a tall tree, which broke Blake's arm. It was a long, cruel list, but Blake survived.

Blake started out high school as one of the smallest and slightest kids at Gordon. He was a little over five foot and about a hundred and twenty pounds. He worked hard on the football field and ran the practice squad. He concocted mock defenses in order to imitate their next opponent. But then, something miraculous happened: his sophomore year, he started to grow. By the beginning of his junior year, he was closing in on six feet in height. By the end of the season, he was 6'1" and starting receiver and safety for a pretty strong Catholic League squad.

His growth spurt had its ill effects on Rich, who'd been bigger and taller than his older brother for several years by then, though Rich could never fight a lick, and Blake could always best him. But now that the tide had shifted, so to speak, Blake recalled the brutality he'd endured most of his life inflicted by a big brother. So, he decided to educate Rich on what it was like to be a hated little brother.

One night, the summer before Blake left for Drake, shit got messy. He'd moved into one of the side rooms in the partially-finished basement. We had a TV and stereo set up down there.

It was about one in the morning, and Rich and Sy sat on the sofa in the basement chowing down on Italian beefs and bags of greasy fries, nodding their heads vigorously to the heavy metal that poured out of the stereo. They were drunk and high, as usual, and on the down-turn from a bright night at the Metro.

The basement door opened. Blake rumbled down the stairs and past the TV console. In one fluid motion, he leaned down, clicked the stereo off, and continued to his room.

"What the fuck?" Rich shouted.

Blake clicked the light on in his bedroom, then popped his head back through the door.

"Get out. I'm going to sleep."

"Fuck you."

Blake ran across the room, leapt onto Rich's lap, and straddled him. Rich raised his arms feebly, and Blake slammed his fist savagely into Rich's nose. The length of Rich's nose mushed sideways. Blood erupted onto his black Pantera t-shirt. Sy jumped up and attempted to pull Blake off.

"Aye, he's your brother God damnit!" Sy shouted, disgusted.

Blake planted his feet on the couch, stood, twisted, and shoved Sy hard, sending him reeling backward.

"Now get de fuck outta here, ya big pussy!" Blake yelled as he leapt off the couch and stomped toward his room.

"You didn't even give me a chance!" Rich yelped as he leapt after Blake. Blake spun sharply and raised his fists. Rich halted mid-step. Then, he sneered and spit a mouthful of blood at Blake that spattered on his neck and his plaid Gap shirt. Blake reeled back, grossed-out.

Rich stomped out of the basement with Sy behind him.

■

I REMEMBER RIDING down to Maxwell Street with Rich in his brown Bronco. He was telling about all the things you could get down at the Maxwell Street Market.

"What kinda things," I asked.

"All kindsa things," Rich said as he opened the flip-up lid of the wooden box he'd built into the space between the seats. A small, chalk-white pistol lay at the bottom of the large box.

"Is it real?"

"Yeah, it's real," he replied as he lifted the pistol out, released the clip, and slid it free. "Dem look like BBs to you?" Rich handed me the metal clip.

I slipped the top bullet out of the structure.

"Damn!" I rubbed my fingers over the smooth brass casing and the heavy, metal tip. "What is it, a .22?"

"Naw, it's a .25 semi-automatic," he answered as we drove down Hollywood.

"Aw, man, that's bad as hell! So you don't got to cock it every time?"

"Just once," he said, glancing at me. I gawked at the small-caliber bullet as I rolled it in my fingertips. "Give me dat fuckin' thing," he said, snatching the clip out of my hand.

I handed him the bullet, and he slipped it back in the clip while steering with his knees. We drove south on Ashland. He picked up the gun from between his legs and popped the clip back in the grip. Then, he placed the pistol back in the box and shut it.

Rich had a way of turning things into these folkloric adventures. As we moved through the city, he gave me a history lesson on the South Loop Skid Row. Then, he eased a slow left onto Halsted through the mob of passing people. We rolled slowly forward as the long line of traffic eked ahead of us. People cut between the cars and trucks as they crossed the street. There was a beat-up, white box-truck near the first intersection, and a green street sign hovered above it that read "Maxwell Street" in white letters.

A series of bums rushed up to my window. Their haggard faces leered inside as they waved gold chains and watches in my face. One thin, black bum in a blue t-shirt blared out, "I got socks!" as he passed. He held up a large bag of tube socks. His crusty fingers and yellow nails squeezed the bag tightly. The socks bulged against the plastic like a balloon ready to burst.

"What?" Rich said, glancing at me. "What's wrong? You look like you're gonna piss your fucking pants."

"What if they ran at the door? What would we do? There's no way outta here."

"That's what the .25's for," he said, smiling. "Go ahead." He flipped the box open. "Hold it if it'll make you feel better."

I slowly reached in and picked up the .25. It still looked fake, but it was much heavier than I expected. I squeezed the white grip enclosed around the spring-loaded clip. The rough, metal-finished barrel was heavy and made it want to point downward. My hand felt big around the grip, like the gun was made for a hand not much larger than mine. I passed it over my lap and slipped it alongside my outer thigh so I could hold it between my leg and the car door. A calm set in my chest as I exhaled a deep breath. The faces of the bums turned comical, clownish even. A fat nose with long, black hairs shot out of each nostril; an old, wrinkle-faced Polack mug with a kid-sized, black and red Chicago Bulls cap stretched around his narrow scalp. I grinned with the knowledge that all I had to do was raise that thing up and squeeze to make them disappear. Inside, I finally felt that powerful aura of Pistol Pat.

I heard the pop from that night at the carnival—that hollow pop that rang out in the midst of all that joy. I thought of where the bullet went. *They all go somewhere right?* The asphalt, the church wall, a ricochet. *Hell, it could have hit me, or a little baby in a stroller. How could he have been so reckless? How could he be so foolish?* A pregnant woman walked past my window with a giant, plump belly. It was like she was gonna give birth right then and there, or explode. *Maybe he deserved to die.*

I could see through the people that filtered past to these glass storefronts filled with racks of clothes, suits, shoes, and gold jewelry.

Up ahead, above the bustling sidewalk, I watched the profile of the street. The 100-year-old, dark brick, three-story buildings leaned and rested against one another like a string of winos in a frozen saunter. Several of the buildings had given way and collapsed in spots. The rubble extracted. Vendors had set up along the sidewalks. Children ran and played behind them in the hilly, glass and concrete-speckled lots.

Twangy blues riffs spouted up from electric guitars every so often. Then, they were swallowed up by the slow thumping baseline of hip-hop that flooded out from the boom boxes of the street vendors who sold tapes.

I could smell a heavy odor of onions caramelizing and rank

fried sausage as we got to Maxwell Street. To the west, there was a large lot that was full of makeshift shacks. Rich parked in front of a hydrant. I put the gun back in the box, and we locked the doors and went shopping.

■

WE PLAYED BASKETBALL on summer evenings in my alley. We used the hoop Dad'd built onto the sloped roof of our garage. I was always just a little bit better than anyone on the block around my age. Only Ryan could beat me and only sometimes. I wasn't the best shooter, but I could always dribble past people and make these running shots. They weren't layups because I was further out from the hoop. I'd dribble past my defender, jump, and sling the ball from my side with both hands with the form of a kid just barely strong enough to shoot on a big hoop. And I'd always bank my shots in using the red box on the backboard as my target. We played most nights. The girls from the block would lean against the far garage, chit-chat, and watch the game. One of them was Hyacinth—a skinny, little Filipino girl who lived on the end of the block at Hermitage Ave. She had thick jet-black hair with long bangs cut straight across her forehead, big amber eyes, and a cute smile. I had a long-running crush on her. She was in my grade at St. Greg's, and sometimes we'd walk home from school together. When she was really sweet and flirty with me, she'd twirl her finger in her hair as we talked. That's how I knew she liked me, too, 'cause I never saw her do that with nobody else. It was an unconscious attraction—a magnetism that had us always beside each other when us kids were grouped up. Our hands thoughtlessly intertwined, then unraveled swiftly when anyone spied us doing it. Our cheeks would blush. Then, I'd have to sock anyone who sang "Joey's got a girlfriend." Slowly, we stopped caring about it, but that was later.

I headed out of the alley after dinner one night. On my way through the dark gangway, I could hear the shuffle of sneakers on concrete and the clank and pank of the game. I opened the gate and saw six kids leaning against the garage across the alley. They watched Ryan play one on one against a kid I'd never seen before. He was thin and taller than me. He wore a tan shirt with a logo I'd never seen, dark green jean-shorts, and Puma sneakers. I walked around the game to where the rest of the kids stood.

"Who's that?" I asked Mario.

"That's the new kid," Mario replied, whipping his long hair out of his face. "He just moved into the apartments over there." He nodded toward the large apartments down the alley that faced onto Olive Ave.

The new kid looked Oriental. He had black, slicked-back hair tied up in a pony-tail, and he was good. He was beating Ryan, bad—seven-zip.

"Where's he from?" I asked.

"California, right?" Mario asked, looking at the girls, who were all giggling and whispering.

"Uh huh, Ca-li-for-nia," Hyacinth said, throwing exuberant emphasis on each syllable. She twirled her finger through her hair and watched the game. My throat tightened, and my palms itched, and I wanted to play real bad. I didn't know why, but I already hated this new kid.

The new kid ended up winning, 11-2.

"Good game," Ryan said as they shook hands. "Damn, you beat my ass."

"Naw, good game," the new kid said as he wiped the sweat from his forehead, then slid his hand along his gleaming hair.

"Aye, you meet Joe yet? He's my best friend," Ryan said, nodding toward me. "Aye, Joe, this the new kid. What you say your name was?"

"Angel," the kid said.

The girls muttered, "Angel, Angel," and giggled.

"What's up," I said, nodding to him. Then, I grabbed the ball out of Ryan's hands. "We shootin' for captains or what?" All the boys got in line to shoot at the long, crooked crack in the center of the alley. I shot first and made it. Ryan shot and missed. I grabbed the rebound and shoved a hard bounce pass to Angel, who caught it by his chest. He glared at me. His mouth hung open, and his dark eyes dampened. Then, he shot and made it.

"Shoot for first pick," Ryan said, passing the ball to Angel.

Angel took it and shoved a hard pass to me. We glowered at each other again. My heart pattered, ready to drop the ball and unload fists into his mug.

"Go ahead," Angel urged.

My heart thumped in my chest. I turned and shot a long, arching one that clanged off the side of the rim. We picked teams, and everyone knew who was guarding who. I stood with my back to the garage, said, "Check ball," and bounced it to Angel. He caught it, looked at it, and passed it back to me. I faked left and went right, then surged past Angel and shot one of my runners that banked home. I jogged back to the far line and smiled at Hyacinth. She grinned back and revealed the small gap in her front teeth.

Angel dribbled the ball towards the check line.

"Naw, we play keeps around here," I said, then snatched the ball from him.

I checked the ball to Angel, then faked a pass. He leapt at it, and I giggled as he stumbled. I put up a shot from right there and instantly knew I'd missed, so I darted to the side of the hoop I thought it'd clang towards. Angel slashed for the rebound, too. The ball jolted high off the rim and arced downward. We both leapt and collided in mid-air, but I had more inertia and toppled him sideways, snagging the ball with both hands before I landed. I then took it out to the side. Angel trailed me. I stopped, then drove straight at him. He stood his ground. I dug my shoulder into his solar plexus, and he stumbled. I bounced back and passed to Mario. Suddenly, Angel cut in front of the pass and stole the ball.

He dribbled back to take the ball out and reset the play, and I followed him. He cut right quickly and surged past me. I pursued as he drove in and went for a lay-up. I swooped in, leapt up, and blocked the shot from behind before I landed full-force onto his back. We tumbled and crashed into my garage with a thunderous boom. Angel spun under me and with his back against the garage and pushed me hard in my face and chest.

A bubbling rage ignited in my shoulders, and I stood up and pushed Angel as he got to his feet. Then, I punched him in the cheek. Mario jumped between us, but Ryan shoved him out of the way.

"Naw, let 'em fight," Ryan sneered.

Angel and I squared-up. His face was all tied up in a knot, and he rushed me without warning. He flung quick fists that smacked me in the head and face; they felt like speeding little stones. I swung wild and missed, and he peppered me as I stumbled sideways. I reached out and grabbed his shirt, and he kneed me in the sternum. All my wind jettisoned from my mouth and nostrils. I collapsed to my knees on the concrete, awestruck at how fast he was, and how he'd delivered all those blows without hesitation or even thinking about it. I gripped my chest, and he wacked me with a hard punch on the side of my head.

"Are ya done?" he asked.

I was about to say 'yeah' when Lil Pat stormed out of the gangway. He plucked me up off the ground by my collar and shoved Angel away from me. He bent down and looked me in the eyes. His beard and mustache were scruffy and dirty. Fried chicken was all over his breath.

"Joey, don't you let that little spick whoop you," Lil Pat said and clouted me across the cheek. "Now get in there God damn it!" He shoved me towards Angel. I closed my eyes, squeezed my fists, and started swinging haymakers.

I stormed forward. My hard, looping punches landed and drove Angel into the wooden plank fence across the alley. Angel smashed against it hard. Then he bent over at the waist and covered his head. I lumped him up nasty. He crumpled and curled into a ball at my feet. These little whining sounds poured out of him. Suddenly, it struck me: this poor kid just came out here trying to make some new friends, and now look at him. Look at me. Lil Pat walked up and grabbed me by the shoulder.

"Atta boy, Joey. Don't ever let nobody whoop you in dis alley," he said. Then, he patted me on the back and walked me away from Angel, who laid there curled-up and whimpering.

Lil Pat grabbed the basketball from the ground where it had rolled to a stop and shot. Angel stood, stumbled, and ran towards his house.

"Well, you don't gotta worry about him no more," Lil Pat laughed.

I looked over at Hyacinth who was watching Angel with her hand over her open mouth. She scowled at me and shook her head. Then, she huffed off towards her house, and the other girls followed. A blue rust bucket pulled in to the mouth of the alley at Hermitage, and we all flinched at its bright, rectangular headlights. Lil Pat walked over and got in, and it eased slowly through our court.

Most of the kids left after that. I didn't feel like playing anymore and sat against my garage. A headache set in. After a while, it was just Ryan and I. He sat down next to me with the ball under his bent legs.

"What was that all about, man?" he asked.

"I don't know," I replied.

"He's an alright kid," Ryan said, shrugging.

"Yeah." I looked down the empty alley where he'd run. "He probably is. Thanks for letting us get it over with."

"No problem."

"He gave me a fat lip," I said, rubbing the bubble along my lower lip.

"Imagine the way he feels," Ryan replied, arching his red eyebrows.

"Yeah," I said, and looked down the quiet, narrow alley.

"Alright, man, I'm gonna head home," Ryan said as he stood. "You OK, right?"

"Yeah, I'm fine," I said, standing up slowly. "Aye, if you see that kid around, man, tell him I'm sorry, OK?"

"Alright, man. I'll tell him."

We shook hands and Ryan disappeared down the alley. I stood there alone feeling sick to my stomach. Then, I went in through the gangway and up to bed.

LOW RIDER

I KNEW MY BROTHER WAS A KILLER. I saw exactly what he'd done. I couldn't lie about it to myself, and the horror of that followed me, always. I loved him—he was a very good big brother to me. Hell, I adored him. It all had me wondering strange things, like if it was OK to kill people. If they shoot at you, then maybe it is. But if they're running away, then maybe not. But what if they came back again next time and didn't miss and killed you? And what was Lil Pat supposed to do, hold the guy there at the pharmacy until the cops showed up? Citizen's arrest, like in that movie *Police Academy*? It didn't work there, neither. I knew the right answer was there, hovering in front of me, and I'd grapple for it in my dreams and sometimes in the days I'd talk with Ryan.

"I've been dreaming about that Assyrian guy again," I said.

"That sucks," he answered.

"Ever think about him?"

"Sometimes. Pretty gross seeing him like that, huh?"

"Yeah it was. I never thought I'd see a dead body up close like that."

"I guess it was gonna happen sooner or later."

"Yeah. I guess so... You think he deserved it?"

"Man... I don't know. I guess he did. He coulda killed somebody shooting like that. Coulda killed Mickey or Pat."

"I can't believe they chased him right off. Those two are crazy as fuck."

"Yep. Hahaha... Down for their crown."

"Ha, yeah I guess. Ever think you're gonna have to kill somebody one day?"

"I don't know. Mickey says my dad killed some people. A Royal and somebody else..."

"They say my old man was pretty bad, too..."

"I tell you what, if anybody ever tried to hurt my family, or hurt you, I'd kill 'em over that."

"Me, too..." I said and exhaled a long breath. "Me, too."

■

ONE DAY, LIL PAT PICKED ME UP alone after collecting. Ryan wasn't there that day; he'd gone to visit his dad in prison. Lil Pat pulled in front of the house and sent me in to grab a Ministry tape. He said it was in his closet, so I ran down there and dug around the disheveled shelves. I dipped my hand into a shelf in his closet and pricked my index finger on something. I recoiled and gripped my hand. A small bead of blood bubbled up along the grains of my fingerprint. I sucked the blood from it, then squeezed my fist together until it stopped. I lifted a dirty t-shirt, and a needle, like the ones Ma used for her insulin shots, sat inside. There was a little ball of brown powder in a plastic bag with a foot-long piece of rubber tubing lying next to it. I'd heard about hard drugs from Officer Friendly when he came to St. Greg's, and it scared me that Lil Pat was using them. I couldn't differentiate between heroin and crack, but I knew that needles were really bad.

I found the tape, ran upstairs, and got in the car. He pulled away as I gripped at the pain in my fingertip.

"What happened?" he asked.

"I pricked myself on something."

"What?" He glanced at me. "What was it?"

"A needle."

"Aw, Jesus, let me see." He grabbed at my hand and looked at the pink fingertip. The blood persistently rose in a small red dab.

"Are you OK? How do you feel?"

"I'm OK. It's OK."

"Jesus. You got to be careful, kid." He sipped his Miller tall boy.

We drove to the beach and parked in a space facing out to the lake. The sun began to set behind us as we listened to Ministry's hard, industrial beats. Finally, he clicked it off.

The lake was choppy. White froth appeared as the dark waves crested.

"Pat, was that drugs in the bag? The brown stuff?"

Lil Pat reclined in his seat and killed his beer.

"Kid, I done seen a lot of things in my life. I done things...." He sighed heavily. "You don't know what I done, kid.... You'll never know."

He snapped the tab on another beer. We sat there for a while, quiet. He gazed way out across the lake like he was floating somewhere. Some place safe. Some place where things were simple. Fishing, or just walking in a forest in the U.P. hunting grouse. I almost said it—told him what I'd seen—but it got all welled up inside. I wanted to tell him he was a good person. He was a good brother. But, where he was, I don't think he could have heard me.

∎

I FINALLY GOT UP THE NERVE to head over by Ryan's house. He hadn't come by that day, and I was lonely. I'd completely avoided the Dead-End-Docks since the fight with Leroy. Ryan'd said he'd smoothed it all over and that no one was mad at me, but my brother should never come back around again. Ever. I knocked on Ryan's front door. No one home except the three dogs that barked and snarled at the square of glass in the oak door. Their puffing snouts pressed against it and fogged their faces.

I walked around back a little nervous. Maybe they were just telling Ryan that they weren't mad so they could get me to come back. When I rounded his garage, I saw a huge shack way over at the far-end of the alley. It was made out of scrap wood, and kids swarmed around it like ants. BB stood atop the 12-foot dumpster near the Ace Hardware loading dock throwing down scraps of 2X4 and plywood to T-Money and a few others. Ryan's prickly, copper scalp emerged out of a square hunk of gray rug at the entrance of the shack. He crawled out. The shack stood waist-high, but it was all slanted and disjointed. Part of the roof was made out of an old refrigerator door, and there was a tan tarp that flapped in the breeze in back. As I walked up, Angel crawled out after Ryan. I hadn't counted on that, and my head swirled uncomfortably as Ryan walked up. He greeted me with a hand shake, and Angel stepped up beside him and smiled awkwardly. His thin lips trembled a little at the creases, and his dark hair was all sprinkled with white dust.

"I was hoping you all would shake on it to squash it," Ryan said as he squinted in the afternoon sunlight. "I still don't know whatchya'll were fightin' about."

I reached out my hand towards Angel and said, "I squash it."

He shook my hand weakly and said, "Squashed."

"Come on and check this thing out, man," Ryan said. "It's almost done!"

We turned and started for the shack. BB spotted me from up high on the filled dumpster.

"Where yo brotha at, mothafucka?" BB shouted down at me, then grabbed a long hunk of 2X4. He hefted it up over his head. "I'a crack dat mothafucka's skull!!!" he seethed through his little teeth. Then, he brought the 2X4 down on the rim of the big, rusty dumpster. The hollow walls bellowed.

"Quit it, Mafucka. It's coo," T-Money shouted up to BB as he stepped to me. "Joe, you cool wit' me. You got heart, boy." T-Money extended his boney, closed fist towards me slowly, and I met it softly with my own—knuckles to knuckles.

"What the fuck is this?" I asked.

"It's de fort," T-Money replied, grinning proudly.

"Yeah? How long you guys been working on it?"

"Since yesterday mornin'. We ain't done yet, boy." He waved us towards it. "Come on, I'll gives youse de tour." He motioned to Ryan and said, "Help dese fools for a minute."

Ryan nodded and went to help catch the falling boards.

Angel and I followed. We crawled on our hands and knees through the gray rug flap. Inside it was dark and musty. Thin rays of sunlight pierced through the roof like golden lasers, and microscopic flecks of dust sauntered inside them. There were long, sixteen penny nails sticking out through the wood everywhere— from the walls, from the ceiling. They were like narrow spikes, and anytime you tried to lean on something you got stabbed at least three times. There was a constant debate volleying back and forth from the various kids about lockjaw and tetanus shots. The conversation grew into a monstrous myth used to run off little brothers.

We crawled in a dark back room in the fort. Twon was there lounging on a green beanbag. A purple and black Vikings ball cap sat on his head. He frowned at us, and then he snatched a can of aerosol off a hook that hung down from a board in the ceiling and sprayed a huge fog of white mist in our direction.

"Quit sprayin' dat shit, nigga," T-Money said.

"It stank in here," Twon replied, eyeing us.

"Whateva, man." T-Money spun around and folded his legs up under him and waited for us to get in. His eyes lit up in the dark, little room. "Now, I gotsta ax y'all a question! Do you wanna be memba's of the dopest, rawest, realest, mothafuckin' click eva?" His eyes bulged excitedly. "KRAZY CREW?"

"Yeah," I said, shrugging.

"Alright," Angel answered, nodding.

"Ok, but den you gots to get V'd in," T-Money added.

"What's dat?" I asked.

"A violation," Twon said ominously.

"20 shots in the chest," T-Money added.

"From who?" I asked, eyeing Twon's huge paws.

"I'll do it," T-Money said.

T-Money had Angel get behind me and hold my wrists behind my back. Then, T-Money started to punch me in the chest—real soft at first, then harder and quicker. The booms of the shots resonated throughout my body. My heart beat traced after them— boom... dmm dmm, boom... dmm dmm, boom.... I lost count in all the pounding, and finally, T-Money stopped, and we shook hands. Then, T-Money showed me how to throw up the "KC" in the midst of the handshake by hooking thumbs. Angel smiled as he got into position. I crawled behind him and held his wrists.

"Aye, Joe, you better count this one. He hit you about thirty-five times," Angel said in a squeaky voice.

"Aight, Joe can count," T-Money said, giggling.

Angel let out some "Ohhs" and "Ewws" between chuckles as T-Money started. Then, he grew real silent as T-Money hit harder. I counted, and when I said, "Nineteen," T-Money wound up and nailed Angel in the chest. Angel's ribs crunched, and then he let out an overly dramatic "Ahhhhhhh" before falling over on the dirty concrete ground, laughing.

"Keep laughing, and I'm gonna do it again," T-Money sighed.

We both giggled as we crawled out of the shack.

"Man, T-Money hits hard!" Angel said.

"That shit was loud as hell wasn't it?" I said.

"Look at this," Angel said as he raised up his shirt. A series of red fist marks bloomed on his chest; the reddest one sat in the center.

"Ahh shit. He fucked you up," Ryan gawked. "You're Crew now!"

"Hell yeah," Angel said, reaching out and shaking his hand.

"What about you?" Ryan asked, looking at me.

I lifted up my shirt. The marks showed clear, bright-red on my pale chest.

"Ahh, man, he really fucked you up," Ryan guffawed.

"Ahhaa," Angel laughed.

"Hell yeah," Ryan said, grinning. We shook hands and threw up "KC."

BB walked up behind Angel and snatched the magazine he had rolled up in his back pocket.

"Ahh snap," he said, flipping it open. Angel ripped it out of his grasp. It was a car magazine that had *Lowrider* written on the cover and an old Chevy Impala ragtop sitting below it. The car was dark-purple with black pinstriping, and it had a crazy-ass mural of a blue and red dragon with bright-orange fire exploding from its mouth. A thick-built Mexican lady bent over the hood. Her healthy curves bulged against her white bikini and hovered over her white high heels. She stuck her huge, round ass out toward the camera and looked back over her shoulder with her long black hair splaying down to her waist.

"Man, gimme dat shit," BB demanded as he reached for it again. "I'ma busta nut ta dis shit."

"Man…" Angel sighed, taking it away from BB. "I don't want your jizzum on my magazine! Get your own, fool."

I peered over Angel's shoulder as he slowly flipped through the pages. A few more kids crowded in. There were more shots of cars with huge murals on their hoods, bright, golden-spoked rims, and white-wall tires. And plenty of hot chicks. Some cars had their hoods up with the engines completely chromed. Then, there was this one car, another old Chevy, with only three wheels on the ground. The fourth wheel levitated three-feet in the air.

"What the fuck's that?" I asked, pointing at it.

"What?" Angel said, squinting at me.

"How'd they lift that car up like that?"

"They got it locked in three-wheel motion," Angel answered and looked at me. I had no idea what the fuck he was talking about.

"Man, hell yeah," Ryan said, beaming. "I'm gonna get a six-foe like dat one."

"That's a '61," Angel remarked.

"Whatever it is, dat shit is bad as hell," Ryan retorted.

"Man, my big cousin's got a six-foe," BB squeaked. "He live out sout' doe."

Angel flipped the page, and there was a large picture of a bike. It was an old Sting-Ray frame from the '60s with the banana seat and springer fork, but it was different. There was a chrome, chain-link steering wheel attached to three thin sheet metal stems that were rigged into the bike's neck. The ape hanger handlebars were forced way down, so the front wheel stuck up between them. It looked like the steering wheel was the more viable option. The old-style springer fork bars were curved and seemed too long, and there was a twisted metal bar where the brace went. Angel went to turn the page.

"Aye, hold up a second," I said.

"What?" he said, looking back at me.

"Man, that bike is bad as hell."

"You like dat?" Angel eyed me suspiciously.

"Man, why would you want a bike like that?" Ryan whined.

"You can't even ride it."

"You can ride 'em," Angel cut in.

"How, bro? The pedals are hittin' the ground?" Ryan tapped the glossy page with the back of his hand in disgust.

"Man, they just got the spring out," Angel replied.

"So, you put the spring in, and you can ride 'em?" I asked.

Angel nodded to me. The other kids had lost interest. They went back to climb in the dumpster and bang on the shack's walls with the tiny ball peen hammer they'd scrounged up. Angel flipped through the pages and then stopped.

"I got something I want to show you guys. Want to come to my place?" he asked.

Ryan and I looked at each other and shrugged.

"OK," I said.

Angel lived in a first-floor apartment on Olive. He let himself in with his own key, and we headed to his room that was up front. He had posters up of all kinds of lowrider cars and bikes. Then, across the room, I saw a wheel with a white-wall tire resting near the door to his closet. There was an old blue Schwinn frame with a back wheel attached that leaned against the wall, too.

"No shit?" I said admiringly. "You got one?"

"Well, it ain't done yet," Angel replied.

"Man, it looks bad ass!" I said, continuing to leer as Angel smiled proudly.

"Here, I'll put the handle bars on." Angel slid the neck and ape hangers into the frame. "Here, grab the wheel." I got the front wheel and brought it to him. "I still got to get the fork, but this is what it's gonna look like." He hovered the handle bars so they were lower than the top of the front tire.

"That's fuckin' dope," Ryan said.

I sat on the bed and picked up a magazine beside me.

"Damn, that's bad ass," I remarked and flipped through the pages.

"Yeah, it's big out in Cali," Angel replied as he sat next to me.

"Man, I gotta make a bike!" I said.

"You're gonna build one, huh?" Angel asked, grinning.

"I got to, man!" I bugged my eyes and we both giggled.

Angel let me borrow a magazine, so I brought it home and spent all night flipping through it completely entranced. A few days later, they tore the fort down. A couple bums'd moved in overnight and freaked the shit out of some early rising kindergartener from the block. Nothing nasty, but the cops got called, and a couple rookie firemen from the firehouse across Clark walked over with an axe and a mallet and spent the warm summer morning hacking it to pieces. By eleven, a swarm of kids stood around them fussing, but the firemen were smart enough to placate to them by letting a few of the bigger kids have a go with the axe. Then, just about the whole of Krazy Crew helped clean up the mess, throwing the mounds of busted wood into the dumpster where it'd come from. It didn't matter much to Angel and Ryan and me. We had another project on our minds—lowrider bicycles. Those bikes would be our obsession for many years to come.

CHAPTER 7

BLACK AND WHITE

COPS ENDED UP BUSTING MICKEY on a gun charge. Later that same night, someone banged hard on our front door. It was Officer O'Riley, a tubby cop in his forties that knew Dad from his repo man days. Sometimes, warrants are needed when repossessing a vehicle, and this one time, a reposessee came out shooting. Dad and O'Riley ducked behind the squad car and took fire. Dad pulls out his .45 Magnum, O'Riley unholsters his .9 millimeter, and they both come up blazing. The reposessee survived, but he was full of holes when they got him to the emergency room.

O'Riley hadn't come to the house to reminisce about their glory days dodging bullets. I listened from my bedroom. Silent, I strained to hear.

"I'm sorry, Pat," O'Riley said in a grim voice. "They said they were coming for him tonight, so I told 'em I'd go along, too, just to make sure it went as easy as it could on the family."

"Well, I just don't understand. Is he being charged with something?" the old man asked, disgusted.

"No, but we've got to bring in all the kids that've been running with the Reid boy," O'Riley replied. "Those boys have gotten themselves quite a reputation around the neighborhood, and I hate to tell you this, Pat, but Junior is no exception."

"Patrick, get up here!" Dad roared.

I got up and went to Rich's door. He was just laying on his back in bed, listening.

"What's going on?" I asked.

"Nothing, Joe. Don't worry about it. Go back to bed."

I went to my room and sat on my bed. A few moments later, Lil Pat walked up the basement stairs and down the hall to the front door. There was a sudden, bursting roar and the sounds of a tussle.

"What the fuck you been doing?" Dad yelled.

Lil Pat cried out in pain. The tussle continued, then Officer O'Riley's voice chimed in. "Now… Now, Pat, we can't let you do this here!" Then handcuffs crunched. Another smack rang out. "Now that's enough, Pat, or we'll be bringing ya in wit' him!" Officer O'Riley shouted.

"You know what? All three of you get the fuck out of my house!" Dad roared. "And you, you piece of shit. When you get back, your shit'll be out on the sidewalk!"

The door slammed shut. Dad rumbled downstairs and tore apart Lil Pat's room. He carried stuff up from the basement and hefted boxes and drawers out the front door, sending them tumbling down the steps. He even lobbed the small black-and-white TV off the porch, and it crashed to the sidewalk and tumbled end-over-end. Glass sprayed the concrete. Ma pleaded with him to stop but he wouldn't. Finally, the light-blue squad car pulled away.

I laid on my bed and sobbed quietly, staring up at the ceiling. The light from the street bled in and cast an orange haze across it.

"I saw that one coming. Fucking junkie," Rich sneered. He stood at my doorway. "Go to sleep, Joey. Don't go crying for that piece of shit."

They questioned Lil Pat, but they couldn't get anything to stick on him. He was in his early twenties by then, and he'd sunk more and more by the day. He even wore long-sleeved shirts on hot days. Rumors spread around the neighborhood. China white had loomed over Edgewater for years by then. Heroin is one of those drugs that's there to stay once it sets in a neighborhood. It was right under our noses. This Greek family, the Genopolises, sold quietly for years before they ever got busted. They lived on Ravenswood Ave. across from the cemetery. Lil Pat could walk less than a block and score. It was too close and too easy. He ended up in the basement apartment across the alley.

I made my walk that Sunday, and Lil Pat pulled up on me just as I finished. He looked sick. He had large, droopy, purplish-brown bags under both eyes, and he trembled incessantly. Ryan was already in the back seat of the Lincoln. He looked ill, too. His face was all pale and awestruck. Not only was his father in prison, but now his only uncle was locked up, too.

"Sorry about Mickey," I said as we pulled off from the curb.

"It's OK, man," Ryan replied. "Thanks." His eyes glistened.

"Hey, Mickey'll be out in no time," Lil Pat said with a low crackle in his voice. I almost didn't recognize it. "Plus, you got Uncle Patty right here, anyways... OK?" Lil Pat's bloodshot eyes strained in the rearview mirror.

"OK," Ryan muttered weakly. He looked out the window.

We went to Montrose Beach. We didn't feel like skipping rocks too much that day. Lil Pat had a few Old Styles, but he could barely drink 'em because of the tremors in his hands. He gave the last two to us.

"You know I love you boys, right?" Lil Pat asked as he looked out across the lake at the gray horizon. "You don't ever forget that, OK?"

"OK, Pat," we said in unison.

"No matter what happens, OK?"

Lil Pat turned and looked at me. I nodded.

Even though I was just ten, I still knew what was happening. He was sick. It didn't matter what he was sick with. I was losing my brother.

■

BLAKE WAS THE GOOD SON. The smart son. The athlete. The one who was gonna get himself out of the neighborhood, and he did. Got all the way to Des Moines, Iowa—Drake University—on a five thousand dollar athletic scholarship. But all it really was was free room and board. Back then, Drake cost about 15K per year, and my parents almost had to take out a second mortgage to keep him in classes. Ma took on another eight kids babysitting, and Dad worked his way up to Superintendent for McQue Construction. Blake was a good high school wide receiver but nowhere near fast enough to be scouted by a Division I school. Drake was Division I-AA, but at the time, they happened to be on an eight-year suspension due to a recruiting scandal. As part of that suspension, they were ejected from their conference and forced to function as a Division III school. This opened the door for Blake. His giant ego most likely propelled him toward Drake for posterity's sake, as he'd always be able to say, 'I played for Drake, a DI-AA school,' when in reality, he probably couldn't have been a towel boy for Drake without the suspension in effect. Blake was like that though—hyper-interested in providing a façade rather than substance. And that attitude was contagious. Everyone revered him, myself included. Grandma even started calling him "Blakey the Drakey."

All was well until the winter break of his junior year when his high school sweetheart and supposed ex-girlfriend, Karen, and her mother showed up at our front door and asked to speak to my parents. They sent us kids upstairs, but we all huddled along the carpeted steps in the dark. There, we listened and peeked in on the conversation in the brightly lit kitchen.

"I'll pay for the abortion," Ma said in a matter of fact tone as she stepped slowly to the counter and riffled through her purse. "I'll cut you a check right now—$500 bucks. Take her over to the place right on Peterson and get it done." She found the checkbook and a pen and slowly limped back to the kitchen table. She sat down in her yellow-cushioned chair at the foot of the table.

"My daughter'll have an abortion over my dead body!" Karen's mom said in a cold, rigid tone with her hands neatly folded over each other atop the oak table.

Dad furiously washed his tall, clear glass in the empty sink. I heard the gush of water and the squeak of his hands and fingers slathering on the dish soap. The suds clapped to the tin sink basin, and his white mustache undulated under his hawkish nose.

Karen cowered beside her mother on the bench, sniffling into a big, fuzzy ball of Kleenex. Her hair was done-up in a giant, blonde perm. Blake paced in and out of the passage between the kitchen and the TV room in his blue-and-white Drake University football letterman's jacket. His sculpted face and long, narrow nose were crunched in a deep scowl. He passed from the dark TV room to the bright kitchen over and over like a defender masking a blitz.

"He's got one year left to graduate. How's he going to do that with a child to raise?" Ma urged.

There was a pop, followed by the sound of glass folding. Dad crushed his cup in his massive paws, and then he softly placed the broken pieces in the sink as not to make any noise.

"He'll have to drop out and marry her," Mrs. Kerney snapped, contemptuously.

"That's not happening," Dad declared, spinning around from the sink. A spray of soppy droplets whisked from his fingertips and clapped to the linoleum floor.

"Well, he'll be a father soon," Mrs. Kerney said as she rose from the oak bench. Karen followed. "He better have a way to provide for the child."

Mrs. Kerney briskly stepped past Dad with her small button nose jutted toward the ceiling. Her eyes pursed, nearly closed, and Karen scuttled after her, still sniffling into the Kleenex wad. Karen followed her mother's gray heels as they clicked sharply down the hall to the front door. Us kids scampered back up the adjacent stairs. Mrs. Kerney swung the heavy door open and slammed it shut behind them.

■

I SAT NEAR MY BEDROOM WINDOW one night when Blake and a few of his friends rambled down the front porch stairs.

"She still pregnant?" one said.

"Yeah," Blake said. "Those things don't go away on their own, ya know."

"Just shove her down some stairs," Blake's friend Steve said, and the group erupted into laughter. "Hell, I'll do it!"

"You'd do that for me?" Blake sighed. "Damn, Steve, you're a real friend." They blasted into more laughter as they sauntered away down the sidewalk.

It made me sick to my stomach to think of it. I saw the protesters outside the abortion clinic on Peterson sometimes. Ma had had one. The child before me was diagnosed with Down's Syndrome, and they chose to terminate it. Even today, I don't know what I'd have done. The quality of life, all the terrible consequences of having a child with serious special needs—it's tough.

I guess teenage girls get abortions all the time, but with Blake, it was different. He was in a relationship with Karen. They were supposed to love each other. And the baby inside of Karen was going to be my nephew or niece—my family, ya know?

I ended up leaving the house and walked down the street toward Hermitage. Hyacinth was out on her front porch doing her homework. I walked up to her, and she frowned at me. I still felt bad about what I'd done to Angel a couple weeks before.

"Hey, I'm sorry about fighting with Angel."

She sighed.

"I shouldn't have."

"That wasn't a very nice welcome to the neighborhood, ya know."

"I know." I hung my head. "Can I sit with you?"

She scooted over, and I sat beside her. It was a cool night. The wind blew in slowly off the lake.

"Something bothering you?" she asked.

"Yeah, well I, I don't know." I dragged my hand through my hair.

"What is it?" She smiled at me.

"My brother, Blake."

"The football player?"

"Yeah. He got his girlfriend pregnant."

"Wow, jeez. That's tough."

"Yeah, he's got a year left to graduate college. He'd be the first to do that in my family since, since, a while, I guess."

"What are they going to do?"

"I think they're going to get an abortion."

"They're gonna kill the baby?"

"Yeah, I think. I think they stick a vacuum inside and suck it out."

"Oh my God, that's horrible." She gripped her stomach.

"My Ma wants to do it, and Blake does, too, I think."

"That's really sad."

"I don't think Karen wants to. I think she wants to have the baby."

"That's so sad."

"I know. Everybody's so proud of Blake. Me, too. I'm proud of him. I want to be just like him and go to college."

"But you're not so proud anymore?"

"I, I don't know what to think anymore."

She patted me softly on the back.

"Maybe it's better if they do it and don't have the baby and he finishes college and can get a good job, and then they could have all the babies they want."

"Maybe. I just think about the baby that's inside Karen. What about the baby?"

I started to cry a little, and I was embarrassed. I looked away and dug my fists into my eyes to squelch the tears. I started to get up to leave, and she reached out and held my arm with her soft, warm hand. She slowly pulled me close to her, wrapped her arms around me, and hugged me. I slid my arms around her and hugged her back. She kissed me on my cheek, and suddenly, my heart was beating quickly, and I wasn't sad anymore. My whole body started to throb. Her front door cracked open, and I shot to my feet and said, "Thanks for telling me the homework for today." Her father scowled down at me from the doorway.

I turned rigidly and walked away quickly. *Maybe she really does like me.* I was confused, all mixed up. I looked back, and she waved with a sad smile. *Maybe she just felt sorry for me. I guess it's pretty sad. I hope they keep the baby.*

■

IT DIDN'T GO WELL FOR BLAKE after that. He'd switched to strong safety from receiver, where he'd been getting less and less reps. He was second string, and by that next camp, he was coming full-bore for the spot. He beat out the starter, and after the first scrimmage game of the season, he ended up at a local college bar. Blake ran into the guy he'd beaten for the position—a black guy from (ironically) the West Side of Chicago. A few choice words exchanged, then Blake made a mistake with his textbook pompous demeanor. He puffed his big chest out, and a wide grin spread on his smug lips. Then, he popped his chin up, turned to one of his pals and said, "Dis guy thinks he can take me."

The West Side brotha did not hesitate to dig his heavy, dark fist into the base of Blake's jaw. All before Blake'd even finished his sentence.

One side of the bottom row of Blake's teeth folded over, and Blake crumbled to the beer-soaked hardwood floor. He missed the first half of the season, and that West Side brotha who'd dropped him got his starting position back. Blake watched from the sidelines with his jaw wired shut and a pair of scissors in his pocket just in case he vomited and started choking to death 'cause there was just nowhere for all that bubbling-hot, mucus-drenched bile to go. Maybe it could erupt from his nostrils, but those two little passages were never gonna be enough.

Blake's son, John, was born around then. Karen moved out to Des Moines, and the two lived in a rented house with several other students. After the season, Blake, who had barely kept his GPA up high enough to be eligible to play football, just stopped doing the work. By the end of the spring semester, he'd failed out completely. He came home to Chicago and got a job as an assistant at an accounting firm by lying and saying that he'd earned his accounting degree at Drake—a degree that he'd completed about half of the coursework for in his four years there. He wouldn't complete the degree until little Johnny was in high school.

CHAPTER 8

SEAGULL

FOR SOME REASON, they'd marched the whole grammar school over to the church for Mass every week. Single-file lines of kids filtered across the school parking lot: the boys in navy-blue slacks and baby-blue, three-button collared shirts; and the girls in their army-green plaid skirts with white, button-up blouses and white, knee-high socks.

I kneeled on the little, cushioned, flip-down bench in my pew. My chin barely cleared the top of the pew in front of me. I stretched and reached my arms up and rested my elbows on the rounded oak that'd been worn smooth by touch. I clasped my palms flat against each other and touched my thumbs to my lips. Mass continued. Thoughts flowed through my head. *Jeez... I hate church...* Then, I realized where I'd be if I wasn't there. *But I hate school even worse!*

Father McCale stood at the altar in his ankle-length, black cloak. His round, bald head and pudgy face beamed red in the low light filtered through the stained-glass windows above. He raised his outstretched arms, palms up.

"We lift up our hearts," he said, his voice booming into the massive emptiness above us children. The heads in the pews slowly ascended. The first graders up front gave way to the higher grades. The heads stepped upward all the way to the eighth graders in the rear pews. The choir balcony hung over the eighth graders. An immense, yellow and red stained-glass window prevailed above the balcony with an image of Christ with a golden crown on his head.

I sat around half-way back through the pews with the fourth graders. Father McCale fixed his eyes in a dreamy gaze far above my head. *Why does he always look up there when he says dat? Can he see God up dere or somethin'?* A huge white marble wall of statues rose up behind Father McCale. It held the figures of Jesus and Mary and the prophets in descending order. Above the white statues, near the steep-pitched apex of the ceiling, two angels were painted in profile facing one another. Their skin was opaque, and their retracted, white-feathered wings were laced with gold. The wings sprouted from high on their backs, and their shape curved way up above their heads, then sleekly flowed down the length of their bodies. At their feet, the wings curled out and away. I wondered what it'd be like to fly, to levitate up out of the pews.

I floated upward. As I did, I noticed the intricate designs in the ceiling. A dashed line ran the length of the pinnacle of the ceiling's apex that looked like a miniature roadway. Suddenly, the room inverted, and the road was in a canyon at the base of two steep mountain ranges. I floated down into the canyon on my belly. Now, I faced the direction Father McCale stared at, and I saw why he looked there. The sunlight struck the stained glass—yellow, gold, red, two stories high and wide—and the flipped image looked like some strange, warped galactic landscape. Nebulous clouds collided. *It must be heaven.*

A sharp slap struck the top of my head as I craned to see above and behind me. The shot sent me suddenly face forward again.

I looked up—it was Sister Angelica. The bitter snarl on her saggy, wrinkled face let me know exactly where I was headed. She grabbed hold of my collar with her thin, boney hands and led me to the back of the church. Her hard-soled shoes clicked on the marble floor as my rubber soles squeaked across it. As we passed the eighth graders, Jan smirked sadistically at me with her chunky cheeks. My face burned red, and my stomach went hollow.

Sister Angelica led me through the open doors into the entrance corridor. She made me kneel on the cold, hard marble floor near a gray porcelain fount filled with bubbling holy water. The only light was a gray-blue glow that seeped through the edges of the oak doors of the main entrance.

"Twenty 'Our Fathers' for not paying attention to Mass!" she hissed in a cutting whisper. Father McCale's voice boomed on in the giant vault beside us.

"Our Father, who aren't in heaven," I began as she loomed behind me. Her golden crucifix tapped on her green, fuzzy sweater, and after I had said a few "Our Fathers," Sister Angelica edged back to the doorway of the main room to watch Mass. I waited until she was just out of ear-shot and settled my weight down on my feet to take the pressure off my sore knees. Then, I looked up into the darkness above the fount.

"Our Father, who aren't in heaven, why the heck did you name her Sister Angelica anyway? She should be named Sister Sourpuss. Thy kingdom come, thy will be done, with going to church and school, so I could play all day with my friends and not have to do multiplication tables. And why did you make Jan'n'Rose so big and strong and mean? And why did you let Dad punch Richard and knock him out? And why did you let Lil Pat kill somebody? Why'd the Assyrian guy have to die? Why couldn't he have lived? Does that mean Lil Pat has to go to hell? What about me, do I have to go to hell, too? And why did you let Lil Pat become a junky? And what's a junky, anyways? And why did you make

Da sick, and why can't you make Da better?" Suddenly, a chill swept through me like the wash of a cold wave at Loyola Beach. My eyes got itchy, and a lump formed in my throat as the thought of what death was slowly set down on me. It became heavier and heavier until it clamped down on my throat from all angles like a massive iron vise. I realized Da would die and be gone forever, and I realized I was going to grow old and die one day, too. Or maybe, I wouldn't grow old at all. The sudden horror of that dark, inescapable contract sent tears rolling down my cheeks that splashed my light-blue shirt. By the time Sister Angelica led me back to my pew, my face was puffy and damp, and there was no question that I'd cried. As I passed, a fifth grader named Marty Espinosa giggled, so later at recess, I slugged him in the mouth and gave him a fat lip. Then, I called him a wuss when he started to cry.

■

I REMEMBER FISHING on the stardock at Montrose Harbor where Da kept his small white sailboat. I cast a minnow lure into the big circle at the center of the dock. The lure jerked and twisted in the greenish water. The shadow of a seagull cut and slashed through the lure as I lazily reeled it in. Da and Grandma were on the boat cleaning and getting ready to take it out. There was a sudden shrieking cry from above and an explosion of feathers in the place my lure was.

"Ahh, no!" Da yelled from the helm of the boat.

I reeled as the seagull flapped, clutching the lure in its beak. It tried to fly and got a few feet out of the water before it wound and twisted in the line and plunged back into the lake. It cried there in the center of the circle of water, and I dropped the rod at my side. Da rushed beside me and snatched the line with his hand and pulled the bird onto the dock beside him. He unfolded his pocket knife and knelt over the squawking and writhing bird. He cut the line furiously as it wound and entangled him. He slit his own palm. Blood lifted up on his dark-brown skin. The bird wouldn't hold still and bit Da's wrist and chest and smacked him with its wings. He cut the line where it wound tight on the bird's neck. Feathers plumed up everywhere. The three prong hooks of the lure clung deep to the bird's beak, face, and neck. The seagull screamed like a child. Da delicately unhooked them as the bird's wings fluttered intensely with the pain. Then, it was free, and it flapped and awkardly flopped back in the stardock's center. It swam around in a slow circle, squawking angrily as Da stood beside me watching. Then, it tried with a great slow flap and rose low out of the water, cut between two sailboats, and soared up into the bright blue sky. Da put his hand on my shoulder.

"It wasn't your fault," he said.

That's what I wanted someone to do for Da now. I wanted them to snap the strings that held him tight to that hospital bed and cut the cancer out of his lungs and his throat and his brain. But no one did, and he died on a hospital bed at Mount Sinai.

■

WE ALL KNEW LIL PAT was a junky. His girlfriend, Angie, one-upped him by being a junky and a whore. He wasn't her pimp, exactly, but he did get high off her hustle. He had a lot a ways to score brown. He was notorious for robbing drug dealers, but the first one didn't go so well. He was driving in his red Ford Escort GT strung-out on a three-month supply of fifty-milligram Percocet, which he ate in two weeks. He hadn't shit in eleven days and had grown a low-slung shit-baby—a large lump of backed-up fecal matter that rose from his pelvis and dissipated at his belly button. He ate when he was high on anything; that deep thriving hunger never satiated. He'd just come home and raid the fridge, but he'd been so high he'd forgotten about laxatives. Lil Pat carried a little, black, snub-nosed .38 he'd grabbed off Fat Buck the night before. He rolled to the tip at Granville Ave. and Winthrop Ave., pulled over, and this teenage black kid in a black bomber jacket stepped up to his window, grinning.

"Whatchu need?" the kid asked.

Lil Pat trembled. He hadn't slept in two days, but he had enough presence of mind to wait until the kid got close. Then, he reached out, snatched the kid's coat collar, and yanked him in through the window. With the other hand, Lil Pat brought the revolver to the kid's temple and said, "Gimmy."

The kid squealed and tried to twist away, but Lil Pat held tight. Suddenly, the kid tossed a roll of money in the window. It flopped in a cup holder.

"Not that—the China white you been running around here."

The kid hesitated. Lil Pat grimaced and cocked the hammer. The kid threw in three little folded-up squares of duct tape, and they landed on the passenger seat. Just then, the front windshield splattered. A thousand tiny cracks splintered across its width. The glass was white at the center where the tip of the metal bat punctured it. Another dude in a bomber jacket yanked and twisted the bat to break it free. Thin little shards clattered atop the tan dashboard.

Lil Pat let go of the kid. He tried to aim the revolver and shot outward through the windshield. The bullet burst a quarter-sized hole through the spider-webbed glass. The bat tugged free as Lil Pat floored it down Winthrop. The wad of cash unfurled and flapped around the center console in the breeze as the Ford knifed through the canyon of red-brick high-rises. Feet pattered at his back. Then, three shots rang out, long and clear, into the daylight.

He drove the Ford around with the windshield like that for three days until he totaled it, high, into the iron pier of a railroad underpass. He fled the scene and reported it stolen the next day.

He still had other less-messy ways to score—ways he'd manage when he was still buzzin' and feeling good. My Grandma was so heartbroken over losing Da, and she loved Lil Pat so much. She'd been kind of a surrogate mother to him in the early days when Ma was just a 14-year-old girl with an infant. I guess Gram was just lonely too. Terribly lonely and sad.

Lil Pat would go over there on cloud nine, take out the trash, and dazzle her with bullcrap about the new job he had. All the while, he stole anything he could get his hands on—cash, jewelry, checks. He had a knack for forging signatures and hustling currency exchanges and bank tellers. Since he had Dad's exact name, he could go to the bank with forged checks, and because Dad had an account, Lil Pat could cash 'em. But after a while, sadly and sickly, Gram started playing into it. They call it "enabling," and old people are almost always the perpetrators. So damned lonely, having so much love to give, wanting to help their son or grandson or nephew, they plop cash in their hands so they can go buy heroin, or crack, or gamble. It's a sick world. I held a lot of animosity towards her about what she'd done, or helped Lil Pat do to himself, years later when I began to understand it all. But in the end, now, today, I can't. They were just two lost people way, way down on their luck. Even ten, fifteen years after Da was gone, she couldn't talk about him without bursting into tears. "Like a wildfire, Joey. I loved him like a wildfire."

■

COPS AND ROBBERS, right. It's a fun game. Both sides have their heroes, both their villains. But I never truly wanted to play the villain. I don't know that anyone does. I always knew Lil Pat was a robber but not a villain. But when the heroin took him, he was the villain—the true villain—in all ways. Though, then, I always allowed that he be detached from himself when he was strung-out.

That it wasn't him who did those things. It was the drugs. There was solace in that, I guess, but it didn't stop the things he did.

■

THERE WAS A NICKEL-PLATED .45 semi-automatic that sat in a sealed plastic bag on a shelf down in the basement evidence room at Chicago Police headquarters for a decade. It was flagged for release. It never got picked up.

I was home sick from school. Or, in other words, Ma got tired of me whining that I was sick at the kitchen table that morning and let me stay home. This was something the old man woulda never put up with, but since he left for work before sunrise, it wasn't a problem.

It was around lunch time, and I'd just finished eating a bowl of Oodles of Noodles. Ma had cooked it up just the way I like it—with an egg dropped in. I headed down the long hallway from the kitchen on my way back upstairs to read my comic books when the front door slowly creaked open. It was always dark there by the door, and the windowless landing at the bottom of the stairs created a gray haze that hung there in the day with the lights out. Lil Pat stuck his head in as the door creaked opened. His eyes bugged out. His usually well-kempt goatee and mustache had grown into an uneven, stubbly beard. Scratches ran down along his cheeks, fingernail thick. He peered over my head as he slowly eased the screen door shut behind him. He glanced down at me with a false smirk and raised his index finger to his lips. His massive body trembled under his tattered, three-quarter-length leather coat, and the smell of burnt fingertips and ammonia swelled into the room with him. Suddenly, all the things my parents had said to me over the past few weeks flooded into my head: *Don't go anywhere with Pat. If you see Pat, run home.* Years later, I'd find out he'd threatened to kidnap me if my parents got between him and Grandma's money. I found this out when he started to make those same threats to my nieces and nephews, but by then, I was grown up and a different person.

He left the door cracked open and tip-toed up the stairs. I didn't know what to do. I walked back into the yellow-tiled walls of the kitchen where Ma stirred a pot of macaroni. I walked up behind her. The sharp smell of melted-butter mixed with cheddar cheese. I stared at her back as she dug the large wooden spoon into the pot. She must have felt my eyes on her because she stopped and turned around to face me.

"What is it, honey," she asked, placing her hands on the small of her back. Her heavy curves slumped.

I couldn't talk. I just slowly raised my head and looked up at the ceiling where Lil Pat's steps creaked.

"What is it?" She repeated. She stepped toward me and undid the strings of her faded-red apron, then glanced up at the ceiling.

The sound of metal sliding across metal and then a sharp click cut through racket of the babysitting kids in the back yard. It was my father's .45mm semi-automatic—the same .45 Dad'd used to make a statement years before. There was this junky that lived in an apartment at the end of the block named Gabriel. He was a mean, skinny Cuban with bushy eyebrows, a mustache, and black eyes. Gabriel was a known burglar operating in the neighborhood—he had to pay for his fix somehow. He'd even been caught a couple times, but it didn't deter him.

One night, someone busted out our first floor back window. The crashing glass triggered an instant nightmare in my sleeping mind. I screamed so loud that my parents were sure it was the second floor window that I slept under that'd broken. Sure that they'd find me, five-years-old with glass dug into my skin. But I was safe, and whoever'd broken the window was gone.

The next night, my Dad saw Gabriel on his way up our block like nothing'd happened, and he stomped towards him. Dad's hands always curled like he was crumbling wads of paper when he was getting ready to do something. Just as he was about to pass Gabriel, Dad suddenly dipped his weight downward. Then, he drove his wide, heavy fist up into Gabriel's jaw with all his might. Gabriel's molars crunched shut with a sharp crack. The force lifted Gabriel just off the ground. His feet levitated just off the ground. His neck stretched like he was hung from an invisible wire. Then, Gabriel descended. His body crumpled like a puppet with its strings cut. Gabriel's head cracked the sidewalk slab with a hollow pop. He lay flat and motionless on the sidewalk.

My father pulled out the .45 and kneeled down over Gabriel's body. He slid the length of the barrel into Gabriel's gaping mouth to wake him up. Then my father explained to him, in no uncertain terms, that he wouldn't be burglarizing homes in the neighborhood anymore. After that, Gabriel disappeared from the block, and the burglaries stopped—for a while anyway.

Ma hurried towards the front door. She dragged her thick, varicose-veined leg under her. Lil Pat rumbled down the stairs. As Ma got to the door, she closed it. She locked all three locks and the chain bolt, then pressed her back to the white-painted wood. I followed her. My betrayal of my brother and fear for my mother churned in my chest. He slowed as he neared the bottom steps and gripped the oak railing. All the family pictures hung just behind him on the staircase wall. They dated back to when Lil Pat was a chipped-tooth boy in the '70s. He hadn't gotten along with her even then.

He stared at her. His eyes widened, and the whites glistened behind the bulged, red veins. His movements were brittle, like taut cords ran through his entire body.

"Get out the way, Ma," he warned.

"Patrick Charles," she said, her voice thundering with fear and outrage. "What are you doing with your father's gun?"

He stepped down the last few steps to the landing.

"Get out the way," he said, flatly, and tilted his head to the side.

"No, Pat. This has to stop," she pleaded. Her body quivered.

"Get the fuck outta the way!" he yelled. "I'll blow your fuckin' brains out, BITCH!"

He twisted and pulled the .45 from his waistband. Then, he extended and pointed it directly in her face. It was like the bottom tip of my crucifix morphed into a point. It elongated, bent, and pierced my skin. Then, it sank deep into my heart and set like a hook. I clutched my chest. She bowed her head and looked away but didn't move from the door.

"Pat," I said, breathless.

Lil Pat turned and looked at me. The pistol trembled. All his teeth were showing—his face flexed. I leaned my back against the wall in the hallway and slid down it slowly. Tears rolled down my cheeks. Confusion swept over his face.

"Naw, Joey, no," He said, lowering the gun. "I wasn't gonna do it... I'm... I'm sorry."

Then, he looked back at Ma. He dug his shoulder into her and knocked her out of the way. Then, he undid the locks as she grabbed at his wrist and hand. He swung the door open and smashed her into the wall with it. The rubber band snapped in her ponytail, and slices of her jet-black hair fell over her face. He thundered down the front steps and was gone.

She shut the door and locked it, taking heaving breaths. And that wasn't the last time there'd be a gun pointed at someone I loved.

■

A FEW NIGHTS LATER, they busted Lil Pat for armed robbery. Nearly all the heroin dealers on the North Side refused to sell to him, and many had even bulked up security just in case Lil Pat and

Fat Buck tried to stick them up again. So, Lil Pat went pharmaceutical. He'd managed to get several high-dosage pain prescriptions, and since the union was still kicking out for insurance, he was getting high almost for free. When the insurance ran out, Lil Pat got strung-out. He went into the pharmacy with the .45 and had them hand over several hundred dollars worth of Oxycontin. He even put the .45 under a pregnant woman's maternity dress to encourage the pharmacist to hurry up. She was a Filipino woman—mid-twenties, with that flushed glow of a soon-to-be mother. She was eight-to-nine months, with her round belly just hovering above that cold-metal .45 pointed up at that life yet to take a breath.

They I.D.'d him easy. There was no way out of it. The cops wanted him bad because of the pregnant lady thing, and they came to the house looking for him. I remember the heavy banging at the door and the officers pouring in with a search warrant. Their hands clasped on their police issue 9s. Officer O'Riley showed up. He frowned—his gray-speckled mustache hung over his top lip. He stepped through the front door slowly, and his Mick-red face bowed. The cops left after the house was searched, and I sat at the top of the stairs and listened to O'Riley talk with my father. I'll never forget my father's cracked voice—the voice of a broken man without the choice of giving in.

"He needs help," my father said. "I don't know what else to do."

"There's nothing you can do, Pat," Officer O'Riley said. "He's gotta face the music on this one."

Later that night, the phone rang, and I heard my father's voice downstairs. I got up and walked to the top of the landing and listened to my father convince Lil Pat to put the .45 in a dumpster behind the Jewel on Ashland. Afterward, Dad called the cops and told them where they could find the gun. Then, later, it was Lil Pat again. I listened as my father convinced him to turn himself in. He ended up getting sent for six years.

It's a strange thing to walk around the neighborhood with everybody knowing your brother's in the Pen. The clean part of the neighborhood looks at you like you're trash and expects you to be bad. I'd be playing with kids like normal when their mothers would call them in. It got so they didn't come ask me to play ball out behind St. Greg's gym no more. I remember the last time I came around to see the clean kids. I saw Mike Thompson walk out his front door with a mitt and bat, and I rode up to him and asked if he was gonna play a game and if I could come. Mrs. Thompson appeared at his front door and called him in. He shrugged and said sorry. I remember how after he passed her inside she stood at the screen door looking at me a long time. Not saying nothing, but saying everything with her frowning bitter face... *My son will not play with the likes of you.* Rifts swelled between me and clean kids. I started to hate them. At the same time, the dark part of the neighborhood looks at you with respect. Guys hanging out and sipping beers on front porches would say things like, "Ohh dat's lil Walsh, Patty's little brother," then give me a sip of their beer while they asked how Lil Pat was doing in there. And the bad kids—the kinds with families just like yours—seem to hang around ya more 'cause the clean part looks at them the same way. So it gets to the point that you do bad shit 'cause it's what the clean part wants. So they know they are nothing like you, and so you know you are nothing like them.

PART TWO

ADOLESCENCE

CHAPTER 9

SIMON

THEY KILLED SY over a stereo. Sounds petty, I know. It was.

This gang called the PG3s sprouted up a few blocks north of us around Granville and Clark. They mainly hung out around Hayt Elementary School's playground, which had this big asphalt baseball diamond with one of those pitched-roof field houses in the corner. The park was encircled by a tall chain-link fence. They were a mixed bag—whites, Cubans, Puerto Ricans, Mexicans, and black's. They were mostly teenagers; there were no real old-school heads 'cause they just didn't have any history. They were renegades, meaning they didn't take sides in the huge rift between street gangs in Chicago known as the Nations. Back then, nearly all the individual gangs in the city fell under alliance with either the Folks Nation or the Peoples Nation. Endless wars raged between them. Being on your own like that in a big city is a difficult thing. It makes you an easy target for both sides, and as result, in the few years of their existence, the PG3s had become pretty ruthless.

One of the big problems with not being part of a Nation was the lack of access to quality drugs. The heroin and cocaine the

PG3s did get a hold of was stomped on vigorously, so by the time they tried to bag it and sell it, even hungriest junkies and crackheads were sticking their noses up at it.

Even their weed was bunk.

Sy had gotten hold of a quarter-pound of kind bud from some Outlaws—this big biker crew from McCook out in the suburbs. Like I said, Sy just knew everybody. He worked part-time at a record store and sold the bud to help pay rent. He'd moved into this little second-floor apartment across from the hospital on Hollywood.

I witnessed the whole thing go down in stages, but nothing could have told me what was coming. It was like watching a bad car wreck in slow motion when the only thing you should do, you can't, which is close your eyes.

■

WHEN I WAS A KID, Andersonville was only considered the shopping district—that strip of Swedish shops along Clark before it hit Ashland. What solidified this for me and all the rest of us was the Edgewater Hospital, which sat at Ashland and Hollywood. It was this towering tan concrete structure that loomed high and wide like a monolith. You could see it from just about anywhere in our little nook of Edgewater. It had an eerie omnipresence, like it was following us. Just above the pitched roofs and between the narrow gangways, there it was, always. We'd all been in that ER at least once with broken bones, cuts that needed stitches, and worse. Many of us had been born there, and more than a few of our relatives had died inside those ominous, concrete walls. The raw, divergent power of that monolith drew us kids like a magnet.

We'd started hanging out at the window sills along the Hollywood side of the hospital. It was something to do, and you could always expect to find somebody hanging out there. Plus, we had benches to sit on. Well, not exactly benches; they were the ledges of these deep-cut windows built right into the concrete wall of the hospital like rectangular vaults that were deep enough that you could fit in four 12-year-old kids sitting Indian style. They were tall, too. Real tall—like ten feet—so if you were standing in one, you couldn't jump and touch the top. The windows were for the accounting offices, so the lights in 'em were out by six or seven at night, and the older guys would curl up in there with a girl to make out, or at least that's what they were constantly bragging about. We were always graffiti'n the inside walls of the sills with markers. They rarely cleaned 'em 'cause you really couldn't see anything unless you stuck your head inside. There were illustrations of strange sexual acts involving men, women, dogs, gorillas, and horses. The drawings were accompanied by silly taglines inside bubbles that read, "Giddy up!" "Give it to me, ya big ape," or "Take it, Bitch!"

Then, there were random curse words, people's nicknames, a big pot leaf, Metallica *Ride the Lightning*, and stuff like "Sue+Angel" with a heart around it. You could spend a whole afternoon just reading the crap the kids had written in all three of the sills. And just when it got cluttered enough and we were running out of space, the city's graffiti blaster'd come in, put some padding on the glass, sandblast it all clean and fresh, and we'd get to start all over again.

The other part about hanging out at the sills that made it fun was that on weekend nights (and pretty much any night) there'd be a steady flow of ambulances. And depending on if the huge black security guard we called Big James was on duty or in a good mood, we got to walk up and get a little peek at the patients coming in. Sometimes, it was old people that just had a stroke or something, but other times, it was car accidents or violence. We saw a lot of nasty crap in that emergency room tunnel. It burrowed through the width of the hospital, paralleling Ashland and continuing to the arterial alley. Looking back now, I can't believe they let us kids lurk around like that, but I guess they couldn't 'a stopped us even if they'd tried, though Big James would run us off sometimes when we got too boisterous and annoying. I guess you could say that it was a sick thing to do, and that if our parents knew what we were doing, they'd have beat the crap outta us. What if the ambulances brought in someone we loved? We wouldn't be wisecracking and ogling the ER patients then, and you'd be right. But kids just don't think like that. What drew us was the same reason people watch reality shows today, or "ER" for Christ's sake: people love realistic drama. Strangely enough, it's a way of readying us for the inevitability of our own tragedies, our loved ones' deaths, and our own. So maybe it ain't so sick after all. We're all curious, right? And we all know sooner or later, it's coming.

It was a little different for Ryan and I than for the others. The Assyrian's dead soul still haunted us. We dreamt of him and of the gore of that night years past, and I think we sought to find a control over our emotions surrounding death and the horrific to fortify our nerves and deaden our hearts to the torment we knew laid ahead.

■

THE FIRST TIME I SAW A PG3, I was down at the sills a couple years after Lil Pat got locked up. Ryan, Angel, and I had become an inseparable clique. My silent connection with Ryan was still strong; witnessing that together at such a young age and losing people to long-term lockups like we had had bound us tight. But getting to know Angel more and more—his weird, perverse sense of humor and his sly way of picking at people—just had me laughing incessantly. Those two were kind of a yin and yang for me: the hard, serious Ryan, and the goofy prankster Angel. We were just punk-ass 12-year-olds trying to find our sense of style. Still ain't even hit puberty and stuck between being little boys and mean teens. Even though we'd seen more than most, we were still playing video games and watching cartoons. We were still liable to fall into a game of tag or hide and go seek with the younger kids, get caught by one another and frozen into rigid embarrassment, and then spend the rest of the day scowling and puffing cigarettes to prove how cold and tough we were, going on about all the guys we'd whooped on and all the girlfriends we had in other neighborhoods. We'd be sitting there at the sills breaking down all the TJO lit we knew. Which gangs were Peoples and which were Folks, and just listing off all the white gangs: Popes, Jousters, Gaylords, Royals.

"Man, fuck the Royals!" Ryan sneered. "They're Folks."

"You said white Stone Greaser gangs," I replied, looking at him confused.

"Yeah, but fuck the Royals. My old man got shot by a Royal. I don't wanta ever hear anybody talkin' bout Royals around me."

"Man, that's stupid," Angel whined, flashing teeth. "What about the Kansas City Royals? What, we can't talk about them?"

"Yeah, fuck Bo Jackson. That bitch is a Royal!" I spat. Angel and I giggled.

"Fuck you," Ryan snarled. "You know what I mean." His face reddened, and his eyebrows trembled.

We let that simmer as we sat on the ledges in wait of something. The yellow streetlights cast dark shadows in the depths of the deep-cut sills like empty bank vaults. Traffic was thick and fast on Ashland, and low heavy metal oozed out of Sy's window across the street. Mike Thompson slouched against the wall beside us. He'd turned into a 13-year-old pothead well on his way to becoming a burn-out. His stuck-up ass mom must have been so proud. He wore these weird pants that were really big and had no shape or taper at the ankle, and the legs looked like two fat, brown sewer pipes. Ryan and I passed a smoke back and forth from adjacent sills. Iron Maiden's rambling clicked off across the street, and a few seconds later, Sy pattered down his front stairs in white gym shoes, jungle-camo pants, and a graying Metallica t-shirt. He strolled across to us. His ragged, dirty-blond hair mopped along his shoulders.

"Thought you said ya never was gonna smoke?" Sy said, grimacing, then he rushed me.

I leapt and dashed away. He swooped up quick. I stopped and cowered against the hospital wall and folded my arms over my head feebly. Sy smacked me, but my hand and wrist deflected it.

"I'm gonna do this every time I catch ya wit' a cigarette," he said, turning away. I unfurled my guard. He suddenly spun back, crouched, and slammed his fist into my thigh. The deep boom sent a chorus of "Ohhhhh!" out of everyone in earshot, then they settled into an uneasy laughter.

"Damn, Sy!" I said, hopping around on one leg. It felt like a heart pulsing there mid-thigh.

I limped to my ledge and sat back down. Grimacing, I kneaded the deep knot. Ryan tried to pass me the cigarette as he smirked up at Sy.

"No. Fuck no. I seen the light! I quit!" I said.

Sy grinned and slid his thin fingers through my hair, then snatched the cigarette from Ryan and took my pull.

"Aye, Sy, where'd you get that pot from?" Mike Thompson asked, whipping his hair out of his face. "That shit blew my fuckin' mind!"

"Don't worry about where I got it. Just remember where you got it." Sy patted his chest right on the empty electric chair with the lightning shooting through it.

An ambulance swung into the ER tunnel with its lights swirling, but no siren. A few of us walked over to see. The paramedics rolled an old lady out on a stretcher. She was unconscious, sucking air through some plastic tubes that ran into her nostrils. A green oxygen tank lay beside her on the sheets.

"Dmm Dmm Dmm, Dm Da Dmm, Dm Da Dmm." Angel hummed the Darth Vader theme as she eased past us. "Pshh, Luke... I am your grandmother," he bellowed. We roared and loped out of the tunnel.

Sy sat in a sill smoking the cigarette he nicked off Ryan and I. He glanced at me disappointedly as we approached, silencing my laughter.

"You guys oughta stop doing that shit," he said, squelching his smoke on the concrete shelf beside him. "What if that was your Gramma? Huh?" He glared at me, his brown eyes somber. I looked away and thought about Da, who was only dead a couple years by then. "What if it was one 'a your parents? Hell, what if it was one 'a you? What if it was me for Christ's sake? You think I'd want to hear you little knuckleheads wisecracking about what happened to me?"

"Naw," I said looking down. My throat tightened. "You're right."

Sy had a way of seeing things—a way of putting 'em to words, too. He was a songwriter, but he coulda been a poet, coulda been a lot of things. There's been a few times in my life where people have told me things out of the blue, or in the midst of doing heavy drugs and drinking. They'd just come out of the fog for a second of clarity and give me something, like a going away present, but backwards. Like they were giving me something while they still had the time, like they knew it was coming and soon. Like a premonition. Like they were telling me exactly what I needed to know before they were gone forever.

"Check this out," Ryan said, nodding down the street.

Four hoods rounded the corner at Ashland. One was a Puerto Rican with a fat head and a cheesy smile. Gold flickered in his ear lobe. There were two other thinner Puerto Ricans, too. One wore a Sox cap, and the other had crazy zigzag graphics cut into the sides of his trimmed, black hair. The last one was a skinny little black dude. His big white t-shirt hung off his narrow frame like a blanket and drooped over his baggy black sweatpants. He had a small head, and his eyes were big and wide open like he was on the absolute edge of committing total mayhem. If I'd a seen a similar guy today, I'd have instantly recognized him as a shooter for whatever gang he ran with. In other words, the go-to-guy when it was time to pop someone. But right then, I just thought he was crazy. Such a little guy, Sy coulda whooped his ass easy. This dangly dude looked like he was ready to whoop any man on the planet, but with the heat he probably had stuffed in his pocket, or snug in his waistband, he coulda.

"What up, Heffey?" Sy said as he walked up and greeted them with handshakes.

"What's up, Simon," the fat one said, grinning and sticking his chest out. His belly swelled against his red Scottie Pippen jersey.

The one with the hat pulled on his brim and asked, "We gonna handle this?"

"Yeah," Sy said. "Just step into my office." He led them across the street toward his place.

"Ay, can I play this on that stereo 'a yours? I just want to see what it sound like?" The one with the zigzag graphics pinched the corner of this clear mix-tape and brandished it.

I stared at the black kid. *Who the fuck's he think he is?* They made their way up the steps, and when he reached the top, the black kid stopped, turned, and shot me a glance. His eyes were yellow and hollow like a black cat. No trace of emotion in his face. No trace of life—like some kinda monster. They filed inside, and a few minutes later, hip hop blasted from Sy's open window like a sin.

■

IN THE STREET, if you can't protect yourself, eventually you will be exposed and victimized. It didn't take long for them PG3s to show their true colors. A couple days later, Angel, Ryan, and me we were out there at the sills as usual. The air was cool and dank. The streetlight above the sills flickered with a tick, like one of those bug zappers. Its audible, electric pulse expanded down to the sidewalk. I wondered how it worked. The sun was a ball of fire, but how did we make light bulbs work? Was there fire in there, too? Maybe it was just electricity, and maybe that's what the sun was: just a big ball of electricity.

Sy sat in a sill with his feet on the ledge, hugging his knees to his chest. His hair flopped down, masking his face. He was silent, so we were silent with him. We even ran off some little kids that were making a racket. Rich and a few metal-heads came up from the corner store gripping glass liter bottles in brown paper bags; it was amazing how easy it was for teens to buy booze in the neighborhood back then. Then, I recognized this tall black one with a spiked mohawk—the guy from Fautches that the skinheads stabbed.

"I remember you," the black guy said in a weird, almost British accent similar to the Ethiopians along Broadway and Granville.

"I remember when you got stabbed," I said.

"This," he pulled his shirt up and revealed a three-inch scar on his stomach, "was nothing." He smiled. "If you only knew how much pussy a scar like this could get you, kid...."

Rich burst out laughing, then sauntered over to Sy.

"What's da matter witchu, fucker?" Rich said, smirking down at Sy. "You look like somebody died."

Sy raised his head, and his hair spliced back and revealed this terrible grimace strung across his burly mug.

"Those fuckin' gangbangers broke in while I was at work. They stole my stereo and part of my stash." Sy spit; it arced out and splattered foamy-white on the concrete.

"Ahh shit!" Rich squealed, stupefied.

"Motherfuckers!" the black guy shot back.

"We're gonna get those motherfuckers," Sy said, flinging out of his sill at Rich. They squared and gazed fiercely in each other's eyes.

"What's a gangbanger?" I asked, looking up at Rich. I'd never heard it said like that. Usually, it was gangster, or by name like a King or a TJO.

"They fuckin' stand on the corner lookin' tough, and then hide behind guns and numbers! They're fuckin' cowards! They're nothing but a bunch of niggers and spicks," Rich said, shooting his crazed eyes at mine. Spittle sprayed from his lips.

"Quit saying 'nigger,'" I said. I looked at the black guy.

"What? Joseph?" Rich nudged the black guy. "Joseph ain't a nigger, he's Ghanaian. Joseph hates niggers more than me!"

"They're not Africans," Joseph sneered. "They're slaves with slave mentalities."

Rich chortled and leaned his face right in close on Sy's. "Let's go up there right now and bust some fuckin' heads."

"Hell yeah," Sy bellowed.

"Let's go," Joseph urged.

"Come on, motherfucker, you scared?" Rich asked, shoving Sy in the chest. They tore off toward Ashland hooting, hollering, and squealing like swine.

I'd have been worried if I'd heard Lil Pat talking that way, but since it was Rich, I just laughed it off. He wasn't known for being all that tough with guys his own age and size.

"Man, you think they're gonna get 'em?" Angel asked.

"Naw, they'll probably get beat up or somethin'," I retorted.

"Yeah, but maybe Sy though," Ryan added, arching his red eyebrows. "He's pretty mad."

"Look what I got." Angel held up a bag. It was small and had green leaves and light-brown stems and a bunch of little, round seeds in it. I scrunched my nose as the pungent aroma struck my nostrils.

"It's weed, man," Angel said, disappointed.

"How we gonna smoke it?" Ryan asked.

"Man, give me a cigarette," Angel said.

Ryan pulled out a Marlboro Light from a tattered Camel pack with an assortment of different-colored butts sticking out. Angel took one and sat down. He crumbled the end in his fingers so about half the tobacco poured out on the ledge of concrete beside him, and we blocked the view from the street with our backs. Ryan took the bag of weed and plucked some of the buds out, then he crumbled 'em into a pile of thin dust next to the stringy lump of tobacco. Then, Angel pinched the green dust in his index and thumb, held the cigarette vertically, and sprinkled it into the hollow end. He filled an inch of the cigarette, then squeezed the paper and twisted it tight. He pulled out his lighter and leaned back. Then, he tilted the cigarette upward, lit it, and puffed hard a few times.

The shit smelled nasty as it swirled up in Angel's eyes. He blew out a small, gray cloud in my face, and passed to Ryan, who puffed and coughed instantly. Angel and I laughed and called him a pussy, then Ryan handed it to me. Maybe it was the nerves or something, but I took a sharp, deep pull and exhaled a huge plume of smoke. This damp, sticky, burning sensation snaked down through my windpipe and into my lungs. Once there, it expanded and twisted into my bronchial tubes like tree roots. I remember seeing Angel's and Ryan's eyes swell wide open. Then, I hunched over and retched, trying to expel the hot liquid, but the only thing that came up was a clear line of drool that dangled down to the sidewalk. It felt like there was molten ooze slithering around inside me. Finally, I recovered and stood up straight. It was like someone had socked me a good one. There were stars. Not the cartoon stars, but real stars, like a thousand tiny dots, flickering over everything. I looked at Angel's laughing face, and his mouth morphed into this giant cave. His big teeth were glossy, wet, and bright. Deep inside the cave, his tiny pink flagella danced and flapped back and forth. Suddenly, it grew eyes. I shuddered and looked away. Ryan sucked hard on the cigarette with his face all tied up in a knot, then the gray smoke poured from his mouth like steam.

My heart thrummed. I was suddenly winded, exhausted, and cold, so I climbed into a sill. My whole being quivered and then crawled up inside my skull. I heard my own thoughts loud in my cranium, and it felt like I could hear everyone else's thoughts, too. First, I heard their words, then their thoughts trailing afterward. They both seemed very far away. Their smiles began to distort into grotesque, elongated masks. They kept trying to hand me the white smoke. The dark-orange ember smoldered audibly. Then, everything went back to normal—time was normal, sound normal, sight normal. Ryan leaned in close and looked at me. I batted my eyes and braced for the next hallucination.

"This motherfucker is fucked up!" Ryan said in awe. I didn't respond. I was scared. *What if I stay like this forever?* Then, it all started again. Everything slowly distorted. My thoughts grew loud. Time stretched.

Suddenly, I heard this familiar voice and turned. Monteff stood at the mouth of the tunnel in some white jeans. The pleats and creases in the jeans created these mountainous glacier legs that flowed down to his Reebok Pumps. He'd said something funny that I didn't catch. They laughed. Monteff's small, bright-white teeth flashed and sent these spiral rays shooting in all directions. He walked up and greeted us with handshakes and toked on the weed smoke.

Monteff was one of the only black dudes from the Dead-End-Docks who would come over by us to chill. He was just one of those vibrant individuals who can transcend race and cliques and haters. He'd surpass those invisible walls and bring his joyful, melodic vibe along with him. But even he was freaking me out in the state I was in. Monteff always arched his eyebrows up when he was listening to something entertaining. Angel was on one of his perverse, sarcastic ramblings, and it sent Monteff's eyebrows stretching up higher and higher. Suddenly, they morphed into the shape of the McDonald's Arches. Then, the tips of his bristly eyebrows melded into the hairline of his trimmed scalp. I was so gripped by it that I couldn't catch what Angel was saying. Angel's voice erupted loudly, then twisted into a chortle. Monteff's eyebrows swelled to form his soft widow's peak, and his eyeballs yawned wide open and protruded out of their sockets. The light-brown flecks caught in the arc lamp. *Man, I really should never smoke weed, especially not kind bud.*

Later, an ambulance roared into the emergency room tunnel. The red-and-blue strobe lit the whole block and struck the full-leaved trees across the street, daylight-bright. A pair of gleaming, phosphorescent-white eyes flashed at me through the leafy branches, then vanished. Angel, Ryan, and Monteff jogged into the alley and up to the ER ramp. I followed, sluggishly.

The ambulance doors burst open. Urgency distorted the faces of the paramedics. It looked like they were all screaming soundlessly. Then, I realized it was the deafening sirens that were screaming.

"Damn, that motherfucker got his ass whooped," Ryan said. A sickness had taken him. Saliva drenched his lips. HIs grimace suddenly elongated until the corners of his lips touched his ears. His crooked teeth wiggled, then suddenly everything warped back to normal. Monteff gawked, then spun away saying, "Ohhhhhhh!" His mouth stretched in a downward "o" like an anteater's snout.

I looked at the guy as the stretcher descended from the ambulance. He was an unconscious, teenaged Puerto Rican kid, and the side of his face and head were terribly swollen and pulsing red. There was a large gash that hung open like a flap and ran along the back of his skull with dark blood leaking from it. There were crazy, zigzagging lines etched into his scalp that ran down behind his ears, and I recognized the face, but couldn't figure out where from. Then, it hit me: he was one of the dudes that stopped by to listen to Sy's stereo.

Years later, Rich'd tell me how they'd gotten that guy. We were riding to work in the big box truck he drove for the construction company. Mancow's Morning Madhouse had enraged him, so he'd shut the radio off. They'd run up into the PG3s' turf that night and saw Mr. Zigzag walk into a corner store. They waited for him along the wall on the dark side street. When he came out with a big plastic bottle of Diet Coke in his hands, Rich'd stepped up behind him. Then Rich smashed his full glass liter of Budweiser over the back of Mr. Zigzag's head with the brown paper still wrapped around it. They lumped him up a little when he went down, face-flat on the sidewalk. Then, they jetted the fuck outta there before anybody saw 'em.

■

SY HAD A GIRLFRIEND over that way, right off of Granville. That's how he met them PG3s when they got word he had some flame bud. Sy went over to see his girl that Friday. Word was out that somebody'd burglarized Sy's place, and that he was sure it was the PG3s who'd done it. The stereo meant a lot to Sy. Music was a big part of his identity. It was his escape from all the trouble he had at home. And he'd saved up a long time to get it. The PG3s didn't like Sy slandering their names in the street like that, and they had their suspicions of who rode on their boy with the zigzag 'do, so when one of 'em saw that Sy had stopped by his girl's house, they sent over their shooter—that same little black kid I saw a few days before. Dude went by the name of Spider. They sent him to stick a gun in Sy's face and tell him to quit with his talking.

When Sy left his girl's place, Spider stepped up to him and pulled the 9mm revolver. He held it at his side, just to show him, and told Sy to keep the PG3s out of his vocabulary. Sy had a certain way of seeing things, so he probably looked at that 15-year-old kid and thought *Screw all this crap*. Probably wanted to talk to him, talk some sense into him. Sy reached for the gun, and Spider lurched back, scared. Pop.

That same night, Angel, Ryan, and I were down there hangin' as usual. Friday night was always a big night—a lot of domestics, car accidents, muggings, knifings, old people off their meds and having strokes and breakdowns. I was sitting on the ledge of my sill, elbows propped on my knees, feeling strange. Sewage rambled below the street and echoed up through the catch-basin along the curb. Angel was next to me chomping on a wad of Gonzo Grape Bubblicious and blowing quick, little bubbles that popped and squished. The noise irritated all the tiny hairs inside my earlobe. Angel could annoy a person like no other. I felt sick and dizzy and a little scared as the full, incandescent moon beamed down on us through the hazy, purplish sky.

"Man, I got a weird feeling about tonight, man," I said, folding my arms over my chest.

"Yeah?" Angel replied, furrowing his brow as he continued to pop away.

"Yeah. Something crazy is gonna happen, man. I can just feel it in my stomach, ya know?"

"What, like that shit—what do they call it—ESB or somethin'?" Ryan said giggling, as he leaned against the narrow concrete partition between the sills.

"Man, I don't know," I said, then licked my dry lips. "I just want to see if it works. That's why I told you. What if I'm fucking psychic or something?"

Angel chortled. "Well, tell me what I'm thinking then."

"Ah, either some kinda joke with hermaphrodites in it, or

about fucking one 'a those big-booty bitches in the Lowrider magazines." I grinned widely at him.

"Shit! He is psychic! Fuck! Watch out what you think around him, Ry. You know, about kissing him and shit like that, 'cause he'll catch your ass."

"Fuck you, you fucking weirdo," Ryan said, flat and cool.

An ambulance strolled slowly through the back way with its lights on swirling lazily, but without sirens. We jogged into the alley. The ambulance drivers helped an old bald man out of the back by his arm. His mouth hung open, and his light-blue eyes were lost. He wore red-striped pajamas with a big wet spot at the crotch.

"Aye, look, he pissed his self!" Angel sighed.

"Man, that old fucker's retarded. Look at him," Ryan said.

"I pissed my pants?" the old man said, bewildered. His mouth gaped, revealing his blackened bottom row of teeth.

"Man, we better stop. Big James is gonna come out here, man," I said as we walked back.

"I pissed my pants?" Angel mimicked the old man perfectly. "That's nothing. I shit myself, too!" Angel cocked his head to the side with his crazy eyes wide open and his bottom lip uncurled.

We were still giggling when the sirens of another ambulance blared onto Hollywood.

"Told you it was gonna be a crazy night," I said. We waited at the mouth of the tunnel.

The ambulance came in hot. Its tires squealed as it rounded the corner, then zoomed into the tunnel. An excitement rushed up, then froze like icicles in my stomach.

The ambulance came to a screeching halt. The driver lunged out, and the one in back leapt down from the back doors. They extracted the stretcher swiftly. Their faces were fierce and panic-stricken. A young doctor jogged down the ER ramp as we stepped up. Big James emerged. I couldn't see at first because of the commotion. Big James pushed us back in his slow, powerful way with the back of his arm. Angel squeezed up in front.

"Ahhhh, dat guy's dead!" Angel said in a silly voice. "Look at him, his brains are leaking out." He turned and walked away with a sick smile. "Yeah, we got a 109: oil leak out of skull." He spoke into an invisible radio attached to his shirt collar.

I chuckled uneasily as I fought my way up to see, and then I saw the face, the beard all wet and dark. The red-soaked hair had familiar, greasy, dirty-blond strands at the edges. The mangled face had dark-red blood smeared all over it. My heart jumped along with my entire body. I turned to run, then turned back to look again. The long hair, the beard, tufts of sinew protruded from the gaping wound in the eye socket. There was blood and a darker, thicker mucus oozing up like tar. I muffled a scream with my palm, spun, and sprinted away. I could hear the ambulance driver speaking with the ER doctor as they pushed him up the ramp: "One round through the left orbital. No exit."

"Oh, shit," Ryan yelled. "Dude got shot in the head!"

I ran as fast as I could. A thousand things soared through my head. I ran home. When I got inside, I bounded stairs to Rich's room and tried the doorknob. It was locked. I banged hard and fast on the thin, hollow wood. The sound thundered over the heavy metal music blaring inside.

"Rich!" I screamed. "Rich!" The emotion poured in a squealing sway.

The door ripped open.

"What the fuck's going on?" Rich said, glaring down at me.

"It's Sy!"

"What?"

"It's Simon!" I hugged him around his waist for some reason.

"What?" Rich gripped my shoulders and yanked me away. "Tell me what's going on dammit!"

"The ambulance, he..."

"What? At the hospital?" Rich jumped, his eyes wide open. He turned towards his room, then bounded out the door past me.

"They—they—brought him in," I said, following him.

Rich stormed down the stairs and out the front door. I followed. He sprinted up the street. The realization that Sy would die sunk into my lungs like two hooks. Wires looped around my arms and legs and bogged me down until I couldn't run. It felt like something'd broken inside my chest. I sobbed and tried to expel the broken thing—to scream it out. I retched, gagged, and vomited air. Then, I steadied and forced myself to walk toward the hospital. Hot tears streamed down my cheeks. I was sure Sy was dead, but then these little sparks of hope started popping inside me, and I thought maybe he'd make it, and I ran again even though the wires tangled me. When I got to the hospital, I gusted past Ryan and Angel at the sills. They looked shocked at having just seen Rich sprint past.

"What's going on, Joe?" Angel said solemnly.

I rushed down the tunnel and sprang through the ER door. Big James snagged me by my collar. "Hold on now, kid, you can't go in there."

I could see Rich down a white corridor talking with a blond doctor. The doctor adjusted his spectacles and said something in a calm, flat tone. A great thing plucked out of Rich in that instant. He crumbled to his knees—clutching his stomach. Silence, then a throttling scream resonated throughout the room. Tears washed down my face as Big James held me there by my arms. The doctor stepped away, and Rich rocked on the floor in the hallway. Beyond him, there was a commotion behind a tall curtain. Doctors and nurses cut in and out of it. Then, the curtain split open. They looked like ants climbing on each other. It yanked shut. Big James spun me and crouched down.

"Why don'tchu go home and get somebody," he said somberly.

When I passed the sills, Angel jogged up beside me. "What's going on? Did you know that guy or something?" he asked.

"That was Sy, man," I answered, staring straight ahead.

"What?" Angel said, repulsed. "No it wasn't."

"It was Simon," I said in a cold tone. "He's dying."

Ryan grabbed Angel's shoulder, and they stopped. I just kept on towards the house. Angel started to say something, but Ryan stopped him. A Medivac helicopter thromped across the sky overhead and disappeared above the leering hospital walls.

"I thought it might be him," Ryan said.

"Oh my God," Angel replied as I fell out of earshot. I went home and told my parents.

When I fell to my knees and prayed that night, it was different than when I'd prayed for the Assyrian. I prayed with a bright and unstoppable hope that Sy would survive and make it and live for a very long time. The hope was so powerful that joyful tears streamed down my face as I imagined Sy walking out of the hospital into the golden sunlight weeks later with an eye patch, smiling; his long, dirty-blond hair draped down over his shoulders.

■

THEY MEDIVAC'D SY to Weiss Memorial Hospital in Uptown, and he made it through the night, but he was on life support and slipped into a deep coma by the next day. The doctors weren't giving him much chance at living, but he was holding on. They put him in their coma ward, but it was all for nothing. They pulled the plug a week later.

After the funeral, Rich went nuts. One day, I was sitting on the porch and Rich and this crazy looking Mexican dude barreled past and inside the house. A few seconds later, they ran out with a bed sheet covering Rich's 12-gauge shotgun. Rich laughed and put his finger to his lips, shushing me as he passed. I stayed quiet, though at night, my mind raced with all the wonder of the war my brother was fighting as shots rang out in the neighborhood.

Rich'd teamed up with the Latin Kings from the set right there on the other side of Clark. They started pulling drive-bys at Hayt Elementary School's playground where, on any given night, you could find thirty or more PG3s lounging along the high fence near the fieldhouse.

Rich told me, years later, how he and Shorty and a few other Kings shot them up almost constantly for months. How the Kings taught him to roll up a main drag, an arterial street, and turn onto a one-way. Do your deed—quick, without words—before they could run or get to their heat. Then, you speed off into the maze of side streets—the capillaries of the city. Get out of that neighborhood, preferably into a worse neighborhood like Rogers Park or Little Vietnam, so if the truck was I.D.'d that precinct wasn't on your shit. They'd have their own crap to deal with. Park the truck near the Red Line, take it to the Bryn Mawr stop. Walk it home. Come back and get the truck the next morning.

Repeat.

Repeat until the shit was getting too redundant and crazy for even the Kings. Repeat until a shotgun slug finally finds someone dead-center, or a .25-round skips along the playground asphalt and tears flesh.

The PG3s began to recognize the big, brown Bronco. One day at Senn, Rich came out of school and every single window had been completely broken out, even the frickin' rear-view mirrors. They sold the Diesel and bought a blue Dodge Ramcharger, and Rich transferred to a public school out on the Northwest Side.

But then, worst of all, Spider got off on self-defense 'cause Sy went for the gun. Can you imagine that? He walked after about two months—walked right out of juvie a free man. Rich saw him one night when he was rolling around near this little playground a half-block north of Senn. Spider was just sitting there on a swing with a Walkman in his lap and some headphones on—the big, padded ones with the input you could plug into a stereo outlet. He was just nodding away, maybe waiting for somebody, who knows. Rich didn't have the .25 on him, or the shotgun, but he had a bat in the truck. Some gnarly, thick-stalked one that Lil Pat'd made in woodshop. Rich drove around the block and parked so he was behind Spider. He got out with the bat and walked up quick, light-footed, trying to be quiet atop the little brown woodchips of the playground. There was no one out. He hid the bat along his thigh as best he could and crept right up behind Spider, who was slowly rocking his head. Rich brought that heavy-stalked bat up over his own head like a two-fisted broadsword and—WAP!— came down directly atop Spider's narrow cranium, cracked his skull, and ended his reign as the PG3s' shooter.

Never did figure out if that's how it really went down. There're police records, I'm sure, and even people I coulda asked, but maybe part of me didn't want to find out. Kinda hope that it ain't how it went down, for Rich's sake. That'd be a whole lot to carry around for the rest of your life, and he already had plenty to haul.

CHAPTER 10

THE OLD MAN

MA BABYSAT LITTLE JOHNNY FOR FREE to help out. Being a nurse, Mrs. Kerney transferred to Edgewater Hospital so she could spend her lunch break with her grandson. A couple of weeks after her regular lunchtime visits started, shit hit the fan. Ma was in the basement with the older babysitting kids cleaning up, doing laundry, and organizing the mountains of toys—new, old, broken, slobbered-on; hand-made wooden blocks; infant, three-dimensional puzzles mixed with big, plastic machine guns, Tonka trucks, and stuffed animals. You name it, Ma had accumulated it over her 20-odd-years of babysitting. Little Johnny had laid down for a late-morning nap upstairs.

When Mrs. Kerney arrived, she depressed the glowing, circular doorbell, which didn't work. Then, she knocked with her brittle, boney hands, which of course Ma couldn't hear. Down in the basement, there was the racket of the children clapping and clanking toys in toy boxes and muttering bored complaints. The vacuum hummed over it all as Ma occasionally cracked the whip on them.

Mrs. Kerney walked along the wide porch to the windows that opened into the living room. There, her deep-red, almost orange-headed, 2-year-old grandson slept atop the couch. She rapped her keys excitedly on the thin glass and little Johnny awoke. He sleepily blinked at his gramma's excited eyes, smiled, and got up scratching the belly of his Tigger shirt. When he got to the window, he spread his pale little arms out wide for her to pick him up. When the glass dividing them wouldn't allow her, sleepy little Johnny erupted into a hysterical cry. She began to fidget angrily with the window, which sent him running around the room with his arms flailing over his head, screeching. Mrs. Kerney banged on the glass with her fists, a deep bass thunder that resonated in the room. Then, she screamed, "Open the damned door!!!"

Little Johnny froze. He looked at his gramma in an appalled horror, then he ran away down the hall and out of sight. Mrs. Kerney returned to the front door and slammed into the wood. The door hopped slightly but remained shut. She turned to the neighborhood and screamed, "Someone call the police!!!"

No one called the cops. Mrs. Sanchez from across the street did call Ma, and somehow, through all the calamitous children, the vacuum, and the tussling washer and dryer, Ma heard the ringer. She rushed to the basement phone and answered it on the second ring.

"Linda, there is some crazy lady on you porch screaming for somebody to call the police."

"What!?" Ma said, then slammed the phone down and rushed up the basement stairs. She heard little Johnny crying and the frantic pounding at the front door. She rushed over and threw it open, and Mrs. Kerney pushed past Ma with tears beading down her wrinkled cheeks. She rushed down the hall to the kitchen to find her precious little Johnny. He looked up at her barreling toward him, and turned and ran. But she was so fast that she cooped him up before he got away and squeezed him to her bony chest.

"Oh, my darling, I'm so sorry. I'm so sorry I let this happen to you!!!" she wailed, then walked back towards the door with him crying and writhing in her arms.

"What the heck's going on? Where are you going with him?" Ma said.

"I won't put up with this kind of neglect! I'm taking him out of here for good!"

"Are you sure you should be taking him? Aren't you going to call Karen and let her know?"

"I'll be having a very, very long conversation with my daughter about the care of my dear grandson. You can guarantee that!" She hustled out of the front door with little Johnny still in hysterics and reaching out a hand toward the only one of the three who wasn't crying.

We all knew Blake thought he was better than us—better than each of us and better than the family as a whole. He was destined for greater things—a greater, larger world of excellence. We'd felt hints of it in his comments over the years, but it was only a prelude to his final, conclusive statement.

That night, Blake showed up with Karen in his CPD sweater and turtleneck. He'd gotten bigger now—fatter from the donuts and diner food. He was stoic. His frozen scowl had a sense of duty in it, and his actions had a sense of long-sustained waiting for this day to come.

"I'm not putting up with this. You people live in a filthy, God-damned pigsty. It's a fucking zoo for Christ's sake." He stood tall as his parents sat at the dinner table with their heads in their hands, all reason spent. "All my life I had to live in it. I won't force my son to live in it now."

"Blake, he was up here alone for fifteen minutes. Fifteen minutes. You've never left him alone for fifteen minutes, Karen?" Ma pleaded. Tears welled in her blue eyes. "He's never woken up fifteen minutes before you?"

"That's enough!" Blake shouted. "I'm not putting up with it! You're neglecting my son!" Blake waved Karen to her feet, and she rose sniffling into a wad of paper towel.

Blake took a deep breath, clenching his eyes closed. "You won't see him or me ever again. You're not my family anymore." He said it with a hint of exhaustion. His shoulders slumped, and there was a sense of completion in the air.

He stomped out of the house with Karen sniffling behind him, and that was it for two long years; we didn't hear a word from them. Until one day, Blake and Karen finally decided to get married, and they needed someone to foot the bill 'cause Mrs. Kerney certainly wasn't going to. Dad coughed it up as a way to get back in his son's and grandson's lives. I guess Blake'd never forgiven Dad for what he was—a hard man.

■

HE USED TO SMACK MA every morning when she came to wake him up for work after brewing his pot of coffee. Just spin off the mattress, back-hand her, and see how far he could send her flying across the room. Until she finally woke him with a heavy iron frying pan crack to the side of his head.

He beat Lil Pat from the time he could walk, and as Lil Pat got older, it got worse. Blake was different, though. He was so sick for so much of his childhood that Ma wouldn't let Dad near him. Blake was a preteen before Dad started to crack him, but he was so good that he rarely got in trouble, so he almost never got one. When Blake came home from Drake with a D-average the summer of his freshman year, that all changed in a split second.

Dad got the news a few weeks into summer. It was late, like two in the morning, and Blake was out drinking at some kegger. When he got home, Dad was waiting for him at the kitchen table with the grades splayed out in front of him atop the lumpy imperfections of the handmade oak tabletop.

Dad said he wasn't gonna pay for those kinda shit grades, and Blake stomped out of the brightly lit kitchen saying he didn't want to hear it with a dismissive wave. That's when he slipped up and said, "What do you know about it? You didn't even graduate high school…." Blake tossed his head back with a laugh. "Not even close!"

Dad stomped after him into the dark hallway. Blake heard him and whirled around by the stairs. He was now a good four inches taller than Dad. Blake cocked back his meaty arm, grimaced, and growled through his teeth. Dad froze mid-step and feebly raised his large, bony hands and petered backward. His whole being trembled.

Blake flashed his All-American, smug grin, raised his chin, and turned back on his path. He sighed to himself, and as the sigh died down, it trickled into a chuckle. Dad sank downward, stepped with him. Then, he swung wide and slammed his heavy fist into the base of Blake's jaw from behind. Blake froze, pole-axed. He began to turn, and his arms and legs locked up, rigid. He toppled forward. Then, Blake plummeted and flopped, belly-down, on the hardwood floor. He laid there, gulping heavy breaths, flat out with his cheek on the cool wood planks.

You could say he was a bad father, I guess. Anyone who beats their kids is wrong and all that, but that New Age, just give 'em a "time out" stuff is bullshit. But my Dad took the reins as the father of his younger brothers at the age of twelve. Imagine that. Dad's dad was gone—crumbled into alcoholism—and with six little brothers to raise, Dad had one way to get their attention. Ever try to tell a gang of wild little boys to stop doing something? To shut up? Cracking a little kid, like it or not, gets their instant, undivided attention. Considering he became a dad at twelve and a biological father at fifteen, I think the old man did pretty good—under the circumstances, that is.

As far as Blake goes, Dad was slaving on the job site, killing himself every day, and he was still living check to check and almost losing the house anytime something unexpected came up. And all so Blake could go to some expensive school to play football when he didn't have a chance in hell of doing anything in the sport. Then Blake turns around and throws that in Dad's face? I woulda stomped him after he went down. But dat's just me.

CHAPTER 11

ASSASSINS

THERE'S PEOPLE OUT THERE that'll tell you racism is a basic tribal instinct—something embedded deep in our collective unconscious. A primal urge to be with our own, to protect our village.
And that may be true, but it doesn't change the fact that it's one
of the ugliest partitions in the heart of man.

Over a year had passed since Sy died. Even though Spider was
gone, sputtering in some home with severe brain damage, there
was still a war raging inside of Rich. The violence in him was
getting more and more misguided and random. A gay bar had
opened up south of us on Clark. Rich drove over there with his
paintball gun one night and waited out front. Two guys in neon-
yellow, tight shirts drunkenly exited the bar's brightly lit front
door. Rich plunked a few speeding red balls that burst on their
neon shirts, then he peeled off. It only leaves bruises, but the sudden, painful sting had them screaming their lungs out thinking
they'd been shot for real. It's sick, I know. Rich'd graduated from
high school and was a first-year apprentice carpenter. They were
riding him hard on the sites like they do everybody, but he wasn't

taking it too good. With his revenge extracted from the PG3s, Rich's general malice simmered into these opportunistic bursts of hatred.

Ryan, Angel, and I were on our posts at the sills, ever-diligent and ready for what was to come. It was early summer, and school'd just let out. I sat in the center sill to keep those two from fucking killing each other. Ryan posted up at the sill nearest the alley and Ashland, which was all struck bright. The orange-yellow streetlight beams emanated above and along the faded-green poles. Angel sat in the other one nearest the thickly tree-shadowed side street. Ryan couldn't handle sitting on that side; he'd constantly mistake the sway of a low-hung tree branch for some enemy trying to get the drop on us. And then, he'd leap to his feet and shout, "Who the fuck's dat!" squinting into the darkness. His temples'd flare until he was worn thin with a headache. Angel didn't see any invisible foes and probably wouldn't have minded if he did. He wasn't scared of much, plus everybody liked Angel anyhow.

I'd gotten bigger, but I was still the smallest out of the three of us. Ryan was the biggest and oldest by about six-months. He'd hit his growth spurt first and grew out and up in equal proportions. His husky arms and legs sprouted red hair.

Our individual styles had begun to form. Ryan wore his hair short, almost shaved. It was a "one" on the clippers, and he had a narrow finger of hair that protruded near the base of his skull that dangled over his collar. He rocked a fake-ass gold rope chain. His face was always knotted up in a snarl, and his eyes were forever challenging and assessing strangers until they looked down or away. Though there was a goofiness about him that came out when it was just us three. But he was easily insulted and slow on his toes with comebacks, which sunk him into his broiling temper that'd eject vicious shouts and quivering sneers. Angel was an expert at bringing out this response in Ryan. Sometimes it seemed that if it weren't for their friendship with me, the two would never hang around each other.

Angel had sprouted up tall and lanky with high cheekbones and long, jet-black hair. He wore his hair with the sides and back buzzed short, and a long, silky shock sat on top. He tied the end of the long shock in a ponytail that hung above the stubbly hair like the tail-feathers of a Blue Jay. Everything was sleek and slick about his appearance, but his temperament was completely the opposite. It didn't take much to crack him up and release his whining, wacky chortle. Then, he'd bare his long top-front teeth, all perfectly spaced and aligned and glossy white. He'd draw the humor out of anything said, goad grins from the speaker, and then send them tumbling into some sarcastic folly of meaning and almost always predictably something sexually perverse. He was one of those guys that habitually took it too far and sent the conversation down into the depths of necrophilia, transsexuals, hermaphrodites, and fecal fetishes. It got to the point where you didn't know whether to keep laughing or vomit, but that was Angel.

I'd taken to wearing my hair slicked back and sprayed stiff with Aqua Net, with the sides buzzed and sharpened into a V at the base of my neck. We'd all picked up on that West Coast style of either blue or tan Dickies work pants with old-school, low-top Nikes, Pumas, or Adidas.

A couple hood rats lurked around that night—dirty, mangy, and loud—trying to impress us and smoking cigarettes. Hood rats weren't so good looking. They wore huge, gaudy jewelry, gold necklaces, and big fake-stone rings. They used cheap grandma perfume and way too much makeup—dark eye-liner and fake eye-lashes. They were all a little on the chunky side—or thick, as the brothas would call 'em—but this didn't stop them from wearing skin-tight jeans with high-tops and big t-shirts that made it look like they had giant tits, but really just hid the bloated lump of their bellies. Half of 'em were pregnant by the time they got to high school, and the other half were pregnant by the time they got out.

Some of the hood rats could fight, and some just thought they could until they got womped on publically. The ability to fight actually mattered to these girls. They were kinda tomboys in a way, but more just girls raised with roughnecks for older brothers, uncles, and fathers. It was the life they knew, you could say. And it wasn't all that difficult to get a hood rat to suck you off in an alley. They were kinda like peewee hookers in training, and they were always screeching and whining about something. But in the end, I guess they were like any other young girls; they were just out there trying to find themselves, looking for romance— and even love—and doomed like so many of us to never find it.

I couldn't stand hood rats. The thought of kissing one, or even letting one slob my thang, made my stomach bubble. Kissing one of them was like smooching the nut-sacks of half the 13-year-olds in the neighborhood. No, thank you. But there was something sad to me then about the way they were, too.

Vicky leaned against the partition separating me and Ryan's sills wearing a short tan skirt and a big airbrushed t-shirt with her name written in pink and purple cursive. She was puffing on a Merit 100 she probably stole from her aunt, and her deep red lipstick was smeared on the butt. She had a ton of Aqua Net in her shoulder-length, light-brown perm, which crinkled every time she tossed her head back to expel a short string of smoke.

Samantha stood across from Vicky and made obviously excited eyes with her like it was some little staged performance Vicky was putting on.

I sighed at the mountain range of pointy blackheads that spread across Vicky's chunky cheeks; she'd smothered and caked them over with makeup. Vicky'd been following me around for a week now, and she'd done the same to Angel months back—he just made fun of her until she gave up on him. Ryan'd bounced her chin off his balls a few times before he got bored. I planned on just ignoring her until she went away.

The lights were out in Sy's old window across the street. Some flowery, yellow drapes hung in 'em, and they swayed lazily in and out of the open window with the breeze.

"Man, I miss Sy," I said.

"Yeah, he wasn't so bad," Angel said as he slid his palm-comb through his oily hair.

"He was like another big brother, ya know?"

"Yeah, but all he ever did was beat-cho-ass," Ryan said laughing.

"Naw...." I shook my head. "He was just playing. Hell, that's what I'd do if I had a little brother."

"Yeah, he was funny." Ryan grinned. "Always yelling out that damned window of his, playing that Slayer shit. I don't know what was worse."

"Slayer ain't so bad," I said, scrunching my brow at Ryan.

"Man, I don't know how you listen to that shit," Ryan jeered.

"I like Slayer," Vicky sang. She leaned up against my sill and batted her darkened, vampire-ish eyes.

"Dr. Dre—now that's some good shit," Ryan said, waving his hand over his head in hip-hop fashion.

"Man, if Mickey knew you were listening to that shit..." I raised my eyebrows.

"Man, Mickey... He's too old-school. This the new generation," Ryan admonished. "Hell, he's the baddest gangsta in the whole neighborhood; Dre's talking about him in dem songs."

"Man, Mickey hates Dr. Dre as much as he hates them Ds up in Rogers Park," I snapped.

"It's different, man," Ryan urged.

"You know dem niggers by your house are gonna flip Stones soon anyway," Angel added, glancing down Hollywood.

"Man, what the fuck are you saying?" Ryan replied in disgust.

"We're staying Crew forever… KC," he bellowed.

"Once they go to Senn, man, that shit'll all be over," I said, cocking my head to the side and locking eyes with Ryan.

"Man, just look at T-Money and Twon," Angel reasoned. "They were Krazy Crew. Now look at 'em; they're Stones. Hell, they started the whole thing."

"Hey look, the TJOs is Peoples, too, so it don't matter," Ryan said, grimacing. His face and scalp reddened.

"It matters, man…" I sighed. "It matters."

"Man, it'll be different. You'll see. We're gonna be Crew forever." Ryan rocked back, swelled his chest out, and threw up the KC with both his hands. "In fact, quit with that 'nigger' shit. Monteff is coming through… He's got some a dat flame 'dro!"

Monteff had gotten a hold of some Hydroponic-grown marijuana and was coming through to share. I think he liked to get away from the Dead-End-Docks—the constant family bickering, the cops always hounding the alley, the redundant gangbanging. Over here at the sills, it was quiet, except when Ryan and Angel were snarling at each other. Plus, we could get away with smoking a bowl right there, too—just crawl in one of the sills and toke. Monteff had a way of keeping the focus of conversation off negative crap, and that helped me a lot in keeping Ryan and Angel from colliding. Sometimes, if we got high enough, we'd even talk about deep shit—black holes, the meaning of life, fate. It was cool 'cause Monteff would defend anyone's wild ideas, no matter how stupid or crazy they were. I liked having him around. We all did.

"Mickey just needs to smoke a J and chill his ass out," Ryan vented.

"Mickey is scary," Vicky sang in a girly-girl voice as she whipped the length of her crinkly perm over her shoulder.

"Shit, Mickey ain't scary," Ryan sneered. "I ain't scared a him."

"He sure is a killer, though," I said, smiling at Vicky.

"That he is," Ryan replied as he looked down toward Ashland and Clark.

I stood and leaned against the same partition as Vicky, and she batted her eyes at me. "We were there when they killed that motherfucker," I said.

Ryan laughed and flicked his cigarette.

"Smashed his fucking brains out with his own pistol!" I added.

Angel and Ryan broke up on that one.

"That's a lie," Vicky said, rolling her eyes.

"Call it whatever you want," I said, sitting down. "I saw the guy take his last breath."

"Tough guy...." She took a short, forced puff off her cigarette and blew it out slow, then looked at me with what was supposed to be a sultry glance. Then, she smiled and revealed the braces encasing her yellowish teeth. I just grinned over at Angel. He giggled.

"Hey, Vicky..." Angel said, cocking his head to the side with his crazed, toothy-smirk. "Do you like to look cool smoking cigarettes?"

"What?" Vicky barked sharply, straightening.

"You puff just like Marilyn Monroe. Did you know that, Vicky?" Angel mocked her girly voice and held an imaginary cigarette in his fingers. Ryan and I cracked up.

"Angel..." She rolled her eyes. "Shut up... God, you are so stupid." She spliced her chunky arms across her chest.

The air stirred, and a tremble rattled up through the metal grate exhaust vents embedded in the sidewalk right between Ryan and the alley. Angel hopped off the sill and stepped towards her. She backed towards Ashland smiling playfully.

"What?" She smiled nervously. The makeup cracked on her cheeks.

"I wonder," Angel said as he took a large, sweeping step and placed his foot between her sneakers. Then, he leant close. "How much attention do you really like? As much as Marilyn did?"

Angel whispered. Then, he tilted his head as if he was about to kiss her.

Vicky backpedalled atop the iron grate on the sidewalk and smirked defiantly. Then, she sucked a quick toke and blew a cloud around Angel's smug smirk. Samantha squealed triumphantly as she followed them. Ryan and I sat up on the edges of our sills, watching.

A deep, subterranean bellow erupted upward through the grate as a subway train howled past. Vicky's skirt caught like a kite and swooped up, elevating above her hips and exposing her panties; they were white with lime-green piping and two little green hearts intertwined above the crotch. She shrieked. Angel stumbled backward, and his short ponytail fluttered upward like a single feather in a brave's headdress. Vicky's half-smoked square dropped from her fingers as she spun and dashed off. It descended a few feet, then levitated in the updraft before the smoldering-red ember disintegrated. A spray of sparks splintered into an upward spiral like a dust devil of fire.

Vicky ran down the sidewalk squealing.

"Angel! You asshole!!!" Samantha screeched as she chased after her friend.

Angel sauntered back toward his sill. I reached my hand out as he passed and he slapped me five.

"That girl can't take a hint," I said.

"Did you see those pasty drawers?" Angel asked, sighing as flopped on his sill ledge.

"If a spark woulda caught in her hair, dat bitch woulda exploded wit' all dat hairspray!" Ryan added.

"I wouldn't be havin' dis problem if you wouldn'ta stopped fuckin' her, Ry," I said.

"Man, I didn't fuck that hoe!" Ryan shot back and grabbed his crotch. "I'd end up with crabs fucking wit' her."

"Ah, you know you got that shit," Angel sang.

"Naw, but what'd it smell like?" I grinned at Ryan.

"Hmmm..." Ryan looked downward and scratched his chin. Then, he sniffed his fingertips, and his eyes darted to mine. "Tostitos!" He shoved his index and middle finger under my nose. "Wanna smell?"

I pushed his hand away, laughing.

Angel scooted way back in his sill and sparked his lighter. I leaned over and looked in his shadowy, concrete cave. His bony face creased in the dark as he giggled. Then, he brought the wood-based bowl to his lips. The flame bent and dipped into the metal cup. He sucked deep, and that ashy stench of two-day-old resin eased out.

"Your ass can't wait, man? Monteff'll be here any second," Ryan whined from his seat.

Just then, there was the throttling ramble of a V8 on Hermitage. I shot to my feet and craned my neck to see down the dark block. Then, tires screeched, and a splash of headlights washed over the façades of the apartments down at the corner.

"It's just that crazy ass brother of yours," Ryan said, standing beside me. He waved it off and drifted back to his sill.

Rich's Dodge raced up, then eased to a stop half-way down the block. My mouth suddenly dried with anticipation. I stepped out to the curb and strained to see through the bright headlights. There was a shadowy figure in the street; it looked small next to the wide 4X4 truck. Rich hung his head out the window and said something—just a whisper. Suddenly, a black streak leapt out of the window. It was quick, thin, and long, like a snake strike. A slashing crack rang out, followed by a whimper. The shadow reeled, then disappeared into the parked cars. Swift footsteps slapped the sidewalk pavement. I stepped back from the curb to intercept it. *Who the fuck is it? Some PG3?* I squeezed my fists closed and bounced on my tip-toes. The foggy figure swept up towards us. Its arms and legs flailed wildly. Rich's Ramcharger paralleled alongside it in the street smooth, keeping pace with his prey.

I'm just gonna crack dis mothafucker when he gets close. Then, the gray glob was a guy—a black kid. As he was just a few feet off, I realized it was Monteff. He clutched the side of his trimmed 'fro. Deep-red blood bubbled up through his fingers. He locked his horrified eyes on mine.

"What de fuck, Joe!"

My hands dropped at my sides. My fists unfurled as Monteff gusted up. His pants blurred into a white whirl as he dashed past us. He bent a left into the ER tunnel. Ryan and Angel stood with their mouths agape, stupefied.

Rich's Ramcharger bounded to a screeching halt in front of the sills. Heavy metal bore out his open window like a gigantic death-rattle on amphetamines. His arm hung down from the window, and he gripped the handle of his wood-blade Samurai sparring sword; its glossy, oak blade was bowed slightly. He aimed it downward. Dark fluid dripped along the wooden blade.

Rich panted. Blood-red veins swelled around his eyes. His wet teeth gleamed inside his overgrown beard and mustache.

"What up, little brotha!!!" Rich called out as he brandished the wooden blade like some boorish relic of the Germanic hordes. "Whyn'tchu catch dat nigger? We coulda had some fun wit' him!"

"Stupid motherfucker," Ryan sighed, defeated.

"Rich, man, dat's my fucking friend." I clutched my throbbing head with both hands. *How the fuck am I gonna explain this.*

Big James's deep voice bellowed out of the tunnel. Rich put it in gear, and the engine surged again. The truck rocked back before accelerating, then squealed a right onto Ashland. Big James emerged at the mouth of the tunnel with his heavy Maglite clanking at his side. His neck swelled as he craned to see the truck, then he snapped his head around, and his eyes flashed at us.

"Hey, get over here you three," he yelled. We broke down Hollywood.

Big James only chased us for half the block, and we stopped running when we turned the corner at Hermitage.

"Man, what the fuck was dat all about?" Angel asked, swallowing deep, heaping breaths.

"Fuckin' Rich, man. He's gone crazy ever since Sy died," I pleaded. "He thinks every fucking nigger's the one who shot him."

"He started some shit now," Angel said, wincing as he leaned over at the waist and gripped his Dickeys at the knees.

"Man, naw. We're cool," Ryan said, rising calmly. He heaved a deep breath. "But we might have to move on your brother now."

"Man, what the fuck?" I spun on Ryan. A trembling shiver rushed through my arms. "Fuck that." I shoved him in his sternum.

He pushed me back. Angel dove between us and pressed either hand into our swelled chests. I craned my neck over Angel and glared at Ryan.

"That's my fucking brother, man!"

"Look, Monteff is Crew!" Ryan demanded. "Crew comes first. Next time I see your brother, I'ma give him a mouth shot!"

"Man, you're fucking crazy... That's my fuckin' brother," I said, knocking Angel's hand away. I reached out to grab Ryan by the throat.

"Look, just chill, alright," Angel pleaded. He caught his balance and shoved me hard. "We'll see what happens tomorrow, alright?" He looked me in the eyes.

"That's my fuckin' brother, Ryan... My fuckin' brother."

"Whatever, man..." Ryan frowned. "Whatever." He flapped his hand at me as he spun, and then he walked away towards the north—to the darkness of those blocks.

Angel walked with me. We crossed Hollywood and turned down the alley we shared—it was empty, dead. The stale-yellow light glimmered off the cracked-up concrete. The garages loomed and seemed to lean out over the alley and leer down at us in quiet judgment. We stopped out behind my garage.

"What the fuck am I supposed to do, man?" I sighed.

"Shit, man. I don't know." Angel shook his head and glanced away. "Man... I don't fucking know."

"Fuck." I raised both hands to my head, then I squatted down on my hams and closed my eyes

"Your brother's too old for that shit. You said he's moving out de neighborhood, right?"

I opened my eyes and looked up at Angel. He stood with his arms folded over his stomach. "Yeah, but not soon or anything."

"Look," Angel said as he slid his hands onto his hips, "I bet this shit blows over." He looked up the alley.

"I hope so, man." I stood up and reached over the gangway gate, unlatched the lock, and pushed it open. I stopped and looked back at him over my shoulder.

"Will you go over there with me tomorrow?" I asked.

Angel looked down. "Yeah," he flinched. Then, he shook his head and looked up into my eyes. "Yeah, I'll go wit' ya."

I nodded and walked into the gangway. The gate swung shut with a sharp bang.

"You'll see, it's gonna be cool. We'll just tell dem mothafuckas at de Dead-End-Docks dat your brother didn't take his meds and thought Monteff was a transsexual pedophile," Angel yelled to me as he walked down the alley. I could hear his laughter over my own until it all faded to nothing.

■

THAT NIGHT, I dreamt I was a little kid. Alone. All the lights were slowly clicking off downstairs in the house. I rushed to get upstairs, where I could hear Ma running a bath. The water roared and clapped into the tub. Her little black and white TV happily buzzed. I got to the base of the stairs and looked in the tall mirror that was part of the old-fashioned mahogany coat rack. The last light went out, and the mirror sunk and swirled into a deep tar black. A magnet-like force sucked me towards it. I tried to pull away, spun, and climbed the stairs. *MA! MA! MOM! HELP ME! MOMMY!!!* The force swelled stronger, and I clawed my fingernails into the carpet, frantically crawling upward. I strained with all I had. I started to scream. Suddenly, from the mirror, a beast rumbled a deep, crackly growl that swallowed my scream. It squeezed a wide claw around my ankle. I turned, and the tar had elongated. It stretched into the shape of a brown-maned monster. Its wide skull morphed slowly into several furred forms: a bear, a buffalo, a lion. It bared a row of small, sharp, white teeth. Then, I awoke panting, sweat-soaked. It was an hour before I slept again.

CHAPTER 12

CIVIL WAR

I WOKE UP GROGGY and laid in bed a long time, just watching the room brighten with the day. Snoop Dogg ambled low from Rose's room down the hall, and it made me sick to think of Rich hating blacks so much. They'd been part of the family before me. I didn't know a world without them. Every memory, every day— my sisters, my family. Skin tone had never been something to divide, and it hadn't meant anything until I got older. That's when people started trying to explain to me about adoption and how they weren't really my sisters, when I knew all along they were— on a level no words could touch. But hatred comes from all sides; no one is immune. We live in a confusing world.

I finally got up and called Angel, and we planned to meet on the corner. I stepped out the front door as Rich headed up the porch steps. His eyes lit up when he saw me, and he sprung right in my face.

"I got dat nigger good last night, huh?" He mimicked the swing of his sword, and I received the blow from the imaginary wooden blade.

"Owwww...," he grimaced in ecstasy. "He was bleedin' everywhere and screamin' like a stuck pig!"

"What the fuck, Rich? That was my friend!" I yelled. Pinprickles swarmed along my neck.

"Who? That nigger? The one walkin' down my street like he owned it?" He flailed his arms and legs wildly like a cartoon pimp. "That nigger won't ever be your friend." He jammed his index finger stiff into my solar plexus. I snatched his hand and shoved it away. Then, I stared into his beady, blue eyes.

"Look, I tried to warn you, little brother, but your day's coming. Them niggers are gonna get you, and it ain't gonna be pretty."

I brushed past him and went down the steps, flicking him off.

"Quit talking like that. The girls'll fuckin' hear you," I said, making it to the sidewalk.

Rich just stood on the porch in front of the door. He folded his arms over chest, and a deep, hacking laughter rumbled from his gut.

Angel met me at the corner, and we headed over, quiet and scared. Looking back, I can see how good a friend he was to me—how obvious it was what was waiting for us.

We got to the Dead-End-Docks at noon. The bright, white sun was high—there was nowhere to hide from it. They played three on three. Somebody'd replaced the milk crate with a rusty rim already bent and warped from people dunking on it. There were a dozen guys out—all of 'em blacks of different shades, except Ryan. He stood shirtless—his deep-brown freckles lined his pale skin. His sweat-dampened scalp glistened bright orange. It was a slow, subtle shift in race. The Mexicans, Puerto Ricans, and Asians slowly evaporated until one white boy stuck out like a flare struck in the dead of night.

Ryan saw us approach and stepped over to meet us. He frowned a little and looked down, bashful and embarrassed. Then, he reached out his hand, and I met it with mine. I could see just then how thick his wrists were—almost twice as thick as most.

"Hey, man... I'm sorry about last night, alright?" he said. His deep-green eyes were still and calm. He pulled me close and patted me on the back with the other.

"Yeah, it's cool, man," I said, hugging him back. "It was all fucked up."

"Hey, Joe, but look, man." Ryan leaned in to whisper in my ear. "Be careful today. Everybody's acting shady."

"Whatchu mean?" I said, pulling back and peering nervously at the others. None of them looked our way.

"I don't know, man. Just be careful, alright?" Ryan urged. I looked into his fiery eyes.

"You got my back, right?"

"You know I do."

I walked up by the fence. The basketball panged. Shoes scraped pavement.

"Who's got next?" I asked.

Three guys raised their hands but said nothing. BB popped off the fence and stepped up to me. He squinted in the mid-day sunlight.

"So what happened last night, Joe?" BB said. "Your brother done kicked some shit off, huh?" He cupped his hand along his brow to shade the sun.

"Man, my brother's gone nuts," I said loudly. "Shit, you remember that day when me and Leroy were going at it, and he jumped out all crazy?"

"Ahh yeah... I remember that day. That was a good-ass fight." BB grinned. "Hell yeah. Aye, remember that fight, Tank? With Joe and Leroy?"

Tank glared at us both but said nothing. His muscularity seemed to grow every day. In the midst of the game, his shirt off, sweat gleamed off his dark, black skin. His wide, slumped shoulders and the thick mounds of his traps swelled. He looked like he'd stumbled onto a bottle of steroid pills and swallowed 'em all in one gulp.

"How's Monteff?" I asked, glancing around for him.

"Ah, he's alright. But don't worry, you'll be seeing him shortly," BB said, smiling. "Ah, look, here he come right now."

I turned to see Monteff walk out of his gangway gate in a white Dago T. He sneered and stepped fast and hostile. There was a large white bandage taped to the side of his head, and he walked directly to me. His thin arms trembled.

"Hey, Monteff. Man, you alright?" I asked.

Monteff stopped a couple of feet from me, looked down, and shook his head. "Now, I'm only gonna ask you this once: was you in on it?" He shot his wet eyes up to mine.

"What?" I took a step back. I heard the basketball bounce to a roll as the others slowly stepped towards us. Their forms crowded my periphery—mountainous.

"You set me up, mothafucka?" Monteff shouted. Spit burst off his trembling lips.

"What're you talking about?" I said, shrugging my shoulders and raising my palms up. "You know my brother's nuts."

"Put it on the Crew…" He looked down and ground his molars. "Naw… you know what? All you honky mothafuckas was in on it! Fuck this Crew! I'm Stones now!" He threw up the Five.

T-Money must've come out of the gangway after him, because I didn't see him 'til just then. He swooped up next to Monteff. Then, he yanked on the brim of his Padres cap and licked his lips. I went to say something; I don't even remember what it was. T-Money's fist sprang at me. I lunged backward. His arm stretched out long and straight like a spear. His fist crashed into my eye socket so quick I didn't blink. His knuckles struck my eyeball. I felt it suck up into the socket, and it got stuck there deep in my skull. I stumbled back and clutched my face. That whole side of my mug flexed hard, and suddenly the eyeball popped back out into place. I couldn't see anything out of that eye. With my good eye, I saw several fists shoot up and crack down on my head and face from all sides.

"What the fuck!" Ryan yelled, then he reached his hand out and grabbed T-Money by the throat. The others swooped in like a swarm of hornets.

I started to fall. Tank punched Angel from the blind side. Angel got taller, then tipped over like a tree cut at the base. I got hit three more times before I flopped on the concrete. I tried to cover up as rubber sneaker soles thumped down on me heavily. They planted into my arms and chest and shot air out of my gut. I peeked up between my forearms. All I could see were black bodies silhouetted against the bright blue sky. They looked tall and narrow and distorted. They were laughing. I could hear little squeaky-ass BB laughing. I didn't recognize any of them. I couldn't believe it was happening. I felt caught inside some wrathful force of nature—an earthquake that wasn't gonna stop 'til it was through with me. I could hear the groans and shouts from Ryan and Angel. Finally, for some reason, they stopped. I heard their feet patter off toward the different gangways.

Monteff slowed and turned. He bounced on his toes. "Stay off this set you honky mothafuckas!" Monteff squeezed his fists at his sides. "This Moe's set now... Black Stone, mothafucka!" he shouted as T-Money went by laughing. They shook-up—some new shit I hadn't seen before. At the end, their left hands patted their chest twice.

Ryan got to his feet and plodded after them. He clutched his temple.

"Motherfuckers!" he shouted. "I'm gonna kill all you motherfuckers!" he screamed. Then, he lumbered back and pulled Angel and me to our feet.

We stumbled back towards Hollywood Ave. My whole body

ached. My heart pumped buckets in my chest. My whole torso swelled up like a balloon. Vomit bubbled in my throat. The sun beat down. The entire neighborhood seemed to shake and vibrate. This neon sheen radiated through the trees' green leaves. Sparrows chirped loud like a clamor of applause. A thousand squeaking murmurs swirled in and out of the air above us. They chirped with the same cadence as the breeze flicking through the leaves.

■

WE WENT TO ANGEL'S HOUSE 'cause his mother wouldn't be home for a few hours. We hung out, bewildered, in his living room. The lights were off, and the daylight seeped in through the yellow drapes. Ryan sat in an easy chair as knuckle-sized red knots blossomed up under his stubbly scalp like he'd been stoned. A red lump swelled on Angel's jaw near the ear. I went into the bathroom and looked in the mirror—my eye was bloodshot. The tissue around it swelled red, and a few purple dots formed inside it like tiny nebulas. It felt like someone had scraped sandpaper across the film of my retina, and the vision in that eye was still blurry like fog on a windshield in the winter. We raided the freezer and grabbed ice and some frozen crap, then I laid down on the couch and flopped a bag of frozen peas over my eye. We didn't say it, but we all knew everything had changed irreconcilably. There was no going back. We were on our own.

After a few hours, Ryan got up, walked to the front door, and opened it. He stopped, looked back, and said, "I'm gonna talk to Mickey tonight."

"Alright." I replied. I didn't know what he meant.

Angel just turned and looked from where he sat at the kitchen table, his head in his hands. Ryan nodded and walked out the door.

■

WHEN I WALKED IN the front door, Ma was on her way downstairs. She took one look at me and flipped shit. "Oh my God!
What happened to you? Who did this? We need to go to the hospital and get that eye checked out!" I just headed past and went
upstairs without even looking at her.

"Ma, it ain't that bad, alright? I'm fine. Nothing happened." I
turned the corner and went to my room. I stayed up there, pros-
trate on my bed, and waited it out—listening. I could hear all the
motions in the house: the kids coming in from the back porch,
Ma slowly stepping up the stairs, running the vacuum, jostling my
doorknob, finding it locked, then slowly easing down the steps.
Later, Dad surged in through the back screen door with his Ther-
mos and lunch pail clattering. Rich rumbled in the front door
and up the stairs into his room. His heavy metal music clicked
on a few seconds later. All the while, I rehearsed answers to their
questions in my mind. Answers to their little comments, ready to
scream, "Yeah, Rich, they fucking jumped me! I wonder why!"
right in his psycho, fucking racist-ass face!

At dinnertime, I went downstairs—weak and hungry because
I hadn't eaten since breakfast. The old man was already eating
at the head of the table. He chomped aggressively as he cut and
jabbed at his mound of mashed potatoes, cauliflower, and bread-
ed pork chops. The whole mound was covered with a heavy sprinkling of black pepper. His eyes flashed at me for a crisp second as
I stepped into the room, then he continued to eat. Rich sat facing
me with his back to the window. His eyes lit up when he saw me,
and he snickered as I walked to the table. I made my plate and sat
down in between Jan'n'Rose on the long bench.

"Now tell me what happened to your eye, honey," Ma said.

I didn't answer.

"You fucked with the wrong motherfucker," Rich drawled,

then burst into laughter. Milk splattered from his lips onto his half-eaten dinner.

Dad slammed his fork and knife to the table, and everyone went silent. He jabbed a finger at Rich. "Stop that shit."

"And whatever, Richard. How many times have you gotten your ass kicked?" Jan said, scowling at him. "Have you ever won a fight?"

Rose choked a little, then quickly grabbed a rag and spit some food in it. Jan's thin lips curled at the edges.

Dad slammed his fist on the table. Everyone's utensils and glasses of milk trembled. "I don't want to hear anymore."

We finished the dinner in relative silence, and I went back up to my room. I took a couple Advil and laid in bed. It was just getting dark, and the orange-red of the sunset painted the east wall of my room. The thin meshing of the window screen splayed across it like chain-link armor. Images of retaliation soared through my mind—what I woulda done, shoulda done. I'm there in the alley and T-Money rushes up, but now there's a twelve-pound sledgehammer in my hands. I squeeze the thick wood stalk and swing wide and hard. The iron sledge slaps into the side of his head. His skull elongates with the collision, then it shoots off his shoulders. Airborne, it arcs end-over-end all the way into Ryan's backyard. There, Bear sits in wait; his wide brick of a head at attention. T-Money's dome flops to a rolling stop at Bear's paws. Then, Bear draws his enormous jaws around T-Money's forehead. T-Money's decapitated body froze before me, his arms and wrists cocked at moronic angles like someone frozen in a pop-lock dance mid-move.

Then, the real images would flash. They'd surge up and wipe the fluttering joy from my chest, and I'd feel it all over again: the betrayal, the shame, the rage, the soreness in my whole body. I'd shove it all out of my head until I'd nod to sleep, then throttle awake. The nerves sparked and popped in my elbows, hands, and knees, jolting me until I was gone. Pitch black. Riding a freight elevator, descending slowly. The elevator shaft creaking and clanking above. Just enough light to see the metal fencing before me. A deep metallic bang as the descent halts. The door slides open rapidly. The light now only from the sky outside. I step out. Millions of stars blaze above. A crescent moon hangs overhead, low, enormous, and florescent white. Suddenly an orb, like a white meteor, emerged on the horizon and careened across the sky with five tentacles flailing behind it like streamers. A whistle blazed faintly, then louder, until it was like the scream of a steam engine. The meteor arced past the moon, then faded and disappeared. The howl fell lower until it came from all around me on ground level. It closed in from the distance. Then, hooves approached over gravel. The only direction the sound didn't come from was behind me. I turned and ran, but the elevator was gone. I ran as fast as I could. My feet dug into the gravel until I fell and sank. The rock splashed my face, and I woke. My screen rattled. Then, pebbles plunked down the roof of my porch outside my window.

I got up on my knees in bed and looked out the window screen. Hyacinth stood down on the patch of concrete that led from the sidewalk to the street. She smiled eagerly up at me, her eyes lit by the streetlamps.

We sat on the front porch steps as the slow night traffic eased by. She had that worried look she got whenever I had a shiner or got banged up, or when anybody got hurt, really. She softly stroked my cheek with the smooth skin of her hand.

"What happened?" She asked. Her auburn eyes were wide and hurt.

"We got jumped," I said, looking away.

"Why? What for?" she urged, mystified.

"My brother... It's a long story...." I waved at the air before me as if the inconsequential truth hovered right there. "It don't matter."

She smelled like coconut oil, and her skin was so soft and cool. I couldn't understand how she could be so cool. All it took was her sitting beside me, our hips and sides touching, and my heart was thumpin' like a rabbit foot. I rubbed my hands together, both of 'em all hot and sweaty. My throat swelled up. I was so fuckin' glad she stopped by that my headache even went away. Her eyes got all watery, and then a tear slid down her cheek and dropped down on her tank-top. I reached my arm around her and squeezed. She was all warm and soft like dough. It made me want to squeeze her tighter, and I did. She let out a little sigh and looked up at me, her breath hot but still sweet in my face. Another droplet fell from her other eye, and I kissed it as it slid down her cheek. I tasted the salty wetness on the tip of my tongue. Mrs. Perez shut her bedroom window across the street, then evaporated. Hyacinth nestled her head into the side of my neck, and I whispered, "I'm fine. It's OK." She turned, and I kissed her mouth, all wet and warm and soft. It made me want to kiss her harder. She just tilted her head up, and we kissed long—her thick, damp lips alternating between soft and firm. Our tongues explored and folded over one another's, and I touched her face, then neck. Her featherlike hair brushed against the back of my hand. She stopped crying, and we kissed like that for a long while—our mouths open, lips smushing. Finally, we stopped, and our eyes met, faces still close.

"Hubba... Hubba..." Vicky's little brother Alex said as he rode past on a beach cruiser that was way too big for him. We both burst into laughter. I flicked him off as he coasted past in the street. Her braces flashed sliver, her eyes sparkled, and then we kissed one more time.

■

I THOUGHT A LOT about things that night. Thought of what Lil Pat would have done; if he'd have seen it coming. Hell, he wouldn't even have been hanging out with those motherfuckers in the first place. I didn't believe that blacks were against us. I knew there was more to life than that. Jan'n'Rose were just normal girls. People didn't have to hate each other. On the other hand, people did hate each other; it was everywhere I looked. Those dudes at the Dead-End-Docks were all full of hatred. Tank and Twon hated us, hated whites, hated blacks. Hell, they even hated each other. T-Money—I guess deep down he was still sore about what Rich had done to him, or maybe he'd sobered to the fact that there weren't any white Black Stones. He was at the bottom rung now —a low-ranking Stone at Senn—and probably pissed off he was an errand boy still getting vetted. But Monteff. I couldn't get over Monteff. He was my friend—my dear friend. We'd talked about all kinds'a shit. He knew almost as much about me and my family as Ryan did, and I knew all about his, too. How all the blacks at the Docks were blood related—half-brothers, cousins, uncles—and how difficult it made everything. How every family argument had the potential to turn into a bloody domestic involving the entire apartment complex. How no one in his family had ever gone to college, and that's why he studied so hard and never got less than a B in anything. How he had to hide that, too, 'cause everybody'd ride on him if he told them he made honor roll. How they'd call him a lame if they knew. He kind of inspired me, really. Made me want to get my ass in gear and get my grades up so I could go to college.

I just couldn't get over it. He knew I wasn't in on it. He even knew about Sy getting killed and how Rich had flipped. Maybe it was about race after all. Maybe we were separated by race— irreconcilably divided. I just didn't have any other way to explain it then.

It was the first time I'd ever gotten beaten-up for real, a true ass whoopin'. There was some solace in the fact that we'd been jumped, out-numbered, and caught off guard, but I still felt humiliated. I couldn't find a shred of nobility in what'd happened. Deep-down, I wanted to be a good and righteous warrior, not some opportunist villain like those fucks had been. I wanted to fight nobly for noble things. To be ferociously loyal to my friends at all costs. I'd watched Evander Holyfield and Riddick Bowe fight. There was nobility in their battles. Win or lose, they both fought with a sense of greatness in their actions and a conviction in their punches. At the same time, they were both quiet, vulnerable. Each of them hurt and battered to the ropes. It was strange how in those battles there was no sense of weakness or humiliation in the loser. Mike Tyson racked up all his spectacular knockouts with intimidation and ferocity. There was no intimidating Bowe or Holyfield. They fought nobly and brave, and I wanted to be like that—a pure warrior. I knew I was far, far away from that, but it was what I wanted more than anything.

CHAPTER 13

THE JUNGLE

BY THEN, Mickey Reid was the most feared TJO on the street. The ones badder than him were all in the penitentiary; terribly outnumbered, they were stacking years on their sentences for multiple in-house stabbing, drug, and murder convictions. Mickey'd killed anywhere from seven to fifteen people (depending on who you asked) over multiple infractions, such as: being a BGD, being a Royal, being an Assyrian King, burning him on a heroin deal, snitching, crashing into and totaling his brand new Camaro that he had neither papers nor insurance for. And one (supposedly) for spitting on his girl, though I can assure you it wasn't because he wanted to defend the hood rat's honor; it was the fact that he'd been slighted vicariously.

He mostly shot people in the head with his .44 cal, but he strangled one and beat a few to death, too. It was all circumstance with him. A spontaneous ingenuity, you could call it. There was no premeditation. Even the Royal they kidnapped and tortured—they were just high, cranked up on speed, drunk, and stumbled onto the kid at a bus stop. They wrangled him into the trunk, took him to a basement, and beat him all night. They singed his eyeballs shut with a heated iron rod, sliced his genitals off. Then, they drove him to the rail lot by Bryn Mawr across from the cemetery and dumped him on the dark stone slope—still breathing. Then, they doused him with gas and lit him up. A TJO'd been stabbed to death by a Royal the month before, and Mickey lived for vengeance. Not just for the identifiable wrongs he'd been doled out, but for the wrongs God had dealt him long before he'd taken his first breath.

■

I WAS UP IN MY ROOM listening to Suicidal Tendencies later that week. I hadn't gone out in days, embarrassed about my eye. I heard a knock on my open door and saw Ryan standing there with his stupid shit-eating grin streaked across his face. The knots on his head had flattened and turned bluish-purple. He stepped in, closing the door behind himself, then he yanked the waist of his sweatpants outward and dug his other hand into his crotch. He pulled up a big, rolled-up, clear plastic bag and tossed it on my bed beside me. I flinched away from it, and then I sat up and got off the bed. I stood and looked down at the unraveling plastic bag that was almost completely filled with faded-green nubs. I grabbed it and dumped some out on my covers. The dank, musty stench of the weed finally hit my nostrils. They looked like dehydrated, flattened-out Brussels sprouts with this orange, stringy fuzz threaded and twirled into them. It was all buds and more weed than I'd ever seen in my whole life.

"Jamaican Red Hair," Ryan proudly said, beaming.

"Where'd you get this, bro?"

"I talked to Mickey." He looked at me with his crazy green eyes. "We're in business."

We burst into laughter.

"How much is it?"

"It's a O-Z, baby." Ryan popped his red eyebrows up.

"How'd you get the money?" I scooped the weed back into the bag, then I picked it up and gawked at it.

"Naw... he fronted us." Ryan sat. "We owe him a hundred. We got two weeks, but it'll be gone before Sunday."

"Hell yeah it will." We slapped palms with a loud clap and headed over to Angel's.

■

HOW TO EYEBALL DOWN AN OUNCE:

A gram scale costs a hundred bucks, and we didn't even know of a store that carried one. We coulda used Mickey's scale, but we wanted to do it all on our own—prove to him that we didn't need anyone holding our hands the whole way. So we broke it down according to the profit we wanted to walk away with—eyeballing it—using simple logic. All three of us sat down at Angel's kitchen table, and Ryan dumped the bag onto the center of it. The buds avalanched down into a heaping pile with a mist of green dust sprinkled on top. Split the mound in half according to diameter and height. Then, you split those halves into equal quarters. Then, into eighths, making sure the ratio of buds and shake is evenly distributed. Now, an eighth should go for twenty-five dollars. At that rate, you're set to make $200 total, but none of those metal-head bong-blowers or hippie-dippy bowl-tokers are gonna cough up twenty-five bucks on a regular basis. Mickey had schooled Ryan that there's twenty-eight grams in an ounce. For the most part, a gram is about the size of a dime-bag, which goes for ten dollars—also known as a sawbuck. Break that gram in half, and you got a nickel bag, which goes for five—also known as a fin. A nickel was our most likely sale. I ran home and stole a fresh roll of sandwich bags out of the cabinet and made it back in a couple minutes while Ryan hit the corner store for a Philly blunt.

You can get two baggies out of each sandwich bag by cutting the two bottom corners into triangles. We broke it down to eighteen dime-bags and twenty nickels and started filling the bags and tying tight little knots in the ends with our fingernails. Angel dug out the funkiest buds, rolled a blunt right there at the table, and sparked up. We started making phone calls from his house phone and bragging about how 'motherfuckin' dank!' this Jamaican Red Hair was. We were set to make sixty bucks each. It was gonna be easy as shit, and we were gonna smoke for free, too.

■

IT WAS A SMOOTH OPERATION. A lot of the business was done over the phone, but we made most of the exchanges down at the sills. We set an old Folgers coffee can under a dumpster in the arterial alley across Hollywood—that way, we could see it from the sills. When a customer would show up, we'd chill and talk for a minute while one of us went to the can for the bag, and then we'd make the exchange. We knew that none of the potheads were crazy enough to try to rob us, and if they did, we'd see 'em doing it and rain down on them like the worst fucking nightmare they'd ever had, so it didn't matter. We moved the entire ounce by early Saturday night.

At about eleven, Mickey's old, boxy Lincoln Town Car floated slowly in front of the sills and eased to a creaky halt. Mickey hung his muscular cube of a head out the window. Mickey's freckles were similar to Ryan's but lighter, smaller, and denser—like close-range shotgun spray. His stubble always sickened me because it didn't grow down like normal facial hair; it sprouted straight out like porcupine quills.

"Look at youse t'ree; you look like choir boys," he said smiling. "Well... get on in here for the sermon."

We got in. Ryan sat in the front passenger seat, and I got in the seat behind Mickey—hiding from him. Mickey's fierce, protruding brow made him seem bigger than he was. He always led with his forehead in conversation, as if he couldn't understand you unless his Cro-Magnon brow was just inches from you. It cast a shadow on those beady eyes like you were looking into two caves with dark-green lanterns lurking deep within.

"Aren't you boys forgetting something?" he asked.

"What, Mickey?" Ryan looked at him confused.

"You did everything like I told you, didn't'chu?" Mickey barked.

"Yeah, Mickey," Ryan implored.

"Well, isn't anybody gonna grab the stash?" Mickey slapped Ryan on the back of the neck.

"Naw, Mickey. Shit. It's empty."

"Empty?"

"Yeah." Ryan reached in his pants pocket, pulled out the thick green wad, and handed Mickey the hundred dollars in tens, fives, and singles.

"No shit?" Mickey's eyebrows raised as he unfolded the roll and thumbed through it. "Well... you keep this up, I'll bumps ya's ta two ounces." Mickey slid the money in his jeans pocket, put the car in gear, and we rolled up to Ashland.

"Yeah, Mickey, we were talking," Ryan said as he relaxed and slouched in his bucket seat. "We think we could probably move three a week."

Mickey giggled. "We'll see... I'll front you two, and we'll go from there." He rubbed his hand through Ryan's buzz-cut. "Fuckin' kids." His eyes flashed at me in the rearview mirror.

"Aye, how's Patty?" Mickey said. "You hear from him lately?"

"He's OK," I answered. I looked out the window as we

turned left on Ashland, away from Mickey's disturbed eyes. "He calls sometimes."

"Dat's one down brother," Mickey said. A smirk slid over his lips. "Just couldn't handle dat brown running through his veins... You gotta be strong if you're gonna mess with dat shit." He tapped his fist against his chest. The Lincoln came to a stop at a red light where Clark slashes across Ashland and overtakes it. Rain pattered the windshield and mixed with the built-up grime. The glass clouded as the rain slowly streaked down in gray, finger-like globs.

"Aye, pass dem beers around," Mickey said as he accelerated. Ryan looked at him mystified. "At your feet, stupid."

Ryan reached down and pulled the Budweiser Tall Boys out and passed them back to us. We cruised on.

"Well, boys, dis is a special night. Dere's reason to celebrate." A grin spread over Mickey's face. "I've decided to bring youse t'ree under my wing."

Mickey took us north on Clark, and we caught a red light at Ridge. A statue of Abraham Lincoln sat across the street in the park.

"Ole honest Abe... If he woulda only knew what setting them animals free would do to this country," Mickey sneered. "Never woulda done it."

We crossed Ridge, and Senn High School burst up from the darkness of the park—bold-white, wide, and tall like a Greek pavilion.

"Dat's gonna be home to you boys next fall, ain't it?" Mickey nodded towards Senn. "Wit' all de niggas and de spicks and de chinks...," Mickey sighed. "It's gonna be tough. You three're gonna have to stick together, tight."

"Now, see, the TJOs," he said as he leaned back in his seat. A sly smile appeared on his cracked lips. "Hell, we got some thirty brothers going to school dere right now... Now dey ain't all there every single day... but if you need 'em, they'll be there for ya." He turned and looked each of us in the eyes, twisting his neck to stare at me in his periphery. The Lincoln magically maintained its lane. Then, he broke eyes with me and drove on. "But see... if dey're dere for you, you gotsta be dere for dem."

"What I'm saying is... is this little crew you three got going, it's under consideration... Now sometimes it takes a couple years, and sometimes it takes five minutes." We slipped deeper and deeper into Rogers Park as the rain stopped; it'd been off and on all day. The wipers screeched lazily across the windshield and smeared the dirt so it built up thick on the glass at the limit of the wipers' wingspans.

I'd never heard Mickey speak more than a few spittle-spouting bursts of hatred. Things were changing for him, too—in his mid-twenties now, the leader. He had more responsibilities than just being a whack-job lunatic. You can only get away with so many murders and handle so much weight in hard drugs before you sink. He'd already tasted hard time, met all the heavies, all the guys from the 70s. He realized his job was to pass some of the responsibilities on to the next generation—to spread it out and let the street start to work for him.

He eased a right onto Howard Street, a.k.a. the Juneway/Jonquil Jungle, the North Pole—take your pick. The rain-slicked street glowed, and the dark neon from the shop signs, stoplights, and the yellow streetlamps splashed the entirety of the lumpy blacktop. The L jutted across Howard on a sharp angle—its underbelly steel-ribbed, dark, and ominous. Even with the rain, the action was thick and frantic. Bum junkies lined the underpass in trench coats and rags, begging with foam cups. A skinny, pregnant mutt lay on its belly and trembled next to a shopping cart filled with black garbage bags that bulged with empty pop cans. Children— wild-eyed, skinny little boys and girls, no older than nine—ran in the light traffic; they dashed across Howard near Hermitage, squealing between taillights and headlights playing tag. A brown four-door Buick coasted slowly alongside three prostitutes in short, tight skirts. Their hooker heels clicked along the sidewalk. Then, one in an imitation fur coat stopped and bent abruptly like there was a hinge at her hips. She peered in through the Buick's passenger window. Her bulbous buttocks jutted high and pointed right at us. The vertical slit of her black panties peeked out from her green skirt. Murmurs floated as they bartered their deal.

A tall black man in a gray hoodie darted across the street and was swallowed by dark blocks to the north; the place known as Jonquil Gardens—a fortress of red-brick Section Eights.

We passed under the L tracks. Across the way there were five black dudes staked out in front of a Dunkin' Donuts. The dreary, brown and orange light from the electric sign saturated the damp sidewalk at their feet. A twitchy crackhead in a tattered pea coat stepped up to a big thug that wore a Georgetown jacket and held a black umbrella pitched over his head. An exchange was made, quick and wordless. I cracked my window, and the stench of rain and sewer drudge filled the air. The sound of roaring water bellowed up through the curb grates.

"You boys know what dis place is?" Mickey asked.

"The Jungle," I replied coldly.

"Very good," Mickey said as he pulled a lazy U-turn and parked so that the car was pointed at the Dunkin' Donuts about a half-block down.

Pigeons slowly swooped in and out of the exposed iron beams of the elevated tracks—securing their way in life. The pulsing bulbs of an all-night diner percolated atop the rain-glossed walkway. Four of the bored thugs slouched against the donut shop's windows, waiting. A skinny one stood across the sidewalk from them; his bright eyes scanned slowly down Howard, north on Paulina, then up Howard, steady like a radar beam.

"Now dere's two gangs in the Jungle: one's de GDs, and the

other is de Vice Lords," Mickey said. "Now dey're both a bunch a niggers, so neither are worth a damn, but see the Vice Lords are Nation, so we can't really go out and start warring with 'em unless they cross us and we get the nod from above." He wiped the saliva from his lips. "But dem Gangster Disciples, now dey ain't shit. Dey ain't Nation, and dey ain't nothing but a bunch of crooked-ass niggers." He slammed his fist into the steering wheel as he stared at the group on the corner.

Angel leaned his elbow on the door ledge, cupped his head in his palm, and watched the group. They hadn't noticed the Lincoln—too busy with the endemic flow of nocturnal souls at the corner.

"In fact, dem niggers shot us up de udder night...," Mickey continued. He leaned back in his seat again. "De house... over on Bryn Mawr... shot all de damned windows out... Fuckin' porch monkeys think they invented drive-by shootings; it was Bugs Moran invented it. The North Side Irish Mob pulled a ten-car drive-by on Capone back in the twenties, and these jungle bunnies think they're onto somethin' new."

Mickey leaned over the center console and removed the false vent. He reached in and pulled out a nickel-plated, snub-nosed .38 revolver.

"Now, like I said, dere's two roads ta becoming a Brother... One starts right here." He held the pistol low, then twisted and looked all three of us in the eyes. "And it takes about one whole second." He slowly pointed the pistol at the four black guys in front of the Dunkin' Donuts. He made a small 'pshhh' sound and mimicked backfire.

"The other road, boys..." He put the gun on his lap, turned back face-forward, and laughed. "Well, from the looks of those knots on your faces, you know all about dat road... And dat road might take ya a couple years."

Just then, a flock of black girls swept up to the Dunkin' Donuts and chatted with the young men. Their voices squawked loudly over the traffic easing past on Howard.

Angel leaned over and patted my shoulder. I looked at him. His eyes urged me with a nod toward the corner. I looked again and saw my sister Rose's mound of puffy, brown, frizzy hair. A sharp needle of rage pierced my temple and unleashed a scream in my mind. *What the fuck are you doing here!* Rose stood in her Duke jacket in front of the big one with the umbrella and smiled at him. His teeth flashed, and then she leaned in and hugged him. My heart palpitated, as if something squeezed around it. *Of all people, Rose! Of all places! What the fuck are you doing hugging some piece of shit in the Jungle for?!* Then, Jan was there, too, in her North Carolina jacket with the hood up. Her round face sulked in the rain as she spoke with one of the other girls. The point dug and twisted deeper. *Jan! You're going to fucking college next year, for Christ's sake! And you're about to be dodging bullets on some gangster shit? WHY?*

"Now, which road's it gonna be, boys?" Mickey said as he turned in his reclined bucket seat. He placed the pistol in his wide, stubby palm and held it low in the center of the cab. The neon lights played on the smudgy nickel finish and created a multi-colored, laser-like sheen along the chambers. He let it hover there. The invitation was clear. Ryan gazed down at the pistol in awe— like it was some mystical instrument.

We stared at it in silence. Brotherhood meant girls, money, drugs, respect, and even power in the neighborhood. I remembered this one day, years back, outside of St. Greg's after school let out. There was a thick mob of high school kids down at the corner, and suddenly Lil Pat appeared. He walked with his chest puffed out, his chin high, and the entire crowd of high school kids parted like the Red Sea. He stomped straight through the opened-up canal like he'd expected nothing less. Being a TJO in Edgewater was like being royalty; it was all Ryan had ever talked about as far back as I could remember. My heart raced, and these wires constricted around my lungs. I could see Ryan's face. He swigged his Budweiser. A sick grin loomed on his mug. Ryan looked up at me. I shook my head slowly—'No.' Ryan's eyes pulsed deep, emerald-green. I imagined him snatching the revolver, twisting, and blindly firing into the corner with Rose caught in the crossfire. Lightning bolts shot down my legs. I readied to just lunge at him, grab him in a bear hug, squeeze him tight, and not let him fucking move. His upturned hand unfurled on his knee, and the thick fingers gesticulated like he was crumbling something. No. Fuck no. Don't you fucking do it. I almost said it. He twitched his hand toward it. I leaned in close. Then, he caught himself and giggled. His smile eased, relaxed, and evaporated. He turned and glanced out of his window, then took another swig off his Tall Boy.

Mickey sighed and put the pistol back in the stash, then re-fit the vents over it.

"Well, boys, if you ever get tired of rock 'em sock 'em over dere at Senn, you just pay me a little visit. Hell, I'll even let ya shoot a chink if ya want," he sighed. "Dem are the ones dat got you boys, right?"

"Yeah, Mickey. Dey're the ones," Ryan lied quickly.

"Kung Fu motherfuckers... Don't go fightin' with dem... What de hell you t'ree tinking? You gotta break dere fuckin' legs with ball bats," he said laughing. "Patty had one, made it in woodshop. We used dat thing all the time. Called her Big Bertha." He adjusted the rearview mirror to see me. "You still got Big Bertha lying around the garage?"

"I'll check," I said, still breathing hard, though the wires slackened. Mickey grinned sadistically in the small mirror.

"You do dat," he said as he put the Lincoln in gear, and we glided away from the curb.

As we passed the corner, they spotted us. One of the slouchy

GDs threw up the pitchforks. Jan'n'Rose peered into the Lincoln, too. Their mouths hung open, eyes wide with recognition. Ryan pointed out the window with his thumb, then he turned slowly to look at me. His eyes bugged out. *'What the fuck?!'* he mouthed. I looked back and shook my head. My heart finally slowed, and I took a large chug from the Tall Boy. The horrors swirled in the cab. *What'd Mickey a said if he recognized Jan'n'Rose? How the fuck could they be hanging out there anyway?* Rage, fear, and anxiety swiftly coursed through my mind. It all churned slowly in my chest like it was inside a steadily cranking meat grinder.

■

IT WAS A COMPLEX DYNAMIC that brought the girls to the Jungle, one as complicated as their bloodline. The girls fearlessly delving into the most violent neighborhood in the area made sense on a few levels. They came across as black girls to most strangers; only Caribbean people could really identify them as Dominican. To white guys, they were pudgy black girls. To black guys, they were thick, exotic, light-skinned girls. Then, when they found out they were islanders, they became even more exotic and coveted. It was only natural they'd be attracted to black guys, too; ethnically speaking, it makes sense. Growing up with roughnecks for older brothers and a fierce father, the Juneway Jungle was a prime locale to find a boyfriend. It just woulda made it a whole lot easier on me if they hadn't had a thing for GD's.

We'd head up to the U.P. of Michigan in the summer to hunt quail and whitetail, but mostly to fish for giant tiger muskie. The lake was named Lac Vieux Desert, and like Lac Ness, it was deep as fuck—two hundred feet in some spots. The muskies would just hover down there in the deep like logs at different depths. Dad had one of those sonar monitors, and we'd sit there and watch it between hour-long bouts with casting these woolly, long lures; they had five sets of three-prong hooks and four different-colored furs. It was exhausting. It'd have been fun if we were hooking into musky, but at Lac Vieux Desert, we spent ninety-five percent of the time beating the water. The girls would be done by the sixth hour of the first day, and they'd spend the rest of the time pouting in the cabin. I really had to feel bad for them. In the same way Dad was only capable of creating male offspring, he didn't have a clue how to engage the girls in a family outing.

There was other crap to do up there, but pretty much nothing for girls, so we'd go canoeing on this river. They have these giant black flies up there that'd bite the crap out of you! And maybe Jan'n'Rose had sweeter blood or something, 'cause those flies bit the hell out of them every year. The sun'd just be blazing down on us, and the girls would be swatting each other and squealing, "Get it off! Get it off!" every five minutes. There were rapids, too—these swift little rapids that'd kick your ass—and the girls were too busy swatting flies to really handle 'em. Inevitably, the girls would capsize and fall into the frigid water. It's amazing how different those two were. Ma always made note of Jan's fiery Spanish blood, but it was Rose, with her much lighter complexion, who carried more of the Spanish genes. Rose was the calm and easy-going one. Jan was always trying to control everything—shouting out orders even though she had no sense of direction and no real ability in a canoe. Dad would try to coach them, but it was hopeless. I remember that summer we eased down a peaceful, quiet stretch of river. Just downstream before the bend, a white heron stood frozen in the shallows watching the water for prey. Jan made some bonehead decision on how to negotiate a rapid and their canoe began to drift and twist sideways, eventually sweeping into one of the large boulders perpendicularly.

"Ohh, God!!!" Rose yelled, gripping the gunwales. There was a splash, and her paddle floated down stream. With their inertia, the canoe slid up atop the boulder and rose until the canoe's bottom hovered momentarily above the water's surface.

"This is all your fault, Rose," Jan hissed.

Rose unleashed a long, frightened moan that ignited a fleet of sparrows in the trees above into flight—even the white heron swept up and vanished around the bend. Their canoe leaned downward into the chute and caught suddenly in the speeding stream. It twisted abruptly and capsized, sending them both plunging neck-deep into the icy water. Rose's arms flung up in the air as her scream tore through the peaceful quiet of the U.P. forest.

Rich chuckled and shook his head. Nancy reached over and slapped his arm.

"What? They did it to themselves," he replied.

The canoe bobbled to the surface and both girls clutched its side. They strained their necks through their life preservers and sucked gulps of air.

Rose screamed and grabbed a gunwale. Her puffy hair spread out like a mop on the surface of the water.

"Help!" Rose screamed, gurgling water.

Rich burst out laughing, and I just shook my head.

"Patrick, get in there and help them," Ma demanded.

"I'm not getting in that water," Dad shot back as we paddled over to them. "Rose, listen to me! It's not that deep right there. Rose—damnit, stand up!" Rose stood. It was about chest-high. Rich still laughed as the girls walked the canoe to a shallow spot.

"Go screw yourself, Richard!" Jan hissed.

"Jan, you're something else," he chortled. "I could watch this all day."

"If it wasn't for Rose paddling the wrong side, we would have been fine."

"You told her to paddle on the right! We all just saw it, Jan!" Rich pleaded.

"Richard, shut it. I'm tired of you teasing them," Nancy complained.

"Oh, they're fine," Ma piped in.

"No. I'm tired of it, Rich. They're your sisters. Put a sock in it!" Nancy argued.

"Girls, girls. You got to tip the canoe over to get all that water out of it first," Dad said.

Jan seethed, "I don't know why we have to go on these stupid vacations anyway."

"You keep it up with that mouth, Janet, and you'll be sitting in the car next time we go out to do something."

"Fine. I don't even frickin' care!"

"Come on, Jan. We're already wet, let's just get this thing going again," Rose added jovially.

"Rose, just shut it!"

"You guys come on already. Just tip it over, and let's go," I whined.

Jan scowled at me, and I knew I'd be on her shit list for the rest of the trip. By the time we got to the end, Jan was still soaked and trembling with rage, and Rose was sniffling and wiping periodic tears. All Dad wanted was some peace, quiet and nature, but from the look on his distressed face, he'd probably have preferred to be managing a hungover construction crew on a Monday morning just to get a break from this. Ma just looked tired and fed up. Ma and Jan had never gotten along since the very beginning; it was always Ma and Rose that clicked—just nature I guess. Jan loved our father. I guess it was something about the way he controlled everything—his power. He is, to this day, a stark individual and a powerful man. I guess Jan wanted that for herself—to find her identity, her power, and it probably was somewhere in that anger and frustration waiting to turn into something.

CHAPTER 14

THE GOOD GIRLS

THERE'S A PRIDE IN BUILDING SOMETHING with your hands that you just can't get from any other accomplishment. It's in the raw physicality—its semi-permanence. It links you into something bigger—the infrastructure of a city, of a country. I've built and rebuilt dozens of streets and bridges all over Chicago. It links you into something bigger—the infrastructure of a city, of a country. You know that spider web of bridges where the Ike, the Dan Ryan, and the Stevenson intersect? That interstate hub would not have remained standing if it weren't, in small part, for my hands and my sweat. Ten years have passed, and the concrete that surrounds the patches I helped extract and replace on the piers is now spotted with new rotten sections. Even so, it's that semi-permanence—that long-endured resistance that the work represents. It's about that glance at a patch you broke out and helped pour as you zip past at sixty-miles an hour. It's the memories of the sweat, pain, and danger. It fortifies your spirit when all your other worldly efforts seem to be failing and crumbling around you.

I'd been working on it for six months, and when you're fourteen, six months is an eternity. Some parts were old-school—scavenged off of junk bikes down at Maxwell Street, or from ones we'd stolen from around the neighborhood. Others, I'd saved for, doing extra chores, selling my old baseball cards and comic books, and, of course, more recently, from slanging. Dollar by dollar, I'd raised the funds and bought parts out of magazines based on the West Coast. All that was left to do was to take the UPS box out to the garage. Cut it open. Throw some inner tubes in the white-wall tires, then stretch them along those Show Chrome, 250-spoke rims. Pump some air in 'em. Hook the back rim up through the rear hub. Stretch the chain on the spindle. Find good tension, and crank the nuts tight with the Crescent wrench. Then, throw that front wheel on the bent springer fork with the twisted braces, and it was ready to go.

I flicked the light on in the garage and just stared at it. It was up on two flipped plastic milk crates. The curved metal fork had flat, twisted bars for braces. The twisted-metal made the light pop white, so it looked like a chain of incandescent orbs end-to-end. The ape hanger handlebars jutted up tall and proud. The fuzzy, black and red zebra print banana seat sagged lazily. The candy apple red Sting Ray frame beamed crisp. Its serpentine bars made the bike appear to surge forward. All the other junk and half-built or broken down bikes slid back in silent homage to my bike's unfinished, un-ridden excellence.

Once the wheels were on, I mounted the bike for the first time. I sat tentatively and listened to the pops and creaks under me. The rubber tires stretched, and the bike held up fine. I bounced a few times and watched the tires for pressure; they held firm, and the white-walls only ballooned slightly. The bike clanked a little, but it wasn't the clank of an old rust-bucket beater; it was the clank of a fresh ride—a new creation finding its groove.

I got up, leaned the bike on its pedal, and opened the sliding garage door. I walked it out into the alley and shut-up shop, then I got on. I took a deep breath and rode under the alley lights. My knees were high up under my armpits, and my back stretched as I reached way out in front to cling to the ape hanger grips. I pedaled the lowrider as the spring popped and hummed like a slinky. The fresh tires loped and bobbed over the uneven alley pavement. Above, the crescent moon beamed down its florescent appreciation.

I reached the end of the alley and turned towards the hospital.

"Ah shit!" Ryan yelled with a goofy, proud grin.

A bunch of other kids were there, and all of them turned to watch me roll up. Angel sat on his sill; the creases of his tan Dickies ran down his long, sprawled-out legs. As I got close, he smiled and nodded. His bike was leant up against the hospital wall. Its midnight-purple gleamed.

"Hell yeah, boy," Ryan said, smirking as I rolled to a stop in front of the sills.

"It looks sick, man," Angel said, looking at me. His eyes were sad, and his lips fought off a frown.

The other kids crowded around and made random comments and asked questions. After the excitement dropped off, I set my bike next to Angel's, and we took up our posts on the sills.

"Man, I'm gonna get my bike out here," Ryan said.

"Do that shit," I replied.

"You already woulda had it out here if you didn't spend all your loot on dat fool's gold," Angel said smiling at me.

"Man, this is 14-karat gold," Ryan said as he thumbed the thick herringbone necklace that hung around his neck.

"Yeah," I muttered. "And it costs as much as my fork and my rims together."

"Ah, but not everybody can be a pimp like me," Ryan said, rocking back and smiling.

"Yeah, all your girlfriends do look like crack whores," Angel retorted. I burst out laughing.

"Fuck you," Ryan ejected, disgusted. He thumbed his herringbone. A faint yellow ring misted into the fibers of his white t-shirt.

A group of girls walked up to the sills; Hyacinth was with them. These were the pretty girls, the nice girls. Always dressing up when they came around. The Good Girls. The Good Girls got straight As. They all smelled like flowers and honey and candy. The Good Girls all covered their mouths when they giggled—their rings and bracelets glimmering. They always had their fingernails and toenails painted the same color and makeup on, but just a little bit. They listened to boy bands and B96. Their voices were girly and light like fairies'. Their skin was like the Noxzema girl's skin—creamy, vibrant, soft, and smooth. They wore lip gloss that tasted like stuff—stuff you'd never think you wanted to taste, but when they were close, the scent of it made your mouth water like a hound dog on a fresh track. They wore necklaces with nameplates written in cursive, and if they wore one with a boy's name on it, it meant they was goin' with 'em. All us guys had gotten nameplates just in case…. The Good Girls always seemed like they knew something was going on, even when there wasn't, 'cause there was always somethin' goin' on when the Good Girls came to hang around wit' us.

"Hey, man, I'm gonna cruise," Angel said as he rose. "Wanna come?"

"Naw, I'm cool," I said. I took a deep breath, trying to keep my heart from thumpin'.

"Aight den, fools," Angel chided in a silly voice as he got on his bike.

"Hey, Hyacinth," Angel sang as he peddled fast and silly towards the girls.

"Hey, Angel," Hyacinth said, smiling at him as he rode past them and into the tree-shadowed walkway.

Hyacinth approached, looking straight at me the whole way.

Her hair was combed down straight to her shoulders, and her bangs cut sharp across her forehead; they framed her round, little face with its small button nose and long eyelashes. Her skin was smooth and perfect and dark. She folded her arms over her stomach. It looked like she squeezed a bouquet of orange, white, and red wildflowers that were printed on the chest of her yellow t-shirt. She walked right up to me with her dark eyes like two almonds, and when she got close, she flashed her bright teeth. I couldn't help but smile back. This warmth rushed all through my chest in overlapping surges like boiling carp in the Chicago River.

"Hey," she said. The heel of her open-toed sandals clacked on the sidewalk. She bumped her knee into my thigh, playfully, and I made room for her to sit beside me in the sill.

"Is this your bike?" she asked, finally breaking eye contact with me and looking at it.

"Yeah... You like it?" My throat swelled with pride.

"It's great." She kicked her legs out in front of her as she gripped the ledge of the sill between her thighs. "It's beautiful." She glanced back at me.

"Beautiful?" Ryan frowned. "Come on... You gotta find some other word than 'beautiful,'" he said.

"Well...." Hyacinth raised her hands.

"'Beautiful' is fine with me," I cut her off as our eyes met again. Her cheeks blushed deep-red.

The other Good Girls giggled and whispered in a huddle like pigeons pecking at a scrap of bread. That's when I saw Monica from next door. She was a year younger than me, and I hadn't paid her much attention, but she'd finally started to grow up. She fit right in with 'em even though she was the only black girl. Her hair was pulled up in some kind of New Wave braids with little white and purple beads tied in on the ends. She made eyes at me— her eyebrows arched way up—challenging me like when we used to play as little kids.

"What?" she said playfully as we both laughed.

Ryan nodded his head towards Monica and winked. His face turned all pink as he showed them gnarly chompers.

I sighed and looked back at Monica. "Have you ever met Ryan, Monica?" I introduced them and thankfully didn't have to do much more, and they started to talk.

"Can I ride it?" Hyacinth asked.

I stood the bike, and she raised her leg up and swung it over the bar and sat down. Her short khaki shorts slid up so her whole thigh showed. It glowed in the streetlight with lotion. She sat down snug on the soft banana seat, and then she reached her arms out to grab the rubber grips on the ape hangers.

"Do you like it?" I asked.

"I like it."

"It's hard to ride lowrider bikes, so I'm gonna push you 'til you get it, OK?" I got behind her.

"OK. Don't let me fall over." I leaned my cheek in close to hers.

"I won't," I whispered.

I grasped the chrome sissy bar and the neck of the handlebars and pushed. Her hair whisked against my face and neck with my chest snug against her back. It felt so good that it instantly eased the tension in my shoulders, and I pushed her like this for a few feet until she peddled away. She made a big loop around the wide sidewalk adjacent to the sills as the Good Girls 'Ooohhed' and cheered. Finally, she rode to a stop in front of me and slapped her sandals on the sidewalk.

"It's a great bike," she said as she got off. "You did a good job making it."

"Thanks." I put it back to rest on its pedal.

Monica sat beside Ryan in his sill. His beet-red face grinned so hard it looked like his head was about to explode at any second.

Hyacinth sat next to me in my sill; there was barely enough space for the two of us. She drew her sparkly lip gloss capsule across her top lip, then glided it along the thick bottom one. She smacked and smushed them together, and the tiny flecks of glitter percolated in the burnt-orange streetlamps. The rest of the Good Girls chattered in a tight gaggle at Angel's vacant sill and drew on the concrete inner-walls with pink and purple highlighter markers. The aroma of Hyacinth's peach-cream lip gloss permeated the vault of my sill, and my mouth salivated instantly.

We sat so our legs and bare arms touched. Her damp, smooth skin pulled like a magnet on mine. It made me want to reach out and squeeze her, then tear off both our clothes so as much as of our skin could touch as humanly possible. Or maybe, just kiss her—kiss her arms, her hands, her neck.

A silence bloomed up in our sill, and finally, she smiled. Her purple lips slowly spread, and her immaculate silver braces shimmered. She reached up and touched the golden nameplate attached to my rope chain that read Joey in cursive.

She inspected it. She rolled her fingers over the smooth, polished gold, and her teal fingernails curled over the letters. I looked at her and her short, straight-cut bangs. The dark, silky strands glistened in the night. My pulse pattered in my thorax, and my ears burned hot. Suddenly it struck me: she'd say yes if I asked her right then. A gush of joy washed over my chest, then popping little pin-prickles spread in its wake and slid up along my neck. My lips quivered, and I started to say it. It came out as this high-pitched squeak, and I swallowed it back as her deep almond eyes rose to mine.

"You wanna be my girl?" It flowed smooth and low like a vibration that'd eased out of my spinal cord. She smiled and nodded. Then, she leaned in and pecked me swiftly, but firmly, and her lips left mine with a moist smack.

I grinned, reached back, and unclasped my rope chain. Then, I slid the little cursive *Joey* off and placed it in my palm. She undid hers and pinched the corner of the *Joey* with her thumb and index to draw the end of her chain through the tiny rings. Then, she asked me to clasp it and turned. Her hair fluttered across my face soft and light as she brushed it over her shoulder. I brought the chain up over her head and laid it down, struggling with the tiny circular clasp.

"This fuckin' thing," I muttered as she covered her mouth and giggled. And then, the ring slid true, and she was mine. I leaned in and softly kissed her neck. The smudge of her lip gloss slid from me and on to her cool skin.

The girls said they had to go and started off down Hollywood, then shouted back, "Come on, Hyacinth!"

Hyacinth looked at them, then back at me.

"See you later," she said smiling.

"OK," I said. She gave me a kiss on the cheek and ran away to catch up with the other Good Girls.

Ryan waited until they were out of earshot. "Man, that Monica is hot as hell!"

"Yeah, man. We been neighbors since we was little," I said. "I think she likes you man."

"Yeah?" Ryan raised his eyebrows, and that awkward squeakiness returned to his voice.

Angel rode up from the tunnel and asked, "What up?"

"Ryan's in love," I said as I shoved a thumb at Ryan.

"Which hood rat now?" Angel replied, flashing his teeth at me.

"Fuck you," Ryan sang.

"Naw, it's my neighbor Monica."

"Mort's little sister?" Angel asked.

"Yeah," I said smiling.

"Got that jungle fever, huh," Angel said as I broke up.

"Man, fuck you," Ryan snapped.

"Hey, but whatcha think Mickey's gonna say about him dating a black girl?" I raised my eyebrows at Angel.

"Well, he'll probably just be happy he finally found a girl

with all her teeth in her mouth," Angel joked, looking away towards Ashland.

"Ohhhhh." I covered my mouth trying to bite back my laughter.

"Motherfucker," Ryan said, jumping up and slugging Angel in the arm hard. "Where's your bitch at?" he shouted.

Angel stood up. They were the same height, but Ryan outweighed him by about twenty pounds. Ryan was a little soft, but it wasn't all fat. Angel's smile disappeared. They snarled nose-to-nose.

"Come on already," I said, exhausted with the way those two got under each other's skin. "Quit already."

They both sat back in their sills and continued to glare at each other like two brothers that had to share the same little room their whole lives.

■

IT WAS LIL PAT'S BIRTHDAY around then, and Ma and Dad felt bad for him—he'd been in the infirmary for some kind of fight—so we drove out to Statesville Correctional to visit him. Jan'n'Rose came along even though they'd never gotten along with him, and at the last second, Rich shuffled out of the house and jumped in the van. There was nothing much to do—it was a rainy Saturday. Statesville is in Joliet and only about an hour outside the city. I was glad to go, glad to see Lil Pat again. I missed him a lot, and we didn't go to visit much; Ma didn't like the idea of us getting tangled up in that world. She wanted better for us. We drove through endless lines of tall cornfields, then passed a sign on the road that read "Do Not Pick Up Hitchhikers."

"Yeah, if Pat ever escaped, he'd probably need a ride into town, huh?" Rich guffawed.

"Quit talking like that, damnit," Dad said, trying to hide his smile as the rest of us the giggled softly.

The van came over a hill, and there it was in the center of a cornfield. The huge concrete prison walls spread widely across the field with the grayish-purple sky hovering heavily above. I remembered it being taller and scarier the first time—I thought it was like Conan the Barbarian's house—but now, it just looked sad and depressing.

"So he's in segregation, huh," Dad said.

"Yeah, I guess he's been misbehaving," Ma replied.

"Ah, what'd you expect," Rich said. "He had detention every day at Gordon."

"Richard, if you don't shut'chur mouth," Ma said, twisting and glaring at him.

It was a long wait. Two lines—one for men, one for women. Step out of your shoes. We were all searched. Ma, Dad, and Jan'n'Rose went in first while Rich and I waited for about a half an hour. Suddenly, Dad burst out of the doors to the visiting room. His face was red and puffy, and he tore across the room to the exit doors where a guard stood behind a glass and mesh window.

"Let me outta here!" he yelled.

The guard buzzed him through.

Ma, Jan, and Rose followed soon after. Ma grinned stoically at us while Jan'n'Rose hung their heads solemnly.

"Go on in. He's only got fifteen minutes left," Ma said.

"You think he should go in?" Rich asked Ma, nodding at me.

"He'll be fine," she replied. "Daddy just got worked up."

"I'm goin' in," I sighed. "I didn't come out here for nothing."

"Go on, it's OK," Ma said, patting me on the shoulder. "He's got a busted-up eye, but he's fine."

I followed Rich through the doors, and we walked down a short hall. Along one side, there was a series of booths—some with people talking and others that were empty. We walked until we saw Lil Pat sitting across the thick glass. His left eye was swollen terribly and sealed shut, and there was a long, twisty string of black stitches running along his brow. He looked anxious and grabbed the yellow phone and motioned for us to pick ours up. Rich picked his up, and Lil Pat spoke fast. I put mine to my ear.

"He's fine," Rich urged.

"Are you sure? He was crying and everything. Jesus," Lil Pat said. His eye bugged out. "Are you sure, Rich?"

"He's fine," Rich sighed.

"Ah, aye, Joey," Lil Pat said, looking at me bright-eyed. "How are ya, buddy?"

"Good," I said. "What happened to your eye?"

"Ah, nothing. I'm fine." Lil Pat shrugged. "How are you, kid? You've grown! How old are you now?"

"Fourteen," I replied.

"Jesus Christ, kid," Lil Pat said as he twisted his head sideways. "I remember when... Ah, ya look great, kid. I miss ya so much."

"I miss you, too." A knot strung-up in my throat.

"So what the hell happened?" Rich laughed.

"Ah, nothin'," Lil Pat said as he eased back on his stool. All his street swagger returned. "Some nigger hit me wit' a hunk of brick rolled up in a sock."

"Ohhho fuck!" Rich gasped. I couldn't believe it.

"Yeah," Lil Pat said. "We was working down in the laundry, and he snuck up on me. Little fuckin' bastard. I'd stole on his boy a couple weeks ago."

"Did you get knocked out?" Rich asked.

"Yeah," Pat smirked. "I woke up like woohoo!" He rolled his eye around in its socket. "But he got his already." He mimicked a stabbing. "The white brothers are doing just fine in here. Don't worry about dat."

"Damn."

In my imagination, the entire series of violent repercussions suddenly unfolded like a row of dominoes falling and clattering on a table. No winners, no losers, just destruction.

"It was good, though. Got me out of the pressure cooker. It's quiet over here."

"Sounds real nice, Pat," Rich said, sarcastically arching his eyebrows.

"You asshole," Lil Pat said giggling. "I heard ya got a real nice girl." He smiled at Rich.

"Yeah," Rich said bashfully.

"Got tired a dem skanks, huh?" Lil Pat asked.

"Yeah," Rich answered and looked away. "She's great."

"You guys gonna get married?" Lil Pat asked.

Rich hid his eyes from his big brother.

"Ah, look at-chu. You're gonna ask her to marry ya, arn'tcha?"

"Come on, Pat," Rich whined.

"What about you, kid? How are things?" Pat looked at me. "You playing sports?"

"Yeah. High Ridge Chargers."

"That's good. How's that knucklehead best friend a yours?"

"Ryan?"

"No! Who else would I be talkin' about?"

"He's good."

"Remember what I wrote you about?" Rich butted in.

"I know, I know..." Lil Pat dismissed Rich's interruption with a wave.

"He's good. We're good, we've been runnin' around fighting and shit."

"Some niggers jumped you guys, huh?"

I glared at Rich. "Yeah," I said, and cleared my throat.

Lil Pat's eyes hardened. "Niggers are the scum of the earth, kid. They'll pretend to be your friend, and then they'll sneak up behind you and stab you in the throat. I seen it in here. I seen it a hundred times," he said, keeping his hard eye on me. "That neighborhood's ours, kid. Don't let those porch monkeys push you around. You got Ryan's back no matter what. No matter if there's six of them. You get beat down together. You go out fighting with pride. Got that?"

I nodded and scratched my thigh nervously.

"It's about loyalty, kid. On the street, it's all that matters. Ryan and you against all them motherfuckers. And don't be scared-a-them neither. You hit 'em good, they're goin' down just like any other dude. Shit, I made a habit a droppin' big niggers in the day-room when I got in here."

His anger flooded through his whole being. His shoulders swelled and trembled in his green smock, and I was scared, to tell ya the truth. He must have seen it. He shook his head in frustration and rolled his shoulders.

"Naw, kid, that's not what I mean. What I mean to say is... Ryan's your friend—your real friend. You gotta hold on to that and protect it, kid. Protect each other. Just be good to each other, like brothers." He leaned his elbows on the small shelf in front of him, and the warmth returned to his voice. "OK?"

There was a beep on the line, and a recorded voice said, *"This visit terminates in the thirty seconds."* Lil Pat put his hand to the glass, and Rich matched him with his own.

"See ya around, Pat," Rich said sadly.

"See ya, Rich," Lil Pat replied.

Lil Pat moved and put his big palm on the glass before me. I placed mine in the shadow of his.

"Ah, Joey, I love ya," Lil Pat said. "I'll be home soon."

"I love ya, Pat," I said, but there was a high-pitched dial tone coming through the earpiece. And that was it.

The whole ride home I kept quiet in the back of the van with my knees hugged up against my chest and thought of what Lil Pat'd said. The storm rumbled on—not a violent storm, but steady. The water mopped down slowly on the windshield. It was fucked up to think about it—to end up in a place like that. Hell, I didn't ever want to end up in there. Made me sick to think of getting hit with a brick for next to nothing. I felt far away from Lil Pat—way far away. A semi-truck blared past us and sent a heavy splash of dark water against my window in its wake. The water trickling down the glass lit a dark-gold like the light inside the back room of the pharmacy where the Assyrian lay dying. I thought of his loved ones having to come to claim the body, and how long it must have took to smear away all that blood and sinew and brain—how that image must have stayed with the loved one forever. I thought of the Assyrian's family driving out to the cemetery to put flowers on his grave. What if he had a little brother or sister, or even kids of his own? I thought of them growing up without a father.

Maybe Lil Pat deserved to be in there.

CHAPTER 15

LINCOLN

WE KNEW DAD had a tough job. Shit could get extremely danger-ous at any moment. He was down in a deep tunnel one day—a three-hundred-foot circular shaft bored vertically through the bedrock. It rains all day when you're that deep; endless water cascading down the stone, and the sky is just a small blue circle above. They were raising forms for the foundation of a small structure, and one of his laborers, Jose, realized he'd forgotten his lunch pail behind the eight-foot plywood wall that they'd just stood and fastened. They both climbed up, and Jose pointed it out in-between the wooden structure and the rough, wet stone. A series of coil rods rigged into the rock-face sat horizontally, plugged into the wall on two-foot centers. It was all kicked to hell with 2X4s, too.

Dad decided to climb down for it. It'd only take a minute, and as foreman, he'd rather it'd been him that got hurt doing something stupid than his best laborer. He climbed the form and shimmied himself in, head first, on an angle so his hands would reach the lunch pail first. It was narrow enough to breathe, but not enough to move quickly. He'd just reached down and grabbed the handle of the red and white plastic pail. He was six-feet deep at the head. His tan boots were still way up by the opening. The ever-present water slid down the stone and slipped under his rain gear, coolly slicking his back. Suddenly, there was a short burst from a foghorn, and he remembered they were setting off blasting caps on site #2, which was a hundred yards north, down a tunnel. He knew there'd be twelve dynamite bursts, and he knew he was fucked.

The thunderous booms from the erupting dynamite layered up on themselves. The echoing reverberation swelled into the shaft and ballooned up to the blue sky. At first, his heart patter accelerated. He struggled to breathe. He twisted and fought what he knew was inevitable. At the seventh blast, he'd given up on trying to twist upright. He braced. The shale, clay, and stone broke above him along the circular shelf face. He knew it was coming, and just when he was sure his pulmonary valve would explode, he gripped a coil rod and breathed deeply. His heart slowed to a hard thump. His vision brightened. All around him grew vibrant and magnified: the oily, brownish-gray thread of the rod next to his pulsing, hairy hand; the grainy, tannish-brown of the many-layered wood slivers of the sheet of plywood. The stone and clay descended and plummeted until it clapped on his legs and side. He was perfectly calm. Then, nothing—a soundless, pitch-black void.

Before the cave-in was even finished, the seven-man crew all stood atop the form. They dug ferociously, clawing the dirt and stone and mud with their fingers and hammers. They gripped the coil rods and bent them by hand. One of them leapt down, snagged a stake-mall, and slung it up to another, who caught it and swung down viciously in one motion. He banged the coil rods and opened a path to him. Dad was a feared boss, but his savage intensity toward the work made him revered. The way those men urgently dug him out and had him hoisted on the deck within a minute—I guess you could call that respect, or loyalty, or even something more.

When he told me the story, he said he had a nice little pocket of air to breath—that is wasn't that bad. But then, I asked Jose a decade or so later while we took lunch break under a bridge way out in Willow Springs. He shut his tattered lunch pail and got real quiet. He cleared his throat of something. His brow creased, and his deep, wrinkled eyes dampened. He shook his head and said, "When we get your Poppa out, he is unconscious. It was very bad."

Within minutes, Dad came to. They'd lowered the big metal box down with the long iron cable of the boom crane and readied to lift him out to an inbound ambulance, but he refused to go. When his men urged him, he shouted, *"I'M NOT GOING ANY-FUCKING-WHERE! WE GOT CONCRETE AT 1:30 GOD-DAMNIT!"* They all sighed—relieved he was his old miserable self again. He grinned and started to crackup, which broke 'em all into joyful hysterics. Finally, he got his shit together and slung his tool belt on. Then, he climbed back in the very same crevasse he'd been buried in, bent the coil rods back straight and true, and re-placed the ones he couldn't. Then, he re-kicked the wall, and they poured at 1:30 sharp. And they made it home in time to eat dinner with their families—their sons, and daughters, and wives who didn't know a thing about it and couldn't ever have understood.

But when each of my father's sons grew into manhood, we did understand, and we loved him with that very same visceral savagery.

■

CLARK IS A SNAKE OF A STREET. There's no sense of order to it. It leaps out of a grassy field next to the railroad tracks at Cermak, then slips through downtown, past the Federal Building, and shoots by that crazy Picasso sculpture and City Hall and the location of the St. Valentine's massacre, past Wrigley Field and the heart of Chicago music: the Metro. Then, it roams north-northwest at its own slithering trajectory creating calamitous intersections and mocking the grid of the city. They named it after the Lewis and Clark expedition because it's an ancient Black Hawk tribal path where many a bloody battle took place; their ghosts haunt it with a mad fury. Our McDonald's is on Clark, just past Bryn Mawr. A block north, Clark overtakes Ashland and drops it a few blocks up, leaving it as nothing more than a side street. Just after that, and exactly seven miles from the center of the city, Clark glides past a statue of Abraham Lincoln, sitting in the park with his back to Thorndale. Then, Clark rides north, strong, and dies at Howard Street right at Chicago's north pole. The parking lot of the McDonald's feeds out onto Ashland to the west and Clark to the east, connecting two of the great arterial streets of the city.

Angel had a beef with this shorty Moe named DeAndre 'cause he called Angel a bitch during summer session at Pierce. So when school let out, it was "On like Donkey Kong." We waited on the side of the McDonald's, silently, passing a Marlboro Light back and forth. Ryan pinched his bright blue and purple collared Guess shirt at the chest and fanned himself, jostling his thin gold rope chain—the only two remnants of his cut of the weed money. Angel leaned against the McDonald's wall and gazed steadily across the lot at the huge, windowless, red-bricked edifice. It had an old, paint-on 7 Up ad that looked like somebody had started to it sand-blast off and given up halfway through. A hot pool of emotion churned inside me. The fear that Angel'd get whooped, then the rest of these bastards'd jump in, and that we'd be on our backs bleeding again. BB's laughter trickled through my memory. The panic swelled until bright flashes pulsed in my cranium. Run, Motherfucker! *RUN THE FUCK AWAY FROM HERE!* But there was this cool, magnetic force holding me right there. Then it clicked: I was trapped. No way out. Accept it, motherfucker. They're coming out here, and it's going down. You better be in and all the fucking way. A growl popped and grumbled up in my throat. I squared with Angel. "You ready!?" I snarled. He yawned in response and kept his long gaze across the way.

The side door of the McDonald's opened, and they filed out. DeAndre in front with the rest trailing in a loose line like a platoon headed into the jungle. There were seven dudes, all our age and younger, and three girls. DeAndre dropped his McDonald's cup on the blacktop as he led them away from us and across the lot. When BB got beside it, he hopped up and stomped it, so the plastic lid and straw popped off. The soda-browned ice gushed out and instantly morphed and melted on the sun-baked pavement.

The afternoon traffic flicked past on Ashland and Clark. The wind gusts doubled up on each other. DeAndre stopped across the lot where there were a few empty parking spaces. He handed his backpack to a fat girl in a baby-blue t-shirt, then he looked down and chuckled. He was a few shades darker than the rest, and there was a line etched into his hair that started at his widow's peak and traced across and over his scalp like the trajectory of a meteor that impacted somewhere behind his ear.

Angel gazed steadily at DeAndre. It was like he stared straight into him and if he peered long enough, whatever was there would disintegrate. DeAndre looked up at Angel and smirked. Angel grinned back slyly like he knew a secret nobody else knew.

"Come on, motherfucker!" I said, shoving Angel. He sighed. Then, he pushed his back off the wall and started toward DeAndre. The group whooped and hollered as we fanned out at his sides. Angel walked cool—like he was stepping into a party where everybody knew his name. As he got close, the group parted and opened a path. Angel smoothly glided toward DeAndre, loose and limber. DeAndre stood with his hands open and spread out at his sides. He raised his chin high. His eyes bugged out. Angel stepped into range, never breaking his stroll, then he just swung right from the hip—deliberate, straight, and true. Angel's fist splashed into DeAndre's upturned jaw and snapped his whole head sideways. A shocked wail rose up around them. DeAndre's knees instantly buckled. He lunged forward and grasped Angel's t-shirt. Angel stepped back. Then, he slammed both hands down on DeAndre's grip and broke it. DeAndre stumbled forward and launched wide haymakers. Angel backed up straight and deflected the punches easily with his shoulders and forearms. DeAndre bulled forward. Angel reeled backward across the lot snapping quick punches that bounced off DeAndre's head until he got to a parked yellow Nova. The back of Angel's legs butted against it, and he toppled onto the car's hood. DeAndre leapt on top of Angel and straddled him. He sat up and throttled vicious punches that penetrated Angel's guard. Angel's head bounced off the sheet metal.

"Whoop his ass, 'Dre!" the fat girl squealed joyfully. The group cheered and swelled in around them. Their eyes lit like a frenzied mob. BB squeezed to the front. He squeaked and began to slap his hands on the car hood beside Angel's head.

The wires looped around my throat and pulled tight. *They're jumpin' in.*

Fear does all kinds of things to people. A dark, cool wave swept through me. Quickly, I rushed up behind DeAndre close, as if I was going to whisper something in his ear. I bent down and gathered my leverage, then I swung up with all my might. My fist crashed into the side of his head near the ear. It felt like hitting a 16-inch softball off a tee. He halted and went limp. Then, he tipped over and flopped flat on the car's hood beside Angel. There was an awestruck silence. Then, one of the girls screamed. Swiftly, I spun as a kid stepped up to my side. I stuck him straight in the teeth. He twisted away clutching his mouth. I heard a hard crack and spun back to see a kid fall at my feet holding the side of his head. Ryan heaved over him, glowering down. Ryan's skin pulsed in a cloudy red.

This monster erupted inside me. "COME ON, NIGGERS! RUSH DIS CREW! RUSH DIS FUCKING CREW!!!"

BB sprung at me. I smirked, twisted, and popped him in the eye. He sprawled backward. Then, he looked pleadingly at everyone, in complete shock. They'd all frozen and just gawked at us. *Thank god Tank isn't here.*

Angel slid off the car's hood. He snagged DeAndre's collar and pulled him to his feet. He reached down and pulled DeAndre's shirt up over his back and head and entangled his arms. Angel began to whomp DeAndre mercilessly with his free fist. The punches were dug and driven in with the absolute worst intention. The sound was sickening, like heavy boot stomps in mud.

The mob of kids unraveled and spread. Their mouths hung open. They ewwe'd and flinched at each punch. All three girls sobbed. As I watched, something rattled up from my sternum and eased out in a vile snicker. Angel was the only thing that held DeAndre up. He repeatedly bent at the waist and ripped uppercuts into DeAndre's head. DeAndre's face dribbled blood all over the blacktop. Angel's fist, shirt, and pants were smeared in the dark-red mess. He didn't seem to notice. His eyes were poised in a focused trance.

A McDonald's worker emerged at the entrance and yelled, "Get on outta here! We called the cops!"

Just then, a squad car with its strobes swirling but no siren swerved in off Clark. The whole group scattered like candy when a piñata bursts. Angel let go, and DeAndre flopped flat on the pavement. We ran toward Ashland when another silent squad car careened in our path, screeching to a halt. A cop with spiked hair sprang out of the passenger door with his gun drawn. He screamed 'Freeze' so ferociously that all three of us stopped mid-step.

Next thing I know, I was belly down on the steaming pavement with cuffs crunched down on my wrists. Angel flopped down next to me. Then, above, I hear the cop shout, "You think you're tough, you little Mick?" Ryan hit the deck on my other side. The cop loomed over him, then he clinked the cuffs down so hard Ryan screamed. The cop cracked Ryan's head off the pavement. Then, he snatched him by his Guess shirt and yanked him so the fabric tore. Ryan's chain broke and thumped on my shoulder. Angel, still un-cuffed, snatched it and dug it in his pocket.

"Fuck you, motherfucker!" Ryan screamed. He writhed, so the cop slammed him on the hood of the squad car.

Angel and I ended up in the back seat together. I leaned forward to keep the pressure off my manacled hands. Someone must have dropped a bunch of fries during the fight because a squad of pigeons were squabbling over them. Then, a small fleet of seagulls swooped in and angrily ran them off.

"Think he's alright?" I asked as an ambulance rolled into the parking lot.

"No."

"Come on, man. You think he's going to the hospital?"

"Yeah. Fuck that motherfucker."

"Fuck." I let my head hang back into the cushion.

Ryan writhed in the squad car across the lot and tried to kick out the windows, screaming so loud we could hear him.

"Ryan's gotta chill the fuck out," I said.

"Man, you know that's the best shirt he's got."

I was scared about what the cops were gonna do, what Dad was gonna do. I didn't feel bad about DeAndre just then. I knew exactly what those guys woulda done to Angel if I hadn't jumped in—what they would have done to all three of us if we hadn't fought so hard right-off like that. All the violent things I've done to people over the years—all those terrible things—it was the fear that made me do it. The fear of them, of the unknown, of what they would have done to me or my friends, my loved ones. But it doesn't change the fact that they've got loved ones, too, and hurting them, whether I like it or not, hurt a lot of people. And that's something that just gets harder with the years—facing down all those terrible things. Looking in the mirror trying to figure out who you are—if you was a good guy or a bad guy. Maybe there just wasn't enough good to go around back then.

We rolled south on Ashland, and the summer afternoon was bright and golden; the neighborhood was obliviously happy. An old lady poured water into flower pots on her front porch—the tulips white and mauve and perky as they unfurled into blossom. Even the dandelions sprung up through the sidewalk cracks with a buoyant, yellow resilience. A little Mexican boy rode his bicycle in the St. Greg's Gym parking lot, and his Grandpa watched, grinning, as the boy tottered on the training wheels. I wished it hadn't happened. *I wish I was a little kid again.*

JAILBIRD

THEY PUT US IN SEPARATE CELLS—three of 'em lined up next to each other.

My cell was small. Two cinderblock beds—one had a gray, plastic bed-roll folded up at the head. There was a metal toilet with a sink rigged into the top in-between the beds, and the bowl was filled to the brim with piss and stale water. There was a foggy trail of toilet paper that floated up from the drain to the water surface like smoke. The three walls were cinderblock, but the fourth was all glass, framed with brown-painted steel. It was an electric system, and when that glass door slowly slid shut, there was a deep boom, like an enormous explosion in the distance. Even then, it didn't sink in that I was a person locked inside of a cage. It was still a game, and a game we'd just won.

Being locked up is primarily an auditory experience. Everything to see is there unchanging. The pale, tan cinderblock walls coated with inch-thick layers of paint. The pitchforks and five-point stars etched into the metal housings. You fall into a world of listening. Footsteps, buzzers, keys jingling; 'I ain't ate all day,

Mothafucka!' reverberating from some long corridor like the echo of all the world's hunger; the cops cracking jokes and talking sports, the Cubbies; newspapers folding; strange Morse codes tapped on steel.

There was a far off scraping sound that came from an air duct in the ceiling. I climbed up on the bed and whispered, "Ryan, you there?"

"Yeah."

"You alright, man?"

"Yeah, man. That fuckin' pig ripped my shirt," Ryan spat, his voice faint like it was coming through a long tunnel.

"They didn't whoop your ass or nothing, did they?"

"Naw, man. In fact, O'Riley showed up and chewed into dat spiky-haired, Sonic the Hedgehog lookin' motherfucker."

"I want my baloney!" Angel's voice whined through the ventilation system. Feet panged off sheet metal. "Where's my baloney at?"

"That motherfucker's going nuts," I said as Ryan I burst into laughter.

"Angel, chill out, man. They're gonna put you in the loony bin!" Ryan yelled in a high-pitched squeak.

"Who dat? Ry-Ry?" Angel said, emulating a cartoon wino. "Aye, man, I got your chain, bra, but I might just have to keep it doh. I kindsa like dis ma-fucka."

The door to my cell buzzed and slid open. O'Riley walked into view with his chin tucked into his tree trunk neck. He took his cap off, and his beet-red forehead gleamed like a freshly painted fire hydrant.

"I was hoping this day wouldn't come, Joe... Let's go," he said. I walked out of the cell and down the hall to the processing room and called home.

Ma went nuts on the phone. "I'm calling your father! And you're just gonna have to wait there for him! So get comfortable!"

she yelled as I eased the receiver into the hook.

"You know you hurt that boy," O'Riley said. His brow furrowed. He frowned at me across the gray metal table between us. "He's staying the night in the hospital." There was a sharp click and flash as they photographed a gnarly bum in a long, tattered, brown coat across the way.

The silence hummed after we'd all made our calls home.

Looking back on it now, I can't imagine how it must have been for the old man then—grinding all day, running a crew and swinging a hammer out there with nobody to watch his back, nobody to look out for him. Got guys on his crew older than him with more years, more experience, and there he is getting by on reputation and proving it true every morning, figuring out the hard shit and fixing the office's mistakes in the real world of concrete, steel, and wood. Cracking the whip on these guys and still beating them on output, setting a pace no one except the crazy hardcore—the kind with blue union pride pumping in their veins; the kind who saw it as their life's work—could ever keep. All this while teaching himself to read plans, shoot grades, and bring it all together to the point where they brought him on as a super. The guy don't even got a high school diploma—not even close—and he's doing a job guys with engineering degrees are supposed to. The whirlwind of those long hours, the daylight burnt trying to break out of the neighborhood. I didn't have a clue. Out there thinking everything was riding on me having my boys' backs, and here he gets a call: Joey's sitting at the police station. Gotta leave the jobsite and come get him.

After a restless half-hour, I climbed up by the vent nearest Angel's cell.

"Hey, we got the story right: it was one-on-one, they jumped in first, and we all fought, right?" I whispered.

"Yeah, man, I got it," Angel replied.

"I mean, dat's what happened, right?"

"Yeah... I mean... Look, man, I ain't gonna say anything if dat's what you mean, alright?"

I paused and took a deep breath.

"Look..." I said. "If worst comes to worst, and he's hurt bad, I'll tell 'em I jumped in, OK?"

"Naw, man, don't worry. That's the story, we're sticking to it: they jumped in, so you guys did."

"Hell, I ain't tellin' 'em a damn thing," Ryan yelled through the vent. "They can go fuck demselves."

Angel's ma came in first. Her scuffed-up Payless tennis shoes squeaked across the cement floor. She wore a white collared shirt with a factory logo on the breast, and there was this stunned look plastered on her face like someone'd just slapped her for no reason at all. They went into a questioning room across the hall, and about twenty minutes passed, then the door swung open, and they came out. Angel looked down at the floor, his face wet. He didn't look up as they left.

The old man came in about a half-hour later. He stepped down the hall lightly in his work boots. His arms were wrapped with curling white hairs and all speckled with sawdust. He shot a fierce glance into Ryan's cell as he ground his molars and pursed his lips. The knot of his jaw pulsed. The door buzzed and slowly slid open. There was a silent, negative charge that radiated from him as he glared at me. O'Riley stepped up beside him as the door finally unlocked.

"What do you got to say for yourself?" Dad asked. His eyes darkened.

I stood and hung my head.

■

THE INTERROGATION ROOM was small and white with a heavy oak table in the center. The arresting officer sat with his back to the door and a pair of gray-framed sunglasses perched atop his thick, prickly hair. The yellow light spread a bronze sheen across the lenses, and that was it for me—dude's name was Sonic. We sat. I had Dad on one side, Sonic on the other, and O'Riley across the way. O'Riley asked the questions, and Sonic scribbled notes on a document attached to a clipboard. I told the truth, except for the part about them jumping in first. When I got to the part where I hit DeAndre, Sonic stopped writing and pointed the butt-end of his ballpoint pen at me.

"So, what did you have in your hand when you hit him?" he asked.

"Nothing. My fist," I answered.

"So, why did your friend," he continued, flipping through some papers under the one he was writing on, "Angel say different?"

"First off, he didn't say different, and second, there was nothing in my hand."

O'Riley sighed and waved dismissively at Sonic.

"Just answer their damn questions," my father snapped.

I finished, and O'Riley took a look at Sonic's notes. He crossed out a few lines, unclipped the paper, and slid it over to me.

"Now read through that, Joe."

It was pretty much what I'd said.

"Is that what happened?" O'Riley confirmed.

"Uhuh."

"Then sign it there at the bottom."

Dad turned toward me in his chair and went to say something when Sonic tossed his pen so it hit the table and rolled next to my hand. Dad snarled. Sonic got up and walked around behind me, then leaned in over my shoulder and placed his stubby hand on the table beside the document. He smelled like Brut aftershave and sweat. Dad shook his head and grumbled. Sonic's starched-stiff uniform scratched my shoulder as he hovered there, and I snatched the pen and signed it quickly in the hopes it would end all of it.

Sonic pinched the corner of the document. Dad muttered, "*I'll slice your fuckin' toes off.*" I turned to him and almost said 'What?'

Sonic began to lift the document when Dad's massive hand lurched out from under the table. It swung up high, then swooped down right in front of my face and banged the document flat, dead-center. The oak resonated. The corner Sonic'd pinched ripped clean off. Sonic grabbed Dad's wrist. Dad squeezed the document, and it crumpled into a ball inside his fist. Then, Sonic lunged to grab Dad's arm and knocked me clear out of my seat. I sprawled onto the dusty gray-tiled floor. Dad burst upward from his seat. He dug his elbow into the center of Sonic's chest and drove him into the wall. A deep thud boomed from Sonic's nostrils. His eyes swelled open. He grasped at my father's elbow and tried to pry it out of his chest cavity. Dad raised his jutting chin and peered down at him clinically, like a physician inspecting a patient's throat. A cloud of white bloomed in Sonic's pink face. His Ray-Bans clattered on the tiles.

O'Riley got up and barreled towards them. "Now dat's enough, Pat! Let up. You're gettin' too old for this crap!" he said, snagging Dad's other arm in some sort of lock. "Let up, or it's gonna get ugly in here!"

There was a throbbing second. Dad snarled and burrowed his eyes through Sonic, who blinked back tears and heaved for breath. The crumpled paper clapped to the floor.

They let up, and Dad stepped toward the door. Sonic bent down and snatched the document, tugged it open, and scowled at it. A little shot of joy blossomed in my heart, and a grin snuck onto my lips. O'Riley caught it, then he grimaced at me, and I hung my head in shame again. We stepped out into the hall, and Ryan was glued to the glass of his cell, all wide eyed. I just shook my head as we walked past.

I'd gotten a few slaps in my day but never a real beating, not like the ones I'd seen Dad give my brothers. He trembled with rage the whole drive home, and I watched him in my periphery—waiting for it. When we got in the house, he said, "Get to your room." I stepped toward the stairs. He followed and I halted. He paused, then stepped in front of me and up the staircase. I followed him. When he reached the top stair, he turned left toward his room, and I stepped right toward mine. I sighed with relief as I walked inside.

There was a whirl, and a heavy palm impacted the whole side of my head. I was airborne. My entire room flopped sideways, then upside down, and I landed on my belly with a hard squeak of bedsprings. Then, I curled into a fetal ball as Dad rampaged through my room. He tore my big Lowrider poster off the low, slanted ceiling, then vaulted my stereo off my dresser to the old shag carpet. "I'm tearing all this shit outta here!" He yelled, smacking my CD cases so they sprinkled over me. Then, he stomped up and snatched a handful of my hair.

"YOU THINK YOU'RE TOUGH?" He planted a punch into my hairline. Then, he smashed one into my lip. Blood poured in through my teeth. "YOU THINK YOU'RE TOUGH?" He chuckled. He released me and surged toward my open door, then halted in the doorway. "YOU THINK YOU'RE FUCKING TOUGH? YOU DON'T KNOW WHAT TOUGH IS!"

I peered at him through the thin crease between my forearms as he vanished into the hall.

Well, that was the first time he cracked me for real, and I spent the rest of that day and night thinking about why. Was it 'cause I'd gotten caught? Screwed up his day? Maybe because I'd jumped in on a fair fight, or because DeAndre was hurt so bad. I never asked. Looking back, I guess he was just scared for me, wanted to wake me the hell up. Sometimes, that's the only way to get a young man to pull his head of out his ass. I didn't though—spent the rest of the day thinking about how to run away and how to maybe hit him with something heavy when he wasn't look-ing. Then, I thought about what was waiting for us out there in the neighborhood. Everyone'd want a piece of us now. I couldn't believe how deep of shit we'd gotten in. I was proud, too, crazy as that sounds—proud that we'd stuck together so tight, proud that we'd fought without hesitation, proud that we hadn't gotten jumped again.

I laid like that in my room all afternoon. No one came to see how I was. I was glad they didn't but lonely at the same time. Outside my window, the block flourished in the full-tilt summer. The little boys played war with plastic machine guns that rattled as they cried out and flopped on their bellies in death throes. *Why do boys have to war with each other?* A Mother pushed her stroll-er across the way. In my mind, I saw DeAndre on a hospital bed with his mom weeping and holding his hand as they waited to do a brain scan. An old man with a brimmed hat walked his muscu-lar pit bull along the sidewalk, and I wondered what Da would think of me now—if he'd be mad with me, or just sad and disap-pointed. An epic, golden green filtered through the full-leaved tree out front. It splattered on the front porch's roofing but fell short of my window. It was too bright, and eventually, I just pulled my drapes closed.

■

I HAD A STEADILY BEATING HEADACHE well into the night. I nev-er turned the light on—just sat there on my bed as dusk saturated my wall in a heavy orange-red. Then, darkness, until the street-lights lit yellow and empty. Sleep would come, and the headache would nudge away. The wires slung heavy in my veins, pinning me to the bed. Then, there was a giant red bubble-shaped organ lying on my belly. It was like a transparent tomato. Wet, slimy, and pulsing, it bobbled there, light as a feather. Its force pinned me, not its weight. Then, light images began to pass through it at a quickening pace like a strobe light: pit bulls fighting, encircled by laughter. Cows quartered with enormous, circular blades. Then, the images took on a terrible speed like someone flipping through a thick deck of cards: the Assyrian's cracked skull, Sy's gaping eye wound, the blood beading through Monteff's fingers, Ryan's purple eye, the stitches along Lil Pat's brow. Then, it froze on DeAndre's eyes, swollen shut and bleeding steady tears that dripped down on me like rain. Then, the bubble clouded and undulated atop me—alive. I raised my hand against the force and dipped my finger into it. It elasticized against my fingertip, recoiled, and floated upward. Then, it burst and flooded down in hot, red ooze, and I awoke panting, covered in sweat, gripping my hollow stomach.

Couldn't sleep after that; I kept sifting through all of it for meaning. I felt somewhere deep inside that what I did was wrong—that I should have only jumped in if they did first. Dad'd beat me like that because what I'd done was villainous and cowardly. A one-on-one fight was sacred bond. Win or lose, there was honor in a fair fight, and breaking that code was a terrible thing to do. It was an unjust thing, and I should have let Angel lose if it had to happen. But in what I did, there was no dignity. Fear made me do it, and that made me sick. I resolved to not do it again. If they'd have moved, it'd have been OK, but since I jumped the gun, I was as bad as they'd been when they jumped us. That sin infuriated and dejected me. A man was only as good as his code. I wasn't a man. I knew that. But I was trying, and I'd failed that afternoon.

■

I SNUCK OUT a few nights later. I walked down the street towards the sills as David Letterman's voice eked out of the Bernhart's open front window and traffic soared quietly along Ashland.

There were a few kids down there. Angel had his midnight-purple Lowrider out, and he gazed solemnly down the arterial alleyway as he sat on his bike. Its serpentine lines swayed and twisted together beneath him. The chain-link steering wheel spouted up from the bike's neck like a chrome crown. The other kids shuffled around him, inspecting it. The tall, wide expanse of the hospital wall behind him loomed, immovable, like the prison walls in Joliet.

Ryan sat in his sill with his legs dangling down, toes barely touching the sidewalk. His scowl was harder than a boy's face should be allowed to scowl—harder than it is was capable of. His freckles were dark and large and spattered across his arms and face, and the skin beneath them was milky white—the type of pale that never darkens, only singes red; the kind of burn not easily forgotten.

Ryan saw me and got up to greet me. Angel looked, then he leaned his bike on its pedal and sauntered over.

Ryan flashed his imbecilic, crooked smirk. "Drown your sorrows," he said, raising a half-pint of whiskey in a crumpled paper bag.

"Thanks, man," I said, taking the half-killed bottle.

Ryan and Angel glanced at each other. The bulbous, purple mound on my widow's peak had dissipated into a hazy orange, but my cut lip was still puffed out.

"So's DeAndre gonna press charges?" I asked, taking a slug.

"Naw, man. I think the cops were just trying to scare us," Angel answered, exhaling hard.

I snickered as Ryan offered me his mint-green pack of Newports. I dug one out.

"I think they did a little more than that," I said, sparking it.

We were silent. I could feel 'em staring at the lump; it felt tight and slid across my skull every time I talked or toked.

"Didn't even see it comin'. Son-of-a-bitch sucker punched me. Believe dat? His own kid."

"Hey man, you alright?" Angel said, putting his hand on my shoulder. His mahogany eyes were soft like a child's.

"Yeah, I'm fine, man. My brothers got it a lot worse den me. Old man must be getting soft or somethin'."

"Didn't he break Rich's nose that one time?" Ryan asked.

"Yeah, broke his nose real nasty. I got off easy."

"Hey, Angel, can I ride it?" a stoner with a threadbare flannel shirt tied around his waist asked Angel, looming beside his bike.

"No," Angel answered, turning and swaying up to it.

"He's drunk, huh? I better catch up," I said. I took a few hard swigs and handed the bottle back to Ryan.

"Yeah, you missed it. We smoked a blunt earlier," Ryan added.

"No shit? What's dat coming out of my cut?"

"Naw, it was outta Angel's personal stash." Ryan took a swig off of the bottle. "Said we were smoking it for you actually. 'For our boy on house arrest.'"

Angel started riding in these wobbly, tightly torqued circles, and a couple of the younger kids ran alongside him. Then, Angel threw his head back and rocked it side to side, gazing into the murky night sky. "My Daddy taught me-ta ride bikes... My Daddy taught me-ta ride bikes..." he sang.

Everybody laughed except Ryan and me. We just walked over, sat in our sills, and watched solemnly.

"Man...," Ryan said and took a swig. "I'd like to say I miss him." His brick of a forehead creased. "All he ever did when he was home was beat the shit outta us. Ma got the worst of it, always with her mouth, ya know? Waa, waa, waa," Ryan mocked his Ma's whiney voice. "Ya know?"

I nodded.

"But still, man, the kinda shit he'd do to her... He'd hit her with a closed fist man... Hard as he could!"

"Damn."

"I'd try to stop him, ya know, but he'd just whoop my ass,

too." Ryan shrugged, defeated. "One time though, Bear got him. Oh, he got him good. Ran him right out the house. Bit his whole hand up real bad. Had to get stitches and everything."

"No shit?"

"That's a good dog, man. That was one of the last times he hit her. It was right before he got locked up."

"Damn, dat is a good dog."

Angel Rode on. His old man had been in the Army, and they'd lived on a base out in California. He had a screw loose from Nam or booze or drugs, and he ended up going insane. He got a medical discharge, and they committed him into an asylum. It'd been ugly. He'd started lashing out at Angel and his Ma—tormenting them with his delusions and horrifying things brought on by some kind of mescaline or LSD. Monsters and demons, and sometimes, even his little boy became the demon. That was just too much for Angel's mother to take, so they got on a bus for Chicago in the middle of the night. She had a cousin here and a job waiting. Later, they found out about the asylum, then the half-way house, then who knows. He sent Angel a letter every Christmas with five bucks in it. Not another word all year round. Angel told me that one night in the garage when it was just him, me. Tears avalanched off his face.

Suddenly, Angel's front tire smashed into the hospital wall. His springer fork gave, and the frame surged upward, but he let go just before his handlebar grips slammed into the concrete. There was a surge of laughter. Angel laughed, too, then stood, grabbed the handlebars, and started crashing his front tire into the wall. The metal fender crinkled. His forearms flared, and his face knotted in a concentrated grimace. The back tire jolted upward with each collision.

"What the fuck?" I yelled, then we sprang up and dashed over. Ryan yanked Angel off, and the bike thumped and clanked to the sidewalk. I picked it up as Ryan held him back. The front fender was dinged pretty bad. The smooth, curved metal dimpled near the neck of the frame.

"What?" Angel giggled.

"What the fuck are you doing, bro?" I pleaded.

"Fuck you. It's my fucking bike to wreck," he said, smiling bitterly.

"What the fuck, Angel?"

"Come on," Angel sang. "It ain't so bad."

Ryan let go, and Angel mounted it. He started to ride again, but the front tire deflated where it contacted the ground and spilled out flat. His smile'd vanished, but he still rode in tight figure eights. The kids'd stopped following, and the tire finally flopped to the side. The rim ground against the sidewalk, and he toppled off and flopped onto his stomach. Ryan rushed over.

"C'mon, let's get you home, bro," Ryan said, picking him up by his elbow. "You're a fucking mess."

Angel bounced up and twisted away, then teetered across the street towards his house.

"Where the fuck you going, man?" Ryan said, following him.

"I'm going home, dog," Angel said over his shoulder with a constrained laugh.

"Let him go, Ry," I urged. Ryan stopped before he got to the street. "I'll put it up in the garage tonight."

Angel loped down the alley atop the uneven pavement and disappeared around the T. I hung a while, killed the bottle with Ryan, then brought the bike home to the garage. I stayed up, patched the inner-tube, and re-fit the tire. Then, I banged the fender back enough to allow the wheel to spin freely—something Angel could have done in half the time and with half the effort, but I did it anyway.

Being fourteen, it was hard for me to see how lucky I was. I thought I was in the same kind of boat as Angel and Ryan—just had a hard-ass for an old man who liked to beat the shit outta his sons. It's incredible how wrong a kid can be. I couldn't understand what it was like to have a dad that was mentally ill or locked up. Maybe none of us could understand what each other was going through, let alone understand what we were going through by ourselves. But at least we had each other to get through it together. At least we had each other.

■

RICH HAD TO SELL the Ramcharger after handmade neon-pink wanted posters of him started to circulate along Clark near the gay bar where he'd shot those guys with paintballs. He'd bought a little black Toyota pickup that had a lift kit and gigantic Mudder tires with gnarly tread.

He said there were some great dirt trails way west near Central Avenue for off-roading, and it was a blast. So, I went out there with him one weekend. It was a long ride, and he didn't start up with the ranting until we were almost there. Once he gets you in the tight cab of a vehicle, something comes over him, and he just starts to let you have it. The confined space shrinks. Trapped, you start having claustrophobia. Somehow he got on the subject of Blake recently becoming a Chicago police officer.

"I can't fucking believe Blakey's a cop. Crazy fucking shit the way things turn out. That accounting job he had flopped. They were paying him like twelve bucks an hour. He was nothing more than a secretary!!! Hahahah...."

We knifed through the tight, winding trails. The deep, water-filled ruts splashed up waves. We rambled on as the overgrown foliage slapped at the windows.

"That's why he took the test to become a copper. All of that money Ma and Dad paid for him to go to school, and he gets a gig chasing down fucking Ricans and niggers on the West Side! And you don't even need a degree to be a pig; all's you need is a high school diploma. I could go take the test right now, but fuck it, I wouldn't! I'm making more than him as a frickin' carpenter!"

We came into an opening, and there was a muddy pit with a half-built concrete manhole structure sitting in the center. Green-epoxied rebar sprouted up from the freshly stripped walls.

"But one good thing's come outta this: all his speechy crap about how blacks, browns and whites are equal and the same and should have the same opportunities—that's all gone now, man."

He floored it toward a path that twisted into greenery. "It took six months for him to wake up to the fact that they're all sewer rats. He's plain-clothed one night, picked up by some special gang unit, and he's sitting there on North Ave. right by Humboldt Park. Him and his partner got out of their unmarked squad car, and they're wearing black and yellow. All of a sudden, somebody shouts 'King Killa' from across the street and—Pop!-Pop!-Pop!— some little Spanish Cobra's shooting at 'em." We ascended a muddy hill, and Rich floored it. When we reached the top, there was nothing. The shocks sprang and locked out, and we vaulted into the air. Rich smirked at me through his tangled beard. We plummeted and landed in an explosion of mud, then we bound on.

Years later, I'd hear it from Blake himself during a lunch break—he was catching some extra hours as a carpenter, and I was working my summer vacation as a laborer.

"So, my partner, this fat Mexican guy named Perez, starts sprinting right at 'em. I figure I'll cut through the alley and head 'em off," Blake elaborated, then took a pull on the straw of his Wendy's cup of Coke. "I'm flying down that alley. I'm telling ya, I'm booking faster than frickin' Carl Lewis ever ran!" He laughed as I took a bite of my spicy chicken sandwich. The traffic on 55 howled past and made the cab of the pickup truck bobble. We sat on the shoulder, right in front of the Harlem Avenue bridge. "I can hear my partner firing on him with the .9—boom-boom-boom! I see an open gangway and cut through it, get to the mouth, and peek my head around, making sure I don't get caught in the crossfire. Then, the shooter screams out, throws the gun, and falls flat to his belly on the muddy grass. But I know he's not hit—he's fakin', playin' possum."

"I shout for Perez to stop shooting, dash out, snag the guy by his shoulders, and lift him up. Then, I realize his feet are dangling two feet off the ground. He's a kid—twelve years old, maybe, his face a smear of tears. But Perez is still running up, and in full-stride he kicks this kid in the balls so hard that he flies right up out of my grip and lands on the hood of the parked Chevy right next to us."

A malicious grin streaked across his face as he finished. My heart pulsed and squeaked. Images of my brother getting shot at flickered through my mind. I thought of his kids. What if Karen got a call in the middle of the night saying he was dead—gone—just like that?

A frowning sneer wrenched onto his mouth, and he gazed out onto the wide, sloping circle of yellow grass between us and the off ramp. "They're animals," he said, and threw the half-full Wendy's cup out the open window. He yanked the door lever and got out, then he slung his tool belt over his shoulders, bent, and yanked the cord on the gas-powered generator. It rippled and petered, then it rambled up to its steady roar. He stepped briskly into the shade of the concrete bridge; the long gray I-beams spanned its underbelly like ribs. The other truck and car doors strung along the shoulder yawned open slowly.

CHAPTER 17

PHYSICAL SCIENCE

IT'S FUNNY HOW WHEN YOU'RE A KID, one little spark can engulf you in flames.

I didn't try on the high school entrance exam, so they put me in the lowest track at Gordon Tech. I didn't really give a shit. School was never my thing, and this would make it easier to do less and still pass. Don't get me wrong—I listened to shit that interested me. It's just almost nothing I'd ever heard a teacher say sounded interesting.

That's when I stepped into the Mr. Dydecky's Physical World class—the dumb-kid physics. The room had faded linoleum tile floors with five rows of long black-topped tables spanning its width that sat four students each. I walked in and sat in back. Then, I flopped my tie on the table, folded my arms over it, slipped my chin into the nook of my elbow, and braced for boredom. A lot of the kids in there were on the football team—the big meathead linemen mostly. Dydecky was a young guy, maybe twenty-something. He was skinny and wore an off-yellow button-down shirt and a frickin' brown bow-tie. He had short, curly, black hair and wire-rimmed glasses. His thick, bushy unibrow wiggled on his face when he talked.

Everyone was bored out of their fucking minds, which was usual with the low-track. On the far side of the back row, a tall, lanky Polish kid exchanged shoulder shots with a pudgy Mexican kid with no neck; his head just popped out of his balloon of a torso like the top ball of a snowman. Both of them snickered and shrieked like a couple rejects.

Then, this guy Dydecky starts talking about physics. The motherfucker's blabbin' like ninety miles per hour about this shit and that. He's drawing multicolored pictures on the big white marker board and jumping from mechanics to thermodynamics without really making any connections. His hands are all trembling like he's got the shakes, and I started thinking the dude was having some kind of a breakdown! But then, he starts in on the universe, galaxies, the solar system, the sun, and what's going down in there. And his beady, brown eyes are glowing behind them glasses like the fuckin' guy's possessed by a demon! But the stuff he's talking about starts sparking shit off in my head. Got me thinking about everything—I mean *everything*.

I'd been hearing all this BS about Genesis for years, but the Hindus had their own creation story. Hell, some of the Native American tribes believed in the god of the Earth or the Sun. That shit made more sense to me than Allah or Yahweh or Zeus. The sun might have been the source of all life. Photosynthesis in plants, hell, even fundamental organisms like plankton needed light to thrive. I mean, what the hell was light, anyway? The shit is elemental to every day of my life, and I had no idea what it was even made out of.

I never spoke in class. Never paid much attention either, but all this talk was about something big—something beyond the bland bullshit of the day-to-day. It got my veins pulsing. All the distrust I had for the whole of education and religion was cleared—right then and there—hearing that scrawny little poindexter talking about physics. And I swear I was the only one listening. I looked a row up, and Owen, the fat-ass starting offensive tackle, was trying to see how many Starbursts he could stuff in his mouth at once without getting caught. Some little half-black kid in the front row with a giant light-brown afro was snoring so loud I could hear him in back. And Dydecky didn't even notice. He just kept going, rattling this shit off until the bell rang.

I found myself reading from the textbook at lunch. Reading! I barely knew anyone in the whole school! These motherfuckers were surely gonna think I was a fucking dork, but I didn't give a shit. I was looking up words: electromagnetic waves, gamma rays, photons.

And by that night, I find myself standing up in the middle of the garage giving a fucking lecture to Angel and Ryan as they worked on their bikes. Ryan was on one knee near the door, and his hands were all greased up with WD-40. The monkey wrench clamped down on the neck of my sister's old Huffy as he tried to get the rusted nut to turn to free the stem and ape hanger handlebars. Angel was sitting on the couch sanding down an old-school sprocket with a patch of fine sandpaper so he could get it chromed. And I'm standing under the naked bulb hanging down from the rafters shouting like I'm on a soapbox.

"The sun puts out, like, a few different kinds of those electromagnetic waves—light was just one spectrum, one energy level. And the colors aren't like you know 'em. Fuck that color-wheel crap you learn in art class—it don't mean nothin'. And white is when all the colors of light focus to one point, and black is the absence of light."

"You're making me dizzy, man," Ryan said, laughing.

"Naw, but what the sun is, is it's a big ball of hydrogen, ya know? Like the most basic element, but what's happening is there's so much of it—it's so dense—that it's compressing with all this energy 'cause of the gravity. It's heating up so fucking hot, and there's this thing that happens way inside: the hydrogen gets changed into helium."

"Like a balloon?" Ryan asked, flashing his crooked teeth at me.

"Yeah, but like, when that happens, it gives off, like, a nuclear explosion and emits all this radiation out into space. And part of it is light, but it also puts out X-rays and gamma rays and all kindsa rays. Gamma rays'll fucking kill your ass quick, but check this out: this reaction way down in the center of the sun... It's called *nuclear fusion.*"

"That's dope. Like lighting a fuse?" Angel asked, looking up for a second.

"Man, that's the name for the crew, man!" I urged.

"I don't know, man. It sounds like some nerdy shit to me," Ryan said as he gave me a dismissive wave, then went back to cranking on the monkey wrench.

"So fusion is like an explosion?" Angel asked, squinting up at me.

"Yeah, sorta. It's like a slow explosion of energy," I answered.

"And that's what makes the sun shine and warm and all that?" Ryan asked, looking up again. His brow furrowed.

"Yeah. It's about the pressure that brings things together to create something new, and then it's changed forever and can't never go back," I said.

Ryan scratched the peach-fuzz under his chin.

"Call it 'Fusion,' 'cause we down forever, and we emit motherfuckin' gamma rays! Fucking photon these motherfuckers!" I shouted.

Angel and Ryan burst out laughing.

Within three nights, *Fusion* was spray painted in neon-orange forty-seven times throughout the neighborhood. We even had to start burning our tag sketches out of our notebooks 'cause so many people were complainin'. Ryan did this big bubble-letter bomb on the side of 7-Eleven's red-brick wall that looked like shit but proclaimed our presence in the neighborhood like a foghorn blowin' in the dead of night.

■

I KNEW TANK wanted a piece of me. He was BB's uncle—seems like some fucked up math right? Well, I knew it was true because Tank had knocked out this fat Mexican kid over it. The kid had poked fun at their age difference and asked if he was sure they weren't cousins. Funny, after all the guys I'd seen Tank whomp over the years, I still thought I had a decent chance. He was twenty pounds heavier than me and not an ounce of it slack. I guess I just believed somewhere way deep inside myself that everyone was mortal, vulnerable. Even Tank.

I stood outside 7-Eleven with a few stoners and a couple hood rats and chatted as we drank Slurpees. Suddenly, I heard a shout up Clark and turned. I saw Tank sprinting straight towards me from about a block down. My heart pumped buckets. I readied—a cool buzz hummed in my fists. A plan unfolded in my head. I was gonna stay real still, wait until he got within arm's reach, then crack him and dodge to the side like a matador. But then, behind Tank, I saw T-Money, Monteff, and Twon, then BB lagging behind them. BB craned his head back and let out a high-pitched battle cry. T-Money clutched a pool stick or a cane—I couldn't be sure. I broke south on Clark along the sidewalk. Tank's footsteps pounded closer. I imagined him making a leaping tackle on me, so I cut out into traffic. A Checker Cab slammed on its brakes and horn as I cut through its headlights. I filed down the center of the two-lane traffic as car horns blew like a Beethoven symphony. Feeling them closing in, I made a split second decision and cut into Calo Restaurant. I decelerated and walked inside, then I strolled to the back and sat down at a vacant booth. There was a serrated steak knife sitting atop my napkin, so I picked it up and clutched it under the table, still breathless. I watched the door. They suddenly appeared at the window, argued, then Twon and BB sprinted back down the street. I saw T-Money mouth "Alley" to Tank, and I wished I'd thought of it first. Then, I wondered if I could have made it through the kitchen or if the cooks would have grabbed me. Hell, I didn't even know where the backdoor was. A waiter placed a black-leather menu on the white-clothed table.

"Anything to drink?" He asked, looking down at me.

"Naw, just water."

I looked up at him; he was a pudgy Dago in his 30's with a black unibrow.

"You alright, buddy?" he asked.

"What?"

"You're breathing kinda hard."

"Yeah, I'm cool."

"Alright." As he walked away he muttered, "What the fuck are those niggers doing out front?"

A Mexican busboy brought me some water and bread, then paused and stared out the front window.

I was surrounded. No way to get a hold of anyone to help me. If they came in, I knew I could stab the first one, maybe slip out in all the chaos of the blow-up. The bus boys'd probably jump in, maybe the waiter.

I had 40 bucks in my pocket, and when the waiter returned, I ordered linguine in clam sauce with some fried calamari as an appetizer. Figured that'd kill some time—make the fuckers wait if they're gonna get me. As the waiter walked away with my order, T-Money stepped through the door by himself. I slid out of the booth, stood, and showed him the blade. He grinned at it. Then, he slid into the booth and nodded for me to sit. I sat, reluctantly. He put his elbows on the table and smiled at me.

"Come on out, Joe. Tank want a word wit' you."

BILL HILLMANN *THE OLD NEIGHBORHOOD* 219

"You motherfuckers're gonna jump me."

"Naw, we ain't. With what Tank finna do to you, we won't need to jump you."

"Fuck that."

"Come out and get what you got comin'," he said as he stood. "Come out, or we comin' in." He walked out of the restaurant.

The waiter walked up after T-Money was gone.

"If those niggers out there are giving you a hard time, we could help you, kid."

"Naw, I'm fine. Thanks."

I tried to eat some of the bread. It was stale, and my hands were shaking real bad. What if they came in? I thought about running to the bathroom and locking the door behind me, but the cowardice of that made my eyes tear with disgust. Maybe he's right. Maybe I should just go out there and fight 'em. Fuck, cut 'em all up.

A dishwasher with a round, shaved head rolled his cart past my booth. "We'll fuck up them negritos wichu, homes," he whispered, then he flashed the crown.

"They're Stones," I said.

"Moe-Moes," he said, shrugging and walking away, "I don't like Moes anyways."

I started to relax a little—grateful for the camaraderie from these perfect strangers. They didn't have to do that.

Matter of fact, we would have been closer with the Kings, but they didn't like Angel. Called him a weto 'cause he was half-white, but it was still nice to know they had our backs.

I ate my meal very slowly, feeling them out there at the door and in the alley. It was so good that I kept forgetting my situation, then suddenly, I'd snap back to attention and arch up to see out the front window and catch one of them slipping past, snarling into their reflection in the glass. I waited for it, devising new plans—seeing the busboys, cooks, and the dishwasher pouring out from the back with rolling pins, frying pans, and butcher knives in hand, all grateful for a break in the monotony. Then, T-Money's face shifting as he made his new calculations. I wouldn't even need the knife then. We'd whomp these motherfuckers up and toss 'em out on the sidewalk.

I started to laugh. The tremble in my hands eased, and I stayed at Calo's for a very long time. I left a ten buck tip, and the Busboy walked out front with me. We looked up and down Clark as it quieted. Across the street, two cute girls walked down the sidewalk holding hands. Kinda funny to think how the TJO's, Stones, Kings, and Spanish Cobras were all warring for power, but it'd end up that lesbians would take over the neighborhood. It was about 11 by then. I'd been inside a couple hours.

"What is you, a TJO?" the busboy asked.

"Nothing. My brother's a TJO," I answered.

"I work here every night of the week, man, OK?"

"Thanks, man." We shook, and he stepped inside.

I took a deep breath and jogged it home, watching the shadows for movement.

■

THINGS WERE GOOD. The potheads were coming from miles around. Even some of the stoners from Gordon were making the trip just to get another taste of them fat sacks of Red Hair we'd been scattering out like birdseed.

We were keeping it cool, but Angel kept sneaking off to toke on his plastic cigarette imitation one-hitter that he'd bought off Rich. He'd come back all red-eyed and giggling. He wasn't skimpin'—he was throwing his money down just like any of 'em. It just made him talk more, and that kept the night moving, rumbling with laughter and that melody of words between people.

"Hey, man," Ryan said as he slid off his sill. "I got to run over to my place real quick and grab dem last few bags."

"I'll go with ya," I said, hopping up. "Alright, Angel, we'll be right back."

"Alright, but if I get kidnapped by some Latin Queens and held for ransom while they try to make me one of their own, it'll be on your guys' conscience."

"Hey, by the time we get back, this motherfucker'll be in mascara," I remarked to Ryan with a smile.

We stepped into the alley tunnel. The fog sifted up from the vents in the sidewalk like there was a fire smoldering beneath the concrete. I glanced back and saw Angel fumbling in his front pants pocket for the one-hit kit.

When we got to the Dead-End-Docks, it was vacant, like an evacuation zone before a disaster. The silence hummed. It wasn't 'til we rounded the lot that I saw them—Monteff and Tank—standing at the mouth of the side alley right where it touched Paulina. It was like they'd seen us coming and were just waiting for us. I was glad I'd came. Glad it wasn't Ryan alone.

We stopped on the sidewalk with only the width of the lot between us. Ryan's goofy grin beamed, and he jutted his thick chin upward as he rocked on his toes.

"What up?" Ryan said. The nervous joy squealed through his throat.

"Shit," Monteff replied, flashing teeth. "Well, my boy here want a word wit' your boy about some'n went down a few weeks back wit' lil BB."

Tank's wide forehead flexed and sent two lines shooting across its width. My heart squeaked in my ears, and it was like one of them dentist's suction tubes instantly slurped all the saliva outta my mouth.

"So it's one-on-one, den?" Ryan asked. Then, he scanned his head to see all the spots they could be lurking: the dark-green dumpster in the corner of the alley; the beat-up, white-paneled van across the street; the warped, paint-peeled corner of Ryan's garage.

"One-on-one," Monteff said, dropping his chin to his throat and glancing down at the tips of his red and black Filas.

"Think I need help to whoop dis bitch?" Tank said, trudging out into the street near the dead end wall. One streetlamp hovered above like a spotlight on the worn, gray and purple blacktop. Its surface rumpled like a thin film of sizzling grease.

Tank hefted his shirt up over his head and flopped it on the ground. His torso heaved. The whites of his eyes beamed starkly against his black skin, and the hulking blocks of muscle at his shoulders and chest levitated over his narrow waist like helium balloons.

It felt like someone tied a rope around my waist and was dragging me out toward the street. The grass felt like mush under the soles of my Pumas. I figured I could make a show of it boxing. I'd run, punch, then run again. I figured he'd be slow with all that muscle. I figured he couldn't hurt me as bad as the old man did. Wrong. Wrong. Wrong.

"Steal off dat fool like he stole on your nephew," Monteff shouted from the curb.

When I got close to Tank, he raised his wide fists to his shoulders. His knuckles were bone gray like the skin was transparent. He bared his teeth in a mid-grimace smile and twisted. A wide punch launched out from his shoulders. I lost it in the darkness as I tried to duck, and it bashed into my ear like a sledgehammer, erupting a screaming siren through my head. I tottered to the side. I could see Tank's face laughing as he hopped backward. The siren faded to a steady, panging bell. I threw a punch from far away that missed by yards. Tank lunged forward, and another punch cracked into my forehead. A pulsing pain filled my cranium. Dark, microscopic circles floated upward in my vision like tiny bubbles. I threw a weak, tentative left into the air. Tank bobbed back. His fists now clasped at his waist. The laughter rose up over the bells.

I heard Ryan's voice moan from the curb: "Come on, Joe!"

I stepped forward and punched again. Tank swung with me and his fist collided with my forehead as I was still mid-swing. I forgot where I was. I felt like I'd just woken up. My legs were like jelly, and my balance drug me backwards.

"Come on, get this shit over wit'! Even I'm embarrassed for him," Monteff's voice swirled in.

Tank stepped forward. I tried to grab him around the waist. He hip-tossed me. My legs cartwheeled up, parallel with my stomach, and I slammed to the blacktop on my side. A swift pain stabbed my ribs, and I clutched them as he swung his leg over my torso. He hunched over me and peered down. He looked like a faceless black ghost as this foggy orange light emanated around his silhouette. Then, from a standing position, he raised his fist and slammed it down, hard. It crashed it into my jaw. I raised my forearms over my face. He crashed his fists into my head and arms.

Ryan shouted, "That's it, man! That's enough!" as he pushed his forearm into Tank's chest. Monteff wrapped his arms around Tank's from behind and pulled him back.

"Don'tchu fuck with my nephew, you motherfuckin' white boy," Tank shouted as he and Monteff walked away, laughing.

Ryan helped me up and gave me a disappointed look. "Man, why didn't you even fight back, man?"

"Shit, that motherfucker hits hard," I said, wobbling, still in a haze.

My head hummed, and I could barely stand on my own. Ryan walked me back to my house. I went up in my room, closed the door, and shut the lights off. I'd realized my chain—my crucifix, the one Lil Pat'd given me—was gone. It must have broken in the fight. I called Ryan, and he went and looked everywhere, but it was nowhere to be found. That was just too much for me to take right then, and after I hung up, I cried for the first time in as long I could remember. I fought to be quiet—I screamed silently, furious with myself.

I'd been a coward.

Maybe I couldn't have beaten Tank. Maybe he was just a better street fighter. A bigger, stronger athlete. But I hadn't even tried—too scared to even go down swingin'. I cried until the anger took over, and this deep upwelling of a cool numbness rose from the base of my skull. It stretched into a tense trembling throughout my whole body—rage pulsed in my chest until I knew I'd rather kill myself than cry another tear, and they stopped then.

I promised myself: never again. I'd never let that shit happen again. Never let the fear of pain keep me from action. Never be a coward. I'd rather die. I figured dyin'd feel a whole lot better than I did right then.

The anger faded, and I continued to grapple with what'd happened. I'd lost a heads-up, mano-a-mano. There was honor in that, or at least that's what I tried to convince myself. But at my foundation, I was innately wrong. Something underneath it was wrong. What I'd done was wrong. This was revenge for jumping in on DeAndre and for punching little ass BB. I realized there was no conviction in the way I'd fought Tank, and it was for just that reason—I was wrong. Hell, I might have even deserved it. Maybe I was punishing myself in the way I fought. That's when I decided to never be in the wrong again in violence—to only fight when I had to and for the right side. To protect and defend. I was sure that I'd fight hard and brave then. Otherwise, there'd be nothing behind me—inside me—and I'd lose every time.

■

MISERABLE AND ASHAMED, I stayed in the next few days.

I was lumped up pretty bad from the ass whoopin', but the

only thing visible was an abrasion along my left temple that dried and flaked off before the weekend came. I thought a lot about what they'd say. Nothing is real until it's been put to words, and the look on Ryan's face that night—the disgusted sneer; the disappointed, droopy-eyed silence—gave him away. Then, there was T-Money and all those motherfuckers. I could hear them talking and laughing in my head—or maybe not. Maybe it was my own mind laughing at what I'd thought I was. People lose fights every day in one way or another. There's lot of losing going on in this world.

■

GRAMMA K HAD ASKED ME OVER to help clear some crap out of a back room in her basement. It was like a tomb down there. Mainly old shit from when she had her doll making school: cracked porcelain baby faces without eyes; tiny, blond nylon wigs; stubby arms with no torsos, like the remnants of some horrible explosion. There were boxes of it, like cardboard coffins stacked up to the ceiling.

After a few minutes of working, the dust billowed up and was swirling around like a dust demon. Then, I came across this plastic milk crate full of books: *A Brief History of Time* by Stephen Hawking, *Coming of Age in the Milky Way* by Timothy Ferris, and several books on the theory of relativity and the Big Bang. I thumbed through 'em—it was just like physics class, except with more depth. It was like physics class was stuck in our solar system. These books were getting out deeper, further back in time and scope, reaching out in all directions.

Gram came down with her wig off—something she only did when it was just close family around. Her hair was short and thinning and combed back straight. I remembered the first time I saw her like that when I was real little. I was shocked, and, not recognizing my own Gramma, I burst into tears. But now, she just seemed worn out, swaying on her arthritic knees. Her house dress dangled like a curtain around her wide belly, and she gripped a chicken salad sandwich wrapped in a square of paper towel, and a glass of milk. She handed me the cool glass, reached in her dress pocket, and came out with a bottle of aspirin. She shook a pair into my palm. "You could use a little protein, Joe. You're running on fumes," she said.

"Thanks." I sat down on a little wooden stool near the crate of books. "You're the best."

"Before he died, Da said you might want these books some-day." She waved her hand toward the crate. "You were his favorite, Joe. You were the one that was the most like him. The same wavelength, Joey." She raised her dark eyebrows.

"Yeah?" I put the empty glass down and picked up the black hardcover of *Coming of Age in the Milky Way.*

"It's true, you both spoke the same language. Pick through them a little bit." She looked at me and added, "I'm sixty-seven years old, and I've yet to see anyone eat a sandwich that fast."

"You make good ones."

"Harry Houdini," she said. "I'll make you another one."

"I'm watchin' my weight," I grinned.

"I know, you're stuffed." She took the glass and turned for the stairs. "Do your grandfather a favor: pick out a few books… Life is an ongoing education, Joey."

I flipped through the glossary in back of the book I was holding.

DARK MATTER: Matter whose existence is inferred on the basis of the orbits of stars and galaxies but which does not show up as bright objects such as stars or nebulae.

I'd never even heard of half of it.

I remembered Da always reading in the kitchen—a mound of

ash and butts in the tray. He'd peer down into the pages through his black-rimmed, rectangular bifocals. His weathered, saggy face creased. The peppering of stubble on his cheeks. His shock of black hair slicked back and shiny. The ceiling light above the kitchen table emitting this hazy, orange glow on him. The silence of the room. The ceiling fan flicking slowly above. I thought of how he was adopted and raised by poor immigrants in a garage. How he had to work as a kid during the depression. How he taught himself to read. And here I was screwing around in school my whole life, never doing my homework and barely passing anything.

I finished up, headed home and up to my room to read.

Da was like that. He thought about other people. He cared about his grandkids deeply. He was a good guy, and I missed him. It was like, by reading these books, I was getting to know him on a different level—not as a kid and a grandpa, but as a young man and an old man. It was like somehow we could commune through the pages.

I was up there for hours, blazing through passages, looking up words. I'd never really liked reading. Never read a novel, let alone a whole book on astrophysics. I was finding something in them that I couldn't find in church or the Bible. It seemed like they were trying to answer something bigger. I mean, if God made the world, fine, but who made God? If the Big Bang was the beginning, then why does it say gasses condensed before the explosion? If there were already gases, then the Big Bang isn't a theory of the origins of existence. Maybe it was a big moment for us, but nothing beside the real scope.

I was looking for something. Call it what you want: symmetry, balance, peace. I figured life, human beings, were chaos. These racing emotions—love, hatred, all of it—were ugly, false, bullshit. We were animals capable of bringing our nightmares into reality. There weren't no answers there.

I was finding answers in these books.

FUSION

YOU CAN ONLY GET CHASED home from school so many times before you either get caught or stop running.

Life at Senn was getting worse for Ryan and Angel. T-Money, Twon, Tank, and Monteff were all full-blown Black Stones now and still bent on retaliation for what'd gone down with DeAndre. Ryan and Angel had to sneak through the halls and go into the bathroom together—one watched at the door while the other ran in and pissed. Then, at three-fifteen, they'd sneak out a side exit and jog their asses all the way back to the neighborhood. The TJOs weren't showing no love. They was on their own—blowin' in the wind.

Gordon had the day off, so I decided I'd go over and walk 'em home. I let 'em know, and they told me where to wait for 'em. I made the lonesome walk to Senn. Hollywood to Clark, past the dusty entrance to the corner store where the sunlight beat down on the chipped-tile entrance way. I passed the flower shop. All the un-bought daisies bowed and browned in the early autumn chill. I cut down Ardmore. Tall, tan-and-red brick apartment buildings lined either side of the street, and tin-sided bungalows and two-flats cowered in between 'em. I found myself looking up along the rooftops half-expecting to see some lookout catch me sneaking through. As I got to Ridge, there was this old lady in a house dress leaning out her third-story window with her hair all full of purple plastic curlers. Her weathered face scowled down at me as she peered out behind huge clear-framed glasses. There was a squad of pigeons in the center of the street near the crosswalk. They squawked as they gouged out chunks from a stale piece of bread. They tossed it up with quick shakes of their heads, and their oily, blue neck-feathers furrowed so they glistened purple in the afternoon sunlight.

Senn was even more menacing up close. It was a block wide and half that deep. The thick Greek-style pillars stretched three stories to the pitched roof, and the crisp cleanliness of the tan concrete gave it a chilling sense of justice and learning. Though, the maroon steel-mesh fencing over the windows hinted at the filth and horror inside its walls festering like innards of a carcass. The park that spanned out behind the school was empty. It was silent like a prison yard during a lockdown. There was the faint trickle of the city water fountain at the far-end. Traffic flicked past in gusts. The peacefulness in the park sat in stark contrast with its history. On weekend nights, its darkness was amplified by the thick-leaved trees. Endemic gunfire lit the heavy darkness like lightning flashes. Many gangbangers'd shot and stabbed each other there. There'd been more than a few horrific beatings with ball bats, fists, and chains along those twisting asphalt paths. I thought of Abraham Lincoln sitting down at the edge of the park.

What would he do?

Ridge Ave. cut through the neighborhood on a diagonal, and the intersection at Ardmore made the tan-bricked building on the corner across from Senn come to a sharp point like an arrowhead. I figured no one could sneak up on me from over there, and I'd have a good view of the side door they'd come out of. The jostling, yellow-and-brown-leafed oak trees cast a deep shadow on Ardmore where it passed beside Senn's south wing. As I crossed Ridge, the school bell let out its low buzz. Suddenly, the building came alive—vibrant, humming like a teakettle getting ready to scream. I hurried across the street and hid behind the jutting corner.

Suddenly, feet clapped the pavement. I craned my head around and looked east on Ardmore. Tank sprinted in a low hunch wearing a black Dago-T. He surged up the shadowed walkway like a fullback hitting a hole, and T-Money trotted after him, gripping the front of his blue jeans so they wouldn't fall off his ass. He had on a black Raiders cap twisted sideways to the left like a clown. I dove behind the corner and pressed my back to the bricks. My chest sputtered as my notion of a safe walk home for Ryan and Angel was shattered like a windshield bashed-in with a crowbar. I slipped my head near the edge of the bricks and peeked around the corner.

"We gon' catch dese mothafuckas today!" Tank screamed. He squeezed his fists at his sides. His heavy arms flared.

Then, Twon shot round the corner in an XL white t-shirt and red jeans. He grinned as he chased after them.

Suddenly, I couldn't breathe. It was like the wires tied up all my chest tubes in knots. I started to jog away up Ridge. My legs felt languorous. It felt like someone was pumping my stomach up with helium more and more. I bent at the waist. Vomit erupted from my mouth and nostrils. Bright orange splattered the cracked sidewalk slab. I hunched over it. My own shadow reflected in the murky pool. I wiped the slime from my lips with my trembling wrist. Goo clogged my nasal passages. My eyes teared. I stood up and took a deep breath—hollow, weak, and resolved. *There was no fuckin' way. If they're gonna stomp us again, it's gonna be together.* I turned back.

I slowed when I got to the corner and peered around it. Nothing. Everyone waited. T-Money and Twon pressed their backs to the wall around the corner from the exit. Tank stood right out front. He rocked his weight slowly, side-to-side. Tank watched the metal doors like a tiger waiting to be fed. There was a dreamy haze in his still face. His arms showed bulbous out of his Dago-T. My shoulder scraped across the gnarly bricks as a rickety Diesel box truck howled past on Ridge.

Suddenly, one of the school's doors burst open. Ryan sprang out and down the steps in his beige Dickies and a loose white t-shirt. He looked back over his shoulder into the closing door.

"Come on, man!" Ryan shouted back as he jogged forward like a guy about to walk blindly into a light pole.

Tank swoop-stepped to Ryan, then he hefted a wide punch from his waist. It thumped into the base of Ryan's jaw and deadened him. He fell clean out onto the grass beside the exit.

My knees were jumping up to my chest before I realized I was running—it was like an out of body experience. I sprinted right into it with absolutely no fucking idea what I was gonna do. T-Money and Twon ran around the corner and yanked on the door handles. I saw Angel in the little meshed-glass window. He held 'em locked. His face'd gone stone white.

Tank raised up his black and red Jordan high-top and stomped down on Ryan's head. I broke from the shade into the sunlight. Not one of 'em so much as glanced back at me. Now, I was on the sidewalk, and I figured out what I was gonna do.

As I got up behind Tank, he twisted his thick neck. His eyes flashed at me. They trembled with rage, or maybe shock, or maybe fear. I didn't stop. I just aimed the meaty end of my forearm at his throat. He raised his arms feebly at the last second. My forearm stuck in like I'd jammed it into a mound of wet concrete. I drove my legs and pole-axed Tank. His feet flew out from under him. The collision jarred me to an absolute halt. Tank landed, traps first, on the grass beside Ryan. The soles of his Jordans appraised the sky as both his hands reached blindly for his thorax. Ryan's eyes flashed to mine from between his arms. He rolled to his side and got up.

"What de fuck!" T-Money yelled, spinning around toward me. He leapt down the steps.

Angel's eyes lit up, then his face disappeared from the window. Suddenly, the door Twon tugged on exploded open, and Angel's leg sprang out with it waist-high. Twon stumbled backward down the steps, trying to catch his balance. Angel leapt out and snagged Twon's front collar, then began to wallop his fist into Twon's shocked face. Twon reeled backward. His hands reached and grasped out at the air for balance.

I was so awestruck with the way Angel was getting down that I didn't even react when T-Money sprang at me and grabbed me in a bear hug.

"We gotchu now, white boy," he whispered. His hot Fritos breath swirled in my face.

I dipped my chin and drove my forehead into his mouth. I felt a click and something gave. He seethed through his teeth and swung a hard punch that planted into the nub behind my ear. I went cross-eyed, and my knees wobbled. I heard a hollow thump and saw Ryan's beet-red face flash at my side. Then, Ryan reeled back again and swung high. I caught the glimmer of the metal seatpost bar we'd cut out of a bike frame. This time, it came down over the top of T-Money's head with a metallic crack, like an aluminum bat just got a good piece of a fastball. T-Money crumbled. He grasped at my shirt to keep from slipping to the concrete.

I looked out at Angel, who'd just shoved Twon out into the street, sending him rolling on his back. Twon's head cracked against the blacktop. His white Reeboks flew up in the air. A green Taurus came to a screeching stop and nearly hit him.

I kneed T-Money straight in the heart. He rocked onto his backside, gripping his chest like he'd been stabbed.

"Ahhh shit!" a voice rocketed over the chaos. Monteff and five others poured out of the main west exit of the school.

Tank got to his hands and knees and crawled out onto the sidewalk in a stupor. Ryan swung his leg back and booted Tank straight in the face. He didn't miss a stride as we all broke across Ridge. The traffic squealed to a halt as we dashed past. When we hit the mouth of Ardmore, the squad of pigeons blew up in a flutter of blue and gray. The old lady gawked from her window perch. Her bottom jaw hung open, toothless.

We ran the whole five blocks back to my alley hooting and hollering like a pack of wild dogs lumbering through the forest. No one even chased us after the first twenty feet. We finally stopped running out back of Angel's garage.

"How the fuck? How the fuck we get outta dere OK?" Ryan asked.

No one answered. All of us hunched over into a loose huddle with our hands on our knees. Our humped backs swelled and deflated. I caught eyes with Ryan, and the emerald-green looked like it'd been splashed with acid. The tiny tentacles in the splatters flared neon, and I saw all the things that made us best friends. His lips started to curl at the edges, and mine did, too, until we grinned. Then, his whole front row of teeth shone at me—all crooked like Stonehenge. Light-red blood lined the bottom row. I bared teeth right back.

"Oh my God…. Oh my God…. Oh my God…," Angel murmured as he sat down on his backside. He laid flat in the thin rectangle of shade cast by the overhang of his garage.

T-Money'd ripped my t-shirt, so I hefted it up over my head and walked out to the center of the alley with the afternoon sun baking my damp skin. Sweat beads dripped off my shoulders, and I started to jump in a rhythm. My sneakers panged off the cracked alley pavement, and I bounded as high as I could. I raised my shirt over my head and swung it in wide circles as electric pulses flashed in my vision like fireworks were bursting inside my skull. This warm joy surged up in my chest, and I had to get it all out. My chest would explode if it wasn't unleashed—I knew that much. Squealing noises erupted from my throat—wild screeches that echoed off the narrow corridor of garages. My heart pounded so hard I could hear my own pulse throb in my ears. I'd completed my quest. I'd been re-born a warrior, righteous and true and loyal to the bone.

■

THAT NIGHT, we were down at the sills when the Lincoln floated up.

"Hey, look who it is," Mickey said, parking the Lincoln in front of the hydrant. A guy they called "Chief" slouched in the passenger seat. He had short, curly, blond hair and a chiseled Nordic face. He peered at us and smirked. Mickey turned to him and whispered something, then Chief nodded and aimed his long, bony finger at each one of us separately while he whispered back. Mickey got out of the Lincoln, which was strange; he never got out unless he had business to attend to. He peered at us with his chin tucked into his wide, hairy neck. A sly smirk slid across his lips.

"Word is in the neighborhood your little crew here is at war with the P Stones," he said, stepping towards us slowly. "Whata you guys call yourself?"

"Fusion," Ryan said, stepping towards Mickey and jutting his chin up like some corporal at attention. His imbecilic smirk snuck into his lips.

"Fusion…," Mickey repeated. His smile grew as he stomped the rest of the distance between them. "Come here, you little fucker." Mickey grabbed Ryan by his head and kissed his forehead with a loud smack. "You whooped them niggers good, didn'tcha?" He hugged Ryan's head to his chest.

"They said it was all three of ya," Mickey said, turning his urgent eyes on me. "What the hell? You ditch school for your boys or somethin'?" He grabbed my shoulder, and I felt the weight and power of his frame, but there was warmth in his hand as he looked me in the eyes. "Your brother'd be proud of you," he said.

"Thanks, Mickey," I said. My eyes burnt as I grimaced.

"And you, I knew you had some chink in ya. Fucking jump-kicking the door open on 'em?" Mickey said, glancing at Angel, then back at Chief in the Lincoln.

"He's the one, right?" Mickey asked.

Chief nodded. His wide smile stretched across his face and made him look like The Joker. His Adam's apple bobbed as he laughed.

"Your last name's German, right?" Mickey asked, looking back at Angel, who nodded. "Hey, that's good enough for me... That good enough for you, Chief?" he asked over his shoulder.

Chief laughed and shouted, "As long as he keeps jump-kicking niggers, it is." They both cracked up.

Mickey walked over to one of the sills and took a seat. We huddled around him.

"Like I told ya," Mickey said, popping a Camel Filter in his mouth. Angel struck his lighter as Mickey patted his pockets. "The brothers have been keeping an eye on ya... But... We can't go breaking up the Nation every time the peewees get into a scrap," Mickey shrugged. "And you three made it out alive. Hell, ya did a whole lot better than making it out alive," he said, smiling and showing his blackened bottom row of teeth. "Big things happening here, boys... Big things." Then, he got up and walked toward the car. "You're well on your way, all of youse... Fusion?" He scratched his head, then he stopped and looked back. "What the fuck's dat even mean?"

I started to answer, but then Ryan piped in, "It's when three combine to make one."

Mickey paused, then he nodded at us and got into the Lincoln. "Tomorrow, you three are all taking the day off a school. Come by the house around noon. We're gonna take a little ride over to old Senn and straighten things out." He threw it in gear. "Fucking kids," he said to Chief as the Lincoln drifted away from the curb.

■

A LITTLE WHILE LATER, the Good Girls showed up with hoop earrings dangling through their crimped curls and shiny nameplate necklaces glinting under their sparkly, lip-glossed smackers. Their New Wave bangs arched up stiffly over their bright eyes. They approached in a tight, little huddle like a flock of chicks, murmuring and giggling. When they got close, the huddle broke and Hyacinth was in the center. Her hair curled in twisted strands as dark-red streaks twirled into it—the color of strawberry jam. She trembled against the mid-September night breeze, and her dark eyes flickered. Her braces flashed at me between her glossy lips.

We decided it was a good night to drink those bottles of wine we'd stolen out of Seth's basement, so we headed to the garage.

Hyacinth and I ended up in the "Boom-Boom Room," as Angel called it. We'd sectioned off a corner of the garage with a metal shelving unit and butted the loveseat against the back of the couch. The girls put on a mixtape with a bunch of Boyz II Men songs and some other hit R&B crap, but it suddenly wasn't crap anymore. All those lovesick, moaning lyrics we'd been making fun of for years suddenly struck a chord. They made my chest ache as I held Hyacinth around the waist with her legs bent and folded over my thighs. My whole body completely relaxed, and I melted into the uneven padding of the old loveseat.

There was the smell of WD-40 and her Watermelon Wave Bubblicious chewing gum. She raised her hand and softly touched my cheek with her fingertips, then her eyes went from mine to her fingernails.

"Almost," she said to herself.

"Almost what?" I said, smirking.

"Almost matched the color." She took her hand from my cheek and looked down at her fingernails.

"To what?"

"Your eyes." She flashed her almond eyes to mine, then dropped them back down to her nails.

"That's the color?" I took her other hand in mine and looked at her dark-blue nails.

"No, just one of 'em. There's like five. They're like two blue fireballs. It's just my favorite one is this one—almost." She looked at her fingernails again.

I stared into her glimmering eyes, and her damp lips collided into mine with a slow smush before I felt I'd even moved. Her body still tense, I slipped my hand on her thigh.

Everything seemed to move faster this night—the endless maze of kissing her neck and lips, the curling and twisting tongues, her breath fast and warm on my face. I slipped my hand up her short shorts and rubbed the edges of her panties. She gripped my wrist but didn't push it away. Then, my finger was under the panties touching the trimmed hairs. I found the opening of warm, wet flesh. She gasped with the music flooding over all of it, then her hand left my wrist and gripped my dick, which was strained tight against my pants. She squeezed hard on the head, then she shocked me—she slipped her hand down my boxers and touched skin. Her hand was cool and eager. I had two fingers inside her, twirling them slowly, and I was amazed by the instant reactions on her face—her eyes shocked—choking back a cry. Then, she stopped me and spun around on the loveseat, panting in my face.

She pulled my dick out of my waistband so just the head peaked out. I put my hand on her back and she slowly bowed-down with her tongue sticking out between her braces. She licked the head—it sent a sudden jolt of electricity through my legs, and I almost screamed. She popped upright, shushing me excitedly. Then, she giggled, and I softly guided her head down. She took the tip of my dick into her mouth. Her whole body trembled. I stared at the top of her head. Just the thought of those perfect lips touching me there—it was too much. I threw my head back into the cushion and came like I was having a grand mal seizure. I heard the moan before I realized it was happening and coming from me. Then, I cut it off as she caught the pumping cum in her mouth. This choking laughter came from the couch behind us, then the rest of the garage broke up. She slurped down the cum and sat upright covering her mouth. She looked at me horrified like she'd just committed a mortal sin. There was a silent second. Both of us froze, then we burst into laughter, and I eased my deflating, wet dickhead back into my pants.

She took a few deep swallows of wine, and we curled up together and stayed like that until she had to go.

I lifted the garage door just enough for the girls to duck under, and they shuffled out, prancing into the alley. Their giggles lifted up to the night.

I shut the door, took a deep breath, and exhaled. Ryan offered his opened pack of menthols. We all took one, and Angel sparked a light for us.

"You ever fuck a black chick?" Ryan asked, looking at me.

"No," I said with an obvious ring. I mean, he knew I was a fucking virgin.

"Man, I gotta get me a black chick," Ryan said, casting his imbecilic grin at Angel.

"There's Monica," Angel said as he puffed his smoke.

"She's too young," Ryan replied with a false tone.

"She's thirteen," I said. "She's just a year younger than you, man."

"She's hot, ain't she?" he said to Angel, then looked at me. "Ain't she hot, Joe?"

"Come on, man. That's like talking about my little cousin or something," I said, spitting in disgust. "Shit, I played doctor wit' her when I was seven, for Christ's sake!"

"How far you get?" he said. His crooked teeth glowed in the garage lamps.

"You sicko," I replied, looking away.

"Ryan's a fuckin' pedophile," Angel said, glancing at me sideways.

"Naw, but what happened tonight? We all heard your ass squealing. What, she jack you off or something?" Ryan asked, his voice squeaking with excitement.

The glow in my face and eyes gave it all away. They both just patted me on the back before we finished the bottles and called it quits.

■

THAT NIGHT I LAY AWAKE. My whole body felt like I was floating two inches off the bed, and every few minutes I'd burst into laughter. The old man even had to call out from down the hall for me to 'Shut the hell up!' When I did sleep, it felt like I was falling. Then, I'm running in pitch-black. I can hear the panting. The heavy, thumping gate behind me closing in—no way out. Running, running as hard as I can. My strides elongate slower and longer. I can't go any further. Then, I just stop. I turn around, and the Beast is before me, hunched up on its hind legs, panting and blowing tufts of steam out of its glossy, black nostrils. I look in its eyes—black mirrors reflecting my own horrified face. Light flickers in my periphery. I peer down at my upturned palms. The flashes pulse. Blue, purple and red strands of light twist through each other like electric flames in my palms. Then they formed into a perfect global sphere like a sun. The power's in my hands now. The Beast tilts its head and looks down at it, then he unleashes a sudden, deep snorting inhale.

Something ripped from his torso and splatter-clapped to the ground. Slippery, black innards dangle from his hollowed out ribcage. Nothing. A full hide of mangy fur levitating. The buffalo head hung. The bear snout and dark lips tremble over small saw blade teeth. Black drool dangles at the creases, falling in long strands. An inch-thick, festering, dark-purple wound starts above its eye and stretches up, then disappears at the top of its skull. Then, inside the wound, miniature white maggots crawl and twist in the flesh. Its frame frozen and slumped like it's hanging from a meat hook. Its eyes like two solid-black marbles. Ape arms, a curved back, and stubby legs like a hyena. It releases a horrified howl, bellowing into the vast blackness. There are mountains on the horizon, and their cliffs are cracked and jagged like the thick chunks of broken ice undulating atop the lake in January. A peach haze above the cliffs silhouettes them. The aura fades sharply to the pitch-black dome above.

I reach up toward its face—the orb of twisting light hovers in my palm. As my fingertips touch his damp, cold snout, he instantly melts into strings of black tar that flop into a puddle at my feet. The strands of light in the sphere reflect off the pool, flickering across the surface.

CHAPTER 19

PEOPLES

THE NEXT DAY, we hung out over at Angel's in the morning, then headed over to the Bryn Mawr house.

Ryan led us up the porch steps and through the screen door. We passed three guys lounging on beat-up couches in the front room watching cartoons who didn't look up when we walked in. All of their eyes were glazed over with dull grins across their stubbled faces. Mickey was in the kitchen with Chief. They sat at a flimsy, white plastic table finishing up their bowls of Cap'n Crunch in water.

We got in the Lincoln and drove around the neighborhood for a while, then we headed over to Senn. School had already let out, and hundreds of kids milled past toward Clark Street. Blacks, whites, Mexicans, Asians—just about every race you could imagine. We pulled up to the south wing.

The Lincoln parked across the street near the corner that I'd hid behind the day before. Brilliant, white light cascaded down and glimmered off of the faded-green leaves of the trees sprouted up on both sides of the narrow one-way street. There were several

Black Stones reclined against the tan building in the shade. Ten or so TJOs huddled across the street. They leaned up against a red-brick apartment building. From their positions, the two groups could watch each other's backs. A set of Kings lurked past the basketball courts and sat at benches along the blacktop path that snaked through the park.

Ryan glanced at me as we got out. His face creased in the bright light, then he nodded to where T-Money stood amongst the Stones, glaring at us. I could hear Mickey's labored, rattling breath as he walked around the front end and up to where we stood on the lawn beside the curb.

"You three stay here," Mickey said. "I'll be right back." He sighed to Chief, who nodded in response. His sucked-up cheek-bones made him look like Frankenstein. Mickey walked up to the row of Stones, and a short, stout, dark-skinned black guy in a gray Dago-T stepped up to meet him. He had two fist-sized five-point stars tattooed at the front of each shoulder.

"What up, Mickey? What up, peeps," he said loudly with a wide, toothy smile. A thick McDonald's straw with the brown and yellow stripes extended from his teeth.

They shook hands and spoke quietly, then walked toward us.

"You guys remember this place, don'tcha?" Chief said as he leaned against the Lincoln. He laughed, and veins pulsed in his long neck. We stood close to each other. I stuck my trembling hands in the pockets of my jeans, Angel crossed his arms over his stomach, and Ryan glowered back at Chief and scratched at the growth of red hair speckled at his Adam's apple.

Mickey and the black guy walked over. The black guy's scalp was a lined-up grid of tightly-bound dreadlock nubs that looked like a series of wilted baby tarantulas. He was all neck. His traps hung like two mounds of dough below his ears. They got within arm's reach and stopped. There was the stench of salty sweat and lime.

"So, Shorty," Mickey said as he squinted at the black guy. "Word is some of your Stones got a beef with these boys. Well, that's gotta stop."

"Yeah, I got word of the scuffle yesterday. Ya know, they put one of my Stones' little cousins in the hospital a few weeks back," Shorty said, squinting. Perspiration glinted off his brow, and a trail of three inked teardrops dripped down his cheek from the corner of his left eye.

Mickey shot a scowl at Ryan, who glanced back, then dropped his eyes to the pavement.

"Now, Shorty, I'm coming here today as your brother in the Nation, and I'm coming to say, as far as you're concerned, these three are ridin' wit' the Five," Mickey said, then raised his stubby hand toward the three of us. All our eyes shot up at him. "As far as their status with the TJOs is concerned... Well, that's my department."

Shorty looked down and took the straw from his mouth—the end was all chewed up and twisted. He stared at us coldly with his head tilted to the side. "So y'all's in when dem Folks run up?" he asked.

We all nodded.

Shorty paused and scanned us; his eyes felt like X-ray beams boring through me.

"Aight den, peeps," Shorty said, smiling wide. He reached out and shook Ryan's hand. First, they gripped, then they slowly slid the fingers away, and then they hooked thumbs and threw up the five. He shook with Angel, then he looked at me confused. "I ain't seen this one before," he said, looking back at Mickey.

"Shit... he's a Cath-lic boy," Mickey sighed. They both laughed. "This is Joe." He put his heavy hand on my shoulder. "He's Pistol Pat's little brother."

"No shit?" Shorty said and reached out for my hand. He tugged me to his heavy chest and gave me a sound pat on the back. "Now that's a down-ass motherfucker."

His coarse fingers still gripped my hand, and we hooked thumbs and threw up the five. Then, he slapped his open palm against his chest twice.

"Thanks," I said as Shorty took a large step back.

"Aight den, peeps," Shorty said as he raised both arms out, palms open. "All that shit's squashed, on de fin." He flapped his arms downward like they were wings. "From now on, we got youse, and youse got us." He smirked as he popped the straw back into his mouth, then turned away from us. "Aight, C. Aight, Mickey."

"Take it easy, Shorty," Mickey said. Chief nodded.

"Ah, man…," Shorty said as he turned and grabbed hold of the crotch of his saggy jeans. "I take it any way I can get it, brotha," he shouted over his shoulder with a grin.

Once Shorty got across the street, Mickey turned. "Fuckin' niggers…," he said low. "Back in the old days, we would have solved this with a couple ball bats. Now I've got to be a fuckin' politician with these porch monkeys."

"We should just kill 'em all and get it over with," Chief said as he stared at the row of Stones.

Mickey laughed and grabbed Chief in a headlock, then he ground his knuckles playfully into Chief's curly hair.

"See, Tommy, that's why I made you Chief," Mickey said, smiling, then let him go. "But God help us all when you make General."

"You boys all right?" Mickey asked as he got back into the Lincoln. "Come on, I'll take ya back to the house."

Across the street, Shorty walked right up to T-Money, who sulked with his chin dropped. He still glowered at us. Shorty pointed toward us, then he plucked the straw from his mouth and shook his head 'no.'

"Fuck dat shit!" T-Money said as he pushed his back off the wall and took a step in our direction. Shorty grasped a handful of his t-shirt at the neck and slammed him back into the wall, then he brought his face close to T-Money's and explained the situation a little clearer. The TJOs across the street had taken silent notice. They chuckled and pointed at us, telling yesterday's story.

The side door opened and a heavy-set, uniformed police officer leaned his blue shoulder out. His pale fist gripped a dark Billy club, and he gazed both ways down the side street and disappeared inside. The door shut. There was the sound of heavy chains jostling and being pulled taut through a set of rings.

We got in, and the Lincoln rolled down the street. Mickey turned left at the corner, and the immense width of the building stretched like some ancient fortress in the shape of a squared-off "C," which created a block-wide courtyard between the two wings. "There they are, boys," Mickey said, nodding as he popped a Marlboro Red between his lips.

What must have been a hundred-fifty Gangster Disciples lounged against the far wall of the north wing. One in particular was a whole head taller than any of the rest. He was busting a sag in his blue Dickies; his orange and brown-striped boxers puffed out at the waist. Shirtless, he rubbed his bulbous belly with both hands. His arms were thick and undefined, and his shaved head was egg-shaped. He stood with his shoulders slouched, and his yellowish-brown skin looked faded in the sunlight. A navy-blue bandana waved in the breeze from his back pocket as he stared out across the courtyard at a group of about fifty Vice Lords sprinkled about on a series of concrete picnic tables near the inner rim of the south wing.

Things got better for Ryan and Angel after that, but now they had to worry about the PG3s (they'd now become a branch of the Spanish Cobras) and, of course, the GDs. It wasn't so bad for me. School over at Gordon was quiet. I didn't know anybody, but that kept me safe at the same time. Most of the kids at Gordon were good kids, but things had changed since my older brothers were there; there just weren't as many white families on the North Side anymore. Most of the white families had moved further west and had their kids in the Catholic schools like St. Patrick's and Holy Cross, or they had left the city completely for the suburbs.

I was a minority at Gordon, and now, the neighborhood that surrounded it was almost completely Hispanic. Mexicans and Puerto Ricans dominated. Some of the kids were screw-ups with good families, just like me, but most of 'em were good kids headed for blue collar jobs or even college.

■

I WROTE LIL PAT A LETTER asking him why Mickey hated the GD's in the Jungle so much. Two weeks later, Mickey hands me an envelope with nothing but Joey written on it. It was typed on a typewriter:

> I wanted to be the one to tell you this story, so I had to get you this letter special delivery, and you got to burn it once you read it. I couldn't put my name on it, but you know who it is 'cause you know who you asked.
>
> We were way up in Rogers Park rolling around in the Lincoln looking for somebody. We cut down a one-way, and there was a car double-parked blocking the street in front of some crack house. My boy Sammy was driving. He beeped the horn to try an' get 'em to move. A shine jumped out the car with a pistol. He walked up and shot Sammy in the chest—just like that. He died in my arms on the way to the hospital. Over nothing. Over beeping a car horn.
>
> We came back that night. We knew it was the

right house 'cause of the smell. Crack smells real distinct where they cook it: burnt baking soda, and the coca plant. We set it on fire—the front and back doors. I don't need to say much more, but no one made it out of that house alive. We've been warring with the Juneway Jungle GD's ever since. They're evil motherfuckers, Joey. That's why Mickey hates 'em. They all deserve to die.

■

I REMEMBER toward the end of our trip to the U.P. that year, we were out on Lac Vieux Desert near this point where a millionaire had a luxury duck blind set up with a TV, stove, and heaters. Suddenly, the light changed—the sky struck this purplish-green that reflected off the water, and the Lac began to swell and chop with a low, swift-moving storm.

Rich and Nancy motored past us. Dad looked at him, frustrated.

"What? It's gonna rain," Rich said.

"A few more casts," Dad urged.

"I ain't stayin' out here no more." Rich revved the motor. "We got skunked. Face it."

The putter of their motor trailed off across the large lake. Dad didn't look at me, just kept his eyes on the water.

"I was out here once with Patrick," he said, flinging a hard, long cast. "Just me and him. The wind changed all of a sudden, to a southern. It was cloudy, and they parted just then and lit the water up."

I cast and began to reel it in. My callused fingers ached. The purple clouds rolled over the tall pine trees along the shore.

"We hooked into five muskies in a row. Five consecutive casts. He boated a five-footer and hooked into something must have been six, maybe more. I got a couple, too. It was really somethin'."

Dad launched a cast out toward the point. The wind surged through the pines.

"He wasn't always..." He sputtered and coughed something back. "He wasn't always like that, ya know?"

The heavy lure splashed into a cresting wave and sunk quickly. He reeled it in hard and tugged on the pole with short jerks to imitate a wounded fish. I thought of Lil Pat—so far away, locked in a little cell in a place with people trying to hurt him any chance they got. I looked out across the wide horizon and saw the dark-green woods sloping up out of the lake. I concentrated and tried to send him that image telepathically, hoping it could somehow work, even if it was just in a dream. Maybe Da could bring it to him, so he could remember there were better places in the world. The rain began to sweep in from far off across the water, and a million tiny plucks spread along the surface with a foggy mist above. I hooked my lure into a line-guide and cranked it tight.

"Here we go!" Dad snarled.

There was a bright-brown flash in the water before the strike. Dad cranked down, gathered himself, heaved back, and set the hook with all his might. The small motorboat swayed, and sure enough, the full length of a five-foot tiger muskie emerged from the water. The fish tail-walked for ten yards, then it slapped hard on the surface and disappeared into the choppy water. The reel squealed. Dad's complexion went stone-white against the darkened sky. The muskie ran hard. The line cut across toward the bow out into deeper waters. Dad gathered himself. He leaned back and cranked hard on the reel. The muskie swept up to the surface and lofted out of the lake on a diagonal. Droplets of water cascaded off its underbelly, then it burst into a white splash and plunged again. Dad leaned, pulled the rod sideways, and turned him. Then, he spun the reel quickly and gained line on him.

"Get the net ready!" he shouted.

I stumbled over near the motor. The boat rocked with the struggle. I clutched the net, then got it tangled in my lure. I worked furiously to free it. A hook plucked into my palm, and I squealed at the sharp pain. Then, I dug it out. My fingers trembled. The barb left a fat gash that bled dark blood. Dad planted his feet into the floorboards and hauled on the sharply bent rod. There was a crisp snap, and the line went slack. And that was it. The muskie's tail fin softly crested the water some 20 yards out on the starboard and was gone—sunk into that dark lake. The only big fish we'd hooked into all trip.

Looking back, it must have been tough on the old man. He was working constantly to support our big family and only wanted to get out on the lake and get into some fish, spend some time with his kids. Having your kid locked in a cage can't be easy, either.

I remember motoring in as the big, cold rain droplets pelted us and the waves crested and gushed up spray on the bow. I remember a welling of tired emotion wrenching in my chest and not knowing if it was just water on my face. That was our last trip to Lac Vieux Desert.

■

JUST WHEN I THOUGHT EVERYTHING WOULD GET NICE and calm down, I strolled down to the sills one day. I'd just gotten home from school and changed outta that jive-ass uniform. I was barely in earshot when Ryan started up.

"The Moes rolled some PG3 Cobra's today," Ryan said.

"No shit?" strolled out of my mouth like nothin'—no weight to it, like a pigeon coasting to the ground.

"Hell yeah. It was crazy as hell," Angel urged.

"Did you guys get in it?" I asked, restless at not being there.

"You know we did," Ryan replied.

"Hell yeah, motherfucker," I said, reaching out to grab Ryan's hand. We shook up.

"Man, nobody even talked about it, man... We were over by the courts. You know the Peoples own them courts by the side door.

"Some PG3s were walkin' through the field right there, and I thought shit would be cool, but, man, then they started throwing up the six-point star an' shit," Ryan said. "And just got rushed."

"How many of 'em?" I asked.

"Like four," Angel said.

"Man, there was like ten of us just stompin' 'em," Ryan said as he raised his foot and mimicked the stomping. The white sole of his Puma was caked with blood-brown splotches.

"So shit's cool now with the Stones, huh?" I asked.

"Real cool," Ryan said. "In fact, Monteff's coming through in a little bit."

"Yeah?" I confirmed.

"Yeah," Angel piped in. "We're gonna smoke a blunt to celebrate; a 'stomped dem fools' blunt."

"But now we gotta worry about them PG3s," I said, thinking back to Sy. I imagined the PG3 Cobras, thirty-deep, all of them lounged along the side of the softball field fence beside Hayt Elementary School just a half-mile up Clark. I wondered how they felt right about now.

"I ain't worried," Ryan said, looking over at Angel. "You worried, Angel?"

Angel laughed and looked Ryan in the eyes.

"Man, they're too scared to come to this side of Ridge, anyways," Ryan sneered.

"What up, peeps?" a joyful voice came from the tunnel.

I turned to see Monteff walk up the alley with little BB sauntering beside him like some comic book sidekick. Both of 'em had big smiles on their faces.

Monteff had a cigar stuck in the rim of his Padres cap that came downward along the side of his face. He wore it tilted slightly to his left.

"What up, party peoples?" Ryan said as he tilted his head to the side.

Monteff looked me in the eyes. Something sad and somber overcame his face. A glint of regret smoldered in his eyes. He rolled his head back and looked away. "Hey, Joe," he said. "Man, come on," he waved his hand toward Ashland. "Let's talk, bro."

"Alright," I replied. We started towards Ashland together.

"Recognize this?" Monteff pulled out my old chain with the crucifix Lil Pat'd given me from his pocket. We stopped. Something reached up and clutched my heart, and I almost fell over. "I been looking at this thing a long time, thinking about things. I wondered if I was right to think you were in on what your brother'd done. I wanted to believe it. It made it all so simple, black and white. It made what we'd done right. But there was something deep in here," he patted his chest, "told me 'no.' I was wrong. You never woulda done nothing like that to me. You was my friend." He sighed. "Your brother, he did what he did. It's probably like you say—he's crazy. Shit, maybe he regret what he did, too. Sometimes people do stuff that don't make any sense. Stuff they regret a whole lot later. Things they could never take back. But either way, it wasn't you that did it. I knew I was gonna give this back to you one day. I just didn't know how." He handed me the cross. "Here you go, Joe. I'm sorry for how it all went down."

"It's cool, Monteff. Thank you, bro. You don't know what this cross means to me, man. My other brother, he's been locked-up a long time."

"Patrick," Monteff remarked solemnly.

I nodded. "He gave this to me before he went away." I blinked and swallowed back some tears. I slid the chain over my head.

"I'm sorry, Joe. You was always a good friend to me. I hope we can be boys again."

"Monteff... man." I took the cross in my hand and looked at it. It was in the exact condition it was in when I'd last put it on. "I think we were friends all along. We just didn't know it."

"Maybe you're right," he said, grinning. We shook hands and hugged each other with our free arms.

"Come on, let's go chief dat blunt," Monteff urged.

"Hell yeah," I replied as we turned and walked back.

As we got close, Angel smiled his slick smile and said, "You two done making out?"

"Shut up," Monteff slugged him. "We gonna smoke or what?"

"I got some Swisher Sweets," Ryan said as he took out the pack.

"Man, fuck that. Use this Philly, man," Monteff said, then reached up and slipped the cigar from his cap.

BB grabbed the blunt from Monteff before Ryan could take it. "I got it... I got it," BB said, shooting his eyes at me. "You know I was about to whoop yo' ass that day before five-o showed up." BB was almost up to my shoulder now. I smiled and gave his sixty-five-pound frame a quick up and down. Then, I just shook my head.

"BB, just roll the blunt," Monteff whined.

"Man, I just had to let a mothafucka know," BB said, walking to one of the sills. His narrow head flexed. "But you know how them pigs like ta whoop a nigga's ass 'n' shit." Angel tossed him a bag as he sat down at one of the sills.

"See, I roll these blunts up nice, mothafucka—not like you white ma'fuckas," BB said. He split the blunt down the center with a small razor. "This how brothas roll a blunt." He looked up at Ryan, who watched intently. BB took his index finger and dug out all the tobacco, then he started crinkling the buds up in the bag so they were almost dust. The rest of us stood around the sill to block any view from the street.

BB sprinkled the green dust into the empty cigar, then lightly rolled it over snugly. He licked his fingertip and used the saliva to seal the crease. Then, he took the lighter and burned the crease to finish the seal.

"Let me see that," Angel said, ready to inspect the blunt. It was smooth and had a near-perfect shape—flat on both ends and ballooning out on a perfect slope.

"Not bad," Angel said, looking up. "Let's see how it smokes, though."

Angel was always serious when it came to weed. It was one of the only times he was serious. He sparked the blunt with his lighter and took a deep hit. As he exhaled, he said, "Nice." The dank, musty smell of the Jamaican Red Hair plumed from his lips.

"Man, Joe... I don't mean to bring this up or nothing,' but man...," Monteff said as Angel passed him the blunt. "What the hell was you thinking going heads up with Tank, man?" He took a long, hard hit.

"Shit," I said and looked down, shaking my head. "Hey, I actually thought I was gonna win, bro," I laughed.

"On the real?" Monteff gave me a serious look as he exhaled. A trail of smoke sauntered up over his shoulder.

"Yeah," I said. Ryan scrutinized me with a glance. "Right up to the point where that motherfucker hit me!" We all burst out laughing.

"Now that's one nigga you just don't fight with!" Monteff admonished.

"Hell no," Angel said, raising his eyebrows.

"Man, he's been knocking motherfuckers out every day over at school, man," Monteff informed us as he shook his head. "Ev-er-ry day!" he shouted, his eyes wide. "He knocked a dude out dat was nineteen years old the udder day."

We all agreed.

"Joe, man," Monteff said. "You're the only one who got him yet, when y'alls went at it after school de other day."

"Yeah," Ryan cut in. "It's a whole lot easier when he ain't looking."

I took a hit, and thick brown flecks sifted across Ryan's face like a migration of dust mites. I exhaled.

"Don't forget, I was saving your ass when I did dat," I said, smiling and pointing at Ryan.

"I won't forget, man," Ryan replied in a serious tone, but the smile remained. "I won't forget."

"You see him still off that spick today, man? I thought he tore his head off," Monteff said, his eyebrows hiked up. "Man, when I saw you guys coming, I was like, 'Damn, these fools is going to the hospital fo' sho' now!'"

"Y'all wanna talk about fightin', man? Now I can straight up box," BB said, jumping off the sill and bouncing on his red Fila high-tops. Then, he threw fast punches into the air with his face all squinted up in fury.

"Fuckin' Sugar Ray Leonard, mothafucka," he said as he punched the air even faster. "I'll whoop Tank... I'll whoop any mothafucka in the hood."

"Oh, I'll let Tank know then, nigga," Monteff said.

"Man," BB replied, waving his hand in the air at Monteff.

"Smoke dis blunt and quit talkin' that crazy-ass shit," I said, handing him the blunt.

"Ah, hell yeah," BB said, snatching the blunt and taking a short inhale. He puffed it out and sucked it up through his nostrils, then he toked a long one and squinted his eyes.

"Man, give me that blunt, you little fool," Angel said, snatching the blunt out of BB's mouth. Then, Angel loomed over him with his tall, thin frame. "Sugar Ray *Midget*," he mocked BB's squeaky voice.

There was the sound of an engine idling, and I turned to see a blue Civic pulled across the walkway lines at the end of the block on Ashland. The light was green. It was parked there at the corner.

"Hey," I said, looking at Monteff and nodding toward the car. There were two Mexicans in it, glaring at us.

BB squeezed past us and threw up the 4-40 diamond as he stared into the car.

The Mexican in the passenger seat leaned his Raiders-capped head out of the window. "Stone killa, nigger," he shouted and threw up the PG3s and that C-shaped pitchfork.

Everybody jumped up, and we let loose with a barrage of shouts.

"Cobra killa!"

"What up den?"

"Moes here!"

"Fuck you, spick!"

"Fusion!"

"What up, flake?"

Ryan ran up and snatched an old Bud Light bottle out of the gutter. He threw it like a bullet, and it bounced once, then crashed on the sidewalk. The broken shards skipped across the concrete and sifted below the Civics' undercarriage. The engine revved, and they pealed out south on Ashland.

"You ain't got V'd in yet, man. Quit doing that shit," Monteff said as he pushed BB.

"Man, I was born to be a P Stone, fool. V me in right now," BB snarled.

"Man, I'll give you a mouth shot right now. Dat's about it."

"Man," BB whined.

"Scared to come across Ridge, huh?" I said, looking at Ryan. He just took another pull off the blunt and stared at Ashland, his temple pulsing.

VIRGINS

MOST HEROICS ARE PURE CHANCE—extreme circumstances thrust onto average people. It resides in all of us. It's there somewhere in the depths of our primal chromosomes, just the same as the rage and fury to murder. The only difference between you and a hero is luck. It's the same difference between you and a murderer, maybe.

It was a muggy, hot September day in the neighborhood. We sat in the garage with the box fan on in the doorway and the sliding door half-up as we worked on the bikes as usual.

"You smell that?" Ryan asked.

"What?" Angel answered, looking up from where he shined his chrome rims with Windex and a gray dishrag. There was the smell of smoke, like from a campfire. It slipped in over the scent of rust, grease, and cleaning fluids.

"Smells like something's burning," I said, inhaling deeply through my nostrils.

Everybody got silent, like we were listening with our noses.

"It's a fire," I said.

"It ain't no fuckin' fire," Angel whined.

I got up and lifted the garage door the rest of the way and stepped out into the afternoon heat. I looked west down the empty alley—nothing. An orange alley cat snaked down along the white coach house with its bushy tail up. I turned and looked east down at the T in the alley where Fat Bubba's yellow-sided house jutted up to its sharp-pitched peak. Beyond it, a thin trail of smoke snaked up into the blue sky.

We waited as the Ashland bus surged past before we jogged across. There was already a crowd forming down on the sidewalk in front of the red-bricked apartment building. Everyone's heads were upturned with their jaws dropped, awestruck. The smoke now gushed thick and lifted fast out of the third-floor window like an upside-down waterfall.

"That's fucked up. I don't even hear a fuckin' siren," Ryan said, turning around to face the street. He cupped his hands around his mouth and yelled, "Hayyoo, call 911!!!"

A fat Assyrian lady next to us looked up with her mouth creased in terror below her thin blonde mustache.

"*Das-Kees-in-deh!*" she screamed, grabbing my wrist. Then, she looked at me with her eyes bugged out, pleading. "*Das Kees in Deh!*"

"What the fuck you sayin'?" Ryan spat at her.

My heart leapt up in my throat. "There's kids in there!" I said, and I sprinted toward the entrance.

"Motherfucker!" Ryan shouted.

"Shit! Joe! Joe, don't go in there! Ah, fuck!" Angel said, then followed.

I ripped the outer door open, and an old lady with a red wig and a walker had just unlocked the inner door. I waited and held the wooden, glass-paned door as she creaked out. Ryan and Angel bunched up at my back.

"Thank you. That's very nice of you, boys," she said in a shaky but ridiculously calm voice as she passed.

We dashed up into the hallway, then found the stairs. They were quick-turning, and we pounded 'em. The smoke stench grew as we ascended.

"This three?" I shouted.

"Yeah, this three, man. This is it," Ryan urged.

I pushed the door open and coughed instantly. Thick smoke hung from the ceiling of the hall at head level. An older black man in a Dago T, sweats, and house slippers stood a little down the hall and banged on a wooden door. He had the shape of a guy who used to be muscular but had sagged with time. He banged on the door with the bottom of his thick fist. It was hollow and steady like a pile-driver. As I got close, I saw he was barefoot.

"This the one?" I asked.

He tilted his head to look at me, and his eyes were all pink with thick red veins flecked in them. "Those little motherfuckers start a fire in dere," he said.

I grabbed the brass knob—it was hot and singed my palm.

"They leave 'em in there all alone. They keep me up all day with this kinda shit," the man said, catching a line of drool sliding down his chin with his palm.

"They start fires all day?" Angel said with ironic disgust.

"Come on, man, just kick the motherfucker down!" I said.

I centered myself in front of the door, pulled my knee up to my chest, and slammed my new Nike low-top into the door. It boomed and rattled but didn't give an inch.

Ryan dove in and slammed his shoulder into it and got the same—the top and bottom just wobbled slightly.

We all coughed now and were heaving for breath. The smoke was thickening. It oozed out of all four creases of the door.

I pushed forward and kicked the door lower. The wobble increased. I ground my molars and stomped my foot into the wood. On the third kick, it gave, and my foot slid right through to the ankle. The wood cracked, and a slice from the puncture stretched up toward the center. I tried to pull my foot out, but it'd gotten stuck. I immediately panicked and started to scream. Images of me burning alive flashed in my head, and I suddenly didn't give a fuck about those little kids in there. The smoke traced up my thigh into my face and burned my eyes. I screamed for help. Tears gushed down my cheeks from the smoke as I yakked and swallowed mouthfuls of it. Angel grabbed hold of my thigh and yanked hard. We both fell against the far wall.

The old man turned abruptly towards the door and threw a straight punch. His fist burst through the wood and sank in all the way to his forearm. Then, he ripped it right out. Splinters of wood sprayed out after it. Ryan drove his shoulder high into the door, and it broke near the top. Angel and I got our shit together and kicked the door low. It broke the lower hole bigger, and flames crackled inside. Sirens slowly built all around us.

"Wait! Wait!" Ryan said as he bent down on a knee.

He took a deep breath then held it. He reached his arm in through the lower hole, and his head disappeared into the billowing smoke. He struggled there for a second. Then, a board banged to the ground inside the apartment, and the busted door folded inward and pushed open.

Three little Mexican kids from about two years old to six ran out in a tight line—one after the other like they were playing Follow the Leader. All of 'em in footsie pajamas, covered in soot. They coughed as they ran right past us like we weren't even there. As they got to the end of the hall, the oldest one yelled, "Sorry!" and ran down the stairwell.

"Sorry? Sorry? Little motherfucker, you sorry?" the old black guy muttered. He walked away from us further down the hall and said, "You done burn my house down, an' you SORRY?" He swung his apartment door open.

"That's all of 'em?" I yelled to him.

"That's all of 'em," the old man said without looking back. Then, he stepped in and slammed his door shut.

"Let's get the fuck outta here," Angel said.

"Fuck that!" Ryan replied, then pulled his shirt up over his mouth and nose before running inside the smoke-blanketed apartment.

"What the fuck you doing, Ryan?" I said, sticking my head in through the door. Then, I reeled back, my eyes burning.

"We gotta get outta here, man!" I yelled.

"I'm gone," Angel said, then he turned and ran down the hall, disappearing down the steps.

"Ryan!" I screamed into the grayness. I got low, below the curtain of smoke, then breathed some good air and readied. Suddenly, Ryan emerged with an Atari and a stack of games on top. He burst past me, and we ran down the hall. As we turned into the stairwell, it sounded like Darth Vader breathing, and a giant fireman emerged, fully geared.

I could just make out his eyes behind the plastic goggles of the mask. He looked at us then looked down at the Atari. "Get the fuck out of here!!!" he blared through the mask. We dashed down the stairs past a whole line of 'em.

In a few seconds, we were back in the garage. We sat, huffin' and puffin', and patted out tufts of soot from our clothes. Angel was inconsolable. He sat sunken into himself and refused to even look at either one of us.

"An Atari?" I said, looking over at Ryan. He sat on a little kid's chair and fondled the game console. "You risk our fucking lives like that for an Atari?"

"Your ass is the one who got us into dat shit!" Ryan shot back, disgusted. He flipped through the games with his brow all furrowed. "I was gonna get somethin' out of it. Ain't my fault their poor asses could only afford an Atari."

I cracked up and sat back on the fuzzy couch. I laughed hard until it turned into a rattling, deep-lunged cough.

We coughed for a week, but whenever a parent or an adult asked us about it, we played dumb. We didn't even talk much about it with the other hoods—didn't want to be called heroes or nothing. But we told the Good Girls about it, and the hood rats, too. Ryan and Angel had unlimited blow job passes with the hood rats and a couple select Good Girls. It went well for a few weeks before they started bragging too much and got their unlimited passes pulled. I didn't take any dibs on that mess, but when I told Hyacinth, I could see it in her eyes—everything went deeper. Her gaze: the saturated almond brown. Her touch: the cocoa-buttered fingertips. She grinned when I told her about getting my foot stuck. I even told her the truth about being so scared I didn't care about them kids no more for a few seconds before we finally broke that door. She paid me extra-special attention after that—said how it scared her that I might have gotten burnt up. Then, she started to tell me all kinds of things, too—secrets she never told anyone before. Silly little things that were more sweet than embarrassing. I ate it all up with laughs, and I never told a soul to this very day.

■

RYAN LOST HIS VIRGINITY FIRST.

I approached the sills where Ryan and Angel sat. Ryan squinted in the late afternoon sunlight with his freckles red as chicken pox. Angel laughed and both rows of his large teeth showed.

"What up, dog?" Ryan greeted me.

"What up?" I replied.

"Man, you ain't gonna believe dis shit!" Angel said, dropping his head and slowly shaking it.

"What?" I asked.

"Tell him, Ry," Angel urged.

I sat down in a sill, and the sunshine slowly burned into my skin. Ryan smiled at me.

"Tell me, fucker," I said, shoving him.

"Well, I told you Vicky's been hangin' around de block, right?" he started.

"Yeah," I answered.

"Well, I thought she was fuckin' around wit' T-Money. Well, I was wrong."

"Ah, shit. What is this fucker sayin'?" I said, looking at Angel.

"Listen!" Angel urged with his eyes.

"So we were fuckin' around, shootin' hoops in the alley, when T-Money comes out. He's leaning against his gate with his shirt off, all sweatin' and shit. Well, he calls us over and tells us he's got somethin' to show us up in his apartment, right?"

"OK," I said, eagerly.

"So we head up to the apartment, and he's got Snoop blaring, right? But when we walk in, we can hear some bitch moanin'. She's yellin', ya know? Somebody's fuckin', right?"

"HAHAHA!" Angel and I hooted.

"So, he opens the door to his ma's room, and there she is: Vicky's gettin' it doggy style from Twon, and BB's in dere gettin' his little dick sucked by her at the same time!"

"Ohh shit!" I said, shocked. "HAHAHA!"

"Then, T-money says, 'Dis bitch gettin' banged into da Crew.'"

"What? There ain't a Crew no more!!!" I said.

"No shit, bro," Ryan said, looking at me seriously.

"So what happened next?"

"Man, we all get in, like, and pulled a train on dat bitch," he said with prideful disdain.

"Oh my God!" I yelled.

"It was crazy, bro. We were all bustin' nuts on her face and ass and tits. She was loving it," Ryan added.

"You got in on dat shit?" I asked. "You sick fuck."

"Man, hell yeah, I did. I ain't passin' up on no pussy. I ain't a faggot!" he said, disgusted.

"Oh my God, bro," I said. "You're gonna get AIDS, man."

"Dat's what I said," Angel piped in.

"Man, fuck dat. AIDS is for fags and junkies," Ryan retorted.

"Ryan, man, you are an idiot!" I said.

"Fuck you, man," he shot back.

"Dis fuckin' guy," I admonished to Angel.

"It gets worse, man. Dey called up Tamika and Tara!" Angel added.

"Big Tara?" I said.

"Big Tara," Angel said, nodding.

"Ryan?" I pleaded—I didn't want to believe my boy fucked a giant fat girl.

"What? Man, forgetchu guys," he said, then took a pull off his cigarette.

"He fucked 'em both," Angel added.

"Oh my God," I said as I jumped up and pointed at Ryan. "You sick fucker!"

"Whatever, man. Whateva," Ryan dismissed us.

"Hey, it's OK. He's just on dat interracial, obese orgy tip," Angel joked.

"HAHAHAHAH!" I laughed.

I couldn't believe it—Vicky going that far, and Ryan with Tara. I couldn't get the nasty visions out of my head. There was the slight pang of jealousy that I was still a virgin, but I knew I didn't want to lose it like that—in a room full of sweaty dudes with girls that meant nothing. As much as I couldn't tell anyone, I wanted it to be special, beautiful even. And I knew I wanted it to be with Hyacinth. Just holding her hand made my heart ache. I wanted to tell her something, but I didn't know what. I knew what I felt was important and that I'd do anything for her.

■

TEETEE WAS AS GAY AS THEY COME. If there are really people that are born gay—if it's genetic—then TeeTee is definitely one of 'em. As far back as Hyacinth could remember, they'd been playing dress up, and as they got older, nothing changed except that they added heels and makeup. When he got to be about twelve, his father tried to put an end to it. He'd caught TeeTee in his mother's white evening gown with dark-red lipstick smeared across his lips, so he grabbed him and gave him a crack to the side of the head that fractured his eye socket but did nothing to stop his dressing; it just sent it underground: backpacks with school books neatly placed atop high heels, skirts, and makeup kits. Hyacinth's bedroom was a kind of safe zone for him. Every once in a while, when he was feeling brave, he'd go out with a few of the approving Good Girls in half-drag. He'd wear tight, bleached blue jeans with high heels, or a tight, girly t-shirt and eyeliner. Sometimes, they'd come by the sills. Ryan was so disgusted by TeeTee that he'd usually disappear when he saw him approaching. When Ryan did stick around, he was a fierce red ball of sneering silence.

TeeTee didn't bother me much. I'd known him since we was little. A year older than me, he used to run around with my sisters. He was a nice-enough guy in his strange, flamboyant way, and Hyacinth really loved him dearly. They were probably best friends on top of being cousins. So, I fought my instinctive urge to run him off with rocks and names like I used to with the other little boys in the neighborhood. But once in a while, my discomfort would show through. He liked to slap people's arms in his limp-wristed way when they said something smart-assed or playfully adversarial. One night, he slapped my arm that way, and an uncontrollable sneer slithered up onto my face. I turned away, but he saw it, and he never touched me again. With Angel, it was different though. Angel didn't mind the slaps and the playful banter. Usually, after Ryan had slipped off on some imaginary task, Angel and TeeTee would chat it up. TeeTee batted his dark mascara'd eyelashes at Angel as he made his ridiculous jokes in his high-pitched, whiney voice. Every once in a while, they'd sit in the same sill together, and the Good Girls'd giggle and clatter as they watched. I tried to ignore it—told myself, *Hey, they're just friends, pals, or something,* but all of that began to fall flat and false at my feet.

A large, silent void rose up between Ryan and Angel. Whenever Angel wasn't around, Ryan referred to him as the 'faggot.' I was always after him to quit dat shit. I said that Angel wasn't no faggot, and that he was our boy and a down one; that he'd fucked around with three hood rats already that I knew of, but Ryan wasn't hearing none of it.

Then, one day I walked home from school after getting off the bus, and there was Ryan. He sat on my front porch steps with his green eyes alight and his elbows propped up on his knees. Both of his thick fists were wedged under his chin.

"What's up?" I said.

"I caught the motherfucker," he answered.

"What?"

"I saw the faggot kissing that sissy."

"Come on, man." I brushed past him.

"I seen it with my own eyes." A sadistic grin stretched across his face. "Don't believe me? He's over there right now at Angel's house." He got up and glared at me. "Go see for yourself."

"You're fucking crazy," I said, walking up the steps.

I went to my room and changed into my street clothes, then I just sat there on my bed pondering it—the possibility that Angel was gay or bisexual or whatever the fuck—until I couldn't take it anymore and found myself walking over to his house. I cut down his gangway, and the narrow passage between the two buildings was dark and cool. MTV Countdown blared out of his open kitchen window. I was quiet with the chain-link gate, and I cut across his lawn and up to his front door. I was about to knock when I heard giggles through his open bedroom window. His yellow drapes swayed slowly with the breeze, opening as they blew backward into the room. High heels clicked on his old hardwood floorboards. Giggling—two voices. I stepped closer and crouched down. I peered into the crease until my eyes adjusted. I saw the two of them. Angel sat on his bed while TeeTee danced and pranced before him in heels and pink satin panties. Then, Angel took him by the hand, and TeeTee got down on his knees between Angel's legs. Angel undid his belt and his blue Dickies. I stepped back slowly from the window. The porch planks creaked and sighed below my sneakers. Then, I turned and went back home the way I'd come.

I never told Angel or Ryan what I saw—never even told Hyacinth—but I started to find things to do whenever TeeTee came by. Imaginary things after Ryan had stepped off. Eventually, TeeTee stopped coming by. It wasn't that I couldn't be around TeeTee no more—he didn't bother me; it was just seeing him and Angel together. I just didn't know how to deal with it right then. At that age, nobody really does, I guess.

■

HYACINTH, TEETEE, AND A FEW of the Good Girls were headed to the beach, and she invited me to come with. It was the last of the nice weather and probably the last swim of the season.

We walked it, only about a mile down Bryn Mawr to Osterman Beach. When we got to the little arched patch of sand, we settled on a flower-patterned towel she'd brought. A bunch of little kids were out with their mothers, scampering around in the sand. Long rows of high-rise apartments rose out of the shoreline to the north with their vacant balconies stacked up like ice cube trays facing out toward the water. I wondered if you could see to Indiana from up there.

We laid on our bellies facing the water and held hands while the others ran in and splashed around in the shallows. The deep-brown skin of her forearm stood out against mine, which was tanned by the summer but unmistakably white. Her skin seemed dark like a Mexican's, and it got me thinking about the migration of Man—the ice bridge connecting Asia and America, and how Eskimos were kind of in-between Orientals and Mexicans, and why the hell they say Columbus discovered America? And about all the distance and shades of color that separated Hyacinth's and my skin, and how it wasn't really much anyway.

The waves rolled in slowly then fizzled near the shore. They bubbled over the damp sand then slurped back. The spotty clouds moved steadily, and the sun beamed through the openings and warmed our skin. We both had a dusting of sweat in the fine hair of our forearms, though she had almost no hair on hers. A golden sheen blazed on her skin from the suntan oil. We clung to each other's hands with a steady, calm pressure, then we alternated from folded palms to spliced fingers.

National Geographic had done a thing on the images coming back from Hubble—all these far-off clouds called nebulae. I'd read about how when a star dies sometimes, it just shrinks to nothing. Other times, it explodes in what's called a supernova, then it makes these things called nebulae.

"They're pretty," she said, sliding her fingertip across the glossy page. Her pink nails matched the purple and red clouds.

"Yeah, they're cool, aren't they?" I replied, glancing at her pouty lips in my periphery.

"They're beautiful," she said as she flipped the page to the next full spread of a nebula. "Then what happens?"

"Well, you see that?" I said, pointing at a little incandescent white dot. It'd formed in the midst of a mountainous, billowing purple cloud that spanned the entire page. "That's a new star forming. It's like a baby star."

"Aw, that's so cute... A baby star." We both giggled and turned and kissed. Her lips were wet and hot and slippery. We kissed for a while—no way to measure the time. Everything ceased to exist. Just the smell and touch, my heart flickering, and the pulsing all over. When we stopped, she folded her hands in front of her and placed her chin atop them, then looked out to the water. The breeze played in the curled strands of her hair. Her lips were damp and swollen from kissing.

"I feel bad for him 'cause everybody picks on him 'cause he's different," she said as she watched TeeTee splash around in the water. His limp-wristed gestures and high-pitched squeal inspired a scowl from an obese mother in a dark one-piece bathing suit.

"But he's not so different. He's a very good and caring friend." She turned her head so her cheek rested on her hands, and her hair feathered in the breeze. Her dark eyes met mine. "Whenever I have trouble, he's there to talk with me and just listen, ya know?"

I thought of all the times I'd burst into laughter with the guys at TeeTee's expense, and how we used to throw rocks at him when we were little and make him run home crying. *Maybe some people were just born like that—look at Boystown. Think all of those guys just prefer having sex with guys instead of girls? Like it's some kinda fad that's gonna pass like frickin' bell bottoms or some shit?*

"He's always been nice," I said. "I remember when Rose would get her migraines, he'd always come by a few hours later to check on her. He didn't have to do that."

She smiled at me, then looked back out at the water. The lake was suddenly enormous in my mind, and I thought about the astronauts looking down at us from space as we slowly spun past. And then I thought about how fast we were moving—hundreds of miles per hour. We spun around like a top. I was suddenly dizzy. I blinked and watched the seagulls cut across the blue sky like tiny dots and thought of the day I caught that seagull with my lure in the center of the stardock at Montrose Harbor. How the bird flapped, twisted, and coiled itself in the line, and how Da had cut it free. How the bird flew away, and how Da was free now, too—free from the cancer and all the tortures of life, smiling down on us all from above.

There was a commotion, and a little blond-haired Polish kid with a big cube of a head ran up and slapped a Mexican boy in the face. Then, he grabbed a little plastic shovel out of his hand.

"Ow!" I laughed as the blond kid's ma ran over. She swore at him in Polish, then grabbed the shovel out of his hand and dropped it at the sobbing Mexican boy's feet. She drug her son away by his wrist, slapping his bottom.

"A little badass," Hyacinth said, raising her chin.

"Yep."

The Mexican boy squealed and writhed in his mother's lap.

"Ow, poor little baby…," Hyacinth said as we giggled. "Why do boys have to hit?"

"Well if you got hit like that, you'd want to hit back, too," I answered.

"I think I would just cry."

"Well, we can't cry."

"Yes you can. Guys can cry."

"Naw, if we cry, then we're gonna cry more and get hurt more, too."

"That's not how it should be."

"Maybe, but it's everywhere I look."

"There's more to life than fighting," she said, brushing her hand through my hair at the base of my skull. A flicker of pin prickles ran down my neck and back. "There's more to life than that, and there's more in you than that."

"Think so?"

She leaned in and kissed me on my cheek, then she lightly bit my earlobe. I turned onto my back and brought her into my arms.

Above, the sky had cleared some, and the blue was deep and vibrant. The clouds stayed back for a while, and something began to loosen from around my chest and stomach like knots unwinding—the wires I'd only just noticed constricting there. And I held her close like she was all I had in the whole world. Then, I said it, like it wasn't me, like someone a little ways away was whispering it. I felt it in my lungs like a rumble.

"I love you."

"I love you, too," she said, like it was the continuation of one sentence.

We watched the clouds. They separated and combined and dissipated as they slowly drifted past.

■

MONTEFF STARTED SEEING one of the Good Girls named Annie Rogers, who was a little blonde from a few blocks over. She and Hyacinth were downtown shopping on State Street. They called, and we set up a double date to walk around down there and then go to the movies. Monteff and I jumped on the Red Line at Bryn Mawr.

"You been contemplating any more of that philosophy?" I asked. The train knifed through the dark high-rises of Edgewater into Uptown.

"Always am," Monteff said as he reclined in his seat. "How about you? I heard you been getting into astrophysics and all."

"Yeah..." I flung my feet up on the empty bench in front of me. "You know that gospel supposed to be written by Jesus? Said lift up a stone, and you'll find me there and all that? Like God was in everything, in the air in you in me."

"Yeah I heard about it."

A bum down at the other side of the train car muttered to himself angrily.

"There's this religion, or philosophy, called Pantheism. It's the same as that gospel, basically. And when I learn about those things—the Sun and the Universe—I feel like I'm learning about God. Except I don't call it God anymore, ya know?"

"Damn, that's deep. You should keep searching into that, Joe, 'cause it really means something to you. You can understand it in a way most a' those dweebs can't—just memorizing it and stuff like that outta a book to ace a test. You reasoned what you know. You know what I mean, Joe?"

I nodded.

"Keep at that, brotha." He looked me in the eyes.

"I will, man. I can't stop thinking about it. It's not just the religion stuff either, man. I feel like the more I know about the Universe, the more I know about who we are an' shit."

"Know the Universe, and you shall come to know thy self."

"What's that?"

"One a those Greek mothafuckas said it, but backwards."

"It's good."

The girls waited for us at the top of the stairs of the Lake St. Red Line stop. We switched to the Brown Line at Belmont and snuck up on them and scared 'em. It was a nice, chill time. I was almost starting to believe shit would really cool off for once.

MA

THE THINGS YOU DO eventually catch up with you.

I came downstairs to the kitchen for breakfast one Saturday. The dry, yellow leaves of the tree in the backyard helicoptered slowly to the ground. Brown, yellow, and red trees rose up over the garages and peeked out between the houses across the alley like the whole neighborhood had lost its complexion.

Ma made me some French toast that was crisp on the surface and soggy and cool on the inside, but I was so hungry it didn't matter. I slathered them with cool syrup and sliced 'em up. Ma had the whole kitchen table covered by the two-fold Sunday Trib, and there were stacks of the colorful coupon brochures everywhere. *The Sun Times* sat down by where my Dad'd had breakfast earlier. The ends of the one-fold paper were crumpled and soaked with the water that hung in beads on everything he did in the kitchen—plates and cups and pans pulled out of the cabinets and rewashed thoroughly.

As I finished my French toast, our dog, Kelly, growled, then she scampered to the back gangway gate. She barked viciously and clanked off the wooden gate. Some invisible bum or kid or neighbor passed through the alley.

"A boy died from the neighborhood," Ma said as she looked down at the paper.

"What?"

"He was your age." She raised her eyes to mine. "It says here he went to Senn."

"Huh, really?" I dropped my eyes back to my plate.

"He got into a fight and got beat so bad he slipped into a coma," she said. "His name was José Alverez."

My heart sank. It had to be that PG3 from a few weeks back. A tremor shot through my shoulders.

"I wonder if Angel or Ryan knew him," she said, looking up at me.

"Naw," I said quickly. "I don't think so."

"He only lived a few blocks from us." She looked back at the paper. "Right on the other side of Ridge."

Silence filled the room, and I quickly finished my orange juice. My hands trembled.

"They say it might be gangs who did it," she said.

"No kidding?" I didn't look up.

"It's so sad, isn't it, honey? A young boy like that." She slid the paper and spun it so it was right in front of me. "He had his whole life ahead of him."

I looked at the picture. It was a school portrait with the fuzzy background. He had a square forehead and short, slicked-back, black hair. He didn't look like no gangbanger, except for that smile. That sly grin, like he was getting something over on someone. Like he was inside the center of some nasty joke looking out at the world.

Then, I realized I knew the guy.

"José! Shit! He went to Greg's for a little bit! Yeah, damn! Until they kicked him out for stealing some books from the library."

I planted my palms on my forehead. "What the hell he wanted with those books I could never figure out," I laughed.

"Joseph," Ma scolded.

"What? Naw, he was an OK kid. I liked him. I can't believe it." It all washed over me. They killed José.

I barely knew him. He had a little sister that stayed at Greg's after he got kicked out, and I remember seeing her in the hall crying that day. A skinny little second grader with a pink scrunchy tied in her dark, straight hair. Not only in a new school, but now in a new school where everybody knew her brother was a thief. *Wonder how she feels now.* Something sharp seemed to pierce my stomach, and it let out a slow grumble. I gazed at my empty plate. The brown syrup sitting atop the glossy, white ceramic plate reflected the room, all murky and dark like a dream.

"Did you hear anything about that fight?" I felt her eyes on me as I stared back at José's face. Who woulda known José grew up to be a PG3? It must have been all over me. My whole body felt heavy. It felt like it was sinking, like slime, like mucky rain water finding the gutter. "Joseph!" She yelled. "If you know anything about what happened to that boy, you need to go to the police!"

"Ma, I don't know anything, alright?" I shot to my feet and stomped out of the room, leaving my syrup-streaked plate beside the picture of José and Ma all alone in the kitchen.

■

I WALKED OVER to Angel's house.

I knocked on his front door, and he parted the light-yellow drapes of his bedroom window and looked out. Still in bed, his hair was all clumpy and matted.

"Man, what time is it, bro?" he groaned through the open slit of the window.

"Man, we gotta talk, now," I said with all the urgency rattling out of my throat.

"What?" he said as he sat up and met my eyes. "Alright, I'll be out in a second."

Angel came out of his front door a few minutes later and drug his plastic palm comb through his shock of hair, then knotted it with a small black rubber band.

"That PG3 died, man," I said as we walked down his front steps.

"What?"

"It's in the paper."

He froze like a raccoon caught in the headlights of a surging car. "Oh shit," Angel said as he walked over and leaned against a thin birch tree. He gagged a few times, then spit. He bowed his head, trying to wrap his mind around all of it.

We walked down to the corner and got the paper out of the little metal stand. Angel read the small article in silence as I lit a cigarette and handed it to him.

"Oh, man, dat's the one," Angel said, pointing to the picture. "The one who started the whole thing…"

"Was it the one Tank hit?" I asked.

"Oh my God, yeah…," Angel looked up at me. "He fucking killed him. Holy shit."

■

WE WALKED OVER to Ryan's. He was out on his front steps working on his tags in a ragged spiral notebook.

"What? What's up?" he said as we walked up the creaky porch steps in silence.

Angel handed him the paper, folded open to the article. Ryan snatched it and grimaced down at it.

"Yeah, man, so what?" Ryan said, shoving it back into Angel's hand.

"It's that PG3 from the other day, man," Angel urged.

"I know, man," Ryan said. His jaws snapped sharply.

"Tank fucking killed him," Angel whined.

"Shhhhhhh." Ryan lifted his pudgy palm toward Angel.

We walked toward the concrete wall at the end of the dead-end street and stepped over a furry, black streak on the concrete—a dead cat. It was flattened to a thin film. The bugs were already out, and its tiny bones were like twigs sticking up through the fur. The profile of the cat's crushed skull showed its fangs spreading open in one last frozen hiss. Ryan led us down toward the dead-end wall. The concrete had crumbled, and rusted rebar showed through where vertical chunks had fallen. He glanced around, then stopped.

"First off... We all fucking killed him. I kicked every one of those flakes in the head at least twice, man," Ryan sneered. "We were all stomping him."

"That kid was out when Tank hit him," Angel said. "You saw how he fell."

"Man, whatever," Ryan snapped sharply. "The cops already been around here looking for Tank. He's hidin' up in Rogers Park, I think."

"The kid is dead, man," Angel remarked, emotion trickling into his voice.

"Man, so what?" Ryan shouted. "That flake never shoulda kicked shit off with the Peoples, man. They shoulda known betta than fuckin' with us. We run dat fuckin' park."

"Man, shit is gonna get crazy now, man," Angel sighed, then gathered himself. His neck strained pink.

"Man, this is how it's always been, man. Mickey's killed like three PG3s by hisself," Ryan replied, flashing his emerald eyes at me. "Remember when they went to war with them Assyrians?"

"I remember," I said flatly. The Assyrian floating in that red pool suddenly flashed in my mind.

"Man, either you're down for your crown, or you ain't," Ryan said, shooting his eyes at Angel.

There was a pause. Angel looked across to the point where Ashland and Clark come together. The weekend traffic buzzed past.

"Man, you know I'm down, man...," Angel said, looking away. "It's just... Goddamn, man! I didn't think it was gonna be like this." His voice cracked as he put both his hands on his head, contemplating it—the guaranteed repercussions, the hundred or more newly sworn enemies. Fear swirled between the three of us, menacing and cold.

"Well, you better get used to it," Ryan said, looking away.

Angel crouched down, still gripping his head like it was about to explode. "It's too late now, anyways," he whispered to himself. Then, he stood back up.

"But, man, we got to get ready," I said. "Them PG3s are gonna go nuts now."

"Shit, they already did," Ryan said. "They shot up the block last night."

"Ah, fuck," Angel said as his cheeks ballooned with vomit before he swallowed it back.

"It was like the 4th of July, man," Ryan said. "You couldn't hear that shit?"

"Naw," Angel and I said in unison.

"Man, it was like three in the morning, man," Ryan said. "They shot up all the apartments."

"Anybody get hit?" I asked.

"Naw, nobody. But I talked to T-Money, and they ain't playing," Ryan said. "I think the Stones already rode out on them last night, too."

"Ah, fuck, man," Angel said.

"I talked to Mickey last night, man," Ryan said, looking me dead in the eyes. "It's war, bro."

My mind reeled. It felt like a hook was dragging through my

gut, and I was dizzy in the late morning light. Images of fire bursting from cars along the street, Tank in cuffs and an orange jumpsuit. I closed my eyes, and the Assyrian had stepped up to my face. He grimaced and bore his teeth at me. His mangled skull flexed as blood streaked down his cheeks and neck. There was a deep rumble, and I whirled on it, expecting a carload of PG3 Cobras—all of them with pistols and ball bats—ready to erupt from its doors. Some old lady craned her neck to look over the steering wheel and dashboard as the pink chain from her glasses jostled on her face.

Everything'd changed. It'd been coming for years, slowly festering. I just didn't know that it would come like that—as phantoms in the daylight.

■

THAT NIGHT, I dreamt I was at the star dock at Montrose Harbor. I watch myself as a young boy casting my lure into the circular center. I fly above in a slow sort of glide. Then, SLAM! The seagull explodes into the lure, and suddenly I'm looking up at Da weeping as he tries to untangle me. There's another one crying—it's a child's cry that transforms into the scream of a gull. White feathers fly everywhere as Da slices at the lines that constrict and dig into me. Then, a swell of feathers gushes past Da's face. Suddenly Da's face morphs into my father's face— cold, grimacing, baring teeth. My father lifts a long blade with a pointed tip and lowers it down, aimed directly at my heart, and I woke screaming, 'NO!!!!!'

PART THREE

JUVENILE

CHAPTER 22

DARK MATTER

THE NEXT NIGHT I was down at the sills by myself when I saw a dark shadow moving towards me. It came down the alley through the rising fog sifting up from the PVC pipe that traced down along the hospital wall. As the dark figure got closer, I saw it was a guy about my size in a large black hoodie. The hood was up; it and hung low and masked his face in blackness like an executioner's cloak. There was something familiar and unsettling about his gait as he hesitated. He turned away, shook his head, and wiped his face with his wrist. I gripped the blade in my pants pocket, then I ripped it loose from where it'd twisted and dug the cloth into a knot. The shadow resolved itself and stepped directly toward me. Both hands disappeared into the large front muffer pocket of the hoodie, and I was thinking: *if it's a gun, break towards Ashland; if it's a blade, let's dance. Where the fuck is Ryan and Angel at? I ain't lettin' dis bitch run me off my own set.* I was hot. The blood flow swelled all over my chest neck and arms, warm and itchy.

I turned to my side. The Assyrian... The Assyrian's little brother coming for revenge. No, a PG3. Pointing my left shoulder at him, I pulled the blade from my pocket and hid it behind my thigh, ready to ride. Suddenly, I realized: there's no way he'd come at this spot without a burner, all alone! Wires seemed to claw up into my mind. I thought that he was a decoy and that they were surrounding me, ready to give me the same fatal beat down that PG3'd just got. Then, he was only a few steps away. Too close to run away now, get shot down through the back. My eyes darted wildly all around—across the street at Ashland, down the alley. Shadows morphed into leering monsters. I couldn't believe I let this go down! Why hadn't I run straight off? *Fuck it! I could at least kill this motherfucker right now!* I squeezed the blade, and then a face emerged from the shadow below the hood: Monteff's yellowish-brown skin, all wet and glistening in the arc lamp. A tear dribbled off his nostril.

"Fuck," I said and exhaled. "You scared de shit outta me. What's up?"

"It's Tank," he said, wiping his mouth and nose with the back of his wrist. "Dey shot him."

"Damn." I was awestruck as I slid the knife back in my pocket.

"Man…" There was a crack in his voice. "I'm gonna kill all those motherfuckers," he said without conviction. "All of 'em."

"Shit, man, what happened?"

"Man…" Monteff hung his head and started to cry. His whole body throbbed with each sob.

"Tank…" He tried to get himself together and looked up at the night sky. "He's fuckin' paralyzed man."

"Oh my fucking God! Are you serious?" I crouched down on my hams in shock and gripped my head with both hands.

"Man… They say he ain't never gonna walk again. Ever."

"Oh my God, man." The news settled down on me like a heavy iron blanket.

"I was at the damn hospital all day. When they let us in to see him, man…" He shook his head, and tears gushed from his eyes.

"Man, he started screaming at us to get away. He ripped all his IVs and shit out. He was throwing stuff at us, even his momma." The images of this flashed bright in my mind.

"They said he tried to cut his own throat, man, with a plastic knife from his hospital tray." Monteff started to cry again.

"Ahh, shit, man." I touched his shoulder. "Are you alright?"

"Man, of course I ain't alright! That's my cousin, man!" Monteff shouted through the tears. I looked down, ashamed. "Man, I'm sorry, Joe, man. I just can't be over there right now, ya know? Everybody's asking and shit, 'How's Tank, how's Tank?' Man, HE'S FUCKED UP! Ya know? He's fucked up, and he ain't never gonna be alright. SHIT!"

I hung my head as the reality of it sunk into me, and I remembered when they killed Sy. The horror of it rippled through my insides, but this was family for Monteff. This was different. I couldn't even conceive of someone in my family getting shot.

"Hey, Joe, man. But thanks, man. Thanks for listening, bro."

"Hey, man, you could talk as long as you want, bro," I said. "I'm here for ya."

"But don't be tellin' nobody I was cryin', man. I ain't no bitch."

"Man, I won't tell nobody, man. You don't got to worry about that."

Ryan and Angel walked up the street. "What up, peeps?" Ryan called out.

"Man, I don't want these guys to see me like this," Monteff said. He turned away from them and pulled his hood down lower.

"Man," I said, then took a deep breath. "Hold up." I walked over to Ryan and Angel.

"Man, you hear what happened?" Ryan asked.

"Yeah, man," I answered.

"Ah, what's up, Monteff?" Ryan said.

"Aye, aye, aye. Look, man. He's real, uh, worked up, man. He just wants to, you know, he don't want to talk about nothin'," I said quietly.

"Ah, man, it's cool. We won't say nothin'," Angel whispered.

"Man. He don't, you know, want youse to go over there right now." I looked at them in the eyes.

"Ah, man. OK," Ryan said. "But we got some custies coming through."

"Shit," I said, scratching my chin. "Well, maybe we'll just go for a walk then."

I walked back to Monteff.

"Aye, Monteff. You wanna step, man?"

We walked in silence. These sudden, periodic fits of tears erupted in him. Grief shook his whole body. I remembered Sy. I remembered how it was when those PG3s snatched the life from his lungs. I wondered how many they'd killed, and when it would all end.

We walked the neighborhood as dark gloom encompassed the small patches of orange light that emanated from the streetlights leering above. It swallowed the light whole, like a ravenous beast. We walked to Bryn Mawr, cut over by the Rose Hill Cemetery, and climbed through a breach in the fence near the Metra Rail lines. Then, we ascended the heavy, blueish-purple stones and walked south a little ways along the tracks. The three sets of iron lines stretched and grew closer together until they evaporated at the gray horizon. To the west, square plots of Metra yards sat before the factories and lumber yards, and to the East, the parish sat quietly. The red-bricked buildings had the pitched roofs of the two-flats plopped between them, and the St. Greg's steeple speared up through the yellowed trees like a gray stone beacon of hope.

I found myself praying for the first time in a long while. I prayed for Tank. Prayed for an enemy—my fiercest of enemies over the past year. Monteff stopped, too. He bowed his head and clasped his hands with his fingers clamped and splicing each other. I prayed for Monteff, and Tank's Ma, and everybody. I even prayed for José and his little sister. The hazy night sky gleamed purple above, and there was the slightest sprinkle of stars hanging overhead that broke through the smog like tiny pin pricks of white light.

I closed my eyes and prayed again for José. Suddenly, I realized his body was probably just across Bryn Mawr—right there over the Rose Hill Cemetery walls that stood 30 feet high like concrete prison walls. His body buried six feet deep and rotting in his best suit—a suit his family probably got from a thrift shop or handed down through generations. Lost in this daydream, I saw him there in the darkness behind my eyelids—the bruises and lacerations remained along his emaciated face. *I'm sorry for what happened to him, may he rest in peace.* Then, his eyes opened and stared at me blank and awake and startled.

I opened my eyes. Monteff stood before me. The orange light from the streetlamps below struck his face even with the large hood pulled low. His swollen lips and nose had crusted dry.

"Let's step, man," he said, cold and resolved.

I couldn't have known then what he'd resolved himself to do, and even if I had, I couldn't have helped him, saved him. There are some actions that are made well before they're actually carried out. Sometimes, you're as much a passenger as a driver, and I could see the momentum building in him heavy and leaden. All there was to do was stand by and watch.

The next day, he walked into school with a 4-inch buck knife—one of the ones we'd been trading around and playing with for years. The gnarly, bowed oak handle with the brass ends and the fold-out blade with that cut-in at the tip like a flame. Monteff encountered six PG3 Cobras in the bustling halls between first and second period. He let 'em pass, then turned and started with the ones trailing in back. He stabbed each in the face, throat, or both. Monteff got one bad enough that they rushed him into emergency surgery at Weiss Memorial and had to bring him back from the other side. The rest of 'em just scarred for life. It took Senn's entire in-house police department to pry the buck knife from his hand. He didn't cry, didn't make a peep. The guys who seen him in first period said he wouldn't even look at 'em, let alone talk to 'em. Guess he was done talking. We thought we'd see him again on the block when he turned 18, but he hung himself a few months later with a white towel at the Audy Home over on Western and Roosevelt.

I remember watching him walk away that night—I'd stopped at my corner at Hermitage for some reason. His black hood up, his narrow frame. The hoodie too big for his slinking blue jeans as he headed north past Edgewater Ave. He walked slowly but with so much inertia. Then, his form melded into the shadows and that was it. The last time I saw him.

■

WITH THE SHIT AS HOT AS IT WAS, we knew we needed a piece. Ryan asked Mickey, and he said no—said we'd end up shooting our fucking dicks off by accident. This may have seemed like a ridiculous joke, but that exact thing actually happened in the bathroom at Senn a few years before. A guy ran up to a urinal in a hurry trying to unzip and 'POP!' The revolver went off and so did his prick. I asked Rich if he still had the .25. I had $200 bucks saved up, and he threw in a box of rounds he had laying around. The gun was even smaller than I'd remembered it—now it fit perfectly into my 14-year-old hand. The chalk-white grip was scratched and worn smooth, and the glossy, nickel-plated barrel had a small notch at the tip for aiming, but I figured there wouldn't be much aiming—this was close-range shit, but who knows.

I lifted up my hoodie and slipped the barrel into the front

waistband of my crisp, beige Dickies. I glanced at myself in the mirror in my closet. My hair spliced back tight to my scalp and sprayed stiff. The light-brown freckles on my cheeks. I checked to see how visible the bulge was—nothing, especially if I put my hands in my hoodie's pockets. I stepped out of my bedroom and started down the stairs slowly, afraid it'd come loose and rattle down my pant leg. Then suddenly, I remembered the guy who'd shot his dick off.

"Joseph, I need you to take the garbage out..." Ma's voice rose from the kitchen.

I froze and wanted to run back upstairs and switch the gun to my back waistband, or just hide the fucking thing under my mattress.

"I gotta go Ma," I said as I opened the front door. "I'll do it when I get home."

Once outside, I took a deep breath of the dry, cool fall air. The gun seemed heavy and loose, and I put my hand inside my muffer pocket and pressed it against my waist. I stepped down the porch stairs slowly.

"Hey, Joey..."

I looked up and saw Mrs. Thompson. She sat on her porch with a button-down gray sweater over her house dress. She smiled down at me as she pulled on her cigarette.

I waved back with my free hand, giddy with the rush of my deception. I walked on down the sidewalk towards the sills. The pistol now felt snug in my waistband, so I took my hands out of my pockets. The muscles of my cheeks froze into a wide grin. I saw Ryan and Angel down at the sills, lounging and bullshitting. I couldn't wait to show 'em. The excitement had my heart pattering in my throat.

An Ashland bus creaked to a halt at a red light, and an un- marked, dark-blue Caprice squad car coasted through it. Two plain-clothed white cops sat in front in ball caps and black shirts over their bulletproof vests. The one in the passenger seat must have felt my gaze 'cause he turned and locked eyes on me. His face smiled as he shook his head 'no' like he'd heard something funny. Then, they were past the intersection and gone—not even enough time for me to get scared.

I stepped up to Ryan and Angel. We shook, and Angel sat back in his sill disinterested and puffing a Winston. Ryan eyed me suspiciously and bare his crooked teeth.

"What's up with you, fucker?" Ryan said, tilting his head to the side.

A warm swell rushed up my neck and face. I smiled so hard it almost hurt.

"Whatcha mean?" I said and shrugged.

"Well, you got that retarded, shit-eating grin smeared all over your face for one thing," Angel said, looking down towards Ashland as some cars swept past.

"Better watch how you talk to me, motherfucker, or I'll pop your ass," I said, then I lifted my hoodie at the waist and gripped the white handle.

Angel shot up from his concrete ledge, stupefied. His mouth hung open in a long, quivering "O."

"Oh, shit!" Ryan's said with his eyes bugging out. "Is dat real!" We huddled together. Our shoulders created a triangle that blocked any view from the street.

"It's Rich's .25," I said, holding it in my open palm. We all leered down at it. The silhouettes of our heads shadowed it from the streetlights and made the chalk-white grip look gray.

"Let me see dat shit!" Ryan said and snatched it from my palm.

"You got any bullets?" Angel asked.

I started to say 'yeah, it's loaded' as a sudden flash ignited in the shade created by our bowed heads. It was followed by a hard 'POP!' and a searing burn in my abdomen. Then, the pistol clattered to the sidewalk. It spun flat on its side to a rattling halt and pointed right between Angel's black Pumas with the fat white laces. A small tuft of smoke floated up from the fabric of my muffler pocket, and I slipped my hand under and froze in scorching pain. I brought my fingertips up—no blood. Angel bent down and scooped up the gun, then jogged towards our arterial alley.

"Come on!" he shouted to us over his shoulder. He stuffed the gun in his coat pocket, and his shiny ponytail whipped around as he went. Ryan and I chased after him.

We hid in my garage. Angel and I panted as we slouched on the couch. Ryan scowled on a low wooden stool across the room. I pulled up my hoodie and looked down at the light-red smudge—it was the size of a thumb print, just to the side and below my belly button. It slowly fogged white. The thin film atop it wrinkled, and the cool garage air soothed the burn. I fingered through the folds of my hoodie, and sure enough, two pinky diameter-sized holes in the fabric. I looked over at Ryan.

"You shot me, motherfucker," I said.

"I didn't even touch THE FUCKING TRIGGER!" he shot back, scowling. His face glowed red.

I had this rumble in my chest that grew, then erupted as laughter—heavy laughter. Angel took the .25 out and placed it on the mangled little table in front of us, between the screwdrivers and wrenches, then he sat back and stared at it. He turned to me with his eyes wide-open and his lips sealed shut, then his long teeth emerged between them. He cracked up with me, and I really let loose then. I bent over and brushed my hoodie against the burn and instantly squealed. Then, I shot back to my reclined posture and let the burn air out.

"You shot me, motherfucker!" I shouted. Ryan still stared out into the darkness in the corner. His forehead folded up on itself, and his eyes turned into squinting black slits.

"What the fuck you laughing about!?" he yelled.

"You shot me, Ry Ry... You shot me!" I joked.

"No, I didn't!" he barked and flashed his eyes to mine—they were puffy, wet, and glossy, barely holding it back. Then, his forehead unfolded. His grimace morphed into a chubby grin, and his torso started to rock on the small, creaky stool.

"I try an' tell motherfuckers not to fuck wit' me; they just don't listen," Ryan said. We roared.

We split the $200 three ways. It was the crew's gun—that's the way I wanted it to be anyway. We kept the clip out from then on. I didn't remember sliding the swing barrel to register a round in the chamber. Fucking Rich must've handed it to me like that. But at least we knew it worked now. Even though it was a small caliber, we could pop any PG3 that came our way in search of revenge. We kept it in the stash with the weed—figured we could get to it quick enough if shit jumped off. And that way, no cop could lay it on any of us if they came down on the sills. Looking back on it now, I can't believe it—how I'd come so close to getting shot for real, and by my best fucking friend, of all people. Years later, I was out on a job site with Blake when he was getting in a few hours with us as a carpenter. We were doing this pin-and-link bridge job way out in Aurora, and he told me how common it was for shit-bag gangbangers to shoot themselves with their own guns. He'd constantly come across 16-year-old kids with bullet wounds in the thigh that had incredibly steep downward trajectories—hundreds of 'em every-year in Chicago alone. I remember laughing—laughing hard—as we slathered white primer on those metal-finished links but keeping that one to myself.

■

I LOST MY VIRGINITY on a Thursday. I was out in the garage with this old scratched-up girls' Schwinn frame clamped tight on the rusted iron vice. Struggling, I cranked the Crescent wrench down on the neck, trying to turn the bolt without stripping it. Then, I hear this light tap at the garage door. I walked over and lifted it up, and there's Gabby. Her jet-black bob cut framed her round face, and those double-D breasts that everybody'd been blabbing about for weeks strained at her white t-shirt. She had this shy smirk on her lips as she twirled her finger in her hair.

I closed the door behind her, and we sat down on the old couch and started small talking. Before I knew it, we were kissing, and I'd clasped my hand onto her large, firm breasts. Hyacinth was my girl—my love really—this was a compulsion. I knew I could get her, but it wasn't that simple. There was this pulsing mystery in those monstrous breasts, and the desire of all the guys my age in the whole neighborhood compelled me. Images flashed in my head—all of the immense tits that'd bombarded me over the years. The enormous jugs that bounced across the TV screen on Baywatch; Dolly Parton's giant knockers; Jenny McCarthy's immense levitating melons. I found myself kissing her neck, and I pawed and gripped her breasts like two large bags of hot dough. Then, my hand was under her shirt, and I pulled down the cups of her tan bra and pinched the fat, dark nipples. Gabby's face was dull and unresponsive as she sighed. I licked and sucked them. I gripped them. My fingers stretched to reach around their balloon-like circumference. There were purple stretch marks near her shoulders. She had her large shirt crumpled up along her collar bone, and her chin pinched it against her throat. She smirked her buck teeth down at me, and the harder I squeezed, the harder my prick got. Finally, I stood up and gripped the top of the couch's seatback. Then, I leaned over her and rubbed my hard on through my jeans against her naked tits. She squeezed them together against it, and her eyes gazed up at me as she panted. Then, I moved up and rubbed it against her face, and she puckered her thin lips. These cold-metal rushes flowed up and down my legs and back. Suddenly, Kelly rippled a short series of vicious barks that boomed through the thin walls separating the garage from the gangway. I froze like I'd had a spotlight shone dead on me. I was horrified. Maybe it was Hyacinth just about to knock on the garage door to surprise me and say 'hi.' She'd heard us through the door and burst into tears. She was outside that door, trembling, knowing everything—that it'd never be the same; that it was over. It couldn't be. I got up and looked out the window; the babysitting kids played noisily in the backyard. Then, I went to the garage door and opened it. The alley was empty. An old gray Ford slowly turned into the mouth at Hermitage.

"What's up?" Gabby said.

"Nothin'. Come on, let's get outta here," I said as I adjusted my dying hard on.

Gabby was taller than me, which made it seem worse and odd as she followed me down the sidewalk. Guilt slid into my stomach, and I nipped at her as we walked to the sills. A few potheads milled around by the hospital.

It was disastrous. The realization of what I'd done and the panging guilt was amplified by Gabby's presence, her bug-eyed daze. She slouched and pouted, then she folded her arms over her stomach. Her mountainous breasts hovered above. I ditched her with the potheads. They gawked at her large tits with my saliva still fresh on them.

I found myself hurrying down the sidewalk to Hyacinth's house. The chatter of sparrows skipped in the branches above. How could I have done it?! How could I have been so damn stupid?! Guilt fluttered in my chest. All the eyes on the block shot accusation at me: Mrs. Simon getting out of her brown station wagon; Mrs. Sanchez reclining in her folding chair on her small front porch. They peered at me, and I wanted to scream 'I'm sorry!!!' My eyes pleaded at them for forgiveness, and I rushed to her, racing the rumors, racing the truth, and begging for just one more moment of that purity we had together. The true ache of love convulsed in my chest.

I knocked on her front door. The sound echoed through the house, followed by a hollow silence. I walked around to her bedroom window, then reached up and grabbed the baseboard of the frame and pulled myself up. It took a second for my eyes to adjust and peer through my strained reflection in the glass. Inside, the covers of her bed were rumpled into a mound that slowly swelled and descended as she napped. Her face was turned away—just the twisted strands of hair in the soft light. I dug the tips of my sneakers into the wood siding and pulled myself so my forearms rested on the ledge. I tapped on the glass with my fingertips. She turned, blinking, and looked at me. Her face was a blur, and I almost blurted out, It's not true! Then, she smiled. Her cheeks bloomed as she sat up, then she lifted the window open and laid her head back down. Her big brown eyes on me, steady.

"Taking a nap, baby?" I asked.

"Yeah," she said, yawning into her palm.

"Is anybody home?"

She sat up and brought her thick purple lips to my forehead. They were warm and damp. She put her arms around me and pulled me into her window. I dug my shoe tips into the siding and climbed through, falling onto the bed with her.

I kicked my shoes off as she opened the covers. She was the warm one now. Her waking breath was hot in my face but smooth like coconut milk. I kissed her neck and cheeks and both eyes. She pulled at my belt, undoing it. Then, my pants, and I felt her smooth thighs through the thick hair on mine. She was so hot I thought she might have a fever. I stopped and looked her in the eyes—hers flickering, dark, watering. Then, she leaned up and kissed me firmly. I kissed her hard back, and I realized she was just in panties. I softly touched her there, and her hips thrust upward against my hand. I was instantly erect. I slid my finger inside the nylon fabric and touched her wetness. She gasped out, then moaned long and low. I slid my finger in, and she grasped at the waistband of my cloth boxers. I suddenly knew that I had her—all of her. I ripped my boxers off, and she grasped my dick in her palm. Warmth radiated into it as it pulsed, and the head nearly exploded. I howled and gently pulled at the hem of her panties. She gripped my wrist. Her breath heaved, and our eyes met. Then, she nodded and helped me slide them down and off. And suddenly, I was there, and I began to push.

"Wait... wait, stop," she said, then brought her palm over her mouth. Her eyes were frightened.

And I did. I propped myself up on my elbows and hung my head down.

"Baby..." I said in a growing whine. Then, I lifted my eyes to her, pleading.

"Tell me you love me..." She said, her eyes watering. "Tell me we'll always be together."

"I love you," I said as I leaned down to kiss her thick lips. "We'll always be together."

Her thighs spread, and I pushed into her strong. The pressure built until there was a snap. She screeched and dug her nails into my shoulder blades. I slid into her, and her voice careened and rose. A splash of hot liquid gushed over my pelvis as I met the hilt. Her cry turned into a light moan as I pumped into her a few times. Then, I froze in orgasm and cried out myself. She undulated beneath me, gasping. Her arms flung around me tightly. My face was against hers. Hot tears streaked across her cheeks and slid down my neck. We both shuttered, breathing simultaneously. I felt her heart beat there.

Slowly, I propped up on my forearms and pulled out. She let out a sharp sigh and clung to me. I still pulsed and strained. I looked down at the red mess of blood and cum, shocked by the gore of it. She tried to sit up to look, but I kissed her and rolled to my side. She rolled on top of me, and we lay there. Her head rested on my chest, lifting and descending until our breathing slowed. I dressed and climbed back out the window. The firm concrete of the sidewalk shocked my jellied, unsteady legs. Then, I pulled myself up on the ledge and kissed her one more time. The silence, not a silence amongst the music of scent and heat, swirled in our faces. I loved her—almost forgetting what I'd done. Almost forgetting everything that I'd done.

NUCLEUS

THANKSGIVING WAS ALWAYS FUN—everybody together watching the game; a huge baked turkey jammed full of stuffing; yams, cheesy veggies, and sparkling grape juice; little Johnny running around playing. But inevitably, we got to talking politics around the dinner table after the meal.

And if it wasn't enough with Blake being a cop and Rich a degenerate racist, Jan had gotten into black Studies at Northern Illinois, and some race-nutty ex-Panther professor took her under his wing. Jan had always been in search of her identity. It was there in her short temper, her prideful stubbornness. She just knew she wasn't white. And in her search for what she was, she'd found a history that set her people against Anglos. Funny, though, how so many of us forget the Spanish were white imperialists and that Spaniards' white blood traced its way through all of the Caribbean and Latin America. How the Spanish language has nothing to do with the Caribbean people, or the Mayans and Aztecs, either. I guess almost all of us have some white in them, and at the root, some black, too. But, to be honest, it was nice to see Rich's and

Blake's crazy shit challenged. It didn't take much to spark it up, and then they were off to the races, full-tilt.

"A racist system?" Blake said, squinting his eyes across the dining room table at Jan. "Where's the racism? What, in Affirmative Action? Yeah, that's definitely racist."

"If it's not a racist system, then why is it that 80 percent of Cook County Jail inmates are African American?" Jan's eyes stretched wide-open, and she raised her short, pudgy hands, fingers spread.

"Well, I don't know, probably because blacks commit 80 percent of the crime in the city?" Blake said, then glanced over to Rich, who burst out laughing. "I'm just taking a guess here, though."

"It's a racist system!" Jan yelled, then slapped her hands down hard on the white lace tablecloth. "How about racial profiling? That is a nationwide problem."

"Listen, when I pull over a car with a young black guy driving it," Blake said, placing his elbows on the table and leaning in toward Jan, "90 percent of the time, he doesn't have insurance, he doesn't have a license, he doesn't have registration for the car, and when I run the VIN number, it comes up stolen." He rocked back in his seat and shot his chin upward. "All a those are jailable offenses, and he's whining about," Blake sneered and cocked his head to the side, "'How you finna profilin' me like dat, bra?'"

"That's a load of bull-crap," Jan replied, dismissing him with a wave.

"No. It's fact, and it's my daily life. And when I pull over a white person, not that there are all that many whites driving around in the hood..."

"Unless they're there to buy drugs!" Jan added.

"That's right. They're there buying drugs, but when I pull 'em over, I got nothing on them. They got a driver's license, proof of insurance, registration, and guess what? They're polite when I walk up on 'em."

"And you let 'em go," Jan said, rocking back and raising her chin, satisfied. "Ahuh."

"That's right. I say, 'Have a nice day, and stay out of the hood. This is a dangerous place.'"

"And that's fair? That's law and order?"

"It's this simple: locking up some suburban business man down there buying a bag of weed is a waste of my time."

"It's your job, Blake," Jan retorted.

"No," he said, shooting his index finger at her. "It's not my job; my job is to get guns off the street, to get drugs off the street, and to get shit-bags off the street." He shot his thumb southwest.

"And that's gonna stop the problem? They're impoverished people. They've got no other way of making money other than the drug trade," Jan argued.

"Get a job at Mickey D's! There's plenty a warehouses on the Wes' Side. They don't want to earn a honest buck—it's too hard."

"No one will even hire you if you're a felon!"

"Well, I don't know about you," Blake said, grinning at Rich, "but that sounds like a pretty good reason not to commit a felony, don't ya think?" Rich choked on his sparkling grape juice.

"That's just asinine," Jan said, pushing away from the table. She grabbed her cloth napkin and threw it on her plate. "You're an asshole, Blake." She stomped out of the room.

"All I'm telling you is the truth, Janet," Blake said, sitting back with a pompous smirk strung on his lips. "You just don't want to hear it."

I stayed out of it when I was still that young, but later I wouldn't. It's amazing—all the crazy debates we've had at the dinner table. Sometimes I don't know how we all stuck together as long as we did.

■

THAT NIGHT, Jan and I were sitting at the dinner table having some chocolate cream pie. She was still steaming about the argument at dinner.

"Do you even know the history of civilization in Africa?" she asked me.

"What? Sure I do," I said, smiling. "The Africans were running around in little tribes in the jungle until the whites came down and took it all over."

"Oh, sure. That's what you read in those Catholic school history books. See, they teach you what they want you to know, but not the truth. Did you know there was a civilization in Africa that had written language and one hundred percent literacy throughout its entire people? You didn't know that, did you?"

"Naw," I replied. "Well, are you talking about the Egyptians?"

"No," she sighed. "See, that's what every textbook says. 'The Egyptians, the Egyptians.' Did you know there was an ancient civilization south of Egypt more advanced than the Egyptians, and the Egyptians came down and massacred them? Massacred them! You never heard that, did you?" She gobbled some chocolate pie with whipped cream.

"Nope," I said. "Never heard that once."

"And did you ever hear of the Moors?"

"Nope."

"Of course you didn't. Did you know that they built all of Spain? They brought technology, they brought everything there. They civilized that whole region."

"So what happened to them?" I ate a forkful of the pie that'd melted some and turned to a creamy-brown, not far from Jan's skin tone.

"They got massacred and pushed out of the country back to Africa. And the Greeks, too; they stole all their philosophy from Africa." She waved her fork around like an instructor's wand.

"Come on, Jan." I gave her a sideways look.

"No, Joe, I'm telling you the truth. I mean, read a real history book for once—not that crap you get in American schools."

"I never heard any of this shit," I said, shrugging.

"Sure you didn't. Did you know that, at the beginning of humanity, there were two peoples in Africa? Way back at the very beginning of mankind. One of those peoples became whites—they had straight hair and light skin; the other was the blacks. The whites were violent and evil, and the blacks went to war with them and ran them all the way out of the continent. The whites were the people who went to Europe and became Europeans and Germanics."

The way she was talking was strange, but I sort of believed her. No one else but Blake went to college, and Blake never really talked with me much. For a minute, I actually believed her.

"Damn, I never heard any of this," I said, shrugging.

"Yeah, you won't either, 'til you get to college," Jan said proudly.

"All they ever teach in high school is the Greeks, the Romans. Hmmm, they're nothing compared to the civilizations in Africa, or the Mayans. Oh yeah, and Christopher Columbus—puhh, he didn't discover America. The Africans were going there for centuries. Just look at the Mayan temples—they're pyramids! I mean, it's just common sense."

I couldn't really argue with her. She just had too many arguments, and they all seemed right, and she was so sure of them. I figured she must have got them from somewhere.

"I don't know. I guess I gotta read some of your history books if I'm gonna be able to talk with you about this shit."

It was funny; with Lil Pat and Blake gone, there wasn't anyone around to ask about it. Dad wouldn't really talk about stuff like that, so I was sort of stuck. But I didn't really give a crap about any of that shit, anyway. I was too busy trying to keep from getting my neck stretched on the street. Plus, it was all messy. It seemed to me that history wasn't really fact; it was all about how you saw it and who wrote the history books. Like, if I told a story about a fight I was in, I'd see it my way, whereas, whoever I was fighting with'd see it their way. The truth was probably somewhere in the middle.

It was still strange the way she was talking, and it weighed on me into the night. I stayed up thinking about it, wondering if Jan really believed all that stuff. If she thought all white people were evil—just born evil—and if she hated them. And if she hated me, too, just because I was white. I thought about it a lot and got angry—thought maybe blacks and whites were pitted against each other. But then, I thought of Monteff and Monica and how they were my friends. Then, I thought of Jan'n'Rose, and I knew he couldn't hate any of them. I thought about the word 'nigger,' and I knew Martin Luther King Jr. was a good man. I wondered what the word even meant. I didn't know, and all the worrying about it just seemed stupid.

"Nigger, nigger, nigger," I said quietly into the dark of my room. A grin stretched across my face. "Spick, chink, honky, sand nigger, dago, mick, polock, flake, pig, fag, dyke, whore, cocksucker, fat ass, bug eyes, big head."

I kept thinking of different words until I couldn't come up with anymore and just started laughing. That's all they were—words. Stupid words that could never describe real people. I laughed so loud, I knew everyone could hear me, and I tried to stop, but it only made it worse. I bit my hand to stop until I was crying real tears and still giggling. Slowly, I drifted off to sleep and dreamt in color—bold and glowing color—all night.

They were good, fun dreams, and at one point, I realized I was dreaming and started desperately to think of things I could do. I found a hot chick and started kissing her and squeezing her breasts and ass. Then, that stopped, and I was inside a packed Aldi grocery store. Everyone was tired and pissed off. They were all mixed races and bickered in different languages, and there were huge lines that stretched far down the aisles. I was giddy and suddenly thought maybe I could fly. I concentrated real hard. Of course I could fly. I wanted to grow wings, and I felt them begin to bulge at my back, but before they could break the skin, I started to float upward. Everyone suddenly stopped arguing and turned to see me. I floated up and towards the door and popped outside. People out in the parking lot gawked as I ascended, rising slowly at an angled trajectory. Then, I looked downward and fell back toward the ground. I remembered I was dreaming and rose again. My whole body flexed, and I flew in a controlled way now. I flew high, and I could see all of the dream beneath me. It was so beautiful. There were these neon-green hills surrounding the store that joyfully and brightly glowed off-and-on and told me how happy they were. I was up in the clouds. The soft clouds bumped against me and shot out of sight. There was nothing up there. It got boring, so I floated back down to the Aldi parking lot, where all the people inside had flooded out to. They fought each other, and there was no order to the violence—it wasn't even along racial lines. Pockets of people punched and kicked each other. Moms punched old ladies, kids jumped up and down on babies, a fat guy kicked another fat guy in the face. No one was really angry, either. They moved mechanically. I focused on them and descended diagonally. When they saw me, they looked up and got mad as hell. I smiled down and thought, *you could fly, too, if you want*. Somehow, my thought was transmitted telepathically to all of them, and they stopped, looked up, and got angrier. So I flicked them off saying 'Nigger, spick, chink, honky, fag, dike, sand nigger...'" as I soared over their heads. Saying the words gave me more power to accelerate, and I flew like that for a long time until I woke up smiling, my body warm. I wanted to dream more but couldn't fall back to sleep. Then, the warmth and the smile wore off in the reality of the day.

∎

THE PG3 COBRAS weren't through exacting their revenge. That weekend, we were sitting at the mouth of the alley beside St. Greg's gymnasium. The parish was throwing some kind of Thanksgiving festival—God only knows what for. The lot across the street from us was inundated with a thick swarm of people, and in the center of it, the swing ride's top spindle rim loomed above glowing neon-green and pink and orange. The chains hung down straight and bobbed some as the riders jostled in their chairs. The ride started to spin slowly, and the chains began to fan outward. The children swirled into a cyclone with their feet dangling sideways from the swing chairs as they gripped the taut chains. The glowing, circular rim of the ride slowly ascended, and the swings fanned out further, so they soared above the heads of the people speckled about on the blacktop. Then, it tilted to the side. The swings spread like the tentacles of some strange amoeba, and the riders squealed so loud it carried out over the building tops.

Ryan had his bike out. It creaked and yawned under him as he repositioned himself on the plastic banana seat. His ape hanger handlebars tilted down and out over the front white-wall tire, and red metallic-flake paint bubbled over the rust spots at the creases of the frame where he'd forgotten to sand them. But they were his mistakes and his ride, all the way. Ryan's imbecilic smirk was irrepressible. He squinted and blinked, and his prideful eyes glowed wet. Lounging, he splayed his arms out on the long handlebars, and his Dago T drooped off his shoulders. His skin was red from the day's long, slow cruise—we'd ridden all the way to Wrigley and back, and the pedestrians'd taken notice. A bum'd gawked at it for 15 minutes between sips on his cheap wine.

I watched the alley for any sign of a PG3, or any Flake really. The thick, slow crowd swayed side-to-side as they waddled, high on cotton candy and funnel cakes. Beyond them, the alley continued on, loping through the intersections. The hospital hung high above the neighborhood just two short blocks down. Suddenly, there was a squeal of tires.

"TJO KILLA!!! FLAKE KILLA!!! PG3 MOTHAFUCKA! CO-BRA LOVE!"

A flash of lights spilt across us, then the black Blazer careened into the alley. I snatched Ryan by the back of his neck and elbow and yanked him right off the bike. The front end of the Blazer lurched up and slammed down on the bike's back tire, then it barreled over the frame. The front tire dislodged and bounced down the alley. Ryan and I fell against the red bricks of the gymnasium.

"Get the fuck out-de way, homes!" Heffey yelled as he stuck his big head out of the driver's side window. An absurd grin spread across his lips, and he reeked of warm beer. The Blazer jolted to a stop.

The passenger's side door flung open, and a mob of PG3s poured out. We broke towards home. We hit the busy alley and sliced through the thick crowd, dipping and dodging people the whole way. The PG3s shouted at our back. Finally, we broke through, and I darted blindly across Bryn Mawr without a glance for traffic. Ryan was never fast, but he booked so hard he broke from us. By the time Angel and me approached Olive, he'd already crossed it. Suddenly, the Blazer emerged and swerved on a diagonal across the mouth of the alley at Olive. It skidded to a stop as I cut around the front end, and Angel leapt up and slid across the black, rusted hood. He stumbled, and I slowed, then he got his footing, and we sprinted across the street into our alley. Ryan dashed to the abandoned garage and ducked down into the stash. I knew what he sought. A sense of relief washed over me, then it was swallowed again by the fear of those dozen pounding footsteps at my back.

Ryan rose from the stash. He gripped the .25 and slapped

the clip in. Then, he stomped into the center of the alley. Angel rounded the corner and paused at the T in the alley. There was a sharp click as the slide barrel registered a round in the chamber. It rang clear over the patter of feet and halted the PG3 Cobras at the mouth of the alley. I stopped, panting, bobbing on my toes. I tried to make eye contact with Ryan, but he just looked down. His lips curled upward at the edges. Tears beaded down and dripped off his sunken chin, sparkling in the stark light. The PG3s shrunk into one glob and gripped at each other's arms; I don't know if it was to keep them together, or to hold their ground. Heffey barged through and emerged in front of them.

"Whatchu gonna do wit' dat BB gun, weto?" he said as he raised his chin and puffed out his belly. The others laughed and bobbed on their toes, still gripping each other like they were walking through a haunted house.

I heard Ryan whisper, "This."

He raised up the .25 and aimed, dead center, at the glob. He squeezed. It was a low pop, but in the darkness, the fire lit the narrow alley like a camera flash. Angel ducked around the corner at the T in the alley, and I dove between two large, black plastic garbage cans, then peaked over the top. The glob of PG3s dispersed instantly, and Heffey wobbled back to the Blazer. He reached under the seat and brandished a large-caliber black pistol. Ryan's second shot rang out, somehow quieter. He kept a steady, crisp, upright pace. His face glistened wet with the .25 aimed, arm stretched chest-high. Heffey ducked down behind the half-open door and cocked his gun. Then, from a crouch, he raised up the barrel and squeezed off a shot. A deep crackling boom illuminated the alleyway. To my horror, Ryan sprinted straight towards Heffey, dead center in the alley. Another PG3 ran around the Blazer and dove into driver's seat. Ryan's third shot burst through the windshield, splintering the glass up high and making it look like an iceball disintegrated across its width.

"Damn," Heffey said, trying to hide his fat belly behind the car door. Then, he raised his heavy piece and squeezed another round off from a crouch. Ryan's fourth shot exploded through the window of the door Heffey hid behind. The glass gushed white, and the center descended as the edges clung like crystal drapes in the frame.

The driver threw it in gear as Heffey drug himself into the door. His feet scraped along the pavement as he gripped the shattered window's frame. The V6 roared as Ryan squeezed the last shot. The pop was followed by a metallic thump as the Blazer disappeared the wrong way up Olive. Ryan stopped out in the street and squeezed the trigger, pointed up Olive. It clicked quietly over and over until I ran up and grasped him by the arm.

"We gotta go, man!" I said as an avalanche of tears poured down his face. He finally snapped out of it.

Angel stepped back around the corner and shouted, "Come on!" We followed him around the bend of the alley and into his garage, where he locked the door behind us. We sat in the dark with our backs slumped alongside Angel's mom's car. Our chests heaved in the quiet.

"Motherfuckers!" Ryan screamed.

"Shhhhh," I said.

"You hit, man?" Angel whispered.

"Naw, that fucking pussy wasn't even aiming for me," Ryan sneered.

"Jesus, man," Angel said. I watched Ryan's mug in profile. He wiped his tear-glossed face with the back of his hand.

"Smashed my motherfucking bike, man," Ryan whispered. "FUCKIN' FLAKES!" he seethed.

"Look… We got to be quiet, man," Angel cut him off as the sound of the sirens swelled in all directions.

"We got to stash the piece and hide out for a while," Ryan said, getting up and looking out the garage door window. A squad car roared down the alley and its blue-and-red strobe lights flooded through the creases of the garage door.

"Nobody's going nowhere right now," I said. "We just need to chill for an hour or so."

"I got a place," Angel said, climbing onto the hood of his mother's car. "Gimme it."

Ryan handed the .25 up to Angel, and he stuffed it into the blackness of one of the rafters.

We stayed in the garage for a very long time just smoking cigarettes in silence. The swirling sirens rose and fell in the distance. I couldn't believe Ryan had raised up the burner like that and rushed up on Heffey with him blasting that cannon! It might sound kinda silly to think it was over something like that—a bike. Especially since we were making so much loot down at the sills that he could buy a brand new bike outta the magazine. But that bike meant a lot more to him than two wheels. Hell it wasn't about the bike at all; it was about work and dedication and the friendships we'd deepened planning and conceiving it. It was scary though. I mean, we'd all sworn to kill or be killed for each other and the neighborhood while buzzin', but to see one of us ride out like that tryin' to make good on the promise—that was a different animal. I could feel him slowly drifting away from us even as we sat shoulder-to-shoulder with him in the middle in that dark garage. Finally, the sirens died out completely, and we slipped off home through the gangways.

■

NEVER DID FIGURE OUT who tricked. Coulda been a neighbor who saw it while walking their kids home from the festival, or my sisters looking out for their baby brother's best interests, or Officer O'Riley got word it was us... Yeah, probably O'Riley, but it really don't make much difference 'cause either way, I had it comin'.

I walked up the steps of the unlit front porch. Traffic passed in sudden jets of air on Ashland down at the end of the block—bursting, then trailing off like a melody of rifle shots in the distance. I slid the key in, turned it, and opened the door. A surge of cool air poured out. I stepped in. No lights. It was darker than the night outside. I heard a sound, like ropes pulled taut and then released. A large figure loomed near in the black. A sliver of light from the alley came in through the kitchen window and down the long hall, silhouetting the profile of a heavy, thick-fingered fist curling and uncurling in the darkness just before me. It could have been an ape standing there—the wide, hunched shoulders, the long, thick arms.

"Get in the basement." My father's growl broke the silence like a sledgehammer through a thin film of ice.

My stomach went hollow like a million tiny pores inside opened and sucked in air. I walked past him down the hall and opened the door to the basement stairs. The light was on. Walking down the slow turn of the staircase, I thought about the time he'd thrown Lil Pat down those steps and broke his leg. The stairs ended almost into the foundation wall. I turned and passed under the bright, naked light bulb that dangled down from the exposed floor joist above. I walked down the long hall towards the back door of the basement, near the washer and dryer. The smell of detergent powder mixed with that deep, stale sewer water smell that never left our basement, or any place below ground in the city.

I walked slowly and thought about my brother Rich and the time he tried to fight Dad in the alley and got knocked cold and his nose broken. I didn't want my nose broken. I was the only one of my brothers who hadn't had it broken yet.

I waited for him. I could hear him swear and work himself up at the top of the stairs, then he rumbled down them. As he turned toward me and passed under the light bulb, I saw him for the first time that night. His skin looked white, like the color of lightning.

His eyes twitched on his angular face. Two knots of bulging muscle gathered where each jawline met his neck. He never stopped his motion, just slowed as he got close.

"Getcher hands up," he spat through his teeth as he raised his clutched, wide fists to his chest. I put 'em up.

It wasn't a punch—you see those coming. His fist just grew and rose in my vision until it was all I could see. The white hair on the knuckles with the thumb pressed in underneath. It slammed into my forehead like a brick. My neck stretched, and the whole of my weight rocked back on my heels.

I stumbled backward and my arms flailed out for balance. The whole room swirled around me like I was a passenger on some terrible Tilt-A-Whirl. I leaned forward and fell toward him. He drove his fist into my chest and sent a booming exhale through my nostrils. My arm sprang out in a wild swing that caught only air. Another fist—I don't remember where it came from—crashed into my jaw. A splash of metallic sparks sprayed through my vision, and I crumbled to my knees. Trembling, I grasped at the concrete floor hoping it would stop the room from moving.

"Naw, no, no. You're too tough for that. You're a big gangster now," my father said. He snatched me up by my shirt and lifted me to my feet. Then, he grabbed my face and throat with each hand and slammed my head into the hollow wood door that closed around the dRyr. The first panel exploded into a shower of small wooden chips, and a thick splinter dug into my cheek, below the eye. The blood beaded down my face, warm. He kept my face pressed against the crumbled door, then he brought his hawk nose and beady blue eyes close. Spittle sprayed through his teeth like a rabid street dog.

"A TJO, YOU LITTLE SHIT! DO YOU KNOW WHAT THEY DID TO YOUR BROTHER? HE WAS..." He looked down and swallowed something back. The veins in his throat strained red. "He was perfect. He was beautiful, and they WRECKED HIM!

YOUR HEAR ME?" He slammed my face into the door again. "THEY WRECKED HIM, AND THEY'RE GONNA WRECK YOU, TOO!"

He let go, and I slid to the cold slab of the basement floor, gasping. Blood seeped in my ears. He turned and walked away towards the stairs. I watched him, and as he turned to go up the steps, I saw his face for a split second—it was wet and hollow and sad. I hadn't known. I hadn't known how much he loved him. Crazy as it sounds, I felt closer to my father then than I ever had in my whole life.

CHAPTER 24

ENRICO FERMI

ACED ANOTHER PHYSICS TEST—big whoop. Everybody was pissed 'cause I was busting up the grading curve. Luckily, the dark-purple welts on my forehead and the cut on my cheek were still fresh. Plus, I had this frozen scowl on my face that looked just mean enough so that nobody wanted to try me after school. Dydecky had pulled me aside and told me about this presentation he'd set up for the Physics Club later in the week. He urged me to come, looking me in the eyes with his bushy brow straight as an arrow. He said it was a guy from Fermi Lab who works with the particle accelerator. I just shrugged and mumbled 'maybe,' but deep down, I was excited by the idea of getting to talk to a big shot like that—a guy making his way in life as a physicist—and with football season over, I decided I'd go.

That Thursday, I stepped slowly down the gray-tiled science corridor. The sounds of thin sheet metal lockers opening and slamming sloped off to almost nothing. Quietly, I stepped toward Dydecky's room, keeping an eye out for any of the football guys. I undid my tie, folded it into a silky mound, and stuffed it into the front pocket of my pants—it crunched the dove sack Antwon was supposed to have bought in third period, but his dopey ass was in the Dean's Office. I figured I could just dip off after this Fermi Lab guy's thing and check the detention hall, and even if he wasn't in there, somebody'd probably cough up the twenty for it.

I heard squeaky footsteps and spun to see some big-ole senior with blond hair and a red face bustle around the corner. He swung a heavy wool coat up and slung his arms through it. Then, he slapped the pole lever on the side exit and dashed out.

Hesitant, I stood just to the side of Dydecky's open door. The windows and ceiling grate lights struck it bright inside and made this hazy yellow light ooze out of the doorway and spread atop the shiny floor. And I'm thinking, *What the fuck are you, some kinda a nerd or somethin'? Going to fucking Physics Club after school?* But it was Ryan's voice I heard in my head, and that recognition slid into my chest and stirred up bubbling, antagonistic knots—like, *fuck it, quit being a fucking pussy. If it's boring, you could just leave, go pass that dove sack off, and catch the bus home.*

I took a deep breath and stepped in. There were nerds all around with big thick glasses, pocket protectors, ill-fitting clothing, and bad hairdos. Right in the center of the room, there's like ten of 'em all bunched up on each other, straining on tip toes. They craned their necks to see over each other's shoulders, hooting and hollering at something happening down low in the center of the mound of bodies. And I'm like, *What the fuck! Are these dorks throwin' dice up in here?!* I step over and strain to see through and over a few of 'em. Finally, I see this frail little guy with his sleeves rolled-up way down in the middle of the deep shade cast by all the leering dweebs. He's doing something with his quick, boney hands. There's this whirling blur of colors: red, blue, yellow, green. These little squares twisted in chaotic vertical and longitudinal spirals in his gesticulating fingers. Then, suddenly: green—solid green.

A dopey kid with a red mop cut and a smear of bright-pink acne on his cheeks wipes his hair out of his face, looks up to the big circular clock at the head of the room, and says "Two minutes, fifty-three seconds!" in this screechy, whiney voice.

Half of 'em sigh and slump back towards their seats while the other half rejoice. The nerd-mound unfurls and spreads out, then, the little super-nerd stands tall and raises the multicolored Rubix Cube, smirking shyly. He's got silver braces with white rubber bands strung in them. This fat Mexican kid with his dress shirt unbuttoned and his big bowling ball-shaped gut straining against his t-shirt is pounding his beefy paw on the little guy's back. Then, Super-Nerd raises the Rubix Cube high with his narrow thumb and index finger on two opposing corners. He starts slowly spinning it with his other hand so it twists like a dice on edge, revealing all of its solid-colored perfection. He wasn't exactly cocky, but showy enough to be entertaining.

"Joe, you came. Great!" I turned to see Dydecky crouched down on a knee. He was next to the slide projector—its side compartment was ajar—and he had a strange, little, oval-shaped light bulb pinched between his pinky and ring finger.

"Take a seat. I gotta get this thing fixed before Tompkins gets here," Dydecky said, wiping his sweat-dotted forehead. "I'm glad you made it." He arched up his eyebrows, then got back to work.

I sat down next to this fat Polish kid with a huge square head and a long, pointy nose. He hadn't partaken in the Rubix Cube contest. He was clomping loudly on something, then dismissively flopped a deflated banana peel atop his desk and eased back into his creaky seat.

On the other side and behind me, this Jewish kid with a dark-brown afro and square, black-framed glasses hunched over a magazine—*Modern Science*, or something. "I told you Tompkins was in the August issue... Right beside lead physicist Peterson.

He's right here, it's this one. Assistant Operations project Top Quark on the Tevatron collider!" he exclaimed.

"Julius, can-it. We all know he's a big cheese," this effeminate black kid sitting beside me said as he vigorously filed his fingernails. Then, he held them up, limp-wristed, before his face with his fingers spread. It was about then that I was sure I was in the wrong fucking room.

Tomkins finally stepped through the open door. He had well-kempt blond hair and a sprinkling of sandy stubble on his cheeks. He wore a fuzzy, green V-neck sweater, dark-blue corduroy pants, and some brown penny loafers. The nerds were instantly prone at attention in their seats. The silence resonated.

He strolled up to where Dydecky still crouched at the head of the class and said, "Hello, Bert. Good to see you."

"John, come on in. Welcome," Dydecky replied as he stood and swung the side compartment closed. "Everybody, this is Mr. Tompkins of the Fermi Lab Top Quark endeavor." Some of the geeks actually clapped. "Mr. Tomkins, this is the Gordon Tech Physics Club."

Tompkins puffed his chest out and grinned condescendingly, like a man who enjoyed his title and position as a lackey on a big project. The Jewish kid with the magazine went to wave, and I glanced over and saw he was actually giving Tompkins the Vulcan salute. Tompkins didn't notice, thankfully, because if he'd a given it back, I woulda leapt up and tore right the hell outta there.

I'd read about the particle accelerator in an old *National Geographic* magazine—we had a few crusty stacks of 'em in the basement next to the furnace that went back decades. I'd also come across Fermi Lab in a few of Da's books in the chapters on quantum physics. I was initially intrigued by the macro: the Universe and its destiny and history. My discarding of religion opened a great, wide void of eternity to explore, and my instincts drew me to find symmetry somewhere out there in all those theories.

I had this impulse that existence must be fluid, constant, though ever-changing and exploding in bright, big bangs. Then, it would recede slowly until all matter had compressed and focused to one point of smoldering near non-existence. Then, the explosion again—a cyclical state, you could say. Most of the contemporary math back then pointed to an ever expanding, open universe, so that all the stars would just continue to drift away and slowly fizzle out. But, of course, the math had been wrong many times before throughout history, constantly proven false by new discoveries like dark matter and new math that was just waiting to swell up and encompass it.

But there was something equally intriguing about the micro: the fundamental parts of matter. If we are all made of energy and matter—and if the sparks in our brains, our memories, and what make up our identities and souls are primarily energy—then the law of the conservation of energy would allow us insights into where we go when our bodies go kaput. Even if it is just to return to the source of all energy—that big ball of everchanging fire; existence, the universe itself.

This idea of colliding electrons and positrons and having them convert into energy and splintering them even further into theoretical particles was incredibly interesting to me. An attempt to find the foundation of matter, and I guess, in the end, it was about finding something out about death in a pure and methodical way without any of the horrific and chaotic emotions tied to human death. It was a safe haven to explore inside of, I guess.

I hated Tompkins right off the bat. He had an aura of answers when he was really in a field of questions. I guess he gave the visitor's tour at Fermi Lab or something—he had a whole spiel.

Dydecky finally got the projector working, so he wheeled it into position in the center of the room and cut the lights.

An image flashed on the pull down screen—an aerial view of plush, green fields, a few patches of dark-green woods, and two immense white concrete loops; the larger loop nearly intersected with the smaller one. Tompkins started his rehearsed spiel. He stood at the head of the class with the wired slide remote in his hand. The late autumn afternoon light seeped in and struck him in a cloudy, gray haze. The sharp, trembling image on the screen splayed across his shoulder and arm. The next slide was of a bison, a buffalo, and a calf.

"There's a lot of real morons out there who think we have the buffalo herd in order to detect hazardous radiation levels, but, of course, that is erroneous," he said, shifting. His pompous grin flickered in the side of the vibrating image. I had a flush of annoyance rush to my palms, and the words just shot right out of my mouth.

"It don't seem that stupid to me," I said.

"What? What? Who said that?" Tompkins asked, squinting in my direction.

I raised my hand.

"Antimatter annihilation is like a hundred times more powerful than nuclear fusion, right?" I asked.

"Well, yes, but...."

"And there's gamma rays present in this annihilation, right? And ain't that what makes living cells mutate when they hit 'em? Gives 'em cancer and makes 'em die and all that?"

"Yes, well, yes, I suppose, but we're talking about finite levels encased in concrete."

"OK, but aren't you trying to find new fundamental particles? Why couldn't there be new energies, too, even more dangerous than gamma rays?"

Tompkins glanced sternly at Dydecky, who lounged atop a desk in the front row by the door. Dydecky just shrugged at him, then looked at me and popped his eyebrows up twice.

Tompkins sighed and soldiered on. I had these warm little needles and pops spiraling up and radiating out of my chest and into my shoulders. I fought back a smile and was glad the lights were off 'cause I was sure my cheeks were burning bright pink. He continued his spiel, basically reiterating everything I'd read already. It was exciting though, nonetheless, to hear it spoken and to see the physical instruments. To think that humankind was achieving near light speed with these particles— it was awe inspiring. Not just on the conceptual level, but the ingenuity in putting it all into physical practice.

When the lights came up, the afro-headed Vulcan Jew kid immediately started slurping balls. He even got Tompkins to sign his copy of *Modern Science*. Tompkins masturbated just a little bit more, then said he had to leave.

Everybody clapped as Tompkins packed up his slides and took off in a hurry like he had some really important tour to give back at headquarters. The nerds started chittering excitedly as Dydecky walked Tompkins out, but I just sat there. The rush of ideas and excitement erased all of my hesitancy to be seen there. Then suddenly, Super-Nerd leans against the desk next to mine, reaches out his narrow hand to me, and says, "Scott."

I shake it and say, "Joe. Good to meet you," hoping this ain't some kinda 'Beam me up, Scottie' joke.

"Interesting stuff, huh?" he said.

"Yeah... Pretty cool."

"You ever hear of dark matter?"

"Yeah, it's that invisible stuff that changes the orbits of stars and galaxies."

"Ever think about it in terms of antimatter?"

"What, like dark matter's made up of antimatter?"

"I don't know, maybe, though—that'd explain a lot, wouldn't it?"

"But, wouldn't there be more collisions and annihilations happening out there in the Universe on a big level?"

"Yeah, maybe there are and we just haven't observed it yet?

Maybe, that's what a supernova is? Or a type of supernova, anyway?"

"Shit, that's trippy, man. Like, what if there's a big-ole ball of antimatter headed straight for us right now?"

Scott looked upward towards the sun and flicked his hands above his face and said, "pshhhhhhhhhhh!!!" and I found myself giggling.

"If that's how this little dot goes, I'm gonna be pissed as hell," Scott chuckled as Dydecky walked back in, grinning at us.

"Alright, fellas, that's it," he said, "Wrap it up, I gotta get the projector back to Mr. Hollander's room before they lock it for the night."

As Dydecky wheeled the projector past, he whispered, "Good comments, Joe." One bushy eyebrow rose way up along his forehead. This ball of pride expanded in my chest, same as when I made an open-field tackle and the coach slapped my helmet when I got back to the sidelines, or when Mickey brought up that fight outside of Senn.

"It was good meeting ya," I said to Scott as I got up.

"Come back again. Dydecky's always bringing in big shots like that guy."

"Maybe I will," I said and stepped out the door.

On my way to the north exit, I ran into Antwon's fat ass as he was plodding outta the Detention Hall and dragging his pick through his messy afro, and I got on the bus twenty bucks the richer. Then, I was sitting there watching the red-bricked world slowly slide past on the packed Addison bus, lost in thoughts about particle physics and the destiny of the frickin' Universe itself. Imagine that.

CHAPTER 25

LOVEBIRD

IT WAS A SLOW MONDAY AFTERNOON, and we all bullshitted down at the sills, hoping for custies, but nobody was really about smoking on a Monday. If anything, they'd toke on resin from the weekend. The breeze blew the winter in hard, stirring up the leaves into these spiraling clusters along the gray sidewalk.

"So you're taking Hyacinth to her homecoming this weekend?" Angel asked.

"Yeah," I said, nodding.

"What about you, Ryan? You gonna go to our homecoming?" Angel said, grinning at me as I winced.

"I ain't goin to no dance," Ryan said, then spit on the sidewalk slab. "Dances're for lames."

"Fuck dat," Angel said, his huge teeth beaming. "You just can't get no bitch to go with you."

"Fuck you, motherfucker," Ryan said, glaring at him. "What bitch you goin' wit'?"

"I gotta take her, man," I said, cutting through the pettiness. "You know how dat shit goes." I took a pull of my Marlboro

Light. "It'd break her heart if we didn't go to that thing."

"I hear you," Ryan said, relaxing his shoulders. His Bulls jersey slumped.

Some of the Good Girls approached the sills: Monica, Hyacinth, and some other one I'd only seen a couple times. Hyacinth wore a white cardigan. She walked fast and kind of led the other two, who were flared out at her sides. Monica had one arm folded over her belly, holding the other elbow like it was broken or something. She had a guilty look on her face, and her bottom jaw hung open a little, showing the blue and red rubber bands in her braces. As Hyacinth got close, her face changed, and suddenly I realized she was furious. Her eyes were all puffy from crying, but now her mouth was pursed. She walked right up to me with her arms forced straight down at her sides. I stood up and suddenly knew. Somebody'd told her. Somebody'd told her everything. I took a deep breath and looked down at the tips of my Nikes.

"How could you?" she hissed disgustedly as I scrambled for what to say. I thought of how to tell her it was a lie. The seconds ticked past. The truth oozed out of my pores and leapt from my defeated, slumped shoulders. Then, she turned, and I thought it was to walk away. I reached out for her hand, then I felt a pop to the side of my face. My head reeled backward. A sharp sting sizzled across my cheek. I just sat back down on my sill. I didn't know how to tell her it was the worst mistake I'd ever made. How I didn't like Gabby—I didn't give a damn about her. How it was like, peer pressure or something. How it was out of my control. I just sat there and watched her stomp away in the same direction she'd come from. The one girl followed her, but Monica sulked at me. Her doe eyes pierced my heart before she turned and caught up with Hyacinth. No one said a word until they were gone. The only sound was my heart beat banging.

"I guess none of us is going to the dance now, huh," Angel sighed.

"Fuck you," I said, my cheeks glowing hot.

I tried calling her, but she didn't want to talk to me. The next night, I tapped on her window, but she just sat up and flicked me off with her thin middle finger. Then, she flopped back down on her bed out of sight, flicking me off the whole way.

■

THE NIGHT OF THE DANCE, I was sitting on my front porch keeping an eye on Hyacinth's house and thinking maybe she'd go with some of her girlfriends, or maybe TeeTee'd take her. But I knew deep down in my gut that she probably had a bunch of dudes from her brother high school ask her and some motherfucker was taking my girl to the dance instead of me. Some motherfucker was taking my girl to the dance instead of me.

A new Nissan pulled up on the corner about 7:30, and some dude in a suit got out of the passenger seat clutching a plastic box. I found myself walking down the block to get a better look. They were inside for a few minutes. I posted up across the street behind a tree. He came out first—a skinny Filipino kid with round cheeks and straight teeth. He smiled and cupped his ear, listening as he waited for her just outside the door.

That chink motherfucker better never come around here again! Stab dat motherfucker in the face!

Then, I saw her. She stepped down her front stairs. Her hair was pulled up in a bun that exploded into a cascade of twirls like the frosting along the edges of a wedding cake. Her cheeks swelled in a smile. Her teeth beamed white and straight without the braces. All the rage evaporated from my chest and dropped into a heavy brick that hung low in my belly. I hid behind the tree and peeked out at her. Her rose-colored dress was elaborately pleated and puffy at the shoulders. It was low-cut at the chest, and the curves of her breasts pushed close. There was a white flower on her wrist. She didn't wear a necklace—my nameplate was in some drawer or trash bin. I wasn't angry. I felt myself whispering, *'I love you, Hyacinth. I love you, Hyacinth. I love you, Hyacinth.'* As she reached the bottom of the stairs, she glanced my way. Her dark, still eyes penetrated me and told me all in one instant that it should have been me taking her hand and helping her into the car. It should have been me in the suit. Should have been me to dance with her, to kiss her out there amongst all the slow-swaying bodies below the corny gym decorations. But it wasn't. It wasn't, and that was all. She bit her lip and got in, and the car was gone with her.

■

ROSE WAS A GOOD SISTER to me. It's funny how guys can ignore their sisters their whole adolescence and then one day—BAM— there they are, right when they need 'em. I was sitting in the kitchen finishing lunch that weekend when Rose walked in.

"Come on, Joe, let's go shoppin'," Rose said nonchalantly. Her hair was all done up in elaborate French braids in the style Da Brat had made famous that summer.

"Huh?" I looked up at her as she grasped her huge ring of keys and Warner Bros gag keychains off the counter.

"Come on, I want to buy you your birthday present," she urged. Wiley Coyote's head hung upside-down from her light-brown hand.

"Ok."

We rode in the green Tempo she shared with Jan. It was messy and had a pungent scent of dank herb and cigars deeply ingrained in the fuzzy interior fabric. Rose plucked a menthol out of the open pack of Newports that rested in a cup holder atop a pile of pennies and dimes in the center console and lit it. The minty smoke clouded over the blunt scent.

"Want one?" she said as she cracked her window.

"Naw, I'm good. Those things burn too much." I patted my chest, then cranked my window down a little.

"OK." She popped in a clear tape that stuck out of the tape deck, and some kind of crazy mixes swelled into the cab—it was electronic but slower than most house music I'd heard.

"What's this?"

"My guy made it—Samson, from up by Howard. He makes beats."

I bit my tongue. I wanted to tell her, 'Why the fuck you hanging out with them GD's up there? They're fucking animals! They're worse than animals!' But I couldn't. She just wanted to spend some time with me and buy me a present that I really liked; something I actually wanted rather than the crap Ma always bought me: socks, underwear, and crappy t-shirts with sports logos for teams I didn't even like and would never wear.

The car lugged northward into Rogers Park.

"Where're we headed?" I asked.

"There's that big Foot Locker on Howard. I know you like jerseys. I'ma get you a jersey," she said, sliding her circular, wire-rimmed glasses up higher on the bridge of her nose with her index finger.

"Ok," I said. My heart pattered. *Why the hell don't we just go up to Evanston, or something?*

By some miracle, we found a spot on Howard right out front of Foot Locker. I'd been meaning to get a Larry Bird jersey. I didn't liked Bird all that much; I couldn't like him after all the hell he'd put Jordan through, although some of those shots he'd made falling out of bounds and all those rings he'd won were impressive. But those Boston jerseys House of Pain wore in their 'Jump Around' music video had all us white boys going nuts. And Bird with the number 33; 3-3 split the 6, it was too perfect. I started sifting through the authentic jerseys, but they were like $40 bucks, so I found some stylized ones on another rack that were half the price. I started sifting through 'em trying to find my size.

"So, you still going with Hyacinth?" Rose asked as she picked through a rack of hoodies a few feet away.

"Naw, well, we kinda broke up," I replied, checking out some of the Charlotte Hornets get-ups.

"You want to be with her still..." Rose said, grinning without looking up from the rack she sifted through.

"Yeah, but she's pretty mad at me." I looked up at her, and she smiled at me.

"Write her a letter," she said with a flick of her wrist. Her maroon fingernails flashed at me for an instant.

"A letter?"

"Yeah, sometimes it's hard to tell someone you're sorry face-to-face 'cause they don't want to hear it and just start arguing or walk away, but they can't do that to a letter."

"What if she just throws it away?"

"She might, probably will. Maybe even tear it up. But give it an hour or so, and she'll be digging in the garbage taping it all back together. Trust me. I'm a girl. I know."

"Maybe you're right," I said as I pulled a medium Celtics jersey with the 33 on it but no name on the back.

"What'chu think of this one?" I held up the jersey towards her.

"Why don'chu get one of the authentic ones?" She walked to the rack I'd been looking at earlier. "Look, they got a Bird right here."

"Too expensive...." I shook my head 'no.'

"Why you worried about how much it cost? I'm the one payin'. Come on, I'm gonna just get it for ya." She grabbed it and turned towards the cash register.

"Alright... Alright." I moped over to take a look.

All they had was a large, but I didn't give a shit—it was getting cold anyway, so I could wear it over my hoodie. Rose bought it, and I slid it over my black hoodie. I strolled out, almost forgetting whose neighborhood I was in, but my dissing of the six-point crown was so elaborate, and seeing how green and black was Cobra's anyway (and they were Folks), no one would have ever guessed I was representin'.

"Ahh, shit," Rose said as we pulled away from the curb. "I'ma pull through here and see if my friend around." Rose turned toward Juneway Gardens. The needle-sharp point of a barbed hook pierced my temple and sent a screeching scream through my cranium. Howard was like the face of the Jungle; Juneway was the fucking heart.

"We shouldn't go in there Rose... I shoul—"

"It's fine. I know all these guys," she said, waving her long acrylic nails towards me. "It'll just be a minute."

We turned down Juneway and were enveloped in the six-story brick Section Eights. They leered on both sides of the narrow street. It was like entering a red brick fortress. The trees were ablaze—scorched brown and red in agreement by the oncoming winter. A bunch of kids ran around in the leafy front lawns, and a bum crackhead limped up the sidewalk with his mouth hung open in a fuzzy black hat with a small bill on it.

Up high in a 5th floor window, a kid with a puffy 'fro leaned out of a drapeless window. His eyes grazed to us, then past us, then he cupped his hand to his mouth and let out a loud and lazy, "We Good." The message was echoed down at street-level three times in succession, each voice further down the street.

"Is dat Stud right dere?" Rose said as she looked at a loose group of dealers standing along a black steel fence. Stud was her pet name for any dude she liked. The big guy with the blue Nike sweatband around his shaved head fit the profile.

"Is dat Stud?" She double parked on the narrow one-way. "Samson," she shouted. The big guy stepped away from the fence towards us.

"Samson," she said as he walked up grinning widely. He

leaned his forearms on her door ledge. "My brotha say he like your beats."

"What up, big man," Samson said, then smirked and reached his large hand into the cab towards me.

"What up," I answered, gripping his immense paw, finding it soft and limp.

A wiry, light-skinned dude eyed us from the sidewalk. He had a dark-blue bandana cribbed on head. The two knotted nubs of the bandana made it look like he hid two horns beneath it. Then, he slowly stepped up behind Samson clutching an aluminum ball bat with a black rubber grip. He peered into the car at Rose with his big lips pouted in an almost perfect circle, and his eyes bugged out—the veins pulsed in them as they trembled in their sockets. He wore a fingerless, black and blue nylon batting glove that rumpled as he squeezed the grip of the short bat. His eyes gleamed with all the menace and suspicion of grade A security.

He slowly stalked around the rear end. I kept him in my periphery as long as I could, until he passed behind me. It felt like he was winding a tight cord around my chest.

"So what'chall up to?" Samson asked.

"Nothin', just got him his birthday present," Rose answered.

"It's yo birfday?"

"Yeah," I said, nodding.

"He smoke bud?" Samson asked Rose, nodding toward me.

"You smoke right, Joseph?" She put the loving inflection onto 'Joseph,' which was the direct opposite of how Ma used it and always made me grin.

I nodded, and suddenly the security passed slowly beside my cracked-open window. He was menacingly close, like a polar bear passing beside the thick underwater glass at the Lincoln Park Zoo— nothing to keep it from breaking through and eating you whole.

"Here," Samson said, tossing a walnut-sized ball of tinfoil in my lap.

"Dat's hydro, boy. Gone have yo ass zig-zaggin'," he laughed. "Why she bringin' dat white mafucka here?" the security asked Samson in a vicious tone. Then, he turned his glower back at me—almost recognizing, almost ignited into action. My urge to leave compounded the pressure of the wires tightening around my torso. He palmed the thick end of the bat that was smudged with brownish-purple spots. The fingers of his naked hand were marred with white scars like teeth marks—like he'd been attacked by a pit bull, or maybe he was the pit bull in the North Side bareknuckle circuit.

I'd never been in the presence of such absolute malice—so cold it was as if he could snatch the life from all three of us in a second, no hesitation.

Later that day, while we toked that very 'dro that sat in my lap, Ryan would tell me his name: D-Ray, the shooter for the Juneway Garden GDs. He'd already been away twice on 'deeds' when he was just a kid, and now at 18-and-a-half, he was head security and prime shooter for the set. The bodies were stacking up. The scars on his knuckles were from fights in juvie, where he'd spent nearly his entire teen years.

As we pulled away, D-Ray snorted loud and disgusted. He must've smelled it on me is all I could figure—the adrenaline, the fear.

We rolled down to Howard, and the wires slowly eased in my shoulders and neck. The realization that my blood, or worse, could have been so easily spilt there on the street seeped into me. It came first as exhilaration, then as rage, and later as sadness that Rose hung out there enough to have a dealer like Samson know her name. He was probably dating her, who the hell knows. I thought of all that was lying in wait for her there in the Jungle.

"Rose, those are some bad people..." I started.

"Samson? Naw, he a football player just like you."

I wanted to lash out at her, scream, '*Stay away from there! That motherfucker is a stone-cold killer!*' But what the fuck ground did

I have to stand on? Mickey was just as bad as any of 'em—worse than most, probably.

I slid my hand down my jersey. The newness of it blazed bright green.

"Thanks for the jersey, Rose. Thanks a lot."

"No problem, little brother. You know I love you, right?"

"I know... I love you, too."

■

I'D BEEN LOVESICK ALL WEEK after the dance. I kept having dreams of Hyacinth on the edge of a dance floor of some gymnasium with the hardwood floor shining below her black heels. She was standing there all alone. The whole room filled with people dancing and laughing as she stood there silently, waiting, looking at her feet. Then, she looked up and tears slid down her round cheeks, her eyes all bloodshot. I tried as hard as I could to rush to her, but all the bodies swayed in front of me, blocking me and holding me back.

I'd written her a letter in pencil on a spiral notebook page— the crinkles all spiky and hopelessly undone. I folded it up tight and wrote 'HYACINTH' on it in capital letters. I snuck out of the house and walked it over. There was no one out. This cool electric pang pulsed in my heart and leapt into my throat. I picked up a dark-pebbled hunk of concrete from a crack in the sidewalk across the street from her house and went to her window ledge. I placed the letter there, quickly and silently, then tapped her window and hurried away. I went home and finally slept with some semblance of peace.

Dear Hyacinth,

I know you don't want to talk to me and I understand. I've been trying to figure out how to say

I'm sorry. I'm sorry. I know it'll never be the way it was. But I still love you the same way that I always did, ever since before I ever kissed you. Before I ever even thought about kissing you, I loved you. Even when you liked other boys, for me, in my head, you were still my girl. I even got in that fight with Angel when he first moved to the neighborhood because I thought you liked him.

I don't even like Gabby 'cause she's dumb and she ain't even pretty. You're the smartest girl I ever knew and not just book smart, you're smart like street smart but more like people smart, you understand things about people and you have compassion for people you don't even know. That was always the thing that made me love you. It's not just that you're the prettiest girl I ever seen, in the whole neighborhood, in the whole city even.

And even if you don't want me back, I'm grateful for all the time I got to be with you, all the time I got to be your guy. I love you and I'm sorry.

Love, Joe

EARLY THAT NEXT MORNING, I woke to pebbles plunked against my window. Then, a clatter as the pebbles tumbled down the roof of my porch and rattled in the white tin gutters. I got up groggy and looked out. The sun'd risen and painted the houses and brick buildings across the street in a reddish-gold glow. The last of the leaves descended from the tree out front, and there she was down on the walkway near the street. She wore a red coat and her Good Council uniform—the blue skirt with the red and yellow plaid pattern and the knee-high white socks. A pink plastic band held her hair back from her face, and she pressed her books to her chest. She looked down the street and waved a finger to her mother, I guess. 'Wait,' she mouthed. I cranked open my window, and she pulled my folded up letter from her books. She waved it at me and smiled. Her eyes were wet and bright—amber in the sunrise. The light just struck her face as it eased above the buildings, and then she mouthed 'I love you, too.'

"I love you," I said quietly, shocked, and then she ran off toward her end of the street happily. Her shoes clacked on the sidewalk, and I watched her as far as I could until she disappeared into the profile of the block. All I could do then was listen until her clicking feet stopped. A car door opened and shut, then the engine sluggishly motored away. I sat back down on my bed in a stupor, not sure if what had just happened was a dream or not, or if I'd gone crazy. Then, a slow laughter billowed up from my chest, and I thought of her riding to school with her mom. I saw her smiling in the morning light as I got up and into the shower.

CHAPTER 26

WORMHOLE

I REMEMBER ONE DAY at the beach near Montrose Harbor, all of us there. I was very young and played in the sand. Dad was off to the side drinking bottles of High Life with my uncle John. I was building sand castles with Jan'n'Rose. I remember digging my feet deep into the sand until my toes found the damp cool. My father back-lit by the falling sun. The sweating beer bottles glowed like light amber orbs in their hands.

There were a few big square-jawed guys throwing a football around, playing tackle. They kicked up tufts of sand and laughed wildly. Then, the ball toppled close to us harmlessly. Sudden, sharp words flared up indistinguishable. The bottles vanished, and one of the square-jaws loomed over my father with his heavy chest heaving. My father's chin jutted long and narrow, and it pointed up at the square-jaw's thorax as he spoke through clenched teeth. The square-jaw's face reddened abruptly. He reached out for my father's collar. My father sprang back and slapped at the larger man's hand; the gesture was at once effeminate and cowardly. Dad turned and stepped away fast. The square-jaw's chest swelled, and he stepped hard after him. My father stopped abruptly and stooped low, like to pick something out of the sand. Suddenly, Dad's whole body lurched upward like a bull placing his horns in the picador's horse. His left arm was straight as a coil-rod. His feet burrowed in the sand. Every bit of the square-jaw's being collapsed inward. My father drove the fist deeper into the base of the man's jaw like the setting of a spear through vitals. The man collapsed on his backside and lay flat atop the sun-sheened sand. His torso heaved slowly. A deep bass hum rumbled through his nostrils. I remember my father peering down at him while grinding something in his molars, examining the man for signs of life. My dad and uncle swept us up and rushed to the van as the other square-jaws huddled about their man.

A perfect silence on the ride home.

■

THIS IS AN EXAMPLE OF WHY, no matter how big you are, you should never go to somebody's house looking for a fight. It was a school night, around eleven o'clock. I lay in bed. I could still hear my parents' TV blaring down the hall. As I started to feel myself drift and fall off to sleep, I heard Rosie's voice raging, "Oh, I know you didn't come up here like THAT! TO MY HOUSE, FOOL?!"

A deep voice grumbled something about, "Where is it, Rose?" I tried to drift back toward sleep. Then, I heard a slap and a scuffle, shoes scraping over pavement.

Rose's voice rippled a vicious "Nooo!" like the hiss of an alley cat. I shot up and looked out the window. My sister wrestled with some large dark figure on the sidewalk out in front of the house. It looked like a grizzly was mauling her. I leapt from bed and rumbled down the stairs. Jan saw me near the front door. "What are you doing?" she shouted from the living room couch.

"Rosie's fighting!" I sprinted out the door. The guy's tall

frame squeezed between Ma's maroon van and the car parked in front of it. Rose grasped at his t-shirt sleeve. They both disappeared into the street. I heard Rose say, "You fucked up now! My brotha's out here!" I followed and squeezed through the narrow space. When I got to the street, they'd stopped. I couldn't figure out what she meant by that, because from the looks of it, I was giving up somewhere around 60 pounds and five years to this guy. Then, I realized it was Samson.

I was standing there in the middle of the street, naked except for the thin wool boxers I'd gone to bed in. Samson lurked a few feet away. His Adam's apple flexed, his skin was pitch-black. The streetlight gleamed off his forehead, which loomed high above his wide shoulders. He stared bug-eyed at Rose beside me. Rose's long, frizzy hair splayed out like it'd been caught in a wind surge from a hurricane. Her torso heaved as she glared straight back at him. My heart pattered. I grasped at Rose's arm with both hands.

"Come on, Rose, let's get in the house," I said in a weak voice. She tore her arm from my grasp, and she stepped directly to him with two long strides. Samson stood his ground—rigid, and leaning back slightly. His chin tilted upward, almost prideful.

Suddenly, her open palm was outstretched at her side, swinging elastic, stretching out longer than it should have. It sang through the air. There was a clapping collision as her palm struck the base of his jaw. The crack echoed through the narrow one-way street from Hermitage to Ashland. His neck stiffened as his six-foot-plus frame gained a couple inches in height. He rocked backward slightly, and then suddenly, his knees jerked violently. He stumbled as his high-tops shuffled along the patched and bumpy blacktop for balance. I couldn't fucking believe my eyes. *She buckled that giant motherfucker's knees with a SLAP!*

I clutched her around the wrist and pulled her toward me as Samson found his footing. "Ah, your brother ain't doin' shit," he mumbled. He cocked his massive, bony fist and leaned into a right cross that slammed into Rose's eye, solid, sending her arms reaching out wildly for balance. She let out a blaring scream—not of pain, but of an animalistic, seething wrath. It's those kinds of moments that show exactly who you are, reveal your bones, naked to all, and more importantly, to yourself.

I leapt at him. He stepped backward with his chin raised, smiling. I swung a quick, straight punch that just nicked his collar bone. He circled to the side, then pivoted and swung again with the right. I tossed my torso backward seeing that massive fist closing in like the grill of a semi-truck, slowed down. With my last bit of balance, I torqued my head to the side. The wind from his thick fist, then his full arm, gusted past. He'd followed through, hoping, I guess, to dislodge my head from my shoulders.

As he swayed back for balance, an electric pulse ignited in my chest that sent both my arms reaching out as if to grab him in a bear hug. Instead, I brought up my hands, fingers spread, and slammed them simultaneously around the soft tissue of his throat. I clasped and squeezed with all my might. His eyes bulged like two mouths screaming. I bent my knees deeply and drove forward. My uncut toenails scraped and dug into the blacktop. I slammed him right into the side of my ma's parked van. His head cracked against the thick glass of the tinted side window; the warped, dark glass reflected the whole block in crisp blacks and yellows all stretched and distorted like a funhouse mirror.

I heard these pounding footsteps. Samson squeezed his hands around my forearms—they enveloped them. But his hands felt weak, like they were just made of water wrapped with skin. His chapped, gray lips gaped, and two lines of frothy drool spanned the distance near the creases. Suddenly, two fists boomed into his forehead, then another and another. It was both of my sisters. Rose stretched and leapt over my back, and Jan had emerged from the side. Both slammed their loose, wild fists into his face.

His eyes started to bob and bounce like pinballs in their sockets, and he began to go again. His knees collapsed like the floors of a building giving way as he grasped at my forearms. I pressed him with everything I had against the van's side window and squeezed so hard that there was no chance his windpipe was open. His neck seemed like it was made of several loose tubes, and I felt like I was deflating them all. Rose leapt over my back so violently that I lost balance and released my grip. Samson stumbled and then rose to his full height again.

I'd decided I was gonna kill this motherfucker—I just didn't know how yet. I thought of the bike chain I had hidden under my bed with the half-roll of duct tape wrapped around one end to make the handle. I leapt between the narrow space in front of the van, sprinted to the house, and bounded the porch steps. Jan's fiancé, DeWayne, burst through the screen door holding a kitchen stool upside-down by one of the foot rungs. His gray-green eyes gleamed out behind his spectacles. I slipped past him. His eyes bugged out as he looked behind me. I turned to see Samson bear-crawling up the steps of the porch. His eyes glowed yellow and black. I stopped and watched.

"Ahh, hell naw, NIGGA! Step off!" DeWayne shouted in his giant baritone voice that dwarfed his medium body frame. He slammed the circular wood seat of the stool directly into Samson's chest. The collision toppled Samson down the front steps. The only thing that saved him was when he grabbed hold of the railing and his torso swung around and bounced off the support bars.

I grinned and sprinted up the stairs to my room. I dove my arm under my bed, and instead of the bike chain, I found a smooth, rounded wood handle. I pulled it out and saw a long, heavy lead file I didn't even remember putting there. I grinned again and got to my feet. I turned and saw my Dad standing in my doorway with his V-neck white t-shirt, yellowed at the creases of his arm-pits, and his saggy whitey tighties. His eyes were fogged over, and

I knew he'd already taken his sleeping medication. He ripped the file from my grasp.

"That's my file," he said, looking at it as he ground his teeth. "Where the hell're you going with this?" he spat.

"There's a guy fighting Rose out front!" I shouted. He grimaced, reached up, and pulled a neon-orange foam earplug from one of his ears. "What?" he said, glaring at me.

"Nowhere." I looked down.

"Well, this is mine. You're not going anywhere with this," he said, turning and rolling the earplug in his fingertips. He walked back toward his room still grasping the file. Then he popped the earplug back in as I walked toward the steps behind him. Ma called out from the bedroom, "What's going on?"

I tried not to run, then ran down the steps, through the hall, and into the kitchen. Rich sat at the old wood table with his hands folded over one another and resting atop the glossy surface. I ran up to the wooden knife rack and blindly grabbed at the many protruding wooden handles. I pulled two out. The cold, steel-gray blade of a foot-long butcher's knife was in my left hand, and a steak knife with a symmetrical point like a dagger was in the other. I could still hear the shouts of the girls and the clatter of the scuffle out front. I sensed Rich's footsteps behind me. I turned and saw him standing before me in the narrow passage into the hallway. He smirked through his full, bristly, unkempt beard.

"Where you going with those?" he asked, grinning.

"There's a guy out there beating on Rose," I roared urgently. "Come on!"

"You're not going out there." He folded his arms over his chest. "Those two got to learn." He put a knowing emphasis on the 'learn.'

"What?" I spat, disgusted.

He just stood there, arms folded over his chest, and laughed with his imbecilic face creased up like some evil clown. I leaned back and bent my knees slightly, then gathered my weight and drove my shoulder into the center of his chest. He gave way like he'd been standing atop a patch of ice. His arms and legs flung out, and he landed flat on his back in one solid thud.

I leapt over him and ran down the hall as Ma stepped down to the landing at the base of the stairs near the front door.

"Joseph! What's happening!" She tried to grab my shoulder, but I tore past her and rushed through the screen door. I stopped on the porch, then spread my arms—blades in both hands. Down on the sidewalk, DeWayne stood in his extra-large Dago T. The stool was broken, but he still clutched its mangled, dangling parts by the end of one of the legs. With his other hand, he held onto Jan's wrist as she slapped her fist into Samson's face for the last time. Rose pulled and finally ripped loose his shirtsleeve. I leapt the full flight of porch steps and ran right up to Samson. He'd gotten hold of a handful of Rose's wild Caribbean hair as she tried to twist away from him. I dug the butcher's knife into the base of his extended shoulder right where the muscle connects to the chest. It only went in a few inches, but it must have struck bone 'cause it ripped from my grasp as he twisted away and fell onto Mrs. Thompson's front lawn. He screamed out. My mother's voice rang clear like a siren over everything and froze us all in mid-motion.

"Joseph!!!" she screamed. I turned and saw her barefoot in her simple, ankle-length white night gown. She tried to step down the front stairs fast with her bad knee and lost her balance, then gripped the railing and just sat on the steps. "Oh, Joseph. What did you do?" she moaned. Her steel-blue eyes pleaded as her mouth hung open. I had such an instant, sharp regret spear into my stomach that I almost cried out in pain. I lowered my head in shame and turned away from Samson as he shouted out and gripped the blade. Blood bubbled up on his hand. Jan suddenly sobered, grabbed my hand, and looked me in the eyes. Her small, round face and button nose were now sullen. She pulled me toward her Tempo parked down the block.

"You got your keys?" she asked to DeWayne.

He nodded.

"Come on," she said as DeWayne glanced down at the mangled stool like he was surprised to see it there. Then, he dropped it to the sidewalk. When we got to the car, I looked back as Rose hovered over Samson. She wept and touched his cheek with her hand as he laid on his back and strained his neck upward. He held her arm. It had all turned so fast, so quick. I wanted to cry; I'm not sure if it was out of regret, fear, or rage. "That motherfucker punched her in face," I spat, looking at them looking at Rose and knowing that she loved him. "Come on, Joe. We gotta getchu outta here man," DeWayne said. I got into the back seat of their small car.

■

WE DROVE AROUND for a while in silence. The hot buzz of the adrenaline faded to a small, hollow tremor. The rush of that instant revenge slowly simmered into the horror of the unknown. How bad was it? The blade had to've gone in four inches. I didn't know what organs it could have hit—lungs, an artery? Hopefully, something not so vital. Some blood had splashed on my hand, and I was shocked at how dark it had turned—like tar there on the trembling creases of my knuckles. I wanted to take it all back, but how? There's something so final about going-to-town on somebody with a weapon. The stakes are forever raised, and with a guy like Samson, they'd be lining up to do a deed on me if he so much as mentioned it. D-Ray would probably walk right through my front door in broad daylight just to light me up. But fuck it, that motherfucker had hit her right in front a me. Stakes had already been raised when I shanked him. And the guns would pour out in my name, too, soon as Lil Pat got word. But I didn't want no one to know. Nobody. I guess I didn't want to make it all even worse for Rose. You can't choose the people you love. As much as I knew, she needed to choose to get the fuck away from that piece of shit and the Juneway Jungle all together.

My love for Rose formed into this warm ball in my stomach, and the fear poked at it like sharp hooks, then the rage twisted wires around it that coiled up into my heart. Then, it slid up my spine and strung taut loops around my mind, which tightened with thoughts of killing Samson. *Just kill him now before he can retaliate.*

We ended up out west by Humboldt Park, passing under those crazy, 50-foot iron Puerto Rican flags frozen in a red, white, and blue flutter. We circled the dark wooded park for a while, then turned south into the neighborhood and passed a few sets that were just ridiculously hot—thirty heads lounging and drinking outside a building on a corner; a dude at the intersection on a GT dirt bike rode in circles through the tight traffic, representing to each and every car; maniac Latin Disciples throwing down the Crown to frightened faces. I just kept my head low, trembling and shivering in my boxers. Jan was steadily wiping tears from behind her glasses, and DeWayne rubbed her neck as she drove.

"We should just take him to Grand Beach," she said. No one replied.

We finally stopped at an Amco station by Western and Augusta. Swarms of crackheads milled about in that brittle, hollow stupor. She pulled up near a payphone with a drippy, blue pitchfork spray painted on the side of the metal housing and got out. She called home, shivering in her pajamas.

DeWayne and I watched her silently.

"Thanks, man, for stepping up like that," I said.

"Hey, Joe, I woulda been there quicker, I just didn't know what was going on 'til den." DeWayne turned his head and reached his large hand to me. We shook.

Jan came back, got in, and shut the door. She took a deep breath and let it out slowly. My heart plunged into my abdomen thinking she'd turn around and tell me he was dead or something, or that the cops had my name and were looking for me. She didn't turn at all—just started talking looking straight ahead at the passing traffic on Western.

"Samson's OK. No serious internal injuries or anything, and Rose said he didn't tell the police who did it, and they finally left him alone. They're about to release him from the hospital." She twisted and looked back at me. Her eyes were all puffy behind her clear-framed glasses. "Dad says we should come home." She sniffled and wiped it quickly with her pajama sleeve. "But, Joe, you gotta hear this: I know you love Rosie, but those two are just drama queens. They're so frickin' stupid. But, Joe, you gotta stop it with all that anger. You're gonna kill somebody with that temper one day. You're gonna go away like Patrick, except longer." She turned back forward and started the car up. "You gotta cool it, little brotha…"

"I know," I said, leaning my head back· in the cushion and closing my eyes. I thought about getting thrown in like Monteff, about the caged wars raging in all those institutions. My hands stopped trembling, and this grateful joy pattered in my chest like a little hummingbird. I reached down and took my crucifix in my fingers and kissed the cool gold. We drove home in silence except for V103 playing low on the radio with the dreary streetlamps easing past my window. I wondered who I was now after all a that? How the monster inside me just leapt out and unleashed its wrath. How maybe I had some a' Mickey and Pistol Pat inside me, and that shit scared me, to tell you the truth.

There was an ominous silence on the block as we stepped up the front porch stairs. I could see a dark patch on the neighbor's dry, dead grass where the blood had congealed and crusted.

We stepped in and shut the door behind us.

I heard Ma's tired voice call to me from the kitchen. "Joseph, come in here a minute."

My back tightened, and just then, Jan reached up and squeezed my traps. The tension burst into a thousand percolating prickles.

"Good luck," Jan whispered as her and DeWayne started up the stairs.

I walked down the hall into the kitchen. Dad sat at the head of the table; the veins in his eyes swollen and red. His gnarly, puffy hair was all sprung up in the back. It was cloudy and whitish-gray with only a little bit of black twisted in. He slowly spun a half-empty, white coffee cup that read *Gone Fishin'* in black cursive.

Ma sat at the foot of the table in her white night gown and rested her large leg up on the long bench. It was hugely swollen and reddish-purple with varicose veins stretching and straining against the shiny skin like mangled tree roots. She watched the old man, waiting for him to say something. I stood there across the kitchen from them with my arms wrapped around my stomach.

"Honey, what you did tonight...," she sputtered, still looking at my father, "I know you just wanted to protect Rose, but you didn't have to..." She slid her hand over her glossy, pulled-back hair. Then, looked at me, but only at my legs—afraid to look into my eyes, I guess. "You can't go around stabbing people. We don't... You don't have to live like that..." She finally looked me in the eyes; hers were steel-gray, sad, and hurt. "This is a safe neighborhood. We could have called the police. You should have just called the police and got Rosie inside." She looked to Dad and raised her eyebrows. Something pierced my liver and sent a sudden rage through me. Cops were nothing but record takers tallying up crimes, taking down stats, and filing reports; they never got there in time to help anybody.

"That guy was punching on her! What, you want me to go inside and dial 911 while he's BEATING HER TO A PULP?" I said.

"We're not going to ACCEPT that kind of BEHAVIOR IN THIS HOUSE!" Dad blared. Suddenly, he slapped both his palms down hard on the table. It swayed and trembled under him, causing his coffee to slide up and splash over the brim.

"WHAT WOULD YOU-A-DONE?!" I yelled, glaring directly into his eyes. His white, protruding brow undulated above them. There was a frozen, startling quiet. He looked at my mother, then propped his elbows on the table and spliced his fingers together before his thin lips in silence, like he was offering up a prayer.

Rose didn't come home that night, and I spent most of it tossing and rolling in bed. All of the horrific possibilities unfolded in my mind. The wires returned and split them into a matrix. If this, then that, what if.... Repercussions reverberated and expanded outward sucking other people in, then swallowing them whole into this confusing, impulsive rage. What had exactly happened? I tried to flip through the blurry memories of the fight, moment-by-moment. The wires cut deep gouges into the tissue of my brain matter.

Violence has no order. The body is just as confused as the mind and spirit. Years later, I'd have bouts like these that would slowly accelerate into flickering images that'd flash in my mind at an incredible pace—gory wounds; a skull split open from the forehead to the base of the neck with purple sinew splurging up and blood oozing slowly out; my loved ones voices screaming; sounds of torture; a robust breast sliced clean off by an articulate bowed carving knife; gang rapes; cars surging towards me as my legs are planted firmly into the asphalt, then uprooted as the bumper cartwheels me upward. And without medication, sedation, I believe these thoughts would have led to a stroke, or something—something unthinkable. There was a horrible throttle pushing them—a surging velocity—that I hope to never feel again and know, of course, I will.

■

I'D WRITTEN LIL PAT a letter about a week before I stabbed Samson. I was all high after the presentation by the Fermi Lab guy and just started thinking of people I could talk about it with. Everybody was completely exhausted by my ranting and raving about astro- and particle physics by then, so I wrote Lil Pat—a captive audience, so to speak. Three days after the fight, I got a letter marked *'Menard Penitentiary.'* I was scared to open it at first and just laid the envelope on my bed. I thought maybe Ma or Dad called him and told him he needed to talk to me. I could still remember all the joy I'd felt just a little over a week back—that rush of ideas and engagement I'd gotten with those brainiacs. I was so far away from that now, and to think about Lil Pat on the inside having to hear about me sticking somebody made my chest knot up. Tears welled in my eyes before I even tore open the letter. It was written on yellow notepad paper with red lines—the kind of paper you get out of the commissary.

Dear Joey,

I'm glad you wrote. I really needed it kiddo. I miss you and everyone so much. I'm glad you started the other day. Free Safety is a good position for you. Ya know, once you hit that growth spurt we all get you'll be starting Line Backer.

To tell ya the truth kid I don't understand half of the stuff you wrote me about Particle Physics but you keep writing about it and you keep writing me about it too, ok. You keep playing football, you'll go to college like Blakey and you study physics, you'll end up working in the frickin' Fermi Lab or something. I wish I woulda kept playin ball, I really do. There's so many things I wish I woulda kept up with. You get to be a little older and you'll see, spending all that time having fun and going around being a big shot, when you look back, it's nothing. You got nothing to show for it. I don't want you to ever feel like that ok kiddo, you gotta go and do stuff. If there's a physics club at Gordon, join the damn thing! Who gives a crap what the guys on the team or the frickin' knuckleheads around the block say. You be you, man, and if that physics stuff is you, be it. Don't go givin' it up 'cause those assholes are raggin' on ya. This could lead to something good for you. And you don't gotta hide it either, you can write me about it all you want, heck you even got me to pick up a book in the library. I ain't been in there in a long time and I read that whole thing and still don't get most of the shit you were writing me, musta got the wrong one or something but you get it and that's what matters. Now go on and go somewhere with it or you'll end up like me, wishing ya did or in here or something… Jesus…

Well, gotta go kiddo.
Love ya little Brother,
-Pat

CHAPTER 27

JAG OFFS

I WALKED DOWN THE BLOCK towards Ashland. The moonless sky was clouded with a murky, purple haze that hung above the canopy of wilting leaves like smoke. As I approached the sills, I saw Ralphy the Junker pushing his empty metal grocery cart out of the mouth of the arterial alley. He crossed Hollywood with his cart rattling as it wobbled on its rickety black wheels. Ralphy stepped behind it in a white hospital coat that'd worn brown and ragged with a black, fuzzy hat sitting atop his gnarled, gray dread-locks. Ryan and Angel glanced around as traffic flicked past on Ashland, then Ralphy stepped shakily to Ryan, and they made an unmistakable exchange. *Ralphy! Ralphy's a hard-banging junky! No way they're slanging H right there?! How the fuck they doing that shit without asking me?! Even telling me?!* Rage roared in my chest. Heroin destroyed my brother's life, and heroin dealers preyed on him just as much as he'd preyed on them. *Fuck dat shit!* I stomped straight up to Ryan as he leaned against the wall of the hospital in his blue hoodie. Ryan grinned at me with Ralphy long-gone down the tunnel.

"What the fuck's up, man?" I shouted. "You pushing H right here?"

"Naw, Joe. Joe, chill out," Angel said, stepping to me with his palm out. His heavy blue flannel hung off of him limply.

"Chill?" I said, shooting my eyes at Angel. "All dat shit carries a felony tag, man! You ready for dat?"

Ryan smirked and jutted his stubby chin upward, which instantly flared my anger even worse. Then, I saw a dark-blue bag under his left eye; it was puffy, and there was some black shit twisted into his eyebrow. His face flexed, and a bulbous lump swelled on the side of his head above his ear like he had a golf ball under his buzzed scalp.

"The fuck happened to you?" I asked.

"The PG3s got 'em, the flakes got 'em," Angel said. His glazed-over, slit-eyed smile revealed his large teeth through his lips.

"Mickey got word-a-what happened," Ryan explained. His chest swelled as he scratched the peach fuzz above his lips and stood squared up with me. "PG3s put a S.O.S. on my ass. Dey were talkin' shit, said the .25 was a BB gun. Piece by piece, he got the whole thing. Said if the PG3s took me serious enough to set out to kill me, then why wouldn't the TJOs take me serious enough to V me in?"

I took a deep breath and swallowed in all of it, not knowing how to feel. There was the rage at the H, the fear that these PG3s were set on killing Ryan, then the jealously that he was a legit TJO, and I still wasn't shit.

"Who V'd you in?" I asked.

"Man, Chief and Freckles... I don't think you met him yet," Ryan said excitedly. "This lil Irish fucker. Man, he's little, but he could bag, man. I squared up with him right away—thought I'd rush him, then deal with Chief. But this fool, man, he had fucking lead in his fists, man." His busted teeth showed wet between his chapped lips.

"No shit?" I asked.

"Yeah, man, it wasn't nothin' nice," Ryan said, touching the stitches along his eyebrow, "but it's over now, boy. I'm in." He smiled, and his green eyes sizzled with pride. "I'm getting my ink done this Saturday. It's gonna be a big-ole party. Mickey says you're both invited."

"Hell yeah," I said. I reached out and our hands clapped together. His was wide, heavy, and stronger than usual.

"I got to talk to you about this shit, too," Ryan said as he sat down in his sill. He pulled out a bag from the front pocket his red jeans.

"What?"

Ryan handed it to me.

"We're gonna start making some real money now," Angel said.

I'd only seen it once up close before, but I knew what it was. The small, crumpled plastic bag. The knot tied around the light-brown powder packed into a tight little ball. It felt so light, so insignificant. But some blackness swelled inside my sternum—a darkness so much larger and heavier than that tiny little bag of dust. The wires looped around it and squeezed, so it evaporated and absorbed into my cells.

"China white," Ryan said.

"Man..." I handed it back to him.

"What?" Ryan slipped it back in his pocket.

"Man, I can't be part of that shit." I sat in my sill beside Ryan's.

"What? What the fuck're you talking about?" Angel asked.

"My brother, man..." I threw my hand up sharply. "Look, I just can't, alright?"

"Hey, man, look. Mickey told me all about that, man," Ryan said, putting his hand on my back. "Pistol Pat, man, he just dipped into his own shit. That's what got him in trouble, man. You can't be dealer and a customer is all."

"Man, I can't, bro. I just can't, alright?" I said, shrugging Ryan's hand off.

"Look, man, we're gonna be making three time as much as we were off that fucking pot, bro," Angel said. "Three times as much, man!"

Ryan pulled out a wad of cash and said, "Look, man. This is what we made tonight." He planted it in my palm.

I weighed it in my palm—it had to be at least a hundred dollars. I handed it back.

"Look, bro, it ain't like we're gonna start doing that shit or nothing," Angel said, pinching the tip of his nose with his thumb and index finger.

"We're gonna stay strong, man," Ryan urged. "Look at all this money, man. This is what we always wanted, bro."

"Hey, look, man, there's something else, too," Ryan said, glancing over at Angel. "Mickey made me chief of the prospects, so you know I'm supposed to be calling the shots'n shit, but you know the way I see it is we're still Fusion, bro, and ya'll are gonna get V'd in soon enough."

I sat back in my sill and thought of Lil Pat. I thought of the last day I saw him as a free man with the gun pointed in Ma's face—that trembling that'd taken hold of his entire being. Then, I remembered the last time I'd seen him in the green jumpsuit—how big he'd gotten, the scars on his forehead and brow like he'd shoved his head in a thorn bush, his eye swelled shut. How he said be loyal to Ryan, he'll be a good friend to you. Then, I thought of the money and of Ryan and Angel, and I didn't know what to do. All three of us sat in silence, listening to the traffic riffle past on Ashland. I could walk away and let 'em count this money, let 'em face the PG3s all by themselves. But the thought of that—of not being there when they needed me—made the wires strain at my heart. It was too much, too much to take.

"Hey, look, man... If it's still Fusion then, man..." I sat back in the darkness of my sill, "I'm down. If this is what we gotta do, then it's what we got to do."

"That's what I like to hear, bro," Ryan said as he hopped off his sill and looked across the street. A bum milled there at the mouth of the alley. The darkness filled the pathway in an off-kilter beat as the alley lamp flickered above the customer. "Aye," Ryan said, standing and nodding him over.

"You'll see, man. Shit'll be cool," Angel said as the bum walked up shrouded in darkness. His face was blackened with dirt or mud or something else, something deeper. A tremble betrayed his steps. Ryan glided up to meet him, and I knew it wouldn't be cool. It wouldn't be cool at all.

■

SATURDAY NIGHT ROLLED AROUND, and the three of us made the short walk over to the house on Bryn Mawr. The front porch steps were full of guys drinking and smoking and scowling. The music blared inside—some kind of fast-paced metal. Ryan led us up the stairs, and Chief stood at the top with his cheeks all sunken and jaundiced like he had HIV or something, but his forehead shook any concern; it was wide and square like the head of a sledgehammer.

"What up, Ryan?" Chief said, reaching his hand out. They shook in the TJO fashion—hooking at the thumbs and throwing up the J. "What the fuck are these two doin' here?"

"Aye, Tommy, they're with me," Ryan answered. "Mickey said they should come."

Tommy nodded at me and Angel, then shook his head in disgust and stepped aside to let us pass in through the screen door. There was nothing but grimy white guys everywhere. The mood was light, but they still had those hard glares in their eyes. Pantera soared on the stereo, and a few of the TJOs leaned against the wall of the enclosed front porch nodding their heads vigorously with their eyes squinted shut. We stepped into the living room. Beer cans and bottles littered the rug. There was the stench of cigarettes, warm beer, and somebody's cheap old lady perfume. The whole room churned in a circus of motion.

A shout came from across the room. "Come here, you little fuck!" We looked over and saw Mickey. His whole head beamed red and glowed in the low table lamp light. His wide grin caused his entire head to flex. Mickey stretched his thick arms out wide as we made our way over to him. When Ryan got close, Mickey clamped his arms around him and planted a big kiss on his forehead. Mickey slid his hand through my slicked-back, Aqua Netted hair, messing it up bad. Then, he turned and karate chopped Angel in the chest playfully.

I noticed this guy standing off to the side by the couch, watching us. He had blond slicked back hair, weathered skin, and light-brown freckles speckling his hard-boiled scowl. His hands were small, though his forearms and shoulders bulged in an undefined bulk. He wore a Dago T and blue jeans that were too big for him at the waist, so they were bunched up on his narrow hips by his tight-slung belt. He stepped to us and punched Ryan in the arm. Ryan recoiled, smiling—his forehead orange in the light. Then, the blond guy grabbed him, pulled him close, and hugged him.

"Welcome to the Brotherhood, kid," the blond guy whispered in Ryan's ear.

"Thanks, Wacker," Ryan said as they broke their embrace.

Wacker was a name that rang out in Edgewater, though I didn't know the whole story just then. He had the most clout in the whole neighborhood, even more than Mickey.

"Who's the spick?" Wacker asked, nodding towards Angel.

"He ain't no spick; he's a chink," Mickey said. "He's the one that's been runnin' around Kung Fu-ing niggers at Senn."

"I heard that fucking story. You're that kid? Put're there!" Wacker reached out his hand to Angel, who took it limply. "That fucking cracked me up, you know that?"

"It's funny now," Ryan said. "Wasn't so funny when it was going down though."

"Almost never is," Wacker said, looking back at Ryan. The light caught Wacker's flushed face. An old scar bubbled-up dead-center above his eye that traced across and disappeared into his hairline. "So this's the new crew, huh?"

"This is dem," Mickey replied, scratching his prickly beard.

"Wait a minute. That makes you Patty's little brother," Wacker said, looking at me shocked.

"Yep," I answered, smiling nervously.

"Ah, shit. I remember when you was in diapers," Wacker said.

"It's a trip, ain't it?" Mickey said, handing me a damp can of Milwaukee's Best.

"Shit, I thought he was gonna piss his pants walking in here," Chief added, sauntering up to us with his angular smile creasing his face.

"You need a change a shorts, Joey?" Wacker asked, smiling. The others laughed.

I shook my head in embarrassment, but more in shock that Wacker remembered my name. They'd just released him from the penitentiary a few weeks back after a long stretch.

"I was with Patty over in Pontiac," Wacker said. His voice saddened. "All he ever did was talk about his baby brother." He put his hand on my shoulder. There was a calm, steady warmth in his hand that I never thought a guy like him could possess.

"How's he doing?" I asked. My eyes burned and watered.

"He's keeping his nose clean." Wacker looked away and stepped backward. "He'll be home soon."

I knew he was lying. They'd just added six months to Lil Pat's sentence for his part in a riot in Pontiac, and they ended up shipping him down to Menard in an attempt to break up the gang's power structure.

"So I hear you've been getting down, too, huh?" Wacker asked. "A young prospect, dropped some big nigger or something?"

"That's right," Chief piped in. "But it was all for nothing; PG3s wasted that nigger the other day." There was a silence. "Blew his fucking brains out."

Mickey and Wacker burst into laughter at the exaggerated rumor. My mind suddenly flashed to Tank in a wheelchair—his legs already shriveled up, his arms looking like they belonged to another body.

"That's the way they all belong," Wacker said as he turned and looked over his shoulder. "Aye, Charlene, get me a fuckin' beer. What the fuck?" he shouted to the kitchen where a beautiful, tall brunette sat talking with some of the other girls. Behind her, a mountain of rotten dishes was heaped in the sink.

"OK," Charlene screeched back. "Geeze." She got up wearing a loose blue flannel shirt tucked into her tight black jeans. Her legs seemed even longer than they were with the tall black heels she was clicking around in. Her hair was dark and wavy, and she had a sharp face with too much make up on it. She grabbed an armful of beer cans from the fridge and stalked over with long, bouncy strides. As she got close, she made eyes with Angel. He stared back, his eyes glazed over. She handed the beers out, and when she handed one to Angel, they locked eyes. She smiled, wrinkling her crow's feet. Angel's mouth hung open in awe.

"Who are these boys?" Charlene asked, throwing her hair over her shoulder. "They're so cute." She winked at Angel.

"Get back in the kitchen, ya tramp," Wacker said, snapping back the tab of his beer. His shoulders swelled as he dismissed her. "What the hell are ya, a pedophile or somethin'?"

She spun back towards the kitchen, and her tight jeans hugged her perfect, high-slung ass. Wacker gave it a hard slap and a deep squeeze as she stepped away. She flashed naughty eyes back at him over her shoulder.

She stepped on. Her ass cheeks twitched through the taut jeans as she went. I nudged Angel, who still gaped at her. I scowled at him and mouthed, *'What-the-fuck-are-you-thinkin'?'* Fucking with Wacker's girl was so far out of the question; to even look her way could mean blood.

There was a rumble on the staircase behind us, and I turned to see a huge fat guy barrel down the steps. He caught himself on the narrow railing that swayed under his grip. It was Fat Buck. I didn't recognize him at first with his head shaved. He had two lightning bolts tattooed above his ears that spanned from his side-burns all the way back to the base of his neck. He wore overalls with black combat boots. A webbed forest of black hair covered his forearms. The hair spouted up from his shirt collar and swam around the rolls of his neck and melded into this full, mangy beard. He drunkenly swayed his way up to Mickey.

"The kid ready?" he asked, jabbing a thumb at Ryan.

"He ain't a kid no more," Mickey answered, putting his arm around Ryan's shoulder.

"Whatever you say, Mickey," Fat Buck replied. "I'm ready for him upstairs."

Mickey looked at Ryan with a sadistic grin on his lips.

"Get on up there," Mickey said as he winked.

Ryan took a deep breath, glanced at me and Angel, and raised his eyebrows.

"See ya on the other side," Angel said, then patted Ryan on his back as he headed upstairs.

"Damn, Bucky, I didn't think you could get any fatter," Wacker joked, poking Fat Buck's stomach as he went by.

"Aye, Wacker. Welcome home, baby," Fat Buck said. They embraced and patted each other on the back. Then, Fat Buck pressed on. "What, do I remind you of your celly? Big bad Bubba?

You probably miss him already, don'tcha?" Fat Buck remarked over his shoulder.

"YOU FAT FUCK!" Wacker roared, red in the face. "I'LL RIP YOUR FUCKING HEAD OFF!" He lunged for Fat Buck, but Mickey restrained him, and everyone in earshot just laughed. "I'LL SHOW YOU WHAT FUCKIN'S ALL ABOUT!" Spit flung from Wacker's lips. "Bust that fat ass of yours!" he yelled as Fat Buck swayed back upstairs muttering to himself.

"Excuse me," Charlene said, getting up from the kitchen table. "But this is the only ass you'll be busting tonight, mister." She pointed her index finger at her perfect butt cheek and twisted it like she was extinguishing a cigarette.

She gave Angel as mischievous smile. He smiled back. Wacker's grimace twisted into a knot.

"Aye, Mickey, can we go up and watch?" I said quickly.

"Yeah, go ahead." Mickey pushed me on the shoulder towards the stairs.

I grabbed Angel around the shoulder, and he finally broke eye contact with Charlene. We made our way up the stairs.

"She's fine as hell," Angel said, stepping up the stairs in front of me.

"I know she is," I said in disgust.

We got to the top of the stairs and heard hard-banging bedsprings and a high-pitched moan from one of the bedrooms. I snatched Angel by the arm.

"Do you got any idea who Wacker is, bro?" I asked, glaring at him. "He will drag you out back in the alley, stab you in the throat, go back inside, drink a six-pack, and laugh about it."

"Come on," Angel said, breaking my grasp and starting towards the open bathroom where Fat Buck and Ryan sat.

"It's your fucking funeral, bro," I called after him.

"What's all this talk about funerals?" Fat Buck asked, leaning over Ryan. The small metal tattoo gun hummed in his big paw.

"This is a celebration." He didn't look up. "Young blood here's getting his first ink."

Ryan clenched his teeth on the toilet seat. His shirt sleeve was rolled up, and Fat Buck went to work on his right shoulder. I noticed the words 'Thieves Junkies and Outlaws' written in cursive at the base of Fat Buck's skull.

"Does it hurt?" Angel sang in an obnoxiously curious tone.

"Fuck you," Ryan spat with his eyes squinted shut.

"Hold still, damn it," Fat Buck growled.

I carefully slid behind Fat Buck, who sat on a wooden chair that creaked every time he shifted his enormous weight. Beads of sweat bubbled up on his creased brow and spotted his scalp. He smelled like a bear that'd taken a bath in whiskey.

I sat on the edge of the tub as Fat Buck slowly stretched the black ink along the outline of a silver dollar-sized five-point star. The skin all around it blossomed up pink and puffy.

"Joe, how's it look?" Ryan asked with his eyes still clenched.

"Badass, man," I said. "Badass."

Ryan smiled for a second, then went back to his grimace.

It took a while. We drank as Ryan squeezed his fists at the sides of the mauve toilet. Underneath the star, Fat Buck wrote 'T.J.O.' in block letters, and it was done.

"I love virgins," Fat Buck sighed. He grabbed his beer can off the sink and poured it over the puffy, red skin that surrounded the tattoo. Ryan screamed and gripped his tat like a wound, then he launched to his feet. The veins in his neck strained purple.

"Motherfucker, Bucky!" Ryan said, then punched him in the chest. Fat Buck's rolls jostled and swallowed the punch, and he heaped up off his seat and snagged Ryan in a bear hug. Fat Buck rocked his hips back, and Ryan's feet came off the white tile floor.

"Welcome to the TJOs, brother," Fat Buck said, then kissed him on the forehead.

"You son of a bitch," Ryan said, squirming in his grasp.

We rumbled back downstairs, and the party was in full swing. A bunch of girls had showed up. All hell broke loose, and we jumped right in it.

In the midst of it, Wacker stormed up and grabbed Ryan's arm with both hands as we were hollerin' at some older girls who giggled up against the wall. Wacker stared at the star and letters and let out a roaring, manic laugh.

"It's final now, kid! No turning back!" Wacker yelled. Drool slipped from his mouth.

"Never even considered it," Ryan said as he looked him in the eyes.

Mickey's voice sprang from the couch next to the coffee table. "Aye, get over here." We made our way over.

"Carve that boy up a line," Mickey said as Ryan sat down.

Chief plopped a pile of white dust onto a mirror on the table, and a sick feeling snaked into my stomach. I stood across the small coffee table as a little guy with slicked-back black hair carved three narrow lines out of the white mound with his state I.D. I walked around and slid in next to Ryan on the couch, then nudged him with my elbow.

"Ryan, man," I whispered. "What about not messing with your own product, man?"

"What?" Mickey said. "Naw, this cocaine, kid." He took a rolled dollar bill off the table, bent down, and snorted a long line. The white grain disappeared into the green roll, hard and fast. Mickey's face surged up at me. His eyes bulged and rolled around in their sockets like he'd gotten cracked in the jaw.

"But you sure as hell better stay away from that stash," Mickey added, pinching his nostrils and glaring at me. "End up like fuckin' Pistol."

"Naw, he's gonna stay away from that, too," Wacker said, jamming his index finger at the coke. "And those are direct orders from you know who."

"Fine," Mickey said, then passed Ryan the rolled dollar bill. Mickey put his hand on Ryan's back and leaned him down to the table. Ryan snorted up his line, then rocked back into the couch cushion beside me. His eyes blinked as he rubbed his nose.

"Want some, Kung Fu?" Mickey asked Angel.

Angel shrugged and sat down next to him on the couch, then leaned down and snorted the last line.

"You boys want some more a-that, you just let me know," Mickey said, laughing. "Gotta do something with all that money you boys are making."

"Come on, Joey," Wacker said, then nudged me towards the back porch.

We sat on the wooden steps out back. It was quiet, and the alley lamp loomed high over the pitched roof of the garage. Wacker opened a pack of Camel Filters and offered me one. I dug one out, and he plucked one for himself. He sparked his silver Zippo and brought the healthy, swaying flame to my smoke. I inhaled. There was a tattoo on his hand where his thumb and forefinger met that read 'TJO' in those same simple block letters.

"Now dem letters there," he said as he showed me the tat, "they've got me in a lot a trouble." The Zippo flame lit Wacker's hardened face. "Kinda trouble I wouldn't wish on nobody, especially not family. Now, I ain't saying Mickey don't love Ryan." He toked his cigarette hard, and the butt roared red like a hot coal. "But, Patty, he really loves ya. You're his baby brother, ya know?"

"I know he does," I sighed.

"What I'm trying to say is, kid, you ain't never gonna have those letters on your skin."

I exhaled a plume of smoke and looked at him. My heart jumped in my throat.

"Patty, he asked me to watch out for ya," he said. "You, you ain't never gonna be no TJO."

"But..."

"I know you're already involved," Wacker broke in. "And he's gonna be pissed about dat, but dat's as far as you go. You're one of us, but you ain't." He looked off northeast toward Senn and the lake. "He wants ya to go to college or some shit, and you better." He pointed at me with his cigarette. "You better."

I looked down as joy flooded my chest, and I missed my brother more than ever. But then, humiliation dug lines through the joy. *Maybe, he thinks I ain't hard enough.* Hooks dragged across my stomach and planted in my gut. *Ryan ain't so bad; I'm the one who stabbed a fucking GD!* Then, my mind suddenly blanked, and I felt like something hugged me from all sides. I closed my eyes and felt like I was floating slowly upward. The hooks plucked free from my stomach, and I grabbed at the wounds.

"Don't take it too hard, kid, and don't worry about nothin'," Wacker said, putting his hand on my shoulder. "You know I'd gut a motherfucker in about a second over you, right?"

I smiled and nodded.

"Oh yeah, and Patty got word of what happened the other night."

My eyes shot at him. My heart raced. *What night?* Shit, a hundred fucking things'd gone down over the past few months.

"If that motherfucker ever comes back around the house, don't do nothin'. You just give me a call, and we'll finish the job," he said. "I know that motherfucker's probably a Stone. That's why you didn't tell nobody, right?"

I went to speak, but he stopped me with a wave of his hand.

"Well, either way, he's gonna have to go. We'll bury that nigger in the fucking alley."

I nodded.

"But, hey, this is a party. What the hell are you doing out here?" He slapped me on the back. "Now go on in and stir you up some of that pussy runnin' around in dere." He nudged me with his shoulder.

I got up and started inside. When I got to the back door, I turned. "Thanks, Wacker."

"Don't thank me, kid." He didn't turn to face me.

I went back inside, and Angel and Ryan were hanging on that same group of older girls who were just laughing at 'em. The night went on like that for a while. I was down, thinking about things too much. I got quiet and wanted to see Hyacinth. I knew she'd probably be asleep, but I decided to go over and check.

"Hey, Ryan, I'm taking off bro," I said.

"What? Why, man?" He had his arm slung on a brunette with frizzy hair.

"I ain't feeling too good."

"Alright, bro."

"Aye, where's Angel?" I asked.

"I don't know." He looked around. "I think he went upstairs."

"I'm gonna go say bye to him and get outta here."

"OK."

I headed upstairs. No one was up there that I could tell. I walked the hall to one of the back rooms, and as I turned the corner, I saw Angel with a girl draped over him. I smiled at him, but he just straightened up, rigid. The girl's head spun around—it was Charlene. I walked right up, grabbed him by the arm, and pulled him away from her, hard.

"What the fuck are doing!?" I shouted in his face.

"Hey!" Charlene said, shoving me.

"You trying to get him killed?" I spat at her.

"What!" Charlene shouted. "Wacker? He doesn't own me."

"Come on, man. We gotta go now before somebody sees this." I pulled Angel down the hall. He drunkenly let himself be dragged with his head bowed. When we got downstairs, Ryan saw us and rushed up.

"What's going on with you, Joe?" Ryan asked.

"We gotta get him outta here, NOW," I said.

"What?"

"NOW!"

"Alright," Ryan replied as we shuffled out the front door. I was last to walk out. I looked back over my shoulder at the coffee table. One of the older TJOs held a spoon in one hand and struck a lighter beneath it. The spoon was full with a muddy, brown liquid. Angel laughed as I hurried them down the porch stairs and up the street. We turned into the alley.

"Now, what the fuck's going on, Joe?" Ryan said as he spun around.

"This motherfucker's rubbing up on Wacker's girl," I replied, then pushed Angel. He fell against a dumpster, drunk.

"What the fuck?" Ryan's eyes widened. "You trying to get killed, bro?"

"That's what I said!" I kicked Angel playfully in the chest.

Angel laughed and curled up next to the dumpster like a sleeping baby, holding his gut.

"I couldn't help it," he pleaded in a childish whine. "You saw her; she was the angel-slut!" He gasped for air.

"This motherfucker is gonna get killed for sure," Ryan laughed.

"Don't I know it," I replied.

We both bent to help him up, then started down the alley with Angel between us—his arms draped over both of us.

"Well, did you touch her ass at least?" I asked.

"Oh my God," Angel squealed, then broke away from us and ran out ahead. "It was like heaven," he yelled out into the alley night. "Like heaven, God damnit."

■

LATER, I WALKED to Hyacinth's house. Her light was on, which meant she was up reading anyway. I was glad; I hated to wake her up. She opened her window, and I climbed up on the wooden sill and kissed her. We whispered in the dark.

"What is it?" she asked.

"It's my brother. He did something for me. I don't know how to feel about."

"Which one?"

"Pat," I sighed. "He made it so I could never be a TJO."

"That's good, Joe. You don't need to be hanging around those crazy assholes anymore."

"I know, but it's like... Ryan, he's practically my frickin' brother for Christ's sake, and he's a TJO now."

"But that's different. Ryan isn't you, and you aren't Ryan. You're you, Joe. I know Ryan's a good friend and a good person, but you're different."

"But, Pat's a TJO. My real brother, my blood."

"But look where he is, Joe," she pleaded. "Look where it got him."

"It wasn't the TJOs, it was shooting that fucking heroin!" I seethed, full of rage. "It destroyed him inside," I spat loudly, then checked my voice. "He was a good guy. He was always a kind brother to me. He was a good person. He is a good person."

"I know he's a good person, Joey. I know it because of what he just did." She reached down and gently stroked my hair. "He's protecting you."

"I don't need no protecting!" I pulled my head away. "I can handle myself out here." I gestured to the street.

"He probably knows that, too. That's why he did it. Joey, you stabbed someone the other day." She started to cry. "That's a very serious thing you did." She inhaled a stuttering breath. "You could go to jail for a very long time over that." Tears beaded down her round cheeks. "They could take you away from me for a very long time."

"I know, I know. I'm sorry. I love you..." I climbed up and

nuzzled my face into her cheeks and wiped the tears with my forehead. "Don't cry."

She caught her breath, then wiped the tears back. "I want to tell your brother I'm grateful for what he did. And you should, too... You should, too...." She broke into a hard sob again, and I did my best to corral it until she stopped. I went home feeling terrible that I'd bothered her with this—that I'd made her cry all over again.

■

THAT NIGHT, I dreamt I was walking down some strange street in broad daylight—some old-style town with fancy lamp posts. Then, the beast walked along the sidewalk across the street from me, and the Assyrian walked behind it holding a chain that stretched to its immense neck. Then, Ryan appeared ahead of them on the sidewalk, and the beast growled. The Assyrian yanked on the leash, and the beast sat. Ryan noticed them. Then, the Assyrian unleashed the beast, and it galloped toward Ryan. Ryan just bounced on his toes, laughing like he had something up his sleeve, like he knew a secret nobody else knew. As the beast got close, Ryan cut down the alley and vanished. The beast disappeared behind him.

CHAPTER 28

ELECTRON POSITRON ANNIHILATION

TO RYAN, being a hype was the ultimate show of weakness. I guess, for him, dealing it was the act of punishing his father for his frailty, brutality, and eventual failure. There was a hunger in Ryan's method. He would not hesitate for a sliver of a second to stick a hype straight in the jaw for the slightest foul in attitude or misconduct. He took a certain pleasure in it that scared me; not fear for myself or for the junkies, but fear for Ryan's own fucking soul. It made me want to grab him by the arms and shake him. Tell him, 'That ain't your old man you just hit, Bro! It's just some poor, bum-ass junky!' And you'd think that kinda behavior would hurt business—it didn't; it only made the junkies revere him. It made their approaches more subtle, made their money right every time—not none of that change and penny bullshit. It got to the point they didn't even talk to Angel and me except to ask for Ryan. Even they'd demoted us to lookouts. I didn't care. The thick wads of green that swelled in my pockets made my skin itch, and I found myself handing money out to panhandlers—sometimes $50 bucks a pop, startling them and making them stumble after me trying to give me a hug with tears in their eyes. But I knew all the while it'd find its way back to Ryan eventually.

■

ONE NIGHT, Lil Pat's old girlfriend Angie showed up at the sills. I thought she'd crawled in some hole and died. Figured being a hooker and a junky gave her about a hundred percent chance at the HIV. There was a brisk, dry breeze that night. The temperature had settled in the teens. Angie was thin, thinner than I ever remembered her, with bleached straight-leg jeans on that only came down to her shins. Her red-striped tube socks were all bunched up in a thick wad at her ankles above her grayed tennis shoes, and she wore this heavy wool red and black flannel that was so big and old it could have been Lil Pat's. Her hair was all crusted and tangled, and she shook in these brittle tremors that made it look like her arms were gonna crack off at the shoulders. Her face was all dried out, porous, and wrinkled. There were dark makeup smudges under her eyes like she'd been crying earlier in the day, or week even, 'cause she smelled like she hadn't showered in at least that long.

"Aye, Joey, can I have a cigarette, honey?" she croaked in her raspy, tired tone.

I looked at Angel, and he flipped open his pack of Marlboro Lights. She rattled her thin trembling fingers around in it until she pinned one down against the thin cardboard. Then, she brought it to her chapped mouth and pulled a small black lighter from her flannel pocket and tried to strike it. The more she focused on lighting it, the more she trembled. Her head even started to wobble. Finally, the lighter clattered at her feet. The whole thing was so pathetic that I bent, scooped it up, and sparked it for her. I had to follow the cigarette tip as it bobbed and swayed with her face like a crusty leaf rattling in the breeze.

She finally pulled, and as she exhaled a thin cloud, she spoke. "Joey, I came here 'cause I'm in trouble. I'm sick. I need a hit. You can see that," she said in her raspy hiss. "I don't have nothin'. I got robbed today; a john beat me up and took everything." She was lying, but I didn't care. I wasn't giving her a fucking thing. She was part of what took my brother from me. She could croak and die right there, and I wouldn't so much as drag her into the ER.

"Will ya help me, Joe? Please! I loved your brother, Joey. I did. I still love him. He would want you to help me."

"Don'tchu fuckin' talk to me about MY BROTHER, BITCH! You didn't fuckin' LOVE HIM; you fuckin' POISONED HIM!" Flecks of spit flung off my mouth and caught in her face and gray eyes.

"Please!" she seethed, blinking. She looked to Angel, who just turned his face westbound down Hollywood. Then, she stared at Ryan. "Please, I'll suck you off... Anything!" she moaned and grabbed at his shiny leather coat sleeve.

Angel snickered, still refusing to even look at her.

Ryan stood up straight.

"Come on den," Ryan said, grinning. "I'll give you a hit if you slob my johnson." He grabbed the crotch of his jeans, and they crossed the street over to the arterial alley near the stash. She knelt down in the salt-grayed snow next to a big black garbage can as he unfastened his belt.

"Can't believe he's letting that nasty bitch suck his dick," Angel admonished, disgusted. "Bitch has got AIDs, let alone her lips are crusty like sand paper, man. They're gonna be over there for half an hour."

It took a while. The whole thing made me sick, like I had two eels slithering around in my stomach. It made me want to just step the fuck off, but I couldn't. Then, Ryan looked over at us.

"Watch dis shit!" he shouted, then took a step backward clutching his dick. A steaming arc of piss gushed outward from his pale, chubby prick, and Angie reached out and grasped the thigh of his pant leg for balance. The piss struck in her gawking, upturned mouth, then splattered on her forehead. It splashed into a steamy, circular mist around the crown of her scalp. The alley lamps caught in it, and it flecked into this foggy orange aura like a halo. She unleashed a screeching hiss, then gagged. Ryan stepped back further, and her hands clapped the murky, snow-covered pavement. She retched. Piss and puke dripped slowly and thick from her lips. Ryan just kept pissing, rippling a steady bead on the top of her head so her hair fell mop-wet and hung down over her face. She continued to gargle, retch, and screech like an alley cat in heat. Ryan, finally spent, zipped up and dug his hand in his deep, 3/4 trench coat pocket. Then, he tossed the nickel of China white in the center of the small pool of piss, bile, and saliva. He walked back toward us giggling.

I can't tell you why, even now, but I wanted to cry right then —for her, for him, for Lil Pat, for me. All of it swelled like warm balloons in my lungs, then the wires bound the balloons and they popped. Ryan grinned, but not his usual smirk. His chin was tucked and it could have been a sneer as much as a smile. His dark, oily red hair was almost black and slicked back like a dark streak running right down the center of his skull. If he woulda said anything to me as he stepped up, I woulda hit him square in the jaw, but he didn't say nothing.

Angel was laughing—tired and wheezy. "Don't come near me, man. You smell of piss and junky whore," he said, squinting at Ryan and pinching his nostrils. Then, he brought the collar of his puffy Miami jacket over his nose.

"Woulda took a hour to cum like dat," Ryan said, glancing at Angel. "She was gonna pay one way or another."

He looked at me with his eyes bold and bloodshot. Just over his shoulder, Angie shuffled to her feet and hurried off down the alley, shivering, screeching, and clawing at her sopping wet hair.

There was the smell of piss, saliva, and drenched sex. Ryan's lips spread and he bared his teeth--one eye tooth grew down on top of the other like a second skin. He was sneering, frowning, and grinning all in one, and then I understood—he'd done it for me. That was how he'd paid her back for what she'd done to me, and I knew then that he was sick beyond all help. He was gone. So far gone from what he'd been the day I met him all those years ago when we were just scared little boys. And I knew he'd never be able to get back to that, like it'd been deleted from his insides. I was sure then that there was nothing in store for him but ugliness from there on out, and he was prepared for what was to come. All of it emblazoned on that pale, acne-scarred mug. That copper fuzz dangling off his square chin. That glossy, black three-quarter trench coat.

We smoked a few more squares, then I dipped over to Hyacinth's. She wasn't home, and I didn't know how I could explain it to her anyway—how that horrible act Ryan'd just done to that poor, old junky whore was an expression of love, and how it made me feel nothing but rage and disgust. I couldn't grab hold of one single thing in all of it. Not one single person or moment to throw my broiling rage at. I just wanted to hold Hyacinth in my arms and not tell her a damn thing. Just hold her and feel all that pure love between us—all that great, giant blue lake of love there, and just be quiet with that for a while 'til it all passed or got swallowed up. But she was gone, probably at volleyball practice, or at a girlfriend's house painting each other's toenails. But there was a kind of solace in that, too. 'Cause at least she was far away from all of that ugliness. Far away and safe.

∎

THERE WERE A COUPLE big busts higher up on the food chain, so we had to go buy a few ounces from the North Pole Moe's connect up by Howard and Ridge. We'd held on to some loot, and Mickey decided to let us buy an ounce of our own as a reward. It was early evening. Mickey drove and Chief rode shotgun. I stared at the light glinting off the back of Chief's blond, curly box cut. All three of us rode in back. They'd beat me to the call, so I rode bitch. We passed a spliff around as Cyprus Hill's "Hits from the Bong" oozed from the stereo. It was a Friday night, and when we pulled onto Howard off Sheridan, there were cars backed up all the way from Paulina. The sidewalk buzzed. A tall black hooker slinked past. Her black weave had blonde streaks curled down past her shoulders, and her huge hoop earrings jostled as she clanked past in tall green heels.

"Your first ounce," Mickey said. "Remember your first ounce, Chief?"

Chief just shook his head and smiled.

"You boys are coming up in the world. Next thing you know, you'll be moving a key," Mickey said, smiling.

Chief laughed.

"The way this money's coming, who knows, Mickey?" Ryan said.

"Ambitious motherfuckers, these three," Mickey laughed to Chief. "You ever here Joey talk about science and his crazy ass ideas? This fuckin' kid...Dumb as you or me, but he knows about shit you ain't ever even dreamed of. Tell him some of that crazy fucking Einstein shit you're always yakking about."

"Ok...." I said, wanting to jam an icepick straight through Mickey's fat head. "So there's this new shit out there they just discovered called antimatter. It's like the parts of an atom except it's made out of all opposite parts—like, you remember learning about electrons?"

"Yeah," Chief said, looking straight ahead.

"Well, electrons got a negative charge, right? Well there's this new thing, it's a kind of antimatter called a positron. It's got the same exact mass and made of the same thing as an electron, except it's got a positive charge..."

"Ok."

"The tripped out thing about it all is that if a positron and a electron ever collide, they annihilate each other.

"Annihilate?"

"Yeah, they destroy each other. They just explode into energy. But you know, like nuclear power, like when they split an atom and made the A-bomb and all that shit. It's called nuclear fusion and fission, right?" He nodded. "Well, when an electron and positron collide, the energy in that annihilation is one hundred times more powerful than an atom bomb."

"It's like they was meant to meet like dat," Chief said in an empty tone. "Perfect enemies. Nemeses."

"Yeah," I said, surprised he'd even listened. "Something like that."

"Told ya," Mickey laughed. "Motherfucker thinks he's a astrophysicist or something." Then, he swung his head around and glanced at Angel. "Aye, Kung Fu, how'd you like dat 8-ball?"

"Loved it," Angel replied.

"Just as good as the other shit, right?" Mickey eyed him in the rearview mirror.

"Better," Angel said as a slick smile slid across his lips. "Had me running around the room with my underwear on my head." We all laughed. "And it was my old He-Man underwear, too."

"This fucker's insane, ain't he?" Mickey said, glancing at Chief and pointing his thumb back at Angel. "I don't know how you guys put up with him over there."

"We need him, that's how," Chief said bitterly.

"What? The GDs? Fuck 'em, they'll be dealt with accordingly," Mickey said, then wiped his salivating mouth.

"It's awful hot over dere, Mickey. They say they're coming for me," Chief said.

"Tommy, of course they're coming for you. They've been coming for you ever since I made you chief, alright," Mickey snapped. "You signed up, now deal wit' it. There's plenty of young brothers who'd love to take your place." Ryan dug his pudgy index finger into his ear and wiggled it.

"I ain't scared, Mickey," Chief replied, looking out the window. "You know I ain't scared to die. But, Mickey, we got to start bringing the heat to school."

"No. How the fuck you gonna get 'em past the metal detectors?" Mickey barked.

"The Stones get 'em in," Ryan piped in.

"Next thing you're gonna tell me, you've been bringing that BB gun to school," Mickey said. Ryan went to speak, then rubbed the tip of his nose. Chief sighed and stared out the window.

"I told you, you ain't bringing no heat to school. We can't afford to lose a brother or a piece. Not right now," Mickey spat. "I'll pick your ass up every fucking day from now on. I'll bring the whole fucking arsenal if it'll make you happy."

There was a silence.

"They ain't never fucking shot in the school, OK?" Mickey said.

"Mickey, I don't want to die if I don't have to," Chief replied.

"Waa waa waa! Maybe we'll get rid of one on the way out. Would that make you happy?"

"Hell," Chief replied. "Why not? They're probably gonna rush us anyways." Chief removed the false vent and put it on his lap.

A hot shot of fear gushed through me as I realized how right Chief was. Five white hoods in the same damn Lincoln we'd been rolling in for years now. It was so obvious to me then. Of course we'd get rushed floating through the Jungle on a Friday night. The street buzzed, and people ushered everywhere—almost all of 'em black, some young, some old, but all with that same bright hunger in their eyes.

As we neared the Red Line stop, crowds of people poured out of the station on their homeward commute. Then, this wiry, light-skinned black guy cut through the current of people. He wore a white hoodie and chomped a wad of gum. The two knots of his jaw muscles flared like the jaw of a Thoroughbred horse. I knew him from somewhere. I knew him. He never looked at the Lincoln, just stepped straight toward it as we eked along Howard. He flipped up his hood so it enveloped his trimmed scalp, and a shadow swallowed his face. He dug both his hands in the front waist pocket of his hoodie. His hands—the knuckles littered with white scars. D-Ray?

Chief was cool as he reached into the stash. He pulled out the nickel-plated 9mm and cocked it quickly.

"I said on the way out, psycho," Mickey said. "Roll that fuckin' window up."

"Ah, fuck," I said with a strange calm in my voice. No one but Chief and I noticed the guy.

"Mickey!" Chief shouted.

"What!" Mickey roared back.

A gleaming, black, snub-nosed revolver emerged from the white hoodie pocket. D-Ray stepped right up to Chief's window and squeezed a shot from the hip. Mickey floored it, swerving the Lincoln into oncoming traffic. Another pop, and a white splash washed over Ryan's window, then the glass broke and descended. Chief twisted in his seat and shot through the gaping window. Time nearly froze. My vision focused and magnified on D-Ray's chest. The black glob of the bullet pressed into the flat plane of D-Ray's hoodie. It pushed deep into it without breaking the cloth, twisting the fabric into a vortex. His mouth gaped—a circular void. His head tilted down. A black hole opened as the bullet sunk into his heart. Dark-red blood burst and exploded into a globular spray. The car jolted forward. I turned and watched through the back window as D-Ray's shoulders wilted inward.

He collapsed to his knees, and his gun clattered in the gutter. I gasped a deep breath, and something tacked against the back of my mouth. It fluttered against the opening of my throat. I turned to see gray and white feathers floating in a cloud around the back seat. Hundreds of 'em slowly sauntered downward. The cold wind poured in through the gaping window, swirling and pushing them around.

"What the fuck is dis shit?" Ryan shouted.

I realized it was Ryan's new coat. He'd turned towards me as the second shot fired. I grasped hold of his shoulder where the feathers spewed out.

"Ah, fuck, am I hit?" he squeaked. I tore his coat open—no blood, no hole.

"Naw, naw, you're good. You're OK," I assured him.

"You sure?" He slid his hand inside his puffy coat.

"Yeah, it just clipped your coat," I said. Suddenly, I realized the bullet's trajectory must have passed right in front of our faces. Angel reached up and stuck his finger in a hole in the off-white fabric of the interior above the door he sat beside.

"You kill that motherfucker?" Mickey asked, squealing the Lincoln around the corner at Clark.

"Yeah, he's dead," Chief answered.

"Yeah," I said. "He caught it in the chest. I think it was... It was D-Ray."

"Motherfucker...," Chief grimaced, panting. "I been trying to kill dat nigger for years."

"You alright, Angel?" I asked.

Angel bent over so his head was near his knees. The Lincoln roared through the streets. Parked cars flew past the windows. Small jets of air slipped through the cab and jostled the feathers into the front seat.

"I felt it," Angel said in a shaky voice. "The wind from the bullet." He rolled down his window and retched into the cold.

Gray and white feathers gusted out over him and landed in his damp black hair.

"Man, I just bought this motherfucker!" Ryan yelled, gripping the puffy duck feather coat. "A hundred'n'fifty bucks! God damnit!"

"Man, just be happy you're alive," I shouted.

"Uh-oh. Ryan, your boys are getting a little shaky back there," Mickey said, grinning as the car crept though the back streets, south towards Edgewater. "Come on, boys, is that the first time you been shot at?" Ryan cracked a smirk. The rest of us were silent. Angel kept his head out of the window. "First time you been around for a little murder?" Mickey nudged Chief. He didn't respond.

"Ahh, you guys ain't no fun," Mickey said, dusting off some feathers that had landed on his shoulder. "Look at dis shit, it's like a fuckin' snow globe." Mickey hacked on a feather. "One last snow before summer."

No one else laughed. Mickey let Chief out near the Morse Red Line stop and dropped us off at the sills.

"I'll just have 'em swing through with it," Mickey said, then pulled off down the alley. "Come by the house tomorrow."

Ryan nodded as we stepped to the sills and collapsed in our spots. I hated the idea of Mickey with our product; who knew what he'd cut with and how much he'd cut, but I was sure he'd step on it. Then, when somebody got sick, he'd say, 'That's what you get when you fuck with niggers.' The Lincoln wobbled through the potholes of the side alley toward Bryn Mawr. Glass still clinked off the window frame and onto the pavement. *Fuck, Mickey's the worst nigger I know.*

Angel was still sick and leaned against the wall. His head hung, and he spit now and again.

"Do you believe that shit?" I said.

"Fuck yeah I do. Look at my fucking coat," Ryan sneered in disgust and pawed at his deflated shoulder.

"Man." I shook my head, then looked over at Angel. "You alright, man? Maybe you should just go home, bro."

"Naw, man," Angel said, then spit again. "I ain't going home now." He looked up with blood-red eyes.

"What's the problem, bro?" Ryan asked. "We're all OK." He looked at me and raised his hands out at his sides. "And we got one less Flake to worry about. One a their fucking shooters, for Christ's sake."

"Man, it's war again, bro, and these D's ain't playing around," I replied.

"Man, you don't even know what it's like at school, bro. We got that shit on lock," Ryan said. "Tell him, Angel."

Angel looked over with the worry all lined up across his forehead.

"Both you motherfuckers are acting scary," Ryan said, disgusted. "Man, come on."

"We ain't scared man. It's just like, like you don't even see how serious this fuckin' shit is, man! These motherfuckers are gonna be gunnin' for us now. They're all killers, man," I pleaded.

"We got a gat, man. What's the problem?" Ryan asked, disgusted. His knees bobbed up happily as he sat, like he'd been waiting for this shit his whole life.

■

LATER THAT WEEK, I was at the dinner table eating. Ma had her little black and white TV on the counter. The volume blared over the clicks and claps of forks and knives and the steady chomping of mashed potatoes, roast beef, and peas. I'd tuned everything out when suddenly the sound of the TV locked in on me from across the room.

"Violence strikes again at Senn High School on Chicago's far northside. Authorities say that at 1:20 this afternoon, Thomas Leaman was shot to death in the school's gymnasium."

They showed a picture of Chief's face, and an electric shock gushed through me. For some reason, I thought they'd caught Chief for the shooting a few days back. Then, it all sunk in: Chief's name was Thomas Leaman, and he was dead. It was then that I realized I was standing at the kitchen table with my palms flat on the smooth oak. My parents and sisters all stared at me. I cleared my throat and sat back down and jammed my fork into my mashed potatoes. I kept my eyes on my plate.

"Don't worry, it wasn't Angel or Ryan. It was just some gang shooting," Ma said.

"Ahh, yeah, it just scared me is all," I replied quickly.

I stuffed those potatoes in my mouth and jammed huge hunks of the roast beef down my throat as fast as humanly possible. My father's eyes beat down on me. I got up and put my plate in the sink. Then, I walked down the hall to the phone in the front room when the doorbell rang. I opened the door and Angel was there in some blue jeans and a black hoodie. He was pale. The porch light above him struck a dark, oval-shaped shadow on his forehead like a black halo. I opened the screen door and walked out onto the front porch. A chilly breeze sent goosebumps up my arms.

"What's goin' on, man?" I whispered.

"They got 'em," Angel answered. His eyes and face had a strange stillness. "Shot him in the chest, then in the head when he went down."

"Let's walk, man. Come on." I led him down the porch steps. He swayed down them. "Man, you been drinkin'?"

"Naw, man, I'm just high." He straightened up. A truck down at Ashland blew its horn long and loud.

"The GDs got' em?" I stepped down the sidewalk towards Ashland.

"Yeah, dude. Ran into the gym blastin'," Angel said. "I heard the shots from the other side of the buildin'. At first, they said it was D-Ray."

Suddenly, it struck me; *they fucking annihilated each other.*
Then, I shivered that away and tried to assure myself.

"D-Ray's dead."

"I know, but that's what they said. He looked exactly like D-Ray." Angel looked hollowed out.

"Fuck, maybe it wasn't him after all?" I sighed.

"No, it was. Everybody knows D-Ray's dead. Hell, we were fighting all day, an' they kept screaming, 'This for D-Ray!'"

"No shit? What the fuck was it, D-Ray's brother?"

"I don't fucking know, man." He shivered.

"So you guys were fightin' all day?"

"Man, they were chasin' us, then we was chasin' them. I think Ryan pulled the .25." He sighed.

"What?! He's been brining dat shit up there?"

"He needs it," Angel said. "They're gunnin' for us."

"So you was fightin' all day?"

"Naw, man." He looked away. "I took off."

"Yeah?"

"Fuck that place." He took a small plastic bag out of his pocket. "Fuck all this shit." He took his school I.D. and shoveled out a bump of the powder.

"You like dat cane, huh?"

"What? Ah, yeah," he muttered.

An old man stepped onto his front porch across the street and eyed us suspiciously.

"Man, I'm about ready to try dat shit," I said, watching him snort the bump.

"Naw, man, don't." He put the bag away quickly.

"Whatever, man," I said, shrugging. "Think we should stay off the sills tonight?"

"Naw, man, I got some people comin' through right now." He walked to his sill.

"Where's the piece?" I asked.

"I don't know. Ryan's got it."

"Where the fuck's Ryan?" I growled.

He shrugged as we both took our seats in our sills. His head bobbed and nodded like he'd drank ten beers. Traffic was slow on Ashland. A woman walked past in a brown Jewel uniform hugging a paper sack against her side. The peace on the street was in bold contrast to my insides. Chief...I never liked the motherfucker, and I wasn't pretending to then, but God damn the bastards had killed his ass in broad daylight in the center of a packed gymnasium. What the fuck was stopping them D's from strolling over here and mopping us up? I felt like they would come at any second. I listened for it. I wanted to scream. I wanted to run and hide somewhere where none of this shit could ever find me. I wanted to go back to the beginning, but I couldn't even tell where it was. Was it me going heads up with Leroy? Was it Lil Pat killing that fucking Assyrian? His first hit of H? His first scrap? They said the old man was bad, too—as bad as they come. It was like I was locked into some rollercoaster, some spiraling acceleration propelling me towards something. Something horrifying and inescapable.

After a while, Wacker's brown I-ROCZ with gold racing stripes pulled up. Angel swayed towards the street. There were two ladies inside. Both of them had tall New Wave hairdos and giant hoop earrings.

"Hey, cutie," Charlene yelled in her screechy voice from the driver's side.

"They didn't get you today, did they?" the other girl shouted to me as she leaned across the cab with her face near Charlene's.

"You got it?" Charlene asked Angel. He stepped up to her and leaned into the window. They whispered.

She opened the door and pulled her seat forward a little, then Angel squeezed into the back seat.

"I'll be right back, bro," Angel said with that same emptiness in his face. I knew he wouldn't be back at all. I raised my hands out, palms up, in a plea for some form of sanity, but there wasn't none. I walked through the foggy tunnel towards Ryan's house. There was a stony quiet at the Dead-End-Docks. As I got close to Ryan's house, T-Money appeared in front of his apartment building with his hands buried in the pockets of his black hoodie. His face was still, and his gray eyes were stone-cold. Then, he stepped back into his gangway, and for some reason, I knew he'd be dead soon, too. There was no jail cell waiting for him, no revelation and escape from the life. Nothing but a pool of blood on some sidewalk. I didn't feel any sadness. Nothing in his being pleaded for pity. There was fortitude in him, a resolve; a simple resolve to die a real motherfucker, and that was all he was living for. A true soldier to a soulless war.

Ryan wasn't home. His Ma opened the door in a dirty pink robe that didn't quite close around her wide stomach and chest. Her eyes were still and bloodshot behind her large brown-framed glasses. "He's not here," she sneered, drunk. Her spiced rum breath was hot and sour in my face. Even the dogs were solemn, mourning. Bear laid on his belly atop the couch with his wide head resting on his paws. The white glare from the TV flashed in his face as he looked at me with his eyelids sagging.

I went home.

■

WHEN I WALKED IN, Ma called me into the living room. "Well, you better try!" she said angrily into the receiver as I walked up to her. She handed me the phone. "Your brother wants to talk with you," she said, looking me sternly in the eyes before walking out of the room.

"What's up, Pat? Are you ok?" I asked.

"Yeah, I'm fine, kid. I'm, I just had to talk to you. I..." He sighed. "You need to know... He needs to know..." he muttered to himself. "I shot heroin because I done things, bad things—things that haunt me every day. I have nightmares. I have anxiety attacks. My heart starts racing for no reason. I shake and tremble when I'm in a crowded room," he whispered. I heard the occupants of the day room chattering in the background. "I'm afraid someone is gonna kill me all the time. I think of killing people, people who did very bad things to me." His voice strained with emotion. "Drugs, they... they took all that away. Heroin, it was like nothing bad ever happened to me in my whole life. I finally felt peaceful. No pain, no hate, no fear, no anxiety. Jesus, I can't even talk about it without itching for it all over, Joe. You can't... You can't end up like—" The phone muffled and clanged against something, then it clattered to the hook, and the line went dead.

"Pat... Pat, you there?"

PIGEONS

THE LAST TIME I made love with her was in the garage on a Saturday in the middle of March. You know the saying, 'In like a lion, out like a lamb'? Well, in Chicago, the lion keeps roaring all the way into April. This night, it roared in the form of freezing rain that clattered atop the wide concrete slab of the backyard. I'd brought this old brown hide blanket out there that was made out of a steer or a buffalo or some kinda beast. I got a bottle of high-end wine—$15. High-end for me back then, anyway. We had the little radiator-style electric space heater cooking, but it was still cold. The lights were out, so I had two tall white candles burning; the wax beaded down them and onto the little table in front of the couch. The scent of her vanilla lotion swirled and twisted around the pungent red wine on her lips and her breath. It exuded from her in a thick steam in my face. The candlelight flickered burnt-orange on her calm cheeks, and her eyes were like two bright amber embers. Her lips were wet and heavy with emotion, and there was the sopping elasticity of me inside her. She panted in my ear, moaning in an impassioned agony. Then, the explosion like an incandescent, white flare struck inside her and me. Then, trembling, trembling. Her tears slid down her face onto mine and sizzled like beads of lava.

"I love you, Hyacinth."

"I love you, too, Joe."

I rolled onto the lumpy couch beside her as steam sifted and streamed up off our sweaty foreheads. Our breath trailed and feathered up like smoke into the bare rafters of the garage. We laid there 'til our breathing slowed.

"Joe."

"What?" I pulled the coarse, furry blanket up higher onto us.

"You think you're ever gonna stop all of that trouble, you're always in?" The four small windows that faced into the backyard were all fogged up and glowed white. The freezing rain roared on, pattering the glass and thrumming atop the roof.

"Yeah... Yeah... One day. One day it'll all stop."

"You think it might happen soon?"

"I hope so." I kissed her temple.

"Me too... Me too."

■

IT WAS AROUND THEN that we found out about Monteff. I've lost people in my life, but that was one of the ones I just never got over. He was just a good person, a bright soul. Even now, sometimes I think of him in there. Some people just aren't meant to be in places like that—locked away inside where the weak are preyed on and tormented and even tortured. When I think of him in there, I want to reach out to him somehow and tell him, 'Kid, if you're gonna survive this, you have to cut out those things, those very tender things: your compassion for others, for the weaker ones. You need to cut all of that out of your heart, and hope that it catches up with you somewhere down the line.'

But maybe some people just can't do that.

■

I CAUGHT UP WITH RYAN the next night over at the sills. He was decked out in a brand new Celtics jersey over a gray sweatsuit. A diamond flickered in his earlobe, and a thick white gold herringbone chain glimmered in the lamp light. Business was good as usual. There wasn't much to say about Chief; he was dead. The war was raging on at Senn, and I knew Mickey would make Ryan the new chief any day now. There was so much I wanted to say to Ryan, but I knew he wouldn't listen anyway. But it made me feel better to see him again. Ryan was my oldest and dearest friend. We'd been through so much, but the silence that had slowly built and surrounded him had spread outward, and there was just no way to cut through it. No way to breach it.

I wanted to tell him, 'This shit's gonna be the end of us. I feel like I'm losing my soul. I feel like I've lost so much already. I'll never be a TJO, and I don't want to be one. You scare me, man. I don't know when or how, but you're gonna kill somebody. If I stick around long enough, I'm gonna kill someone, too. I'm probably going to hell or something like it, and so are you. We've got to pay for all that we've done.' But nothing came out. The whole world was resting on his shoulders and mine as we slowly fed the neighborhood the same poison that'd gotten my own brother exiled in earth's living purgatory and his father the same.

As the night wore on, Angel stumbled up to the sills wearing an opened red and yellow flannel shirt. His upper lip curtained his top row of teeth, and the bottom lip hung low in a loose 'O.' His eyes were distant. His shoulders slumped—every joint in his being languorous. There was some kind of wet spot on his undershirt that I kept seeing in slashes of as his flannel swayed with his shoulders.

"This motherfucker," Ryan said.

"What the fuck… You been drinkin'?" I asked with a smile.

"Yeah," Angel said, sniffling back a clear drip that hung from his nose.

"What'd you get? Some cane?" I asked, looking at him sideways.

Angel giggled. His eyes were glossy, vacant.

"That ain't cane, man. Look at him!" Ryan growled at Angel. "He's fallin' asleep." Ryan's neck and head blossomed red.

"You fucking with that shit?" I asked Angel, still looking at him sideways.

"Naw," Angel said, smiling. "I just got it mixed up with that last 8-ball."

There was a silence as I looked at Ryan, shocked. Ryan's chin sucked into his neck. A vile grin slashed across his mouth.

"It's cool, man. I don't even like it," Angel said.

"You fucking idiot," I said slowly.

Ryan's torso swelled below his Celtics jersey. He bobbed on the toes slightly, then his flabby fist slapped into Angel's jaw. His jaw compressed into his throat. Angel slowly fell away with his eyes closed, a slight smirk on his lips, hands limply at his sides like he was playing—like he was falling backwards expecting someone to catch him. No one was there except the cold sidewalk. I lunged and reached out to try and snag his shirt, but it was too late. He fell flat out, and his skull splashed and bounced on the concrete. His eyes retracted up into his skull and flipped like two movie reels hitting their ends. A hum came from his mouth. Blood pooled under his head.

"You're through now, motherfucker!" Ryan shouted.

"Ah, shit," I said, crouching down and cradling Angel's wet head.

"You son of a bitch," Ryan snarled, pacing back and forth. "One thing. You couldn't do one thing for me."

Angel's eyes were half open, still flickering.

"You gonna be alright, man," I whispered to him.

It shocked me that Ryan had that much pop in him. None of us'd ever put anyone clean out. I'd never known who'd win between all of us heads up, and to see Angel dealt with so easily had me embarrassed for him. It had me wondering if I was all wrong about my speculation and if Ryan really was the baddest with his hands after all.

I saw a light come on in a house across the street. "Ryan, man. Take off, you're blowing up the spot."

"Son of a bitch," Ryan shouted.

"Go on. Get the stash, and get the fuck outta here," I whispered. Ryan hesitated, grimacing. "NOW, MAN!"

Ryan jogged across the street, then squatted down, grabbed the stash, stuffed it in his sweatpants pocket, and started walking down the arterial alley towards the Bryn Mawr house. A squad car pulled into the alley in front of him, and he froze in the bright beam as the car came to a halt.

"Be cool, man," I whispered to myself. I watched Ryan and the dark figures in the squad car staring at each other. I knew the squad could see me and Angel on the sidewalk—him bleeding and me holding his head up. I tried to play it off. I smiled and grabbed him by the arm. I tried to pull him to his feet, but he was still out. His head slumped limply.

The cop flicked a switch in the squad, and its blue and red strobe lights twirled alight. Without hesitation, Ryan broke down my alley out of sight. The squad roared after him, strobe lights spinning. The siren careened as the wheels squealed around the corner.

"Fuck!" I yelled. "Wake up, man! We gotta fuckin' hide now, you asshole!" I pulled Angel up by both his arms. "Wake up!"

Angel got to his feet, kneading the back of his head with his palm. I pulled him along towards my house by his elbow, and by the time we got half way, he had it together enough to jog. We cut through the gangway to the garage. Other sirens popped on around the neighborhood as the whole shift slowly committed to catching Ryan. I only hoped he could ditch the stash before they got him.

I sat on a milk crate near the garage door listening until the sirens stopped, and I knew they'd snagged him. Angel was a mess. His jaw puffed and reddened where Ryan'd cracked him. He had this far off look on his face as he slouched on the couch. Finally, his eyes just slid shut, and he drifted to sleep. I watched him as the low light crept in the small windows of the garage. His mouth hung open, and his skin was like brown porcelain—calm, at peace, and pure, like a child dreaming.

After about an hour, I woke Angel up and walked him home. We didn't say much; he was too out of it anyway. I headed over to the house on Bryn Mawr. Wacker sat on the front porch smoking a cigarette. His thick arms flared as he saw me. His face was worn and wrinkled. The scar was more prominent now—like he'd been branded.

"What the fuck happened?" Wacker said, standing up.

"You guys got any loot laying around?" I asked as I walked up.

"Yeah... Mickey's already over there bailing 'em out." He sat back down with a defeated exhale. "Well, we hope anyways."

"What?"

"We don't know if they're gonna let him go," he said. "He got caught with some weight all bagged up. It's distribution."

"Ah, fuck. They got it?" I sighed as the shock set in. How much weight? What's the law for a minor?

"You fuckin' kids," he said in disgust. "I don't know what Mickey was thinking puttin' youse three to work."

"We were just packing up shop, and the cops rolled up." I raised my shoulders.

"You think they was watching you or something?" He shot me a cold look.

"I don't know." I shrugged.

"Were they watching you?!" he said, leering over me.

"We ain't had any trouble 'til this," I said, raising my hands, palms up.

"Fuckin' Mickey! Puttin' kids out there like that." He looked out into the street. "That fuckin' asshole! Your old man woulda never put up wit' shit like this!"

"What?" I said, mystified.

"When your dad started this shit, he never woulda even considered putting kids out there like that. Back then, kids got to be kids. The older guys dealt with the serious shit."

I tried to swallow what Wacker'd said. Could it be true? My old man started the TJOs? It couldn't be, but he was so pissed, I didn't pursue it. I didn't believe him. Maybe that shot to the head made him nuts—who knows? We sat and waited in silence for an hour or so. I was sick to my stomach, and I gagged a few times but didn't throw up.

"You look like hell, kid. Go home," he said, flicking a half-smoked cigarette. "I'm tired of lookin' at ya."

I stood up and paused.

"Go on. Everything's gonna be alright. It's a first offense. They'll let him go, we'll get him a lawyer, and he'll be fine." He shook his head and looked down.

"You living here now?" I said as I started down the stairs.

"Naw, I got my own place down on Granville with the niggers, working nights at the college. I just came by when Mickey called. My only night off, and I got to deal with this shit."

"What'd'they got you doing?" I asked.

"Janitor."

"They make good money, right?" I raised my eyebrows.

"Yeah, lucky me. It's this parole shit. It's only six months though."

"Yeah?" I rubbed my eyes.

"Yeah," he said. "Now get outta here, kid."

"Alright, Wacker." I stepped off the stairs, and he got up and walked inside the house in silence.

I walked towards home slowly. I was mad and sick, and my heart filled with hatred for the neighborhood. *Every time we get past one thing, another thing that's even worse pops up. When's this shit ever gonna just let us be?*

■

I FOUND MYSELF WALKING towards Hyacinth's house. It was just past midnight, and a near perfect silence hung on Hermitage. All the parked cars were bunched up on each other like deadlocked traffic. An alley cat scampered around the corner of the hospital parking garage. Deep down, I didn't want to bother her, wake her out of the peace of sleep. I could see her in my mind as I walked—her angelic, golden-brown face; those large eyes softly shut, flickering, dreaming. I thought about her future and what happens to pretty girls on the honor roll. She'd be going away to college. She'd end up a doctor or a lawyer, drive to work in a Beemer or an Audi, have a family, be happy and good. Then, I thought of where punk-ass drug dealers end up. I figured I was headed to jail or maybe dead. If I was lucky, I'd end up swinging a hammer like my old man my whole life. *Maybe I could go to college, I don't know.* I was getting an A in physics, but with a 1.8 GPA, I wasn't exactly college material. *Ah, hell,* I sighed. My chin tucked into my chest as I stepped over the cracked pavement with tiny little weeds wilted between the cracks. *I ain't on shit—can't even get V'd into a gang I've been riding with for years, and now I don't even know if I want it.*

I walked up the sidewalk to her window, pulled myself up, and tapped on it with my fingertips. She suddenly shot up straight on her bed, turned, and hurriedly pulled the window open. Her scared eyes searched mine as her chest heaved under her nightgown.

"I had a dream about you. I was dreaming that you were drowning out on the lake, and it was the dead of winter, and there was ice, and there was... I, I just couldn't get to you, and you slipped below the ice in-between...." She threw her arms around my shoulders and buried her face into my chest.

"It's alright, baby," I said, kissing her on her forehead as she nestled her face into my neck.

After a few moments, she looked up.

"What's up? What's going on? Why are you here?" She looked up, lip trembling.

"It's just..." I wished I hadn't come. "It's Ryan. He got arrested."

"He got arrested? For what? Selling weed?" she replied, shocked. And for some reason, I couldn't lie to her then. I couldn't lie to her anymore.

"Naw, he was selling something else."

"What?"

"Heroin...." My eyes burned.

"Oh, my God...." She recoiled away from me with her mouth gaping open. "You, you weren't part of that?"

I looked away and tried to shake the guilt from my face. My throat ached.

"Your brother, Joey... How could you get involved in that?"

"I don't know."

"You got to get away from it," she said as tears welled in her eyes.

"I know...," I said, finally able to look her in the eyes.

She started to cry in heavy, loud sobs, and I reached out and stroked her hair. She just kept crying. Her eyes shifted from horrified to hopeless, and I could see all I'd been doing to her—how I'd been hurting her, how I was so fucking bad for her, like a poison. She was the sweetest person I'd ever known. She loved me so much. She was my first love, and this was what I did to her? This is all I'd been doing to her for months—making her hurt, making her cry.

I finally calmed her down enough so that I could go. We kissed one more time. I whispered I love you over and over in her face and ears. Her lips were hot and damp, but this time for another reason—the wrong reason. She shut her window, and I walked home.

■

I WASN'T WORRIED that the cops had called or came by. I knew better that Ryan wouldn't talk, but then I thought, *What if O'Riley walked up and just threw it all on the old man's lap?* My shit'd already be out on the lawn by now, so that'd be the answer. It wasn't. I went in and got into bed wondering what it'd be like to face a real charge—a felony—shit that they were gonna slap years on you for. Then, I thought of Lil Pat. Thought of how he'd gotten older in there, how he'd grown up in there, really, and how hard that must be to have to fight, cut, and kill just to survive day-to-day. That's not the life that I wanted. That's not what I wanted to be. I saw Lil Pat years from then, as a carpenter, as a father, owning some house way far away from here. Tears welled up and burned my eyes because I didn't know if I'd ever see my big brother again, and all for this. All for nothing.

It took a long while, but I slept and dreamt that I was stepping through a thick, dark-green jungle. No path, only a tangle of vines and thick bamboo stalks that rose up toward the spliced blue sky. Steam rose from the black ground. I had to reach my legs up towards my shoulders, then stretch my feet way up over the entwined green before me to make any forward progress. Birds flicked up at the tips of the bamboo, and tall, bustling trees swayed above, drifting like dark-green clouds. There was a slow roar and a light trickle in the distance as flies buzzed and swarmed about my face and ears. I moved towards the roaring trickle of water that would end this tarring oppression that was twisting tightly around me. I fought and struggled for a long, long time, until the roar was all around me. Still, no break in the slimy vines and foggy steam. Then, I reached out and split the bamboo as if it were a drape drawn closed before me. The world opened, and a light-blue river rushed and swirled past. On the far bank there was a stone shore, with a sparse forest and hills beyond. Then, a fire. Three men stooped above a carcass—a chest-high mound of mangy and knotted brown fur. The beast—head in profile with his purple, crusted tongue dangling below his snout. The men worked without words, hacking into the ribs of the beast with short blades. Then, suddenly, the smallest of the men was Ryan. His bare, pale arms slathered with deep-red blood that dripped steadily from his wrists. All three of them were bare-chested and smeared with dark, chunky blood. I knew the other was Mickey and was horrified to see Chief's emaciated face. He stared at me. The side of his head was peeled open, and black organs pulsed through a gaping wound at his solar plexus. He stood up. Blood dropped from his fingers in heavy globs. He stared at me, long and without recognition or expression, then he burst into laughter, his torso hunching. The black organs swelled from the wound and jostled with each laugh. My chest convulsed with rage at all the disdain he'd shown us three. The disdain he'd shown the world even. When he killed, it was without hatred!

"What!?!?!" I screamed, but no sound escaped me. Ryan and Mickey busily drew and strung their blades through the carcass, slicing hunks of meat below the pulled-back flaps of hide. 'What!?!?!' I screamed, then ran out into the river and found no bottom. The water gushed up, encompassing me. I was drowning. The river was suddenly an incandescent violet with white foamy swirls surging and thrusting me downstream to the deeper roar. I fought to the surface, finding air and water. The roar rose into a rumble so powerful that it shook even the water. I saw a wide, deep canyon with a steam cloud rising up to the heavens at its center. The sun played in it like a golden haze and ignited it into water droplets that fell instantly. I descended, cascading and careening into the dismantling fog below, then I exploded into consciousness and awoke on my back, bouncing atop the mattress. The springs squeezing as if I'd just landed.

■

THE NEXT MORNING, I walked over to the house on Bryn Mawr. I didn't want to have to face Ryan's Ma, but when I turned the corner, I was shocked to see Ryan sitting on the porch steps. He still had the earring and herringbone necklace, but now he wore a big black hoodie. He scowled against the breeze with his face all dried out and chapped. I hurried up to him, but he didn't get up—just reached his hand out, and we shook.

"You alright?" I asked, sitting down next to him on the steps.

"Fuck," he said, grinning and looking away. His face was all pink and splotchy like he'd just woken. "Ma kicked me out. Said she wouldn't go through this again."

"Damn." I sat down.

"Fuck it. I've been paying half the bills anyway. She's gonna get fucking evicted."

"You think so?" I looked in his eyes.

"Man, I didn't know," he replied. We both looked down. "She didn't care where it was comin' from as long as it was green. Now, all of a sudden, I'm a criminal."

"Damn..."

"But I'm gonna bring Bear over here. Fuck her," he sneered.

"Well, with those other two, I think she'll be alright," I said.

"Yeah, T-Money and dem said they'd keep an eye out for her," he said sadly.

"That's good, man." I took a pull off my cigarette. "What'd they get ya with?"

"Only a few bags. I ditched 'em in two spots." He smiled.

"Good man," I said.

"Yeah, that fuckin' Sonic can run, man! He chased me three blocks and caught my ass."

"On foot?" I asked, eyebrows raised.

"Hell yeah, on foot! He was talking shit about his football days when they were bringing me in."

"They didn't fuck you up, it don't look like."

"Naw, the fucker was so happy. He was jumping around and shit, celebrating like he scored a fucking touchdown."

"Dat asshole," I laughed. "You didn't fight or nothing?"

"Man, I was too tired to fight, man." He laughed. "Too many of these, man," he added, holding up his smoke.

"Hell yeah," I agreed. Both of us laughed. "How much was bail?"

"They can't hold you, I guess, if you're a minor, so they just set a date."

"What'd Mickey say?"

"He was mad, but you know, he was just happy I didn't talk." Ryan flicked his cigarette. "You know how he is."

"Yeah." I leaned back on the steps.

"He's closing down the sills though. Said we failed the test."

"What?"

"I told him about Angel. I guess Wacker wants to talk to you." He shrugged. "You better start looking for a day job."

"Ah... You serious? I just talked to him last night."

"I guess your brother's been after him about it, so you're back to choir boy status." He smiled, then he took a deep breath and let it out slowly. He turned his head east down Bryn Mawr. The traffic moved slowly, and the sunset struck everything in a bright orange glow that hung in the air. Tiny specks of dust sifted downward, and Melon Park was all lit up. The children rushed and laughed and squealed. When he turned back to look at me, there was a scowl on his lips. His eyes were all squinted up, and he looked old—old and tired.

"Your brother wrote me a letter…" he said.

"He's been writin' me a lot, too."

"You know, man," he said, pinching his nostrils. "You shouldn't be runnin' around wit' us… You got… You got more in you than this, man. You could go to college… I don't mean it like that bullshit 'Everybody could go to college.' I mean, you're smart—smarter than me and Angel and Mickey. You got a "A" in physics. I never got a "A" in anything in my whole life, even when I tried. And I tried before. The only thing I ever been good at is this."

"That ain't true, man."

"Fuck dat, Joe. It's true, and you know it. All I ever wanted to be was a TJO. You got something in you that's different, and if you keep hanging around here, you gonna waste it, and that'd be some stupid ass shit that I don't wanta have to fuckin' watch…"

Joy overwhelmed me in a warm haze. He was a true friend. I wanted to tell him there was so much more to him than gangbanging. How he should go be a soldier, a Marine. How great nations were built upon the backs of fierce warriors like him. The wires sliced through the joy, and I knew he'd just laugh at me. Then, I thought of Lil Pat writing Ryan those things—I never told Ryan I got an "A" in physics. I realized Lil Pat was asking Ryan to let me go. *But I don't want to let go. It's all I know. But then again, maybe it's time to give it a try.*

"Ah, fuck it…." I tossed my smoke down to the sidewalk. "I'm through," I said.

"Yeah?"

"Yeah, man." I looked Ryan in his bright-green eyes. "At least for now."

"Ah, that's good, ya know." A smile crept over his face. "You're still down though, right?"

"Of course I am, motherfucker." I punched him hard in the arm.

"Just checking." He smiled, rubbing his bicep.

"You son of a bitch," I said. "I'll be down forever."

"For-ever?" Ryan replied in a mocking, shocked, high-pitch tone as he raised his red eyebrows.

"Forever," I assured him. We both laughed and went on talking like neighborhood boys do as the afternoon traffic strode past on Bryn Mawr.

CHAPTER 30

COLLIDER

THEY BUMPED ME UP to honors physics, screwed my whole schedule up. Looking back, I still can't figure out how I maintained an "A" through all of that bullshit I was going through. I guess it was my refuge—the sterile concepts, the great expanse I could dissolve into and the chaos of my life would just evaporate.

One day after class, Dydecky pulled Scott and I aside after all the kids had left. He shut the old oak door and turned around with his bushy eyebrows trembling in a straight line above his glasses and stark, dark-brown eyes. He waved us to sit on the desks in the front row as he eased down onto his desktop. He wiped his lips with the back of his hand.

"They're starting a new summer program at Fermi Lab for high school students with exceptional aptitude and interest in the field of particle physics," he said, splicing his fingers and wrapping them snugly around his partially bent knee.

"There're only 20 openings, you stay at the facilities the entire time, and you're trained to do hands-on work with the accelerator and converse with some of the top physicists in the world.

It's a three-week program starting this June, and I was asked to nominate one student for it. I decided to write a letter petitioning that I be allowed to send two. My finest student," he nodded towards Scott, who batted his eyelashes bashfully and looked down, "and my student with the most potential." He looked at me stone sober. His eyebrows percolated. "I just received the letter today; they've accepted both of you."

"There are no fees involved; you just need to show up June eighth at 3pm," he continued. "If you don't have a ride, I can drive you. These forms need to be signed by both of your parents and brought back as soon as you can, and I mean tomorrow." He pulled two thick brochures from his cluttered desk and briskly flung them out into our waiting hands.

"You're going to be there with some of the finest students in the state of Illinois. Joe, I know you're struggling with some of the math, but I wouldn't have nominated you if I wasn't sure you could handle it, and if I wasn't sure you had something to offer to the program. Scott, maybe you can help him a little bringing him up to speed."

"Sure," he replied.

"Thanks," I said.

"Now, this is a great opportunity. I wish I'd had an opportunity like it when I was your age." He rubbed his thin bottom lip with his index finger. "But at the same time, I want you to know that you've both earned this, and I'm proud to be sending the both of you." His brow bent and curved slightly as a stern grin crept on his pale lips. "Any questions?" He slipped his glasses off and cleared a smudge with a silk handkerchief he'd drawn from his pants pocket.

"Naw." I shrugged.

"Nope." Scott clapped his hands together softly.

We all stood up, and Dydecky walked us to the door with the world buzzing by behind the wire-flecked glass—a swirl of faces, flapping ties, running shouts, hollow metal locker slams, and hurried, squeaky steps. Dydecky, between and behind us, was rubbing both of our shoulders. My traps were tense, and his steady squeezes released warm electric prickles that sifted out across my back and arms.

The door opened, and the sound of the chaos erupted. Scott stepped out into it; I paused and turned back.

"Thanks, Dydecky."

"Don't thank me, Joe. You've accomplished a lot this year. Thank you." His brows popped up and stayed there. Long, horizontal lines layered up and stretched across his forehead below his thick, curly black hair. "It's been fun to watch." He patted me on the back as I turned and stepped out into the hall.

When I got back to the block, I didn't know who to tell, so I went to tell Hyacinth. She sat on her front porch flipping through Seventeen magazine, still in her blue and red plaid Good Council uniform. I swooped up the steps and flopped down next to her. She nestled her face into my neck as I stretched my arm around her warm shoulders and squeezed. I kissed her forehead.

"What's dat?" she asked.

I'd forgotten I still had the forms from the physics program in my hand. I'd been reading them over and over all the way home.

"I got nominated for this physics program."

"What!" She was awestruck. Her amber eyes suddenly brightened, and the afternoon light flecked in them as they swelled wide.

"Yeah, it's pretty cool. I'm gonna be gone for like three weeks this summer out at this big laboratory out in..." I glanced down at the papers. "Batavia."

She reached out with both hands and grabbed my cheeks, smiling wildly in my face. Her deep-brown skin flushed lighter, and then she kissed my lips, hard. "I can't believe it, Joe! Congratulations!"

I laughed, my cheeks burning.

"Is it the one? The one you're always talking about? That Fermi place?"

"Yeah, it's the same one."

"I can't believe it, baby... I can't believe it!"

"Me neither." My chest filled with this warm joy as my whole life seemed to unfurl and blossom right there in front of me. I sat on that porch squeezing her soft, warm hand in mine. The crisp, almost spring air sifted over us, and it felt, for the first time in a long time, like all those deep, heavy, purple clouds had finally parted—that the wires were gone. Like a new life was blossoming.

■

Hi Kiddo,

Well you probably done heard by now, you ain't gonna be no TJO. That's the best thing I ever did for you. Remember that. May be the best thing I ever did in my whole messed up life. Sorry about the phone call. I just couldn't talk nomore and I had to hang up. Ya know there ain't never an hour passes I don't think about that Assyrian kid. I know. I know you was there. I imagine him at home with his mom and dad, sisters and brothers. I imagine him working in some office or driving an L train or on a construction site or just hanging out with his buddies. He'll never have those jobs. He'll never hang out with his buddies. I imagine him talking to beautiful chicks he'll never meet. Crying at the birth of his kids he'll never have. And he'll never do none of these things because a' me. 'Cause I took them away from him. And I can never give 'em back. Never. I didn't have the right to do that, Joey. I don't even have the right to do it to myself. Killing somebody, it's like you kill parts of a lot of people and you kill a big part of yourself too, a big part, a real precious part. There ain't many good laws in the world and you just broke the best of 'em. The only path from there is down. You can't make that same mistake I did. There's more for you out there in the world than the four walls I gotta stare at and the shitty memories in my head. Go on and do something with your life. Kid, go make something you could be proud of.

Your Brother,
Pat

CHAPTER 31

SUPER NOVA

WHEN IT FINALLY DID GO DOWN, it was like our world exploded into a supernova and sent us all tumbling into an irreparable nebulous cloud.

I sat on the front porch steps of the house on Bryn Mawr with Ryan beside me. There was only a narrow path on the steps between us. The railings framed us at the sides with blue-gray paint peeling from the twisted metal support bars. The large windows of the enclosed front porch spread across the width of the house behind us. It was early evening. The March weather'd broken slightly, but you could feel it readying to roar again. I looked up Bryn Mawr to Ashland, then Melon Park across Ashland—empty of children and dark. St. Greg's loomed across the street like a medieval castle. Even though the laws were changing about slangin' in school zones, they were still runnin' H outta the Bryn Mawr house. I was through. I wasn't getting paid, just keepin' Ryan company as he played spotter and gatekeeper. There just wasn't much else to do.

A hype stumbled out of the side alley, and Ryan dragged his tongue across his lips. The yellow streetlight brought out the pale white on his thick-muscled forehead as he puffed on a Newport. The crisp menthol smell somehow brought out that smoldering winter scent that'd break soon and give way to spring. As the hype got closer, I saw it was Angel. He'd lopped his hair off, and now it was an uneven and spotty mess. It glowed black and greasy under the streetlight like the fur of a sewer rat.

"Look at dis motherfucker," Ryan sneered, staring at him as he approached.

"Man, give him a break," I said, shaking my head and looking away from him.

"Naw, man, fuck dat." Ryan flicked his cigarette toward the street, and it sailed in a long arc out into the darkness in front of us like an arrow lit on fire. "He's out, dat's it."

"I don't give a fuck what happens." I stared at Ryan's profile. "Dat's my boy 'til death."

Ryan peered at me and whispered as Angel got close. "Look, man. I got love for 'em, too, but dis shit's gotta stop."

"What can we do, man?" Something stirred in my stomach like a swarm of flies attached to strings. "Put him in a fuckin' hospital?"

"Somethin', man. We gotta do something."

As Angel got close, I could see his hands were trembling. His Pumas were scuffed up; the fat, graying laces had frayed at the ends and flapped as he stepped. He glanced up at us. His eyes were pink with red veins spider-webbed behind the deep-brown irises. His face was sunken—the bone structure revealed—like all the baby fat got eaten up. He lowered his head and started up the stairs towards us.

"Hey," Angel said as he turned his shoulders to squeeze past us.

"Man, hold up a second," I said, raising my palm towards him. "We gotta talk."

"Man, I'm in a rush. I'm just picking up a bag for these guys, make a quick buck, ya know?" Angel paused on the steps. His bottom lip hung open. His upper lip covered those large white teeth, so all there was was the blackness of his mouth.

"Angel, man, look at you," I said. "What the fuck happened to you, bro?"

"What?" Angel answered, then looked down at his long-sleeved undershirt, stained a brownish gray, and his ripped jeans. He looked back up at me like he didn't see a problem with the way he looked. I could smell that acrid ammonia stench mixed with his body odor; he smelled like a straight-up bum junky.

"Angel, man, you're hooked. You're fucked, man." I looked him in the eyes. "They tell me you ain't even been at school all week."

"Joe, I don't know what you're talkin' about, man. I, I don't fuck with that shit. I just smoke, man. There ain't nothing wrong with dat," Angel said fast. He rose to his full height on the steps and rubbed the tip of his nose with the back of his hand. Then, he turned and looked back from where he'd come.

He folded his arms over his stomach and looked back at me. There was nothing in his eyes. Nothing. All the spark I'd known was gone, and I realized he hadn't smiled that slick, toothy grin of his once since he'd walked up.

"Look at you!" Ryan yelled, grabbing hold of Angel's wrist and yanking his shirtsleeve up with his other hand. Large blue veins streamed down to his wrist. Yellow, pus-oozing pockmarks littered them—undeniable tracks.

Angel shoved his sleeve back down to his wrist. Ryan growled and looked down at his own feet. He gripped his head with both hands. "Don't fucking lie to us! We're your fucking friends, man!" He shot to his feet. His eyes blazed like two emerald flames.

"Hey, look, I gotta go, man. These guys are waiting on me." Angel tried to squeeze past us.

"You motherfuckin' hype!" Ryan yelled, then smacked his wide hand against Angel's neck. Angel yelped and gripped Ryan's wrist with both hands. Ryan clamped down on Angel's narrow throat.

I reached out and grasped at Angel's moist, soiled shirt as he fell back against the steel railing. His torso bent and arched backward, way out and off the porch, like he was gonna cartwheel down to the muddy lawn below. The sharp squeal of tires at Ashland froze us all. There was the roar of an engine, then a floating quiet.

There's a sense of knowing something's gonna happen before it does. It's in the air—a shift. It's a sudden, flat silence—a sense that everyone is listening; the whole neighborhood holding its breath.

The blacked-out windows of the maroon Intrepid descended smooth and soundless as it slowed in front of the house. The barrels of several metal-finished pistols extended out of the dark passenger's side windows like a gunner deck on a battleship. Then, Samson's head emerged over the barrels. His eyes sparked when they hit mine. His teeth flashed.

"Di-Ci-Ple!" rang out clear into the silence that had surrounded us. You see the light first—a tuft of fire before you realize the sound is happening. It jars you and blunts your eardrums even though you can still hear the casings clamoring atop the pavement and see their arcing motion shining brass—gold in the streetlights as they flip end-over-end and shower down hollow. I couldn't believe how many shots were fired. They were short, fast, and vicious, overlapping each other like the barks of many dogs at a junkyard gate. I remember the sound of glass falling. I felt the old, worn brown carpet of the enclosed front porch against my cheek. Small shards of glass sprayed my eyes before I could shut them. My eyelids closed around them, then blinked and spewed them out.

The silence rose up and swallowed the shots. The peel of the tires swirled again. That's when the other sounds came—the yells from inside. Mickey leapt over me with the .45 in-hand, then Ryan behind him with the .25. They rumbled down the porch steps. Then, there was the low moan from the base of the stairs.

"Ah, fuck," Ryan screamed.

The moans continued, and I knew what it was. I got up shaky. The glass clinked and dribbled off me. I walked out onto the top step as the ground shifted side-to-side like a slow motion earthquake. A blur clouded my vision. My mouth was all dried out.

"Somebody call an ambulance!" Ryan yelled.

"Fuck that," Mickey snapped with his wide, squared-off head flexed. "Gimme dat piece." He yanked it out from Ryan's grasp. "Do what you gotta do."

"Joe!" Ryan shouted as he crouched over him. Angel laid on the slab at the base of the stairs. I stumbled down the steps.

One shot in the stomach. The blood radiated out in a perfect circle and soaked through his dirty shirt. There was a fog in his eyes like he'd just woken. His pupils swelled so that they nearly eclipsed the deep-brown irises—seeing nothing, throat spasming. That low moan continued from his gaping lips like a slowed down deep bass scream.

"Fuck the ambulance," Ryan said, then reached out and grasped my wrist.

The next thing I remember, we were carrying him. Ryan had him by the legs with his arms wrapped under his kneecaps, and I had my forearms up under his armpits. I squeezed him around the chest, cupping my hands and locking them together. His torso and hips slumped and hung down like a sack of potatoes ready to burst. I couldn't believe there was so much blood. Globs of it slapped the alley as our rubber soles pattered along the pavement. The lamps atop the splintered wood telephone poles lit our path through the alleys. The thick black cables that spanned between them gleamed a wet gold. The tan monolith of Edgewater Hospital towered above like a giant limestone cube.

The wires constricted tight around my mind and cut deep gouges in the flesh. This voice started up in my head. It was my voice, and I knew it was coming from me. *I'm gonna kill some-body—I'm gonna kill somebody—I'm gonna kill somebody—I'm gonna kill somebody...*

As we got to Olive Ave., Angel slipped some. The blood slathered my forearms and hands. It was warm. Now, I held him with my hands cupped up under his armpit. My nails dug into his shirt and the skin beneath. There was a straining tug like I had piano strings pulled taut from the tips of my fingers through my hands, arms, and shoulders, all the way to the pit of my back. I looked down. His neck stretched back, his face to the night sky. The skin pulled tight to his cheekbones. His up-per lip still pressed down over his top front teeth. The bottom lip hung open as dark-red blood slid down his cheek, thick like ink, from the black chasm of his mouth. His eyelids squinted into two thin slits. The irises bobbed and flickered beneath them with each step like two matches struck in the breeze. Ryan and I drew closer as we carried him. The backside of his jeans scuffed the pavement with each step. Tears gushed down our faces—a mirror of each other. Our necks strained, breath quick and loud. We bore our load.

As we crossed Hollywood, I saw Big James in his crisp, dark-blue security uniform. He stared at me as he stood there in the center of the alley with the tunnel framing him. The bright, cold light made his skin gleam like polished ebony. He stood still as a ghost. Then, he looked me straight in the eyes. His lip sneered un-der his pencil-thin black mustache. He pulled hard on the menthol clasped between two fingers. Then, he came alive. He tossed the cigarette and, in one motion, twisted into a sprint up the emer-gency room ramp. We entered the tunnel. The bright white lights illuminated the alley tunnel like a landing strip. As we turned up the ramp, Big James exploded out of the ER door. His basketball-sized hand pressed against the gray-painted sheet-metal. He held it wide open, and we entered without slowing.

The room was a white blur of motion. A nurse in her 40s with light-red hair pulled back in a ponytail shouted, "Here!" She swung a heavy, gray drape wide open that surrounded an empty gurney. It took the last of my strength to hoist him up into the bed. His limbs dangled, slippery. His body mushed into the thin mattress like a king salmon stung with a club melts into the ice chest. Suddenly, a black nurse in a white-and-green-checkered smock took scissors and sliced his sopping red shirt from waist to neck in one motion. That's when I saw I was correct—one quarter-sized black hole just between the sternum and the belly button. The deep-red oozed up slow and thick like slime.

Ryan ran to the payphone as the red-headed nurse pushed me away from the bed and pulled the curtain shut between us. I crossed the room to the wall beside the entrance, turned, and leaned my back against the wall. Then, I slowly eased down it to the ground and sat, legs out straight. The blood had spotted my jeans purple. It was splattered all the way to down my ankles and white Nikes. My ears still rang. The lights in the room seemed to flash bright then dull in sudden jolts.

Ryan walked back to where I sat. He stood over me and said something, but I couldn't hear it through the ringing in my ears. He said it again.

I read his lips and reached my hand out. He took it and pulled me to my feet. Our hands stuck; the blood still congealing.

We made our way out of the emergency room. Big James watched us go, silently. The two of us were covered in blood, our faces wet and puffy from the tears. We walked past him and into the tunnel.

"They'll be here in a minute," Ryan said. We stood in front of the sills, waiting. "They're bringing the .25 and something for you."

I knew what was coming next. I didn't care—didn't care what happened. The Lincoln crept down the side alley towards us. The fear'd gone from me now, though I still shook with anger and shock. I watched Mickey coming—coming for me and Ryan and that destiny that'd sat before us for years now—to ride for real. To kill.

The wires squeezed deeper into my mind in a steady, contracting rhythm. It started again: *I'm gonna kill somebody—I'm gonna kill somebody—I'm gonna kill somebody...*

As the Lincoln passed through my alley, my father's small, red pickup pulled in front of the sills. He slammed on the brakes. Then he leaned over the passenger's side seat and glared at me. His chin tucked as he ground his teeth. He threw it in park and swung the door open, then he got out and stomped towards me. His red suspenders spanned his bulging torso and clasped to his work jeans that were scuffed gray with concrete dust.

"WHAT THE FUCK!" he said sharply. He clamped his wide hand around my forearm, then he raised his jutting chin and glowered down at me. "What the fuck did you do," he said, then twisted his neck and shot his scowl at Ryan. "WHAT THE FUCK'S GOING ON HERE!"

Neither of us said anything. We just stared blankly at Mickey as the Lincoln stopped in the arterial alley across the street. Dad followed our eyes to the Lincoln.

"GOD DAMN THOSE MOTHERFUCKERS!" He tugged me, so I lurched forward towards the truck. He glared at Mickey in the Lincoln. Mickey squinted, then his eyes widened when he recognized my father.

"YOU MOTHERFUCKER! YOU DRAGGIN' MY KID INTO THIS SHIT?" my father roared towards the Lincoln. Spit burst from his teeth. He pointed his thick index finger at Mickey with his free hand. "WELL YOU CAN'T HAVE HIM! YOU HEAR ME? YOU CAN'T HAVE HIM!" he blared savagely. Mickey threw the Lincoln in reverse and slowly backed down the side alley. I could see Wacker's spiky hair beside Mickey and Fat Buck's huge head in back.

My dad opened the passenger's side door and threw me in. All the blueprint plans and tools he had piled up on the seat avalanched to the floor boards. He slammed the door shut, stomped around the front end, and got in. I glanced back over my shoulder through the window and saw Ryan lumbering down the alley in a slow gait towards the Lincoln. I could see his pale face above the open passenger's side door. The wind-wrinkled, black plastic garbage bag stretched across the door's window where that bullet had passed. The light streaked the plastic like a splatter of lightning. Then, his face disappeared behind it, and the door shut. It was the last time I'd see my friend. The Lincoln turned and disappeared down my alley.

My father turned and drove into the alley, and for a second, I thought maybe he was going after them—going to get Ryan and pull him out of that car. But when we rounded the T, I saw the Lincoln's taillights way down at the intersection. It swung northbound on Hermitage. My father parked out back behind the garage. My whole body trembled uncontrollably. He walked me in the house, and I went upstairs and sat on the foot of my bed in the darkness. I bowed my head. The streetlight seeped in the window at my back and cast a massive black shadow onto the wall that loomed before me like a monster.

FLIGHT

IT WASN'T TOO LONG before the phone rang. For some reason, I thought it was Ryan. I quickly stepped down the hall into my parent's room. Forgetting the light, I rushed in the dark to the bedside table where the phone sat, picked up the receiver, and put it to my ear. Static, muffled screams, sirens. "Please, Darnel!" I heard Rose's friend Tonya's sobbing voice. My mom picked up.

"Hello," she said into the phone. "Rosie..." A guy's voice, then a scream rose up and blurred into static. Then, a quick murmur: *"Rose got shot!"*

"No, honey. Rose just left. She's out for the night—" Click.

"No, God damnit, ROSIE JUST GOT SHOT!" Click. My heart started pulsing fast in my chest. It pumped outward and up like it'd burst from my chest at any second and undulate up to the ceiling and out the window into the March night sky. But the wires clung tight and kept it stuck there inside. I hung up the phone and walked downstairs slowly. The buzzing rose up in my ears again. Everything seemed to vibrate with electricity. These tiny electrons jumped out of the walls and up from the carpet, then fell off in the periphery like feathers. I walked down the hall into the gleaming, yellow-tiled walls of the kitchen. I'd never noticed how they looked like they were made of honey. My father ate at the head of the old oak table he'd made with his own hands and stared at the tall, sweating glass of ice water in front of him while Ma dug into the refrigerator. My father's eyes shot at me as I entered. His protruding brow made his eyes look like two black voids.

"What are you covered in, Joseph?" Ma asked, leaning her head out of the fridge and looking at me. Three lines appeared and stretched across her forehead, then she disappeared again behind the refrigerator door.

"I think Rose got shot," I said.

The phone rang sharp, blaring. The wires constricted and sent my heart pattering again. *I'm gonna kill somebody—I'm gonna kill somebody—I'm gonna kill somebody...* I held tight to the counter's ledge expecting the wires to snap and my heart to explode through my ribcage. My father got up and picked up the receiver from the wall mount. Ma stepped back, closed the fridge and looked at me.

"What's happening to you?" she asked.

"Rose." My grip on the countertop was all that held me up.

"Rose's gone honey. She left a half-hour ago."

"What THE FUCK ARE YOU SAYING TO ME?" my father growled into the phone.

Ma put her hands on the back of her hips and arched her belly out. "Honey, what are you covered in?" She scrunched her pudgy-featured face.

My dad slammed the phone into the receiver.

"Mary, where're your keys?" he asked.

"What the hell's going on here!?" Ma said, turning to look at him.

"Rose just got shot. They're taking her to St. Francis," he said flat and clear.

We took Clark. As we passed Senn, a police car swerved up with its lights flashing, swung itself diagonal across all the northbound lanes, and slammed on its brakes. I could see a commotion a couple blocks up at the intersection at Granville. There were several squad cars, two ambulances, and what looked like a tow truck.

"Oh, God. Do you think this is where it happened?" Ma asked.

"She doesn't hang out around here," Dad spat disgustedly. "Does she?"

"Naw, it looks like a car crash," I said as my dad turned down a side street to cut around the chaos and over to Ridge. We headed up north across the border of Howard into Evanston.

The emergency room was a bustling maze of halls and doors, rooms and curtains. It was strange timing, but when we entered the reception area, they must have been moving her into surgery. A door swung open, and there she was on a wheeled stretcher. Her chest was covered with a blue wool blanket, and her milky, light-brown skin showed naked underneath it. An IV was already started. The clear rubber tube dangled and curled beside her. She wept as she laid flat. Then, she strained her neck to sit up and turned her head to see us. "Mom!" she yelled in a weak voice. The door slowly swung closed again. Ma rushed over and burst through the door hard so it locked open. For some reason, the doctors let her and stopped the stretcher there. And for some reason, my father and I stayed back. I could hear Rose sobbing and saying, "I'm so sorry, I'm so sorry," over and over.

Ma grasped Rose's hand with both of hers and leaned over her so their faces were close. Ma raised her chin. Both of their soft, rounded features somehow resembled each other, even though their blood was severed by continents. "Rosie, you have to fight now. You have to fight, Rosemary."

Rose muttered and shook her head 'no,' then Ma said, "I don't want to hear that. You fight, Rosemary. You're gonna pull through this." A male nurse appeared at the foot of the stretcher in light-blue scrubs and said, "I'm sorry, miss... They're ready for her." He pushed Rose off into an operating room, and Mom came back. Her face was pearl white. Silver streaks jetted up her tightly pulled back hair. Wrinkles stretched and spread out from her crow's feet like the roots of two oak trees. Just then, I realized that she was getting older right before my eyes, that I was part of what was doing it to her, and the guilt of that pushed barbed hooks into my Adam's apple. Doctors kept coming up and talking to my parents, telling them it was a .22 that hit her. Then, no; the officers on the scene have confirmed it was a .25 by the bullet casings. I wanted to scream *WHYTHEFUCK DOES IT MATTER WHAT SIZE ROUND IT WAS!?* right in their dumbfounded faces, pull the chalk-white piece and jam it in their fucking mouths and tell them *SAY IT AGAIN, SAY IT AGAIN, MOTHERFUCKER, AND I'LL BLOW YOUR FUCKING HEAD UP.* Everyone seemed to be running but me. I felt like they were just ushering me—pushing and dragging me here and there. The lights in the ceiling grates kept dimming and flashing bright in the all-white emergency room, and I couldn't figure out why.

■

I FOUND MYSELF SITTING in the waiting room. It was a wide rectangle with several long rows of chairs that spanned its width, all of them filled. There must have been 50 people in there of all ages, from old ladies to kids. But mainly, it was people in their early teens like me to guys and girls in their twenties. This one little girl sat on the floor, maybe five years old. Her hair was half-done in braids with little blue butterfly clips, like they'd gotten the call in the middle of it. The other half of her hair sprang out in a long-arcing afro that hung down to her shoulder. She sat with her legs bent underneath her and played with a naked, white Barbie doll by what looked to be her grandmother's feet.

The only one I recognized was Rose's friend Tonya. Her large torso filled her chair, and her short black hair was pulled back in a tight ponytail. Her back heaved as she wept. Her black and white high-top rose from the floor as she rocked. She was afraid to even look our way from shame. My mom, me, and my dad were the only whites in the room. We sat near the door that led out to the exit and the operating rooms. Our chairs were backed up to the wall. The large TV rigged into the ceiling hung down above our heads. The entire wall across from the TV was made of windows that ran almost floor to ceiling. The darkness outside made the reflection of the room colorful, and like it was double its size—like some war zone ER.

For some reason I kept thinking, *it's not so bad, she'll be alright. People don't die if they make it to the hospital alive.* I didn't know then that she'd already died. Her heart stopped beating on the sidewalk right under the Howard L stop where the bums' piss makes a stink like the cat cages in the Lincoln Park Zoo. Rose lay there with her light, chocolate-milk skin glowing under the streetlamps—her oversized Loony Toons gangster t-shirt of Tweety Bird as a thug with a hole at the side of her belly. The hole was just between the lung and the liver where the .25 caliber round entered and did some bouncing in her ribcage before it exited the way small-caliber rounds do if they exit at all. I didn't know that they'd brought her back once, and that the heart had stopped again when they got her to the ER, and that it would stop one more time that night. I didn't know any of this, so I kept thinking she'd be alright 'cause nobody dies if they make it to the ER alive.

At first, there was a lot of tears and sobbing and praying. I watched them all hugging each other, and I wondered why we weren't hugging each other. The three of us sat side by side with me in the middle—we didn't even touch at the elbows. I realized I couldn't remember the last time I'd hugged either one of them. They must have still wondered about the blood I was covered in. I was so gone by then that I didn't even remember it. My mind raced to where Ryan was, wondering if he'd rode out with Mickey in the Lincoln and shot up those D's and if he would come to the hospital soon, so I'd have someone to talk to. Right then, the memory of Angel being shot, even though it was just an hour before, was completely blacked out of my mind. Years later, a doctor friend of mine would tell me it was PTSD, but now it was the only thing that kept me from melting to the floor and screaming until my lungs spewed blood.

Suddenly, I was on the dock, nine years old. The seagull flapped and screamed. White feathers sprayed everywhere. Da beside me with his hands bleeding as he cut the fishing line. The seagull swooped up into the sky, free, then it was gone. I remembered how I wanted someone to do that for Da with the cancer, but how he was free in death now. *But then, if that vision came now, did that mean Rose was dying? That she was already gone, and any second the doctor would come to tell us?* The wires twisted up my spine. The doctor didn't come.

After about an hour, the crying had almost completely stopped. The younger ones were all blood-caked. Their dark-brown skin'd turned ash-gray like they'd been standing close by watching the city burn all night. Ma stepped out into the hall to the payphones. Suddenly, a tall, young girl jumped up beside Tonya. Her face was a smear of makeup and drying tears.

"Look," she said. She jogged over to the TV and turned up the volume. Then, she darted back to her seat as a newscaster's voice flooded into the room.

"We are at the scene of a deadly shooting in Chicago's Rogers Park neighborhood—a triple homicide. The shooting led to a high-speed chase that ended in the arrest of three men and one juvenile. All four are being charged at this hour with three counts of murder, and the shooting of several other youths. Nine total were hospitalized. The incident took place on the corner of Howard and Paulina directly under the Howard Red Line stop—an area known to the local hoodlums as 'The Jungle.'" I realized the bottom tip of my crucifix was sunken into my heart again. Even so, I got up and walked toward the center of the room and stood in front of the TV. On the screen, a female reporter stood with her back to a line of yellow police tape that trembled in the breeze.

"Police are not certain at this hour whether the shooting was gang-related or racially motivated. This was the scene where the police chase finally ended at the 6700 block of north Clark Street."

The camera switched shots and panned to Mickey's Lincoln. The front end was wrapped around a green stoplight pole. The two headlights seemed to point in toward one another like they'd gone cross-eyed. The smashed windshield had two skull-sized holes in it—one in front of the driver's seat and another in front of the passenger's seat. A tiny white fracture spread out from each hole and stretched across the entire windshield. The black plastic bag in the rear passenger's side window flapped and sucked in with the breeze as if the Lincoln was gasping for breath. Ryan and Mickey's absence from the Lincoln was even more ominous than if they'd shown their mug shots on screen.

"Motha-Fuckas! I'm gonna kill all those white honky motherfuckers!"

I turned, and one of the black guys stood across the room from me. His voice crackled over the newscast, and spittle splashed from his thick lips. He was tall and lanky, and his arms trembled as he squeezed his fists at his sides. Then, his eyes panned down to mine—they gleamed red behind the black irises.

"AND WHO THE FUCK IS YOU!!!" he said, pointing his long, thin finger directly at my chest. Even though he was still across the room, it felt like his finger jabbed straight into my sternum and jammed my crucifix in even deeper. Two other guys jumped up, grasped his arms, and pulled him back toward the full rows of seats. Tonya shouted, "Quit it, T. Dat's Rose little brotha!" The two guys glanced back at me, squinted their eyes, then thought better of it and pulled harder. They yanked him into the only vacant seat in the wide room. T turned and glared at Tonya as she sat in her seat with a ball of mauve tissue paper clutched in her dark hand.

"WHY DE FUCK HE COVERED IN BLOOD DEN?" T screamed as a glob of drool dribbled like a teardrop from his bottom lip. "HE WADN'T EVEN THERE!" His voice thundered, and all the eyes in the room suddenly landed on me—the two guys' holding him back, Tonya's, even the old lady's and the little girl's. Then, I remembered Angel. I looked down at where his blood had slathered my t-shirt and jeans hours earlier; it was now brownish-purple on the white cotton over my belly. My jeans were stained black at the thighs. I raised my hands from my sides slowly and stood there underneath the still-blaring TV. Though for me, the room had gone silent. I looked down at the dry, coarse blood splintering off my fingers in tiny flakes and dropping to the scuffed, white-and-black-checkered, linoleum-tiled floor slow like feathers. I slowly opened my hands, palms up. The uneven, loping surfaces; the lines—heart, money, fate—all of 'em leading to the life lines like dry riverbeds. That brownish-red caked over both my hands like the surface of Mars. I still resisted the belief that the nightmare earlier was real.

Suddenly, my father's massive hand slammed down on my shoulder and clutched my shirt into a ball. I turned to see his face. Pinkish splotches hazed around his pale skin at the cheeks like a spattering of clouds on the horizon at dawn. The stale gray light from the ceiling panels glared off his forehead. His lips curled into a frowning grimace and trembled under his thick white mustache. He'd put it all together—the blood on me from a shooting, and this nightmare the retaliation. What would have happened if he hadn't stopped me from getting into that Lincoln earlier that night? He knew it was the same TJOs that had taken his firstborn son from him years ago. Hooks dragged through my intestines. He yanked me toward him. Something snapped and clinked to the hard linoleum floor. He shoved me forward and through the door that led out into the hall. My sneakers felt like they stepped atop mush, and I heard Tonya's voice rise up again. "Quit it, T! Rose in dere! She might be dyin' right now!"

"Well, you shot yo own sista, mothafucka! How de fuck dat feel?!" T's voice twisted and followed me down the corridor like the blistering tail of a comet.

My legs felt loose, like two strands of cooked spaghetti. They just dangled and fell, one by one, in front of me. *Why? Why the fuck would he say that to me?* I cupped my heart where the wound was. *Why would someone say something like that to me? Why.* The nurses and doctors in teal scrubs rushed in all directions. We passed Ma at a payphone. Rich and his wife Nancy had arrived. They all spoke with urgency in their eyes.

"Stay with her," my father spat at Rich as we rushed past. "And stay out of that goddamn waiting room."

Rich nodded as his jaw dropped around his beard. He stared at me, at the blood.

Dad pushed me through the doors and out into the cool black air of the parking lot. My sneakers caught and scraped over the blacktop. The wind rushed up off the lake, cold, and sent a spray of goosebumps across my neck and face. When we got to the passenger's side of the van, he spun me around and shoved me against it. My back slammed into the side panel, and I felt the sheet metal give, then pop flat against my back. I looked down at the ground and waited for it. I hoped it would put me out cold and drive me deep into some black-tar abyss that would erase all of it. It never came.

"Get in," he said flatly.

We pulled up in front of the house. The block was calm and empty. The trees rocked slowly in the wind.

"Go in there and pack a bag," he said, looking straight ahead as he gripped the steering wheel. His knuckles bulged out like large white marble stones. I swung the door open and started to step down. "And say goodbye to that house, that's the last time you'll step foot in it." He brushed the back of his hand across his lips.

I went in and packed a bag in the dark. I didn't know where I was headed. Dad switched to his pickup truck. A warm, throbbing tremble coursed through me, rising and surging like it would snap the wires at any moment, explode through my skin, and float up free.

I stepped out onto the porch and saw my block one last time as resident. *Guess I am the baddest kid on the block after all*—it only summoned a great wealth of sadness. I walked down the steps, turned, and looked back at the house. The old, gnarly siding, the wooden porch where I'd had my first real kiss. Suddenly, there was a hand on my shoulder. It was soft and strong. I turned and saw my father's trembling blue eyes.

"Ahh, Joe.... Ah, Joe...," he said softly, his lips nearly motionless under his mustache. I felt that connection again, like when he'd told me about Lil Pat in the basement that night.

■

WE TOOK ASHLAND TO FOSTER, cut over to Lake Shore Drive, and rode south. The small pickup rattled as gusts surged off the lake and got up underneath the small truck bed, lifting us up like we were riding the wind. The buildings slowly thickened, rose, and sloped upward. The lake was a black-gray glob swaying and peaking to the east. The moon was full and low on the dark horizon, emitting a brownish-orange glow that fluttered and flecked across the undulating surface of the water. Ahead was the Drake Hotel's gleaming, neon-pink sign. The John Hancock seemed to rise up straight out of it like an Erector set of cold steel and black glass.

We took Lower Wacker to the Dan Ryan and drove past Comiskey in that canyon-like valley. There were five lanes both ways with the Red Line tracks in between them. He never even looked my way. We drove on past the high-rise projects of the Robert Taylor Homes—all of them lined up like dominoes, ready to fall. The red smudge next to my belly button began to tingle. A lotta shit ran through my mind. I thought of Rose, and I thought of Angel. Then, I thought of Ryan and our .25, and the first day I held it in my hand so many years ago when I was still a little boy riding with Rich down at Maxwell Street—the deceiving weight of it; how my hand felt big around the squared-off, white grip enclosed around the spring-loaded clip and those five small rounds; its nickel-finish barrel; how the weight of the barrel was too much for the grip and made it want to point downward; how holding that pistol made all the fear in my 9-year-old mind disappear and marvel at all the potential right there in my hand; how it made me grin like I knew a joke no one else knew. Guess the joke was on me.

He shot her. It was an accident, but Ryan shot my sister. The wires cut deeper into my mind. My skull slowly filled with blood.

I realized it was over. The TJOs would never survive losing Mickey, Wacker, Fat Buck, and Ryan to murder raps. No matter what guns the bullets were traced to, each of them would eat the three counts. Ryan might get out in four years when he turned 18, or they might charge him as an adult. Either way, it was over. I thought about the neighborhood without them—without the trouble that followed them at every step. The street numbers on the exit signs rose. A northbound Red Line train roared past, rattling up a spray of sparks, then it was gone and left just the sway of traffic and the burnt-orange, ever-present light that stained the concrete.

"Somebody told me something the other day," I said, looking to the side out the window. "Said you started the TJOs."

Just then, Da swept in through my open window with the street lights. He swirled around in the cab and slid over our shoulders and kept our arms and hands from moving. Da swallowed all the rage that was there in that truck.

I could almost hear Dad thinking as he shifted and gripped the wheel. Many years later, he'd put those thoughts to words. By then, I was a grown man with a family of my own, but now they just floated and swirled with Da in the cab of the pickup between us. I leaned against the door with my arm resting on the ledge. The wind poured in through the half rolled-down window and splintered my slicked-back hair. The streetlights approached slowly, then darted past in my periphery like so many sunsets.

'I started Bryn Mawr after Devon broke up... It was different back then... Back then, it was about protecting the goddamn neighborhood so your grandmother wouldn't get mugged walking home from the grocery store. There were drugs around back then, sure, but nothing serious; a garbage bag of rag weed, a couple sheets of acid, a few stolen cars—small time, you know? Kinda stuff kept food in your kid's mouth when you were laid off. Back den, it was about street fights—maybe someone gets hit with a ball bat. There were guns back then, too, but you didn't go shooting into a crowd of people! You wanted somebody gone, you go in and get 'em. Get it done right—close enough to be sure, bury 'em in the fucking alley... I hand it off to Ganci and Kellas, and they want to run it like a goddamned syndicate. Collecting from the businesses on Clark Street... Come on, that's not what dis was about. I tell him 'no.' Tell him he's got to change the name... TJOs, the judge in that juvie court was right. That's all they are: a bunch of jag offs... And what they did to those black kids at the school; it was wrong. Then, heroin comes in, lays the entire North Side on its back, from Uptown to Howard Street. And these little jags think they're big dealers. They're selling that crap to each other, can't they see that? It's gotten so there ain't no neighborhood left to protect. It's gone... Tearing my family apart. It's over.'

He didn't say none of it. Not a word of it. He just glanced over, reached out, and gripped my shoulder with his calloused, brittle hands.

"I love you, son." It was the first time he'd said it that I could remember.

I looked him in the eyes, then I looked ahead and squinted. One healthy tear rolled down from my eye. He didn't see it. "I love you, too, Dad."

We took 90 towards the Skyway. It was empty. I looked across at the flat and slanted rooftops that floated past at eye level. I could see the Skyway Bridge—it loomed ahead like a steel-framed mountain. Then, my father's voice broke the silence.

"We're selling the house. You're gonna stay up at Grand Beach 'til we get this all sorted out." He paused. I said nothing. "We've been looking out in the suburbs, near your Aunt Cindy." He looked straight ahead at the bridge he'd spent years building and rebuilding. They'd been planning it for months, with the trouble Rose and I'd been getting in, knowing there was no doubt we'd soon be locked up with Lil Pat or dead if they didn't get us away from the city. It was their last chance to save us. Their only chance.

We creaked to a stop at the toll booth and strange Middle Eastern music leaked into the cab of the truck. I looked over, and there in the booth was the Assyrian—five years older than the last time I saw him dead on those green tiles in the pharmacy. There was no wound, no scar—no sign of any harm or hardship. He'd cleaned up, wasn't gangbanging no more. There were family photos in the booth with him—children. He did have children. The Assyrian sang along to the joyful, flowing, rhythmic whine. He grinned and gave my father the change.

"Thank you, sir. You guys have a nice night," he said with almost no accent.

Dad waved, and we pulled off. I glanced through the back window as we rolled away. The Assyrian watched us go. He looked me in the eyes with a pleasant smirk on his lips and waved goodbye. I waved back. All the wires that'd twisted so tightly around my heart and mind for so long, something sliced them, and they fell away. I sighed, turned forward, and whispered, "Goodbye."

It wasn't the Assyrian, of course; it was just another person who deserved to live.

My throat ached as we began the steep ascent. I thought of Hyacinth, and I knew I should let it be, let it go. I thought of Ryan and Angel and Rose and Lil Pat. I felt for my crucifix, but it was gone. Then, I looked out off the bridge at the steel mills and silos that towered beside us; their burnt-orange lights in the windows blazed like lit torches. A pack of seagulls disturbed by the windstorm soared in the light. I glanced back from where we'd come from. A murky, purple nebulous cloud hovered over the city, and the street lights pierced the haze in tiny gold dots like baby stars. I gazed out at the lake. The shoreline arced and spanned out northwest and northeast to the horizon. Then, it vanished into the vast black void of the night sky, and I wasn't scared anymore. I thought about the neighborhood, and I wondered what life would be like in the suburbs.

ACKNOWLEDGMENTS

I met my wife the same day I started writing this novel. Enid, you fanned my flames from the absolute beginning. I wouldn't have made it here without your love fortifying my life. Thank you.

My family: I apologize if any of the characters resemble you in any way. These characters are not some twisted opinion of or vendetta against you. These characters are monsters who live in a dark world and do strange things. I forbid any child in my family under the age of 18 from reading this book. Also, if you can't comprehend the concept of a fictitious memoir, stop reading now and don't pick it back up until you can. I love you all, you've all give me tremendous gifts that I am truly in awe of.

I was diagnosed with learning disabilities as a child. Brother Peter Hannon and St. Joseph High School taught me that hard work and focus overcomes all. You changed my life, Brother. I want to thank the Elmhurst College English Department and Ron Wiginton, who inspired me and acknowledged I had something and gave me the tools to pursue it. Thank you, Chicago Boxing Community and the Chicago Golden Gloves, you opened the doors to sacred places both physical and spiritual that changed me very deeply and you showed me the world.

Thanks to Fred Burkhart and your Underground for the deep upwelling of inspiration you gave me. I want to thank Marty Tunney, who picked me out of the choir. Thank you Marc Kelly Smith for helping me find myself on stage. Thanks to the Columbia College Fiction Department staff and the Story Workshop Method for supplying me with the tools to take my work to the next level. Thank you Johnny Brown for believing in me and giving me so much. Thanks to Thom Jones for the help and inspiration. Thank you Nichiren Daishonin for giving me and the world the tools to change our destiny. I want to thank my dear friend Jacob Knabb who believed in the novel from the beginning and chose it for publication. Thanks to Victor David Giron and his beautiful publishing house, Curbside Splendor. I want to thank Leonard Vance and Naomi Huffman for their excellent work in editing this book.

Thank you, Irvine Welsh for your friendship and taking the time from your insanely busy schedule to read my manuscript with care, and for working closely with me on re-writes. You are one of my heroes. It was an unreal honor.

Thank you to the haterz, all the people who stood in my way. Karmically speaking, you may have given me more than anyone else. Please keep being the petty, malicious, people you are. No, but really, I wish you all well and hope you find happiness.

I want to thank all the people who opened doors for me, patted me on the back, picked me up off the floor and encouraged me in any way. You helped me more than you'll ever know and I am forever grateful.

For my father and for the Old Neighborhood.

TOMORROWLAND Stories by Joseph Bates

"Tomorrowland is a revelation, combining slightly skewed or fantastic conceits, a darkly comic tone, and wonderfully nimble, funny prose, all in service of a surprisingly serious, touching vision. These inventive stories mark the debut of a major talent." —**Michael Griffith,** *author of* Trophy

Joseph Bates's debut short story collection *Tomorrowland* offers stories full of strange attractions and uncanny conceits, a world of freakish former child stars, abused Elvis impersonators, derelict roadside attractions, apocalyptic small towns, and parallel universes where you make out with your ex. At its core, the world of *Tomorrowland* is our own, though reflected off a funhouse mirror—revealing our hopes and deepest fears to comic, heartbreaking effect.

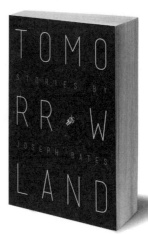

MEATY Essays by Samantha Irby

"Blunt, sharp and occasionally heartbreaking, Samantha Irby's Meaty *marks the arrival of a truly original voice. You don't need difficult circumstances to become a great writer, but you need a great writer to capture life's weird turns with such honesty and wit."*

—**John August,** *acclaimed screenwriter and filmmaker*

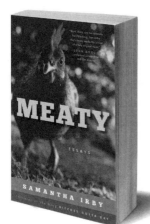

Samantha Irby explodes onto the page in her debut collection of brand-new essays about being a complete dummy trying to laugh her way through her ridiculous life of failed relationships, taco feasts, bouts with Crohn's Disease, and more, all told with the same scathing wit and poignant candor long-time readers have come to expect from her notoriously hilarious blog, bitchesgottaeat.com.